ELEMENTS OF POWER

THE METALIST'S JOURNEY, BOOK 2

KD LUMSDEN

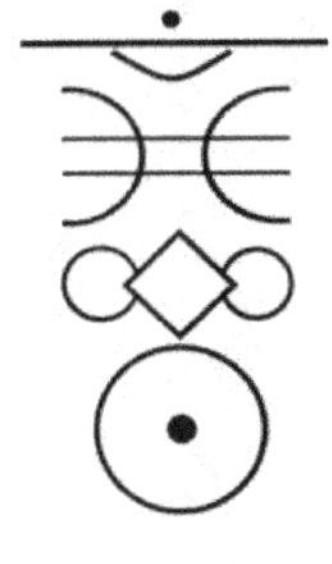

KD LUMSDEN

A KD Lumsden Production

Edited by Camille Cole.

This book is published in the United States and Internationally by KD Lumsden.

ISBNs

Paperback: 978-1-959679-02-8

EPUB: 978-1-959679-03-5

www.KDLumsden.com

This book is dedicated to those who strive to be better than their ancestors.
You are making a difference. You are amazing.
Do not let anything stop you!

Irwin believes in you.
So do I.

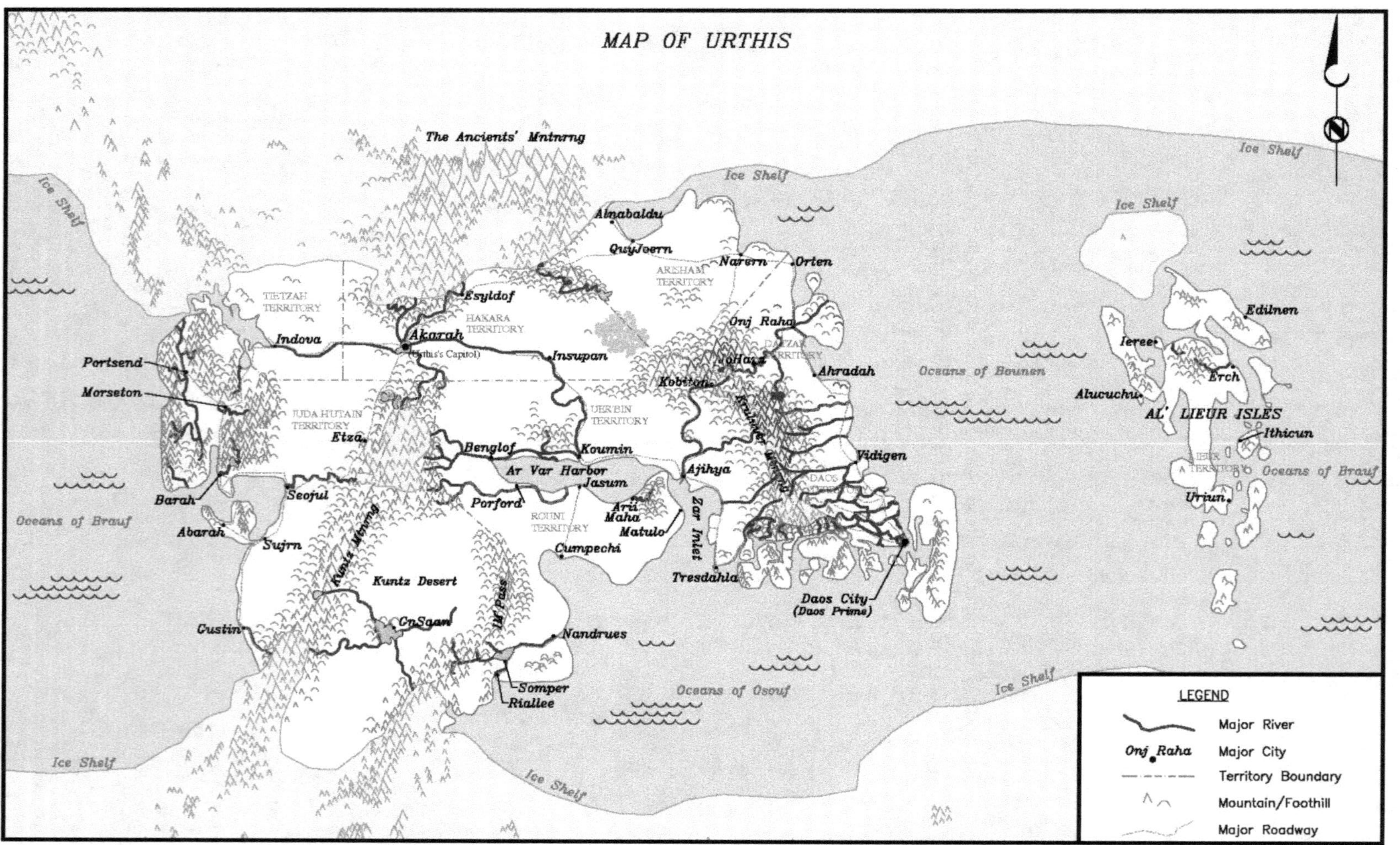
MAP OF URTHIS
The Ancients' Mntnrng
Ice Shelf
Ice Shelf
Ice Shelf
Ice Shelf
Ice Shelf
Ice Shelf
Ice Shelf
Almabaldu
QuyJoern
Narern
Orten
ARISHAM TERRITORY
TETZAH TERRITORY
Esyldof
HAKARA TERRITORY
Akarah
Indova
Insupan
Onj Raha
Edilnen
Ieree
Portsend
Morseton
JUDA HUTAIN TERRITORY
Etza
UER'BIN TERRITORY
JoHaza
Kobitan
Ahradah
Oceans of Bounen
Erch
Alucuchu
AL' LIEUR ISLES
Ithicun
Benglof
Koumin
Ar Var Harbor
Jasum
Ajihya
Vidigen
Oceans of Brauf
Uriun
Barah
Seojul
Porford
ROUNI TERRITORY
Arii Maha
Matulo
Zar Inlet
Oceans of Brauf
Abarah
Sujrn
Kuntz Mntnrng
Cumpechi
Tresdahla
Kuntz Desert
Daos City
(Daos Prime)
Ill' Pass
CnSgam
Custin
Nandrues
Somper
Riallee
Oceans of Osouf
LEGEND
Major River
Onj Raha
Major City
Territory Boundary
Mountain/Foothill
Major Roadway

THE METALIST'S JOURNEY
Book 1 ~ Secrets of Urthis
Book 2 ~ Elements of Power

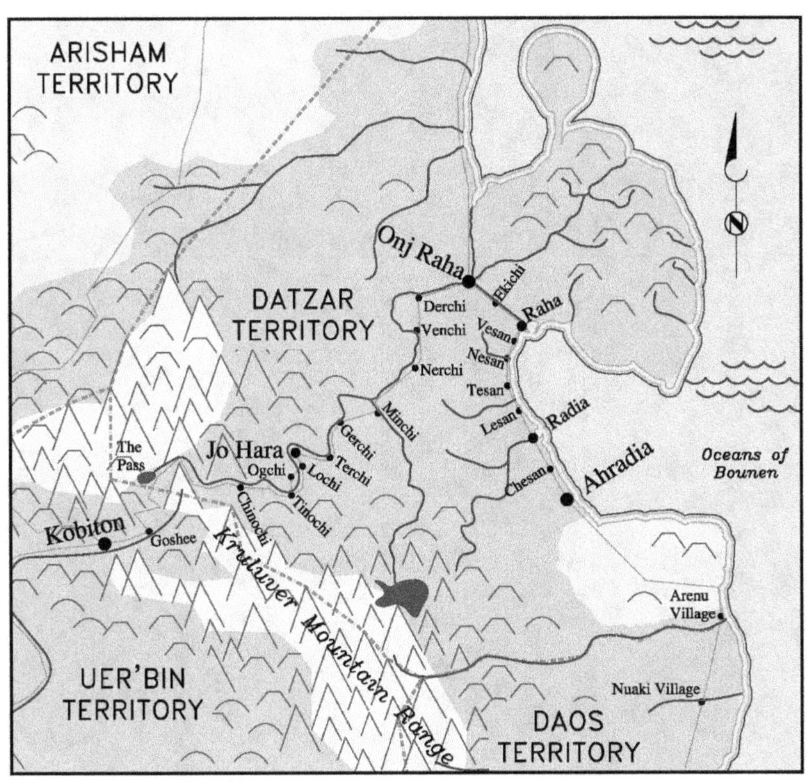

Contents

1

THE PCP HALL

Captured.

Irwin had spent all morning diffusing telepathic spells. He followed Kipp's nose, here and there, in search of their beloved friend Yace. They were supposed to be protecting her, but late last night she disappeared just hours after collapsing across her father on his deathbed.

Now they were surrounded by gruff Erthin soldiers. It was apparent to Irwin that this was likely part of Yace's father's, Lord Master Dephen Ishik's, devious plan. He had tricked them.

How will they ever find Yace?

More pressing, how will they escape the clutches of these goons?

There was no way other than to fight. Irwin had already tried diplomacy, but he was not a talker. Yet if they had acted violently when accosted, a worse situation might have ensued. One of them could have been hurt, possibly killed. For now, they must go along.

It could be worse.

Samuel Irwin Miner and his best friend, Kipp Hauler, were being forced to follow a squad of darkly dressed Public Constable Patrol (PCP) soldiers. These dark-skinned warriors were seen by Mortals as all powerful, and they were. The soldiers that surrounded them were capable of harnessing the five elements, but there were others who had the ability to transform themselves into carnivorous animals. And yet there were others—here on the planet Urthis—more wicked, men who could change a man's mind without them even knowing what was happening. There were many different species of man and woman, most of them yielded amazing powers that could crumple a Mortal man or woman. This he knew.

Irwin sat tall astride their giant war-horse. Kipp jogged alongside through the crowds covering the streets of Onj Raha. All the locals knew to part for the procession.

This was not a good place to be; Irwin was aware of the trouble they faced. And the look Kipp kept shooting at him didn't help his anxieties. This was a challenge, but especially for him. He has known all along to downplay his abilities to use all kinds of metals to cause great harm to those in his way. He knew to be aloof. But as they made their way, the ringing melodies from every metallic thing persisted to chime in his head. He didn't want to lose his control of his Metalistic powers, but it could happen in a place like this.

He was perched high atop their only horse—Yace had stolen the other two, and now she was nowhere to be seen. Kipp was tied to one of the Squaddies' saddles and raced alongside the quick moving horses. He was a fleet-of-foot Clan-Duin, but he was Clan-Duin and the Erthin Squaddies didn't like him. They seemed indifferent toward Irwin, whose powers were unknown to them. Irwin was a Metalist, a Ferro-kineticist, a rare being who could manipulate any type of metal to do his bidding. Only those closest to him—his family of birth and his new friends—knew of this power. This amazing talent could easily kill anyone, but Irwin was altruistic and kind by nature. He preferred to have fun with his Metalist gifts instead of provoking or harming others. A favorite trick of his was to use some gold or silver and mold the metal into a perfect spere while levitating it above his hands. This was something Yace had recently taught him. Remembering their lessons together made his eyes water.

His loyal donkeys, his beloved Jennies—Jenn Jenn and Nee Nee—were in tow behind his horse, Bodi. They kept in stride. From time to time, he would glance back and try not to fret. He felt the worry wrinkling his face.

I hope nothing bad befalls us.

From his perch on the giant black horse, the city of Onj Raha was a constant buzz of color and sound. The locals continued to stop for the clamoring horses and continued to avoid eye-contact with the looming soldiers. Irwin and Kipp were being escorted towards a block-sized building called the Hall. It rose six stories toward the clear blue sky and mirrored the other buildings in the center of town. Their loud procession passed around to the backside of the towering building. Irwin remembered seeing the gigantic gates they were about to enter earlier that day while they had been searching for their lost friend, Yace. They were only a few blocks away from Lord Dephen Ishik's residence, where she had disappeared early that morning.

We will get out of this situation, and we will find Yace.

Will we?

I need to remain positive for Kipp's sake.

They passed four guardsmen, who stood in front of the giant open gates, dressed alike in dark indigo uniforms. Four more soldiers stood near the middle of the courtyard talking among themselves. They stopped and watched the incoming squad of soldiers and their prisoners—watched them enter the large and busy PCP Hall. Many more moved across the wide, cobbled square.

Irwin's chest pounded. He could barely swallow.

At first glance around the courtyard, he calculated half the guards were Erthins—their fiery red hair well-kept. The rest were Clan-Duin mixes—brown skinned and thick bodied. Every guard carried at least one blade. He could sense these things; he could feel any present metals. The sound and the song of the guard's metals hummed throughout his body.

Kipp had objected to coming here with these thugs. But what else could they do? To have fought would have brought about worse foul play, Irwin was sure of it. They had to find Yace before it was too late, but for now, they had to go along with this charade of capture. They had to bide their time. For the moment, Irwin made note of his surroundings; the obedient young boys following alongside the resident Telepaths—gruff middle-aged Clan-Duins turning up their noses at him. And there were the horses clomping and dogs barking and growling. He even sensed the amount of light still in the sky.

Once inside the PCP Hall courtyard, they faced a pack of guard dogs—Clan-Duins, humans transformed into canine creatures—tethered to stone walls by thick chains; others roamed freely around the yard. All the hounds wore metal collars. And when they caught Irwin's scent, many barked and yowled as though a behemoth wolf had entered their den. He tried to ignore the racket while studying the massive brick and mortar building surrounding the courtyard.

Men dressed in matching indigo uniforms came and went in pairs and quads. There was an array of tin and wooden buckets piled around a stone well in the middle of the atrium. Stacks of empty barrels and crates lined the exterior walls of the magnificent building—this PCP Hall. A large metal caged carriage and several flat-bed wagons—heaped with manure—sat unattended along another wall. Someone from across the yard shouted at the barking dogs, and they fell silent—a few whined and whimpered.

Irwin dismounted.

Kipp was released from his bindings. He stepped up and took hold of Irwin's horse, and whispered, "I said it before, and I'll say it again; we shouldn't be here."

"Do not worry, I will get us out of this," Irwin kept his voice low and moved to untie the small gray donkeys from his saddle.

A young Clan-Duin stable attendant rushed toward them. His brown clothes matched his skin color. His eyes were amber and glowed like the sun. Irwin held up his hand to stop the eager boy. "It is best we deal with our own mounts. They have never been in the care of anyone else and would take offense to strangers handling them."

"Bossman says it's my job."

"Bossman?"

The boy wrinkled his nose, showing his disgust at Irwin's odor, an odor that has offended all the Clan-Duins he has encountered since his journey away from his mountaintop began. The stable hand pointed toward an older man in a pale gray uniform with red stripes along the seams—different from the indigo uniforms the other soldiers wore. The ones who brought them here had already dismounted and crowded around their superior. Their horses were ushered away and out of the late day's heat by other young brown clothed stable hands.

Irwin felt all the metal throughout the Hall and its property. It was everywhere, rattling him to his core.

Keep cool, breathe.

His body wanted to pull for it.

I must fight the urge.

Every muscle wanted to tighten against his internal commands. And suddenly it became almost impossible to inhale and exhale.

Breathe!

Bossman stepped up to Irwin's face. He had a broad nose and his bright blue eyes, an obvious telepathic trait, glowered. He was dark-skinned, well kept, except his breath that smelled of smoke and booze. Irwin noticed hints of gray in those blue eyes, like the same hints of gray that never left his own eyes.

Right away he groveled as he would have done in his father's presence. Eyes at once upon the ground. "We want no trouble, Sir. We are tired and want to go home, that is all."

"Yeah, that's all we want." Kipp's expression then changed, fell flat—a change in his nature that Irwin noticed right away.

I bet Bossman is using Kipp. How is it that a Telepath can do that? Taking over another person's mind should not be allowed.

Bossman waved his hand. "That is fine. Haesen; show them to a stall on the south side." Kipp held firm to the lead line. Irwin walked along the other side of their great black mount, donkeys on either side of him. Neither said a word as they were led into a lantern-lit stable where stalls lined both sides of the corridor.

The young stable hand named Haesen showed them to a large and freshly cleaned stall that the donkeys and the large warhorse would share.

The stable boy held the stall door open. "There ya go."

Kipp and Irwin pulled their animals inside, and the boy shut the stall gate behind them.

Haesen stepped aside and stared blankly across the corridor. He appeared empty of emotion or self-direction.

Why do they always appear so mechanical?

Kipp began methodically removing tack and packs from Bodi, their towering black horse.

Irwin put his hand on Kipp's forearm, and the Clan-Duin stopped, shook his head and blinked. He looked around, confused, but then anger washed across him.

"Dang it," Kipp grumbled. "I don't know who I hate more, Telepaths or Erthins. We shouldn't be here. You don't know what I know about places like this."

Irwin kept his voice low. "We must do whatever it takes to stay in this city and find Yace."

"Oh, to be with the Gypsy right now. What I'd give to see my family again." Kipp paused from removing the bags, paced to the stall door, and peered out. Haesen was still there beside the doorway.

"I will get you out of here and back to your Gypsy," Irwin whispered. "I promise."

What am I saying? I should promise nothing. I have no clue what I am doing, but neither does Kipp.

He carried on removing bags, setting each aside on the hay covered stable floor. Kipp turned back to help.

They stood side by side pulling packs off the Jennies. "How will you get us out of here? This is the brig. This is where they'll tear us down, break us, and then remake us to their liking. Nothing'll be the same after this."

"Why are you so fatalistic?"

"Olei and Alio warned me about places like this. This hellhole is just like what they described." Kipp's eyelid twitched. "First, they'll interrogate us. They'll wanna know everything about us. And I mean everything! And what we don't tell them, they'll pry from us by any means. You think you can save me?" He cackled and looked around like a caged dog. "We're gonna die here."

Irwin knelt and put his hand inside one of his bags. "You really think so?" He was careful not to pull anything out of the baggage that Kipp could see. "You have so little faith in me."

"How will we find Yace in here?!" Kipp began to howl, but quietly, as though off in the distance. He kept on removing tack. "We won't; we'll be locked up forever." He glared at Irwin. "You said we should think like Yace, and this is what you come up with? What are you doing down there?"

By now Irwin was used to Kipp's canine side—his ability to change from man to dog and his dog-like nature. He responded softly. "I have about ninety pounds of pure silver I need to keep hidden. Most likely, they will go through our baggage while we are not here."

"Ninety pounds of ...?!" Kipp gasped, his eyes as wide as his mouth. "How?"

"I will tell you everything, but until then ..." He signaled for Kipp to kneel and placed a hand on his Clan-Duin friend's arm. "... I need to make sure you are Kipp. That Telepaths have not taken your mind. I never realized how easy it is for them to do it."

"You know that after they enter your mind, they'll know all about you, Irwin. And once they do, they'll never let you leave. Dang it, I told you to let me do the talking."

"They had you by the neck! Besides, if you had, I am sure you would be dead."

"No. I'd be alive and still searching for Yace." They frowned at each other. "How are we gonna get out of here?"

They both listened for the sound of anyone approaching or breathing. All they could hear was Haesen. They remained at a whisper.

"We need to think like Yace."

"She'd never think like this!"

"If she did leave us on purpose, would she feel safe enough to be without protection? My gut answer is no. As she has put it, 'women need to be protected by men'. I believe Yace would hire someone—maybe go to a saloon to find that someone?"

Kipp's body shook with silent laughter. "A saloon? Like the one across the way?" Now his voice pitched higher, his eyes darted around the stall. "I don't know about that. These dogs aren't gonna let us go to any saloon."

"We are innocent Kipp. We have done nothing wrong other than not check in with the local Hall. We did not know the rules."

Several pairs of boots echoed as they approached down the corridor. The man called Bossman and another male telepathic assistant, stepped up and looked over the edge of the stall door. Both wore matching gray uniforms, more decorated than the indigo garb of their subordinates. Behind the Telepaths, the indigo-dressed brigade of Erthins that escorted Irwin and Kipp to the PCP hall hovered.

Bossman pressed, "We're wondering where you got that gelding."

Kipp stepped forward. "He was loaned to the Lady who requested our escort. This is her mount."

Bossman rested his arms across the stall front. "And to what household did you take this Lady?"

Kipp looked at Irwin. There were many names for this father of Yace's. He turned back to the Telepath. "Lord Dephen."

Thank you Kipp for not disclosing his full name.

Bossman assessed Kipp with his piercing blue eyes. "Lord Dephen?"

"I believe that was his name. But maybe it was Master Dephen," Kipp said. "All we know is that he was old and dying. We delivered her to a residence in that dark-spired building a few blocks over."

Once again, Irwin witnessed a telepathic exchange. Bossman focused on Kipp, who fell silent—staring forward, void of thought or emotion. Irwin's sleeveless forearm made contact again with Kipp's hairy arm while Bossman attempted to peer inside Kipp's Clan-Duin mind. Kipp blinked while the Telepath struggled to take control; it did not happen, but then it did, and did not again. The Metalist's innate power was grounding out the telepathic link being pushed onto Kipp, and Irwin persisted to maintain contact with Kipp's body.

I need to get their attention away from him and on me.

"If it pleases you, Bossman Sir, we are interested in finding a job that takes us back home—back to Kobiton. We were not told we would be kept here. We completed the request only for our families. If there are no brigades to join, may we please go home?"

Bossman flung open the stall door. His assistant followed. The Telepath stepped closer to Irwin until they were face to face. "I'm told you're Erthin?" He peered into Irwin's eyes. "But I don't see it."

"My father was part Erthin. My mother, Hakra, rest her soul, was Mortal. She died when I was very young."

"Hmm. Not even your eyes hint that you are Erthin." Bossman kept staring at Irwin. Their eyes were locked in a battle of wills. His right hand reached out in an attempt to make skin on skin contact, a mind-to-mind connection. "You're lying."

He is trying to scare me.

Arching his back, his eyes firmly on Bossman, Irwin asked, "And if I were, what would you do to me?"

He does not know me. He cannot see into me. Breathe.

"We usually maim or kill those who lie."

"How would you kill me, exactly? Is it with a rope? Or a blade? Or do you incinerate?"

I dare you to try to kill me.

Bossman glanced at the younger Telepath who had shadowed him into the stall.

"I've been told you regenerate. Show us your Talent!"

He is trying to inflict his will on me. But his powers have no effect. I must remember to keep arms-length from the Telepaths. I hope none of the Erthins try to hurt me.

He knew what Erthins could do. The two Telepaths were an unknown variable. Still, he had the upper hand. Everyone in the stall was—unknown to them—standing on a layer of silver beneath the straw bedding.

The brigade of four Erthins entered, and he and Kipp were outnumbered should anyone decide to act.

Breathe. Relax. Do not worry. I can kill everyone in this crowded hellhole if necessary. Keep calm.

Bossman, the senior most Telepath in the room, tried to read his lack of emotion. Irwin could tell that he and his apprentice were trying to figure out what type of creature he might be. Beyond Erthins, Clan-Duins, and Telepaths, there were other creatures who resided on the planet of Urthis with amazing mystical powers, beings who could turn invisible, or teleport, and there were others who appear as the person you most desire. These men knew this, but Irwin did not.

Kipp stiffened as the Erthins filed in. Kipp, a Clan-Duin, wanted to stay out of the confrontation, but he was now clearly in the middle of it. He took a step away from Irwin and bumped into their horse they had stolen from a PCP brigade who had attempted to destroy them many moons prior. Fortunately, the animals were docile now that they were out of the sun. Kipp patted Bodi's belly, leaning against the large animal.

Irwin approached the Erthin man at Bossman's side.

Keep calm for Kipp.

He looked at Bossman but instructed the Erthin. "Take your blade across my arm."

He had to concentrate on not absorbing the metal, all the while studying the Telepath's gaze. The Erthin was slow to slide the blade deep into Irwin's forearm. It was painful at first, but Irwin did not flinch.

Blood trickled down his arm, and Bossman chuckled. Within seconds his skin fused back together. Only a few dribbles of blood remained. The Erthin then took his blade and stabbed Irwin in the shoulder.

He winced when the blade slid in. He had accidentally absorbed the metal. No one saw it happen. And as the Erthin pulled out the blade, Irwin made his flesh grip the metal as it was withdrawn. He had to remake the blade as it was removed. The metal had to stand as thick and full as it had been before he absorbed it.

His clothing was torn, but there was not a mark on his body. Bossman nodded, "Impressive." He studied Irwin, and everyone squirmed and shuffled. "So, you believe you're just a healer, but you have not tried to heal anyone else?" The Telepath glanced over at Kipp.

I do not like where this is going.

The same Erthin stepped around Bossman toward Kipp. Irwin's Clan-Duin counterpart was unable to run away, but clearly wanted to.

At this moment, there was no way to ensure Kipp's safety. Irwin never wanted any harm to come to his best and only friend.

There is iron in the Erthin's blood. Pull for the iron.

Not meaning to show off too much, he threw his left hand forward, and using his Metalist's power, he metaphysically grabbed the Erthin's metal-laced blood and the blade now firm in the Erthin's hand.

Keep it solid.

He knew to keep the knife whole, to not liquefy it. But his powers wanted to. Bossman made a noise, eagerly watching the powerful display.

Abruptly, the Erthin's arm turned and popped out of its socket. He screamed in agony and dropped the blade. Irwin loosened his Metalistic grip. Kipp was now safe, and that was all that mattered to Irwin.

The Erthin wailed, fell to his knees. One of his comrades rushed to his aid and carried him out of the stall.

"Now that was interesting," Bossman said, his voice flat and empty of emotion. "That wasn't an Erthin move. An Erthin cannot control another in that way. That looked more like telekinesis, but didn't feel like it. I would know; I'm a Telepath—I can feel more than you ever could. No. No. You're not Erthin. Nor are you Telekinetic." The Telepath stepped toward him without warning and grabbed Irwin's forehead with his long spindly fingers.

Irwin closed his eyes, afraid of the contact. He flashed back to his childhood. How father Albert and grandfather Jebadia beat and tortured him. His mind fell into a painful thought mode, recalling every agonizing experience he had ever endured. He had been beaten by open hands, metal encased fists, spoons, and belts; he had been sodomized, burned, and tortured in so many ways. He had been verbally and mentally assaulted his whole life while working in the mines for his father and grandfather. He played the most disturbing episodes over and over in his mind, hoping to scare the Telepath off his flesh. This was a technique Yace had spoken of, only once, and he was running with the idea now. All the images—all the horror—made Bossman recoil.

"You're a troubled individual," Bossman said, and looked around the stall, perhaps trying to forget the images he had just seen in Irwin's mind.

"My life may seem like a living hell, but I look forward to reuniting with my father," Irwin said while trying to ignore the singing of copious amounts of metal—much like a horrible bout of deafening tinnitus.

I do miss the quiet mountaintops.

Bossman considered Kipp again. "Chuck will escort you, Clan-Duin. And while you two are being interviewed, we'll look for markings of ownership." The man appeared at once larger and looming. "If you're soldiers' sons, you'll have none. That'll make you mine. And if you have markings, we will contact your owner. Those who leave employment prematurely are returned to their owners and forced to work the rest of their days."

To Irwin he said, "You follow Leon." Bossman then turned and strode from the stall.

The only Erthin left, Leon, stepped up to Irwin. He was a fire yielding Erthin, a creature who could incinerate on contact or toss flames from his fingertips. Kipp had always feared this specific type of Erthin. Irwin was not scared. "Ya will com' wit me." Leon motioned for him to follow.

Hoisting his bags to his shoulder, Irwin watched Kipp walk away with his own baggage slung over his back. He felt a pang of fear. He did not want to leave his donkeys behind. They left the saddle and packs, mostly empty, leaning against the stall's interior wall.

He followed Leon through the stables. Chuck took Kipp in the opposite direction. Irwin felt the sting of regret and hoped to see his only friend again—soon. "In the tavern, you said you were from Porford. Where is that exactly?"

"Far rup Ar Var Har bar."

"What brought you to Onj Raha?"

"Wok."

"Did you always want to be a soldier?"

"Shut ya damn ansaws ta later." His grin told of greed.

He is not very smart.

"You mean hold my questions."

Leon did not look back at Irwin as they ascended a spiral staircase. "Ya be folla."

2

Releasing Attachment

A Telepath was waiting for him inside a small room on the fourth floor. With shoulder-length blonde hair and pale eyebrows partially camouflaged by the same color of skin, he wore the same gray outfit as Bossman. This middle-aged Telepath named Gerome was waiting, apparently, for the interrogation session to begin.

Once Irwin was inside, Leon stood with his back against the closed door.

Gerome instructed Irwin to sit and to confess about himself—all of it—like some sort of therapy session.

Irwin spoke freely, talking about everything that had happened to him throughout his life. He spoke about the horrors endured—how he had been beaten every day, how hard he worked for no recognition. As he confessed his life story, Irwin realized he missed that life, if only slightly and only at that moment. He cried. He professed how much he wanted to return to mining after all this was over. Everything he said was true, in that instant, but not completely revealing of his genuine nature.

He didn't talk about his powers. And though he shared much about his life, he left out crucial details about his time with Kipp and Yace, about their journey to Onj Raha. Instead, he talked about the mundaneness of their time together. He made it all sound bland, hardly worth living, hardly worth repeating. In the end, the Telepath showed empathy for Irwin.

Irwin felt a certain amount of relief when he talked about what he had suffered as a child. And though he had been holding onto many horrible events from his past, Irwin was willing to let go now. The Telepath did not seem to judge the content of his story. He listened and encouraged the conversation.

Once done, Irwin was asked to strip down and show his body, completely naked of tattoos and markings. He was then given an updated indigo uniform. And after he dressed, he was escorted out of the room and up another narrow spiral staircase to the fifth floor.

I wonder why I was not telepathically probed.

Leon, the Erthin, led Irwin through the barracks, through long open sleeping quarters separated by stairwells and lavatories encircling the upper floors of the massive Hall.

They wandered the fifth floor looking for available beds. There were none. He followed Leon up to the sixth floor where Kipp was staking out a bunk at the far end of the long barracks hall.

"As ya seeya, we've gotta lotsa stuffa hereya to do," Leon said. "Dere isya, da rec'ya rooma over dere." Leon stopped at a dormer window and pointed down to the third-floor windows across the courtyard where there were men moving about. "Weya gotta some chores. Diligent pays ofya, rounda hereya."

"We will do what needs to be done. We just want to go home."

Leon spewed a verbal list to Irwin about all that was offered if the rules were followed. There was free food, housing, and clothing; everything else cost. And everyone had a job in order to pay their way in the Hall. Laziness was not accepted.

There were several men napping in the upper floor barracks; some talked quietly amongst themselves; some played card games between bunks. There were only a few open beds, all the others were claimed with bags, colorful blankets, and a variety of personal items.

The unclaimed beds were nestled next to an open gabled window with an eastern view—a view of the sunrise. A young Erthin near Kipp was playing a four-card guessing game, and his opponents were losing money to the shifty card dealer.

Leon pointed at Kipp. "Dere be ya fend. Supper be soon. See ya den!"

"The dining hall is on the second floor, below the recreation room, correct?"

"Yessiree, ya."

"Thank you." He flung the heavy baggage hanging from his shoulder onto the bed across from Kipp's. "I am sorry, Kipp."

"Sorry won't cut it, Irwin." Some of the men stared at them. "They saw my tattoo. They know I'm Gypsy. I'm not so sure about you, but they said they'll make me into one of their courtyard sitters if I don't obey." He was referring to the dogs chained in the courtyard below. "They do that to Clan-Duins they can't control."

He felt Kipp's energy churning. His Talent for growing into a canine had served them well along their journey thus far, but not now. They both felt the trouble to come. He would have to come up with a plan, and fast.

"You better have a damn good reason ... some way ... some sort of idea to get us out of here. Because if you don't, I'll find my own way out and leave you behind."

Ouch!

"I deserve that."

I need to make sure Telepaths do not possess him before we talk any further.

He leaned in, his arm grazed Kipp's, but the Clan-Duin recoiled. They had made contact, but Kipp clearly did not enjoy any gesture from Irwin at this point.

I should say something positive.

He whispered, "My plan is simple. We will find Yace."

"We would've had a better chance finding Yace if we hadn't come here."

Irwin continued to speak softly. "Had I not changed my clothing, we would have been passed on by. And had we not rode together, they would have overlooked us. As it is, we did not know what we were doing, and because of that, we drew too much attention. We did not look the part, so they picked us up. We were doomed from the start. Had I not listened to you and taken charge, like Yace would have—"

"None of this would've happened if you hadn't been so flippant!"

"I was not flippant. I was trying to take charge."

"It's all your fault we're in this mess."

What if Yace, or Dephen inhabiting Yace, is trying to get rid of us? It definitely seems like she-he wants us off their tracks. Is that possible? Has he taken over Yace's mind and body alike?

"Do not blame me, Kipp. It is quite possible that Yace had a hand in our being taken into custody."

"No, this was all you. We both know there was another option besides coming here."

"Yes. Yes, there was. But I do not believe that would have ended well. Most likely you would be dead, and I would have been captured."

"If you'd let me talk, we could've had a chance at freedom. As it is, we're both captured!" Kipp was drawing attention. "How are you gonna get out of this?" The young Clan-Duin was oblivious to all the eyes on them. "I might be able to exit sometime in the future in a brigade, or if Nonbry comes and claims me. But you-you ... you're doomed! They'll either lock you up here forever or send you someplace far worse than here."

"This is a bad predicament, Kipp, but we have both lived through worse. Did they hurt you physically or mentally?"

"That Telepath tested my patience and my abilities. Then he probed me and stripped me looking for my tattoo." He pointed at his left shoulder where he had an insignia showing he was owned. "They said they'll contact my owner. Nonbry's gonna be so mad."

"Same thing happened to me. They did to us as they said they would do, and they did not hurt us. They did not beat you or berate you. They only want to know about us, our background. They want to know who we are. That is all. Do not worry. We will be alright. Remember that we need to be fluid with our thoughts and not hope for a specific outcome. If we become heated with our emotions, they win. You know this. You are the one who told me that." This had been at the core of Kipp's training with Alio back in the Gypsy camp. But Kipp, a young Clan-Duin, was forgetting all that. Irwin recalled the guidance Kipp himself had shared back when they were just starting out on the journey to bring Yace to her father, to get her to Onj Raha before the old man died and she would supposedly, magically, learn from him how to use her amazing Coterie powers.

The Erthin card-dealer called to them. "It's only four cards, my friends." He repeated this several times. "Find the ace, make a silver! It's quite simple."

"You're not helping." Kipp glared at Irwin in the same way he had all those moons ago—the night they met in the dark camp along the river past the Gypsy caravan.

Kipp had accused him back then of being 'Death' in living form, of having the odor of Death. They had come so far since then.

Kipp rose from his bed and approached the Erthin hustler. "What's the game?"

"Find the ace, win a silver." The Erthin's eyes were dark brown, his skin pale and heavily freckled, his hair fiery red.

"And what do I put down to win this silver?"

"Anything you have in your pockets, preferably a silver."

Kipp glanced back at Irwin but did not make eye contact.

Irwin felt a flush of relief. Kipp knew he was holding several pounds of silver.

Kipp tried to brush off the Erthin. "Sounds like I'm better off keeping my coin."

"You find the ace the first time, make your silver back; find it a second time, make three silvers for the price of one. Simple, my friend! You're Clan-Duin. You'll make your coin back, guaranteed."

Irwin was now intrigued by the game. He wanted to join but knew to give Kipp his space. He watched, not wanting his friend to stray too far. He had to keep him protected. Slowly he approached, leaving their baggage on the beds. He stepped alongside Kipp and knelt at the same level as the Erthin and his card game.

Four cards lay face up on a small wooden platform. Kipp placed down a silver piece. The Erthin flopped all the cards over and began moving them around. He was quick, but not so quick that Kipp could not find the ace the first time. So he played again. This time the Erthin's hand moved faster, and Kipp could not find the ace. He lost his silver.

Kipp retrieved another coin and placed it down. Again, the cards flew around too quickly for even a Clan-Duin to catch which one was the ace. He lost another coin and stepped away from the game.

Irwin decided to take a try, impressed by the Erthin's maneuvers. He was given the same speech. Again, the cards moved around, slowly the first try so Irwin would win and bet again. On the second try, Irwin could not find the ace and lost his silver. He studied the Erthin as he flipped over the cards.

"Oh, so sorry for your loss," the Erthin said with a greedy grin. "Maybe try again?"

"Yes. I will try again." Irwin peeked over at Kipp who was obviously ready to move away from this dubious game. "How about this ... I will give you three silvers if I cannot find the ace. You give me three if I do." He placed his coins.

The air smelled of greed. This Erthin clearly liked the wager. "You're on, young man." He smiled and began to shift the cards around faster and faster. He was a wind yielding Erthin and was using his powers to rig the game. He stopped and asked Irwin to pick the ace.

Irwin's hand floated slowly over the cards. The ace was not on the small wooden platform, but up the Wind Erthin's loose and long sleeve. "It is not on your table," Irwin then pointed. "It is up your sleeve."

Clearly stunned, the Erthin shoved the three wagered silvers back toward Irwin. "This game is over." He grabbed his cards and makeshift table and left.

Kipp scowled at Irwin. "I don't know how you knew which one was the ace, but you shouldn't have done that."

"I laced his ace with a piece of metal. Now that he is gone, we are the only ones up here. Quick! Let us figure out how we are going to get ourselves and the animals out of here tonight."

Kipp studied the sleeping hall. "Wait. What? Where'd everyone go?" He pointed at the rows of vacant beds.

"My smell," Irwin replied. "It comes in handy."

"The plan is to find Yace," Kipp said, clearly not succumbing to Irwin's attempt at lightheartedness.

"It is. But we cannot do that here. I like your idea better—being out there and not enslaved."

"Now you know how I feel. Dang me, Irwin, once those gates are locked tonight, we'll be shut in. And there's guards everywhere! Erthins. Telepaths. Barking dogs. I'm not sure what your plan is, but mine is to leave the animals and get the Hell out of here. They can keep the horse."

"I am not leaving without my Jennies. Besides, I have all that silver down there."

"When they clean that stall, they'll find your silver."

Keep calm. Breathe. I will get us out of here.

He heard the ringing of all the metal—all the many types of ore located everywhere around called to him. Iron, tin, copper, silver, gold, lead, aluminum, zinc, nickel, and combinations of more; all of it sang to him.

I need to keep control. Breathe. Keep calm. Ugh! It is not working.

The longer he stayed near all this metal, the more his head hummed. He never had this problem anywhere else, until here, until now. He tried not to pay attention to what was now calling to him from every direction. As much as he struggled, the metallic songs kept playing loudly in his head and throughout his body.

Keep control. Be calm.

He walked over to the window and looked down at the courtyard. He saw many of the metals within range. The metal carriage with its thick wrought iron bars on all sides stood separate from the other wagons. The metal axles and steel-lined wheels spoke to him. At the same time, he felt all the axes and hammers, shovels and buckets, brackets, levers, nails, hinges, horseshoes, stirrups, bits, spurs ... on and on! His eyes, his mind, and his body were drawn to this metallic choir.

Kipp came over and stood next to him. They watched the soldiers below, watched the switching of guards at the main gate. Several dozen red and black-haired soldiers rode in and out of the courtyard. Young, brown-skinned and brown uniformed boys were taking horses to and from the stables. Irwin endured the metal horseshoes colliding against the stony ground. The slobbery horse bits inside warm mouths. Argh! He was keenly aware of everything metal moving around the building—the soldier's belt buckles, gold teeth, pouches full of monies, rings, earrings ....

"We must leave here tonight. I cannot stay longer than that."

"You alright?"

"Hardly. If I wanted," Irwin pointed at the metal caged wagon, "I could float that vehicle into the sky."

"Please don't."

"I could make those horses slide around as if they were on ice. The soldiers with swords, I could probably impale them all, or slice off their heads. And those gates .... I could break them open with a snap of my fingers. I could overturn all those lanterns—light all that hay on fire. And the well's buckets ...." His breath escaped him.

The caged vehicle rocked back and forth. Kipp put his hand on Irwin's shoulder. "Alright, calm down. We'll get out of here. In the meantime, don't do anything that'll get us killed."

The clanging of the supper bell rang out. Those who were allowed to eat were hustling into the building. Kipp licked his lips. "I guess it's time for our free meal!"

As a Clan-Duin, Kipp was heavily motivated by his stomach. Irwin was aware of this as his friend pulled him along, following his nose and the other soldiers to the dining hall. They clomped down many stairs, along unfamiliar hallways, as they followed everyone to the food. The dining hall was louder than the ringing in his head. This new racket made it too loud to hear his own thoughts. The line advanced slowly, allowing him time to take in the patrons surrounding them. Most of these people were of varying shades of brown skin, and there were many Clan-Duins in the bunch. Half as many were Erthins, and they sat in one section of the boisterous room. The Telepaths congregated along the two tables closest to the entrance of the mess hall. He noticed them studying him and refocused his attention on the soldier in front of him.

The meal was being served by those like them who stood behind counters wearing cooking hats and food-splattered aprons. The line of soldiers waiting for food was long. He heard Kipp's stomach growl even though the meal of overcooked soupy stew did not look appetizing.

Irwin helped himself to baskets of cheese chunks, bread rolls, and bowls of fruit that had been left out for grazing. He picked up two rolls and put them in his soup. He walked over to a counter covered with tall cups filled with silverware. Summoning a silver spoon into his hand, the chorus of metal was still overwhelming. He was struggling to stay calm—he wanted to let go and allow the metal to dance.

Once more, he surveyed the room. He felt out of place amongst the red-, brown-, and black-haired people. His own gray locks stood out. He was thankful Kipp was there and kept to his side. He pushed him along until they were confronted and invited by the gang of Erthins, who brought them in, to sit at their table. It was clear they were all still keen on finding out what type of Talents Irwin might possess.

The dining hall was filled with men who had some sort of weapon attached to their body. Irwin felt every blade. Holding his urges at bay, he did not want to engage these Erthin soldiers. He looked at his food—the only way to ignore the metallic songs.

Keep focused.

The leader of this small gang pried, getting under Irwin's skin. "Sounds like Bossman will want you teamed up with one of the Master Erthins tomorrow morning. They're planning on putting you through the rigors."

Kipp shoveled his food; maybe he thought these soldiers would take it away from him.

"Yup, eat up boys, tonight's your only free night. Starting tomorrow, it's work, work, work!"

I need to take hold of the conversation.

He put his silverware down with a hard thud. "Well then, that means we need to hit a saloon tonight!" He patted Kipp on the back. "I promised my friend here I would take him to a saloon full of pretty ladies once we were done with our job. I figure one of you will know a good place to find us some whores?"

The Erthins were clearly enjoying this. "We really need to get you on our team." One Erthin soldier slapped Irwin's back. "But first we'll need to thicken you up some. Come fighting time, you'll likely be the one with broken bones."

"Speaking of broken bones," Irwin drew up a spoonful of watery soup. "I am sorry about earlier. I never knew I had that in me. Never knew I could use my power to break bones."

"That's alright. It's what the Healers Hall is for. And those healers are beautiful. Best place to be mended up, if ya ask me," said the Erthin with a menacing grin. He whacked Irwin's shoulder this time—leaving a sharp sting on his skin. "If you'd like to meet a few of them, I'll break your bones for ya."

"I bet you would." If his bones broke, all he must do to instantly fuse them back together was to hold any sort of metal inside. But bones fusing back together hurt worse than having them broken. Nevertheless, his mind was elsewhere now. He was working on getting himself and Kipp outside of the compound, alive and ready to find Yace.

Smile. Keep engaging these contenders. They will help make this night go our way.

He continued with a caustic politeness. "I guess we could find out now."

Several men grinned.

"Fighting's not encouraged at the Hall," the Erthin said. "But over at the saloon, they've got a boxing square. We could go a round, or two. That is, after an ale or two."

"Really! Maybe we bet against one another." Irwin wanted to encourage this line of banter.

"You'll wager money against me?"

"I am a wild kind of man. Why not? If I get to meet some pretty ladies out of the deal, why not?"

"Holy Hakra, you're a fun one!"

The Erthins began pulling coins out of their pockets. "I'll bet five silvers on Arny."

A man from a neighboring table hollered, "I'll bet seven on the scrawny guy!"

The lead Erthin said, "I'd enjoy a chance to make money for breaking bones tonight."

Irwin heckled back, "I would like to see you try!"

Kipp glared at Irwin, who smiled back.

Do not worry, my friend. We will get out of here tonight and with no broken bones. I hope.

He was having fun egging the Erthins on. They settled in and ate quietly; none of them bullied Kipp or Irwin out of their meal. They did, however, excite other Erthins at the surrounding tables into going over to the saloon for a rowdy time. When all the meals were finished, at least another thirty men were interested in the idea of a lively night.

Irwin said he needed to relieve himself before they went out. He left the mess hall, but instead of pissing, he raced up the stairs—bounding to the sixth floor; he hurried to place his hands on their bags. He made sure the contents could not be ransacked. But if they were, he would know. He laced his metal throughout the bags' fibers, knowing he would be back soon.

He returned to the dining hall, where the gang of Erthins and other soldiers were ready to head for the saloon across the road. Once again, Irwin and Kipp were surrounded by Erthins. The crowd marched down the stairs and out into the night. They passed through looming wrought-iron gates. Irwin kept his eyes forward, trying to ignore everything except the saloon ahead.

3

A Drink and a Whore

The mass of soldiers led them into a grand saloon where serving wenches maneuvered around hordes of drunken men. Many of the women were scantily dressed and acting flirtatious. They were a colorful backdrop to the sea of indigo-dressed soldiers. There was a stage on the left side of the room, half as wide as the room, decorated with patterns of woodland scenes, of birds and butterflies. Long curtains were intricately embroidered with flower stalks, dangling ivy, and boldly colored flowers flowing from top to bottom.

Irwin gazed across the busy barroom and the many faces. The men in the main room were all sitting or finding their seats. All the ladies rushed about—most were mixed race with pale skin-tones; some appeared Mortal. They were dressed in bright colors, tight and short clothing, showing off much skin for the men—it was like looking at a meadow filled with flowers.

From the middle of the giant room, off-duty soldiers and servants hollered at their cohorts as they entered the saloon. About twenty moved in unison toward one of many the long wooden tables; the others set off for the gaming room where there were a dozen giant timbered slabs full of men trying to make money while having a good time. The Erthin soldiers pushed Irwin and Kipp onto short benches lining the closest table. Irwin looked across the table at Kipp who kept his head down.

Do not worry, Kipp, we will get out of here.

Irwin scanned the massive room, trying to get a glimpse into the gaming area.

The Erthin leader, Arny, shouted at a server nearby. "Round of ale for the men!"

Irwin turned to Arny. "Do they have whiskey?"

"They sure do."

He smiled and motioned toward Kipp. "I would like to buy my companion here a shot or two. Ah, maybe I should buy a bottle if they can spare one."

"Sure thing," Arny said. He then shouted, "Margy! A bottle of Kobiton whiskey for my friend here!"

Irwin's eyes lit. "They have Kobiton whiskey?"

The serving woman nodded at Arny. He laughed and patted Irwin hard on his shoulder. "Figured you'd like a shot of home."

"Kobiton makes the best whiskey." Irwin glanced at Kipp who was still head down.

So-far, so-good.

"We tend to enjoy ales—they be cheaper than the hard stuff, but if you're buying ...." Arny slapped Irwin again. "I'll take a whiskey drink!"

He could tell Kipp was nervous to be surrounded by so many Erthins. His brown eyes peered up at the women on the walkways along the third and fourth floor promenades. They were the house whores. All of them were naked. Some cooed at the men who leered up at them, others huddled with sad faces. Every one of those ladies was chained by their ankles. Many had scars on their faces or on their bodies. Some had tattoos, metal piercings in more places than just their ears, nose, eyebrows, and lips; others had enlarged ear lobes or a bone through their nose. Only the youngest were not yet marked. Most were Clan-Duin. He noticed a couple with half an arm or just a stub remaining from whatever fright they must have endured. Many of the ladies gazed down at the crowded saloon floor with solemn faces and blank eyes.

Irwin tried not to feel their pain. "I would like to buy me and my friend a night to remember. If this is our only night of freedom, our only night to enjoy the women before we are put to work, I want to make the memories last."

Kipp's eyes widened. "You want a woman?"

"I have never wanted a woman like I want one now."

I do not want a woman. All I want is the metal. But I cannot.

A cool dribble of sweat trickled down his spine.

I want to summon it all!

No. Keep focused. Breathe. Figure a way out of here.

The ringing of all the metal in the saloon was making him feel crazed. "I know you want to have some fun too, huh, Hauss? If this is our last night of freedom, we might as well."

Kipp looked apprehensive, but mercifully went along with the ruse. "A night with a lady would be nice."

Arny had been talking to a soldier on his other side and turned to engage Irwin. He leaned in and aggressively grabbed his hand. "I wonder if we chop off your fingers if they'd regenerate."

Not wanting to deal with that conversation again, Irwin looked back up to the third floor and pointed, "How much for one of them?"

The Erthins all turned their gazes up to the women on the upper floors. "One of the whores? Depends. If you want all of them, it's four silvers for time in bed. If you only want a hand-job, it's two. They're not cheap bitches. But they can be wild in bed! That's why they all look the way they look."

Kipp was not laughing, but Irwin went along with the banter. "Why are some without arms?"

"Those are the ravens," the youngest of the Erthin squad said. "Their wings have to be clipped so they don't fly away. Not to worry, though, they're always allowed one arm. They have to pay for themselves in one way or another—if ya know what I mean. If their privates don't work, their hand will!"

The server returned with a tray of ale-filled steins.

She placed the bottle of whiskey next to Arny and a plate of six shot glasses. Irwin handed over ten gold coins for the whiskey, which was more than enough, but he did not care. He needed to appear carefree—out on the town and ready to enjoy a wild time.

He grabbed the bottle, pulled the cork out with his teeth, and pulled the plate of glasses toward him. He took two, filled them to the top, and pushed one over to Kipp. Then he topped off the other shots.

"We salute you and your comrade," Arny declared. He held his mug up in one hand, the shot in the other. "Congratulations on finding Onj Raha. Enjoy your night of freedom." He tossed the shot of whiskey down his throat, and then the stein full of ale. The other soldiers guzzled their drinks.

Irwin was grateful that Kipp was being cautious about becoming drunk for once. He watched him sip his whiskey. He smiled at Kipp and poured him another. "Tonight is going to be a night to remember."

I have missed Kobiton's whiskey. Alcohol, for me, is like it is for Yace. It calms me down.

Their blue-eyed server apparently did not need to be signaled to know all their steins needed to be refilled. She hustled to their table with a carafe in either hand. Every stein was topped off. Arny and Leon were exploring up her short lavender skirt. Irwin watched and tried not to act offended or angered. None of the groping hands seemed to faze her as she managed her duties. She nodded at Arny and walked away.

Irwin feigned drunkenness. In fact, it was the harmony of metal everywhere that got him going.

The alcohol is not working. Shit! Did it just get louder in here? I need to stay focused.

His breathing became labored. He turned toward the stage, the one place where there was not a lot of metal. His toes tapped inside his boot as he asked Arny, "When does the show start?" He swigged another shot of whiskey.

The older Erthin looked at Irwin. "Soon. We never caught your name, or your friend's."

"I am Samuel Miner, and he is Hauss Hauler." Irwin contemplated his empty glass. The alcohol was having an opposite effect tonight, amplifying his desire to summon the metal. His foot beat the floor.

Nothing is helping. Plan. I must figure out a plan.

"A son of a miner and a hauler. What did your father haul, boy?" Arny glared at Kipp.

"Crops."

The Erthins all chuckled. Arny focused on Irwin. "And you are a miner's son. What did your family mine, boy?"

Irwin stared back at Arny.

I could kill you right now. Do not provoke me. Keep calm. Breathe. Ignore him. But I want to heckle.

His foot stopped tapping. "I am no boy."

"You're younger than me; that makes you a boy."

"Then all your peers are boys."

Slightly drunk, Arny glanced at his companions. "Huh. I guess so."

"My family mined coal."

"Coal, eh!"

"Mining coal makes you a man." Irwin saw Kipp fight back a smirk.

"Huh, I guess it would." Arny's attention was called away from that table to the next one over.

Everyone at their table was wound up in their own discussions.

There are so many people. So much metal. We need to get out of here!

His nervous foot resumed tapping.

Keep calm. But it's calling to me. I want to release it all! Breathe. Must breathe.

"I think I'm ready for a woman on my lap. Kipp, what about you?"

Kipp glared at him.

The banter in the saloon became deafening. The main floor was stuffed to capacity for the first show of the evening. Sweaty men wearing day's old clothing, some reeked of alcohol, others emitted smokey scents; more had horrible breath—he felt sorry for any Clan-Duin with too keen a nose.

A tall female piano player with long red hair strode across the stage with a short, somewhat stocky, lute strummer. She swished her ruffled skirt. A percussionist wearing a low-cut red dress followed five steps behind. The musicians gathered their instruments and sat down, ready to play. They were the only fully clothed women in the saloon. The curtain rose and dancers appeared in sparkling dresses, faces painted more dramatically than Irwin had ever seen. In several beats, the dresses were half-off, parts and pieces strewn across the dance floor.

There was not a man in the house who was not enjoying the sight of the mostly naked women—except him. Irwin watched with saddened eyes, but he knew to keep up a façade.

Here I am again in the midst of debauchery. When will it end? When will women be treated with respect? This is disgusting!

Screaming, shouting, clapping, and stomping their feet, all the men's eyes were on the stage, on the women.

Kipp pushed into the tabletop. His lips barely moved. "Is this your plan?"

Irwin winked at his friend.

Yes. Thank you for reminding me. Stay focused! We will befriend them and use their weakness as our strength.

He joined in with the banter and urged Kipp to do the same with a nod and a smile.

Once the show started, the women up on the promenade were not as flirtatious. They sat back and watched the dancers. Those directly above the stage looked down at the men. Irwin waved at one of them, and this encouraged Kipp to glance up.

"Which one would you like, Kipp?"

Kipp's brow furrowed. "You pick!"

Irwin pointed to one of the Erthin ladies whose room faced the street they had crossed. "That one?"

Exiting out onto the roadway through a window might not be so easy.

"Or that one?"

She will have a room facing the interior courtyard. Yes, let us take that room.

Irwin realized he had picked out the woman who caught his eye the first time he looked up. She appeared lonely, resting warily against the wall of her bedroom. When she noticed Irwin pointing at her, she hunkered down. "That one is a good one."

They watched two dances. During the second dance, the ladies had chains hanging from their hips, a few wore bells on their ankles. It all became like a raging migraine. Irwin kept consuming shots of whiskey to calm his nerves. Those pretty dancers were only there to provoke the men, and it was working.

Shit, I need to get out of here.

At the end of the first set of dances, Irwin leaned toward Arny. "I am ready for that woman."

"One woman for each of ya?"

"At four silvers apiece, we will share." Irwin felt Kipp's gaze on the side of his face. He nodded at him, hoping his friend would stay mute.

"Ya just had some gold pieces!"

"Yes. And that bottle of whiskey took all I had been paid. All I have now is five or six silvers. Hauss might have a few pieces left, but I told him I would buy."

Arny leaned forward toward Kipp. "You two like to share women?"

Kipp stiffened in his seat. His voice rattled. "Well, Samuel usually likes to watch more than take part. But now and then, we do have some fun."

"I am thinking of a threesome tonight!" Irwin closed his eyes and took a deep breath. All the broad swords, short knives, and nails holding soldier's boots together, fake teeth, jewelry, ladies' hairpins, buttons and hooks on clothing, and monies in soldier's pockets generated a symphony of metal. He could barely keep from exploding. When he opened his eyes, small bits of silver speckled around his iris. He gazed at Kipp. "I want a feisty woman tonight! How about you, Hauss?"

Kipp nodded. "We should probably go get one then, before they're all taken." He poked Irwin's forearm with his finger.

Arny jabbed Leon's elbow, indicating for him to take over chaperoning.

Irwin stood first. Kipp was slow to rise, and looked at Arny, as if to ask permission to go. The Erthin signaled for him to leave the table and follow his friend.

Leon led them across the crowded room. They pushed past patrons, many of them were Clan-Duins with sour faces looking at Irwin. A line of men congregated at the bottom of the stairs. The Erthin signaled Irwin and Kipp to lead the way. They were stopped at the third-floor promenade. Two robust men sat on either side of the stairs, taking the silvers needed to access the whores.

A Clan-Duin bouncer was hesitant to allow both Irwin and Kipp into the one room. He sniffed at Irwin and glanced at Leon behind them. Leon assured the bouncer, "I be makin' sur dey donna 'eckle da ladee muchya."

For the price of six silvers, they were allowed to pass without further incident. Leon followed. Irwin in the lead, Kipp remained one step behind. They were slowed down by naked women hoping for some attention. All these women were chained to heavy locks in their bedrooms attached to sturdy wooden bedframes; the sight turned his stomach.

Keep focused, find that wounded bird. There she is.

"Hi. I am Samuel. This is Hauss. We would like some time with you." He glanced at Leon who clearly looked eager to join in.

Irwin and Kipp stared at the battered Clan-Duin woman they had picked out—a mixture of Mortal and Clan-Duin. Her light-brown body had been scarred, and she bore many piercings; her right arm had been taken at the elbow. She was visibly ashamed of her partial limb and bashful about looking at either man. She said her name softly. "Augusta. You can come in." Her head was bowed low as she beckoned the men into her room.

Irwin closed the door before Leon could enter, who then knocked to be let in. He wanted to see into the room, but Irwin would not allow it. The bedroom was small and drab. Her bed was nothing more than a wide cot with a tattered and stained knit blanket. There was a small bedside table with nothing on it. And on the wall behind them, there were two hooks for a gentleman's clothes. Other than that, there was nothing else in the room, no lantern or candles, no dresser or cabinet, no paintings or curtains, no color whatsoever. But there was a window!

Irwin felt the warm nighttime breeze while considering the square opening. A tightly woven grill of iron bars stood between them and freedom. Not even a small bird could slip through. There was no way anyone could get out of this room without going past Leon at the door—except Irwin.

Leon yelled through the door, "Iya wasa 'opin' ta watchya."

"Nope, I did not pay for you to watch."

Leon shouted again, "Iya locka da room on ya tree, anden burn ya'll!"

Irwin opened the door and handed him two silver coins. "Go pay for one of those things they do with their hands." He motioned toward one of the wounded birds on the floor. "She could probably help you out." He shut the door.

Irwin placed a hand on the door and locked them in the room.

Kipp was staring at Augusta. "What happened to you?"

"I dared to escape." She pulled her long hair across her partial arm. "That's what happens here. If you try a third time, they take it off at the pit." She averted her eyes and went to the bed, pulling at her hair, watching the two men.

Kipp asked the naked woman, "What else do they do if you dare to escape?"

"We get three strikes. Fourth time, you're beheaded." Her eyes averted away from his, down to her skinny legs. "I'm sorry." She lifted her dark amber eyes. "What would you like me to do?" She began a sultry dance.

Irwin put a hand on both Kipp and Augusta. "I need you two to be good."

Augusta froze under his touch. "I am always good, sir." Her voice shook, as did she, but there was no change in her behavior. He was thankful she was not under telepathic control.

"Good." He walked over to the barred window. Kipp watched with apparent confusion. Irwin drew the tightly welded metal window casing into his flesh. Full of metal, his arm hairs stood on end. The window was now wide open, and the nightly breeze wafted through the otherwise stale-smelling room. He looked back at Kipp and Augusta and placed his fingertip to his lips. She was visibly frightened, but said nothing.

"Kipp, I need you to enjoy Augusta until I call for you." He wiped dry his sweaty palms and climbed up on the open windowsill.

"Wait a minute!" Kipp wheezed. "What are you doing?"

Irwin held himself steady in the window frame. It was a three-story drop to the stone courtyard below. Drunk on ore and whiskey, he whispered, "I am about ready to erupt." He looked down again. "We will escape soon. But first I will cause a distraction."

Metal sang to him from everywhere.

Keep calm. Do not let go. Not yet.

Sweat flew from his brow when he shook his head. He was trying his best to keep his eyes and thoughts straight. "Now I know why my father did not want us to be inside a town or city for too long. Kobiton did not prepare me for this place." The metallic humming was almost more than he could bear.

Shit! I cannot control it. I want to let go. Ugh, but not here. Not around Kipp. Not yet.

All the metal within a block's radius was screaming for him to summon it, to release it, and mold it into his own creation—into himself.

I cannot let go. Not yet!

Kipp was definitely horrified. "I hope you know what you're doing?"

The hunger for the ore was taking over. Silver swirled in Irwin's eyes; his irises were consumed by it.

The woman on the bed sat back against the wall, fear rattling her eyes. With a snap of his fingers, her ankle cuff and chain were summoned into Irwin's hand. She gasped, quivered.

A gold piece floated to the table next to Augusta's bed. "When that moves, Kipp, so should you. Stay here until then. Oh, and do not forget to enjoy yourselves!"

4

Get in. Get the Baggage. Get Out

Irwin hung onto the stone lined windowsill. Dropping this far would kill most anyone. Long ago he had thrown himself off a cliff, a little higher up than this, and survived. Using some of the metal he had just absorbed, he created disk-like footholds and cemented them firmly into the brick-and-mortar façade. Pushing metal into rock was as easy for him as pulling it into his skin. He scaled down the tall building and left the footholds for Kipp.

He crept along the edge of the courtyard wall, where adjacent alleyways were flanked by five and six-story buildings. He followed the pull of his metal located deep in the Hall's stables. For the moment, the streets were mostly barren. Yet he heard distant conversations and felt metal moving everywhere. Slinking through the shadows, he found his way toward the avenue between the barracks and the saloon.

Stopping at the end of a zig-zag alley, Irwin was barely out of the street's light and could see only four PCP soldiers guarding the closed gates. A few people of Talent passed by the narrow alleyway, unaware of him there in the darkness. He held still—held his breath. Metallic melodies beat at his brain. He shook his head, trying to hold his perspective. The world rattled and tilted sideways.

I am ready to give in. No. Keep it together for Kipp. But he is not here. I do not have to keep myself in check. I just want to let go. NO!

He wobbled, struggled to keep his compulsions at bay. But the music of the metals was too loud—a symphony calling for him to conduct it.

Remember the plan. Keep it simple. Get the horse and donkeys, baggage, and metal, and get out. Shit, this is not going to work.

He could barely control the rush of power.

Keep it together. You know what to do. Go in, get our belongings and get out.

There were Erthins and Clan-Duin guards standing around, unaware of the brutality about to be unleashed.

Do no harm. Be safe.

He took a deep breath and walked out into the open where four guards stood idly chatting on either side of the massive closed gates. A small open doorway in the right gate allowed foot soldiers access into the courtyard. With a quick motion of his hand, both iron gates automatically spread open.

A guard was hit and flew out into the roadway, his head slammed against the cobbles. He lay still, possibly dead. The other startled guards turned toward the threat. One of them was an Earth Erthin. He tried to engage Irwin with his earth power, to up-heave the surrounding ground. But his first move was his last.

An odd sensation enveloped Irwin. Suddenly he could feel what this Earth Erthin was made up of: dozens of types of trace metals, minerals, and elements. With little movement from his hand, he disintegrated the Erthin who became fluid like a river. His whole body turned into moving molecules—he ceased to exist. That Erthin's essence then floated into Irwin's flesh. He had absorbed all the tiny pieces of that Earth Erthin.

For only a moment, Irwin paused and gazed around.

What just happened? What did I just do?

Do not worry. Keep focused. Breathe. Get in, get the animals, get the baggage and metal, and get out.

He forced himself to move and strode through the giant gated doorway into the Hall's interior compound.

He was not fully aware of what had just transpired.

The singing. I want to control it. The melodies are overwhelming. Keep focused. Do not worry. But I must fix the songs! Keep focused. Get in, get the animals, get the baggage and metal, and get out.

The other two Erthins guarding the entrance launched an aerial assault. Half a dozen fiery balls flew at him. Irwin was a magnet for their flames—they landed on his exposed arms and were snuffed out immediately. A low growl gurgled in his throat. His eyes reflected the iron held with his flesh—reflected the inner demon screaming to escape.

Do not oppose me! I could kill them all. Shit, no! Stay focused. No. Kill them all. No, stay in control. No. Kill them! No.

Sweat dripped down his sides and back, his shirt clung uncomfortably inside his pants. The urge to control everything made of metal grew stronger. It was just like his father's screams, demanding a reaction.

Keep focused. I want to kill them. I cannot. Keep focused. I want to let go. Kill them all. No! Stay focused!

The Metalistic energy oscillated throughout him, screaming to be released.

NO!

He blinked and exhaled. A sense of calm rushed through him as he succumbed to the will of his own cumbersome power. Irwin could not contain himself any longer. He was overwhelmed by his Metalistic energy. He had been restrained for too long. His whole life had been a series of lessons in learning to contain these inner demons. But finally, he let go of his urge to control his power and at once there was a sense of freedom he had never felt. He did not have to hide who he was from anyone anymore—a state of ecstasy rushed through him.

Samuel Irwin Miner was a Metalist—and something else.

A dormant Coterie power had been passed to him from his mother's family. And the combination of Coterie and Metalist powers was unlike any other. That dormant power had now been triggered the instant Irwin gave into his Metalistic desires. An electrical charge took hold over him, and the damage he could now inflict was far greater than anything his father ever wrought, and not something Irwin would or could gain control over now.

The Fire Erthins did not give up their attack. They pummeled Irwin with their fire, and he absorbed it. Unrelenting, they tried all their tricks—but to no avail. Fire blasted from their hands, then all around him; they even tried to incinerate him from within, but Irwin moved on. With a flick of his fingers, he extinguished their lives, absorbing the two Erthin soldiers who assaulted him with their fire. As they dissolved into tiny pieces, Irwin watched their oxygen and hydrogen molecules move around him, as if on a breeze, and then he pulled all of it into his flesh. On he marched, still not fully aware that he had just taken two more lives.

Three Clan-Duin soldiers, hidden by shadows but not to him, were shocked by what they had just witnessed. They were frozen, not wanting to advance as they probably smelled him; saw what he was—Death in human form.

He stepped further into the compound without any more confrontation. The courtyard sitters barked wildly, trying to alert those above in the barracks and those across the road. Irwin had little regard for life now. He had succumbed to his powers. He was not even seeing everything going on around him.

Get in, get the animals, get the baggage and metal, and get out.

He moved his hands, and all the metal collars crushed the canine's throats, killing all the barking dogs instantly.

Soldiers in the Hall had become aware of the horror going on below. Many lights flickered on. Everything in the courtyard that was metal began to move. All things metal swirled toward and around Irwin—he did not know what he was doing, but he did know where he was going. The silver cache in the stall spoke to him. As he left the courtyard, all the axes, hammers, buckets, nails, and other metals churned into tall, thin cyclones—moving around the courtyard and magnetizing other metal items. Even the iron carriage and wagons shifted from their idle positions. The iron carriage levitated around and thrust destruction against the exterior walls. The other wagons over-turned their manure loads, swam along the cobbles, ramming into everything in their path.

Irwin strode into the stable. He snapped his fingers, and all the stall doors unlocked and opened; except for one. He put his arms up, and all the horses with horseshoes were forced to move—startling other enormous beasts into moving, whether or not they had shoes on. They all ran toward the courtyard and freedom.

Pandemonium had struck the PCP Hall.

Buckets, blades, nails, latches, chains, hoists, hardware, small equipment, wagons, and the iron carriage all swam in the air, smashing into the building's façade, horses, and PCP soldiers. The first men to arrive in the courtyard had to dodge the deadly metal twisters. They were still trying to figure out what was happening. Not even the Telepaths knew from where the destruction came.

Within the Hall's walls, pieces of metal were also disturbed, flying this way and that—swords and knives, goblets, pitchers, trays, utensils, pots, pans, vases, pictures, nails, doors, and drawers. Not one item of metal was left untouched. Screams echoed from inside the Hall and all the sleeping quarters above. He moved toward his goal.

Get in, get the animals, get the baggage and metal, and get out.

No one could stop the carnage.

Metallic cyclones veered off-course, drawn to any Erthin who tried to use their powers—bodies were diced and left in bloody pieces. The Coterie spell put in place impacted the building most of all. Erthins' powers were used like boomerangs in a windstorm. Those who harnessed fire were set aflame; those who held water drowned. Those who channeled air had their breath sucked away; those who touched earth split into atoms and floated into oblivion. All this, and Irwin had no clue what type of power he had unleashed. More and more soldiers were reduced to nothing and then absorbed by him.

This was all about freeing Kipp, retrieving the animals and his metal. It was also about finding Yace. He could not stop what he had started. And there was no one in the city of Onj Raha with comparable power. Those in his way would not prevail—not even those who possessed telekinesis could stop this destruction.

Irwin was lost in his own world.

His mind was focused on one stall—the donkeys and the warhorse.

Get in, get the animals, get the baggage and metal, and get out.

He put the packs on Jenn Jenn and Nee Nee and saddled Bodi. The silver on the floor levitated up into perfect spheres and floated into his bags. He tied the donkeys onto the horse and led them out of the stables. Their footfalls echoed as they followed their master. They parted through a wide doorway into the chaotic courtyard. Irwin lifted his hand high into the night. Their personal bags, laced with metal and nestled under their claimed beds, burst out through the glass window and flew down to him.

He secured their baggage and mounted the massive black horse—watched his metal twisters churn around the courtyard, chewing up all in their path. Any Erthin who dared to challenge him was absorbed without hesitation. He had no care in this storm of his own creation for any life but his own, his animals, and Kipp. Dead bodies of the two-legged and four-legged lay scattered across the courtyard.

A young warhorse was stuck in the corner next to the open gates. It had avoided a twister but found the corner and was panicking. Rearing several times, the horse calmed as Irwin and his animals approached. Irwin tossed a rope around its neck and pulled it along and then escaped the Hall.

Hundreds of Erthins and Clan-Duins were waiting out on the roadway, waiting to block his getaway. They had come from the saloon, from down the streets, and out from neighboring buildings. They were mostly men, but several women stood ready to fight, ready to kill. But they were no match for Irwin's newly unleashed power. Without warning, the gates flew off their hinges, smashing dozens to their death.

Having wiped clean a swath of people in the road, he was ready to leave—no matter what. Those who tried to smother him with their Erthin powers were instantly absorbed. Anyone daring to stand in his way was either smashed with the gates, pummeled with pieces of metal, or sliced to death by the metal twisters he released into the streets. Irwin was immune to all attacks. None of the PCP soldiers were prepared to fight this monster. He directed and deflected energies, absorbing soldiers while slicing others into bits and pieces, the whole time keeping himself and his animals safe. He rode down the street on horseback, hoping to avoid a chase, meanwhile heading for Kipp; any Clan-Duins who tried to get to him were taken out by the pieces of metal he rotated around himself and his animals. Anyone who got in his way would not survive.

The Saloon rattled. Screams echoed throughout the building. Chaos erupted. It sounded and felt as if a war had broken loose and that the giant structure would soon collapse.

The gold piece Irwin left behind levitated off the table in Augusta's bedroom and floated toward the window. Kipp followed the coin down the wall and across the courtyard.

The coin flew along a narrow alley until Kipp bumped into the rump of a warhorse.

"That is your mount." Irwin had backed the horses and donkeys into the alleyway in an attempt to keep out of sight.

Kipp used the wall to climb up onto his tall steed. He had no saddle or bridle to hold on to, only a long and thick horse's mane. "Should I ask what all that was about?"

Irwin was preoccupied. There were still armed soldiers on horseback and on foot, racing around, trying to find him. Those who were left alive were out for revenge. He looked back to make sure Kipp was mounted and ready to run.

"Stay close." He kicked the black horse onward.

Hoof falls cracked loudly against the cobbles as they raced out from the shadows. The donkeys were fit enough to keep up with the warhorse to which they were attached. Irwin prompted his horse onward. He did not look around as they passed through the intersection next to the Hall and the saloon. He sensed that Kipp was looking around, smelling the blood, seeing the carnage. Thankfully, his friend stayed close, had mercifully left Augusta behind.

They crossed the main thoroughfare and headed due south. Clan-Duin soldier dogs, no doubt having caught his scent, pursued them with vengeance. Brigades of Erthins on horseback, alerted by the barks and howls, trailed close. The chase was on. He did not know where he was going, but he wanted to get them out of Onj Raha as fast as possible.

϶϶ ϶϶

For the first few kilometers, the horses did not tire. Even after they were outside the city limits, Irwin did not let up and neither did their pursuers. Dogs, large cats, and even birds of prey trailed close behind. The band of Erthins on horseback tried to match the pace he had set. There was a legion of PCP after them. Luckily, Irwin and Kipp's horses were up for the nighttime run—more so than a run during the day when it was hot and humid.

They were chased into the darkness. It soon became noticeable that none of those hunting them were trying to harm them. It appeared that the PCP wanted to make sure that Irwin and Kipp did not return to Onj Raha. The main base for PCP in Onj Raha was wrecked. Several hundred soldiers were dead, and those remaining pursued with caution.

The horses and donkeys were lathered up and breathing heavily by the time Kipp could catch Irwin's attention. They had to slow down. The Clan-Duins on foot had halted their chase. And those on horseback had slowed their pace.

"Irwin!" Kipp shouted repeatedly. "You need to stop! IRWIN! You're gonna kill your Jennies."

Irwin ceased the break-neck speed, letting the out-of-breath animals have a reprieve.

Kipp slid off his bareback mount. "What's wrong with you? What in holy Hakra did you do back there? I saw bodies, and the stench of blood was ... was ...."

Still atop his blowing steed, Irwin swooned—rolled off and hit the ground.

"Irwin? Dang it! Are you alright?"

His head hurt. His lungs tingled. His body ached. It was a short time before he came to and rolled over. "I think I am going to be sick." He gagged and lost his meal, the alcohol, and the metal in his body. Food and drink spewed from his mouth. Metal pooled out from his hands and lay semi-liquid on the gravel road.

"What the fuk happened back there?"

Irwin heaved again.

Kipp brought him a canteen. "Do you know how much carnage I saw? You broke the Hall and the saloon!"

Irwin steadied himself; he rose slowly to his feet. Everything was spinning.

Kipp handed him the canteen and stepped back. "Now I know why my first instinct when I met you was to run away."

Irwin looked at his hands. "What have I done?" His voice shook, and so did his body. He remembered everything he had done. "What did I do?"

"I'll tell you what you did," Kipp snapped, "you murdered dozens of men and women. I saw at least a hundred Clan-Duins lain to waste! They're gonna pursue you until you are dead. You know that!"

Irwin coughed and dry-heaved; he drank down the flask of water. "One hundred and seventeen," he hiccoughed, "I feel them all." He squeezed the last drops of water into his mouth. "I am a monster."

"Yeah, you are. I shouldn't be with you. I should leave you," Kipp muttered under his breath and walked away.

"Yes, you should! You should not trust me. I am not to be ... I should be put away. Now I know why my father was so ...."

His mind swirled, recalling everything he had done, accidentally and on purpose. He had created a spell unknown even to him—from some dormant power. It was a Coterie spell of reaction and deconstruction, a spell with a more deadly effect when combined with his Metalistic abilities. He shuttered from its effect. Irwin's powers had not ceased when it came to manipulating metal; he had always wondered, but now he knew. This latent power he had just unlocked was unlike his father's. His newfound ability allowed him to see and affect all the basic elements at an infinitesimal level.

Realizing the depth of his destruction, he cried out. "I can feel them," he spluttered, "one hundred and seventeen—I can tell you how many and of what type they were. Thirty-five Fire Erthins. Forty-nine Earth Erthins; ten Wind Erthins, seventeen Water Erthins, and six Healers. I can feel their energy signatures, their elements—all the pieces of them are in me." He stared at his hands. "I want to die, but I cannot." He was lightheaded, and his body swayed.

"How'd you do ... why would you ...? I told you not to do anything that would get us into trouble—get us killed. This'll make it harder for us to blend in. I thought you would've learned by now that there's an order to things."

Crickets and frogs chanted from the darkness, from the fields beside the road. Irwin did not hear soldiers advancing, but he knew they were not far off. He studied the night sky, trying to figure out their direction.

Kipp's head craned sideways, and he stepped in front of Irwin, sniffing several times until his nose caught a scent. Then he stepped ahead of the horses and walked off into a grassy field. "She was here. She stopped here to relieve herself."

"I am so sorry, Kipp. I never meant for any of this to happen. I only meant to save us and the animals, but I was overwhelmed by the chorus. The metal. It sang to me. It was so loud. You were right. We never should have gone into that Hall. I am sorry for not trusting you."

"Yace!" Kipp called out again.

"What?"

"Wait, I was right?" Kipp wailed as he returned to Irwin. "I knew I was right! Being in that Hall. But had you not been so crazed, we would've been converted into PCP by now. Had they any clue about your power, they would've locked you away and turned me into a courtyard sitter. So, I should thank you for rescuing me, rescuing us." He patted Irwin's shoulder. "Besides, you found her trail. Not thinking like Yace got us Yace. Her scent isn't fresh, but it's not old either." He looked around. "She passed by here earlier."

"Actually, I was thinking like Yace," Irwin muttered. Then he realized what Kipp was implying. "Wait a moment, you mean we actually found Yace?"

"Well, kind of," Kipp said, inhaling the night air. "It seems she's heading in the same direction. You're the luckiest fool of them all, Samuel Irwin Miner."

"I do not feel lucky."

"Not only did you save us from doom, but you also got us onto her trail. Had you not been so brazen, we wouldn't be so lucky."

"That was not luck. It was stupidity."

Horses approached in the distance. "Sounds like our reprieve is over," Kipp said. "Come on!"

Irwin mounted up at the sound of the thunderous hoof beats. Their horses and donkeys were not ready for a full gallop, so they started out at a fast-paced walk. After a while, they began to jog. Irwin raised his arm as if pointing at the stars. "Should I stop them?"

"I feel like you're gonna do what you want, regardless of what I have to say."

"I did not want to kill anyone, but I will if I must."

Kipp harrumphed. "Maybe it's better if we carry on. Engaging them further might cause something we're not ready for. They might kill us. Or they might be chasing us into a trap. Who knows?"

They began to go a little faster; Kipp kept his horse alongside Irwin's. "In any case, we need to be prepared for more soldiers up ahead. We already know what's behind us."

5

Learning to Compromise

They saw no soldiers on either side of the horizon all the next day.

The land they rode across was gentle and rolling and lay like fat fingers spread on the ground, pushing eastward from the foothills of the Kruluver Mountain Range. They loped along a road that paralleled a man-made canal which started in Onj Raha and continued southeast to Raha. Well-kept crops, off-shooting lanes, and aqueducts followed the rolling landscape and did not allow them to see very far ahead or behind.

Nevertheless, they continued to put distance between themselves and the soldiers on their tail. They had to find Yace. The wind blew at them, and her scent lingered as they persisted southward. They raced their horses from before first light until well beyond sunset. The PCP followed, but without confrontation. Meanwhile, the two kept their sights focused on what lay ahead: Yace—the woman they both cared about so much, the woman who had brought them on this journey to find her father, to learn how to use her own Talents and gain knowledge about her own heritage before he died. She was his heir; she was their friend, and now she was in deep trouble. Irwin did not want to speak of what he sensed to be true.

"Why would she run?" Kipp grumbled as they slowed their animals to catch a breath. "Why south?"

"I am guessing that Daos has something to do with it."

"We don't wanna go to Daos. That's the worst place. There's no way she's going to Daos!"

"Where is she going then?"

"We'll find her soon." Kipp strained his head as if to see something. "She's just up ahead somewhere. We'll confront her, and she'll tell us why all the running around."

"You actually think she will tell us why she is running away?"

"I hope."

They passed a line of workers. After about a hundred strides, Irwin picked up the conversation again. "We have seen no evidence of her since that scat sighting."

"Her shit was about half a day old. We're so close!"

How can he be so certain?

"I still smell her." Kipp stared ahead and began describing Yace's scat. "There was sheen and moisture, even though it was beginning to dry out; that means she did it in the heat of the day or just after. And there were several flies on it, also indicating freshness. We should have seen more since then. But most likely, like you, she's not eating much."

"Do we need to discuss excrement right now?"

"Yes," Kipp, the Clan-Duin, barked, "That's how we know it's her. That's how we can figure out how far ahead she is. If she shits again and I smell it, I can tell you how old it is and how far away we are from her—how much faster we need to push our animals." He patted his horse's sweaty neck. "I'm not giving up on Yace, but I'm not running these horses to death either."

There was a long pause. They rode for a while in silence. Workers tended green and brown fields—harvesting, transplanting, transporting, and sowing new crops. It was all well-orchestrated. They still had not seen any other patrols of PCP in front of them or behind. There were many white-washed plantation houses, rows of flourishing crops, fields with cows, sheep, and horses along the roadway.

"I can't believe she is Ishik!" Kipp bemoaned. "Why does she have to be Ishik?"

"You say it as if it is a bad thing. Even if her family background stems from generations of manipulating hundreds of thousands of Mortal people into eternal servitude and suffrage, it does not mean she is that way." Irwin paused to recall the way things had been on this journey with Yace. "I know she has ordered us around, but it was for the good of us all. Yace is a kind and caring person."

"This means she's at least half Coterie!" Kipp panted. "We can only hope her mother's Mortal; but for all we know, Yace could be full Ishik with the incest and all."

"She told me her mother abandoned her."

"And why would a mother abandon her baby?"

"Because she could not care for it. I know nothing about babies, but I know I was hard to deal with as a child. And I had three caretakers."

"Come on, Irwin, don't you understand the power she has just come into? That Oracle told you Ishik's are powerful, and I tell you the same. Dang it. What are we gonna do?"

"Oh, I understand the power she has inherited." Irwin reflected on his recent revelations. "Maybe, since she found out she is Ishik, she decided to go home to her people." He needed to think this all the way through, gain perspective from all angles. "Maybe she was not taken over by Dephen like I first believed. Maybe he told her of his homeland, and now she wants to return to her biological family. Maybe they are the ones who will help her."

Kipp turned up his nose.

"As you have said, Kipp, she always wants something she cannot have. Maybe she believes that going to Daos, back to her family, will bring her that happiness—eternal love and inner peace. Think about it, Kipp. What would you do if you found out you belonged to a grand empire?—forget the fact that they kill those with Talents and have enslaved Mortals? Maybe she just wants to be pampered. You know, have things go her way. She has never wanted to work hard for anything. We know this. She just wants to be bestowed with all the treasures. And now that reality is being handed to her on a golden platter."

"Whose side are you on, Irwin?"

"Hey, I am just trying to run through all the options, find one that fits the proof we have. All I know is what I see, and all you have is what you smell."

"Don't think that my sense of smell doesn't alarm me. But this goes way beyond smell," Kipp said. "It's like that first night with you. My hackles went up. Your smell, your look, everything about you made me wanna run away. But this ... this is worse. Every part of my Clan-Duin nature tells me to drop this hunt."

"Clan-Duin nature or Yace trying to control you?"

"But then a voice in my head says, 'It's Yace you dumb fool', and turns me back around."

"Sounds like a smart voice."

"Sounds like Dana to me." Although they were many days removed from the Gypsy troop, it seemed Yace's adoptive mother was still trying to guide them.

Irwin waited while Kipp drifted—perhaps back to the Gypsy camp.

Finally, Kipp said, "You think Yace's trying to control me?"

"At this point, anything is possible."

"Dang it! Just like I did with you when we first came together, I feel I've gotta compromise."

"At least you are willing to compromise."

"It's not like I want to. I have to. When it was you, it was Yace who kept me from attacking you or running back to the Gypsy. I probably would've run off into the woods and not gone home. I don't wanna compromise again."

They rode on.

This is tough on him. We need to get to Yace.

Irwin stayed in with his own thoughts, watching the road ahead, but occasionally glancing behind.

"You said you believe her body's been taken over?" Kipp was still stewing, still lost in his confusion about Yace. "That she would've said goodbye instead of deserting us?"

"It is one of my theories—the strongest one, really. Unless she is willingly returning home to Daos." Irwin shuddered. "But that exchange with Yace and her father at the manor, I know something happened beyond what we could see or smell. I saw that room dim and felt it get colder." Kipp's stare burned on the side of his face, so he turned to engage the Clan-Duin.

Kipp's eyes dropped. "You're more watchful than I am."

"Why do you say that? You observe things at a completely different level than I ever could. Your sense of smell is uncanny."

"It's your views on behaviors. I see behaviors, but you see the slightest exchange—I just use my sense of smell to tell if someone is angry or fearful."

"I was trained at a young age to watch and not react, Kipp. My father and grandfather were reactive to everything I did. If I did not pay attention, I was beaten. Most of the time, before making any decision, I had to figure out every probable outcome before I made any move. And I constantly feared I would make the wrong move. But after a while, I just figured I would always make the wrong decision. I accepted the fact that I would always do and be wrong."

"That bites."

"Yes, yes, it did."

Kipp held silent for a long time. "I ... I've come up with a compromise."

"And that is?"

"To listen to you."

Irwin chuckled. "You think I have the answers?"

"Yeah, I do."

"I have no answers, only questions."

"But in asking questions, you get answers."

"Ah, you are summoning Yace again, I see."

"No, really Irwin, what is your best idea about why we're going south? Why Yace left us?"

Again silence. They passed several large and long outbuildings. "You really want to know what I think?"

Kipp nodded.

"I believe she has been abducted, so to speak—mentally and physically."

Kipp frowned.

"Think about it. Her actions, the lies—the misleading trails she set for us—why would she do that?"

"She wouldn't."

"Why would she go to such great lengths to get rid of us? If the truth was simple, she would have said goodbye. We could have handled it. This is not Yace leading us around, this is Dephen's doing."

"Why would he abduct her?"

"I do not know. Why did Nonbry not answer any of my questions?"

"He's an asshole!"

"No, that is not it. Although he gave me no verbal answer to my question on Telepaths taking over another person's body, his pauses, and the looks he gave us, I believe he knows more about Dephen than he wants to tell us.

"And when I asked Mistress Guveir about souls of deceased people taking over the living, she too hesitated, said that was powerful magic. But she did not disclose more. So, my guess is that it can happen, but Telepaths do not want anyone knowing that they have the ability for their souls to remain immortal.

"Or the other option is that Yace heard a calling to return to Daos. Maybe during that brief exchange with her father, with Lord Master Dephen Ishik, he somehow told or showed Yace her heritage. Maybe, like I said before, she yearns to be with her true family. Why else would we be heading for lower land? Yace told me that the waterways from Onj Raha lead to the ocean. Daos is by the ocean, correct?" A gust of wind blew Irwin's hair across his eyes.

"From what I understand, not knowing exactly where Daos is located on Urthis, if she takes up passage on a ship, she could return home in a matter of a few moon cycles." He contemplated in silence. He was still in awe of his journey thus far. It had felt expansive—long and drawn out—even though he had only traveled a small jaunt compared to the actual circumference of Urthis.

The Clan-Duin shook his head like a wet dog. "Yace hates boats and the open ocean. One time, a while back, Captain Hari took the two of us out into the Ar Var Harbor when we were following the road to Ajihya. It was windy, and the boat rocked back and forth. She was terrified. I've never seen her like that. She swore she'd never step foot on any boat ever again."

Irwin's curiosity percolated. "Do you know where Daos is located with relation to Onj Raha?"

"If Yace were here, she'd draw us a map in the sky. She used to study Captain Hari's maps with the other kids in camp. I was supposed to, but never did. All I know is that the Daos Territory is south of the Datzar Jungle. We'll find Yace before then." Kipp's shoulders shook, and his brown eyes grew wider than usual. "I've been told about the violent animals in the Datzar jungle. They like eating people."

Again, they rode in silence. Irwin did not press the issue; the Clan-Duin would heat up again.

The occasional plantation buildings, flanked by enormous trees, sat nestled along the roadway. But for the most part, trees were sparse despite the rest of the luscious green landscape. The further away from Onj Raha they rode, the fewer shady spots were to be found. It was only along the canal that a plethora of tall cottonwoods and evergreens grew. And still, they could see workers tending cultivated land, enduring the scorching sun and humid air. An overabundance of dark-furred animals grazed down hundreds of acres of grassland beyond the gardens. An amazing sight.

They ate the second loaf of bread the Inn lady, Gladis, had given them back in Onj Raha. Had there been time, they would have filled their ration bags at one of the local markets. As it was, they ate the last bit of dried meat, half a sack of nuts, and a small portion of rolled oats. After that, Kipp was pressed to steal food from the fields, and he did so that evening after the workers returned to their houses. They plucked what they could from the plants closest to the roadway. Herbs, onions, carrots, corn, an assortment of beans, tomatoes, and peppers would provide enough food to go on.

It was late into the night when Kipp agreed to take a reprieve. They agreed that by then the soldiers in pursuit had most likely stopped to make a camp.

They noticed a fire glowing from the middle of the roadway atop a knoll far behind them—about two kilometers to the north. Shadows moved around the blaze, no doubt the soldiers who were still in pursuit, following.

Irwin and Kipp rested together in the dark. Irwin faced north and Kipp kept an eye on the south. They passed the bag of stolen rations back and forth.

Kipp handed the last pepper to Irwin.

"Oh, no, please, those are making my stomach turn."

The Clan-Duin took the pepper and stuffed it back into the half-full bag.

Irwin asked, "What are we going to do about those soldiers?"

"Nothing. They're probably steering us toward the Hall in the next city."

Irwin studied the road to the north. "If that is the reason, I want you to leave me before we get there. I do not know what I might do if confronted by the PCP again. And you cannot be around when it happens."

Nocturnal animals sang loudly all around them. Irwin knew that Kipp was focused on nothing but Yace. Every other time they had conversed in length that day, the Clan-Duin shared his worries and regrets.

"Sorry Irwin, but I'm gonna leave. I smell Yace. She's close enough that I must go. Alone." Kipp stood to leave.

Irwin was tired and not yet ready to move. "Are you sure about this? You think you will be safe?"

"Yeah."

"Maybe I should come with you. That way, I can be near if you need help."

"No. You stay here, Irwin. Take a nap." Kipp glanced longingly down the road. "I just need validation that this is her choice to abandon us. If she wants us to leave her alone, then we will."

"Wait! No, we cannot abandon her Kipp; we have gone back and forth on this all day. We cannot keep flopping around like fish out of water. If she has been taken in the mind and body by a supposedly dead Telepath, we cannot forsake her." He stood to face his companion in the dark. "Profess your loyalty to her, if you must. Tell her that we want to protect her, that we are here for her. We both know she needs that; she needs us. Besides, there is no way we can go back the way we came. And if we can still be her escorts, then we have nothing to worry about." Kipp had a far-off look. "Are you positive you want me to stay here?"

Kipp took off his boots, and then his clothes, stuffing his belongings into his saddlebags. "Yeah. One of us needs to get some rest. I promise not to provoke her. Hopefully she won't spellbind me like she did the others back in Onj Raha—Gladis and Paulur, and who knows who else."

Somewhat disappointed that he would not be with Kipp, Irwin replied, "I am hoping she will not outright kill you like she did her father's servant Paulur."

"I think I've got better odds with Yace not killing me," said Kipp, rolling his eyes, "without you around."

The residual pain from the chaos he had created back in Onj Raha hung in Irwin's chest. Though he was good at masking his emotions, he was exhausted. He threw up his hands. "If I could have stopped everyone without killing them, I would have. I did not mean to annihilate all those Erthins or to kill all the

Clan-Duin dogs in the yard—not even those who opposed me in the street. I wish I could say it was all an accident." He stared at Kipp; remorse ate at his gut. "But had I not surrendered to my power, we would still be there and not here on Yace's trail." He shook his head, recalling all that he had done. "Everyone would still be alive. Those faces ... the blood. I should have sacrificed myself."

The tension in Kipp's voice was nearly as thick as it had been the night they first met by the roadside past the Gypsy camp. "Get over yourself, Irwin. I've gotten over the fact that you're a mass murderer." The Clan-Duin said nothing more and then mutated into his four-legged canine self.

Irwin watched as Kipp trotted off down the road to follow Yace's scent.

The first bit of morning light kissed the eastern horizon. Irwin climbed onboard his horse and pulled at the other animals to follow. The soldiers would be up by now and riding toward them. Still alone, he headed southward. The donkeys and horses were easier to goad, having napped and eaten. And with a meager load, just over one hundred pounds, the donkeys were compliant.

Kipp had not returned. Irwin knew to keep distance between the soldiers, but he wondered just how far ahead of them Yace had really been.

I hope Kipp found her. Maybe they are still talking. That would be great! Hopefully, she wants us to follow along. What if she does not? Breathe. It will all work out.

He let his mind wander as he rode, keeping an eye out for Kipp.

He traveled almost a kilometer before spotting his hairy friend. The Clan-Duin canine was jogging along, panting heavily, his brown eyes forward and intent. He was unsure Kipp saw them when he passed on by.

"Kipp!" Irwin shouted at the canine version of his Clan Duin friend. He spun the horses around, shouting. "Kipp!" He jumped off his horse and tackled his friend.

He had taken Kipp by surprise. The Clan Duin mutated back into his human form.

Irwin gave Kipp a hand up. "Did you not hear me shouting your name?"

Kipp looked around, clearly bewildered. He studied the sky and then glanced down the road toward the south, then toward the north. He reached up and took his clothing from the saddlebags. He dressed, not speaking a word to Irwin. "Are you alright Kipp?"

Using the stirrup from Irwin's saddle to mount his own saddleless horse, Kipp signaled for them to turn around. "Come on." He sped off on his horse. Irwin turned and followed, trying to keep up.

"Well? Did you see her?"

"Yeah, I am sure I did. I know I did. I think I talked to her, but I don't remember. I don't know what I said. But I know what she said. I know she told me to go home. And her eyes were not hers. Her mind isn't hers either. That's Yace's body we're following, but she's not present. Once we get to the next major town or city, we need to seek out the Talented District and find an Oracle. I need to speak to Nonbry. I need him to tell us what he knows."

After a while, they passed the point where the Clan-Duin had found her. He confessed that he could still smell her horses perched on the roadway. They had pooped, but the manure had been kicked to the roadside. There was a slight divot in the roadway made from her saddle. It appeared that she may have used her saddle as a pillow. Everything Kipp had seen, and how and where she had camped, was unlike Yace. She was not using her tent or any of the pounds of pillows she loved to use for bedding. She was sleeping completely out of her comfort zone. Any remnants of her camp had been swept away—leaving no trace of her existence—but her smell lingered.

Kipp said he had gone to her in earnest, hoping for the best—wanting to know the truth. Before he could speak, she had commanded him to leave.

Irwin watched as Kipp scoured the land all around the deserted campsite.

For the rest of the day, Kipp's mind wandered as they rode. They could still see the trail of dust from the PCP soldiers in pursuit and continued to maintain a distance. By late afternoon, they rode into a small town adjacent to the wide canal that carried supplies from Onj Raha to Raha. There were no PCP soldiers waiting to stop their forward progression here, which Irwin found odd.

Two-story buildings lined the two main avenues through the small agricultural community. Several shops sold home goods and other items to the local farmers. Most of the buildings were wooden—carved and painted with fancy designs. They stopped long enough to purchase some dried food. But this town would not have what they really needed—an Oracle.

6

Amanus Lunas

They continued to chase Yace's scent, but she was never seen again on the southern horizon. Three more days of bone-jarring riding brought them to Raha—an ancient city with white-washed buildings, impressive archways, and layered walkways. This magnificent architecture modeled the flowing ocean and arch of the sun across the horizon, some arches more rounded than others. Stucco facades were flourished with motifs and mosaics. In some places, thick timbers held colorful awnings. Newer construction flowed into older buildings well-chiseled by time. Bright flowerbeds and gardens lined pathways, up and down stairs, and along narrow streets—the bold colors of the red and purple climbing flowers accented the white-washed buildings. The wide canal they had been following flowed through the heart of Raha and emptied into an oblong harbor protected by a great sea wall of stone. Beyond that point, the Bounen Ocean churned and glistened from the nighttime sky.

In what would have taken the average rider twelve traveling days, Irwin and Kipp had made in six. It was twilight when they arrived. The sky turned dark as they rode down the mostly empty roadway. Most of the storefronts were closed. Lights glowed behind curtained windows where most likely city folk were enjoying an evening meal.

Irwin and his steed led, but Kipp's nose told them where to go. They found a large inn with a stable yard and a forge next door, not far from the closed markets and the harbor. So far, they had not been confronted by any PCP.

He continued to ponder their fate. Had the pursuing soldiers lost track? Or lost interest?

As they always had done, per Yace's instructions, they dressed in specific attire. Kipp wore his uniform, playing the part of a passive soldier working for a wealthy merchant, Irwin. Adorned with his rich attire, Irwin had to remember to order his Clan-Duin partner around. It was a tough spot to be in, especially since he considered Kipp an equal. He had to remain alert and keen to their mission and their masquerade.

When in any civilized place, Irwin kept his metal on him, either in coin or knife form. His pale skin, platinum-grayish hair and eyes made him look Mortal, and older—distinguished. He was quiet and charming when paying for a night at the inn. Both remained wary of extraneous interactions in front of others. They sat unobtrusively in the shadows of the dining room. Neither spoke while they gobbled up a hot meal.

He had bought them a bedroom to share, laundered clothing, and hot baths—making good use of the inn's facilities. The animals would also be well kept. They had been fed, watered, and housed for the night. He used the gold Yace had left behind to persuade people to do for them without question.

The two men did everything together. The inn was nearly silent when they ventured out into the dark streets of Raha. It might have been late into the night, but Kipp was keen on finding an Oracle. They needed to contact Nonbry. Yace had not been seen since Kipp's brief encounter. And now that they were in a city, her trail had gone cold.

Irwin took the lead and looked the part, but still they kept to the shadows. There were fewer PCP brigades in Raha compared to Onj Raha, and those they had seen were on horseback. The sound of horse hooves echoing down darkened streets wrought an alarm every time.

Irwin whispered over his shoulder, "Do you not think it is too late, even for an Oracle?"

"I've been told they do most of their business late into the night."

"Do you think Nonbry will be awake?"

"One can hope."

"Do you think he will talk to us?"

"I think you're thinking too much."

The Talented District, an appropriated place where most Talented people lived, was only four blocks large and more rambunctious than the rest of Raha. They detoured away from the local Hall at the edge of the district—Irwin had noticed it from a block away. This Hall was a quarter of the size of the one in Onj Raha but was kept the same way. Large gates loomed two stories tall and opened into a tiny courtyard. Although it looked foreboding, the building wasn't as towering as the other had been. Fewer soldiers, less to worry about—maybe. He led Kipp, still following three steps behind, as they walked the dark and barren streets looking for an open Oracle den. There were no workshops, no whimsically lit storefronts along the avenue.

It was late. Only two taverns and one saloon were open. Irwin was leery of going into any of these establishments. He could feel men with sacks of coins and blades moving around inside. After peering through the windows of two of the bars, he concluded that every establishment in the Talented District had soldiers enjoying libations. How were they to know if any of those soldiers were the ones pursuing them? No doubt there still was a brigade in pursuit, but they had not seen them on the roadway for the last two days. Their caution wavered.

We must remain calm and thoughtful in our mission while we try to gain information.

But Kipp had other ideas—to ignore the notion that they were still being hunted.

The Clan-Duin said, "If we have not seen them yet, we probably won't. The PCP don't seem all that organized."

That is not what Yace told me.

Kipp's thoughts, Irwin knew, were hyper-focused on finding a reputable Oracle and speaking with Nonbry. Nothing else. He insisted the solution they sought would only be available in a local bar somewhere here in this District. After peering inside each establishment, they finally entered the smallest of three.

They stepped quietly into the Clucky Ducky Tavern. It took Irwin's eyes a moment to adjust to the bright lights. The soldiers they had seen earlier through the windows were now gone. Only five people of Talent sat around enjoying drinks. They all wore servants' clothing and were huddled around a bulky table, clamoring over their daily events. The one barkeep was female, a young vibrant Erthin with freckles across her face and bright green eyes. Her auburn hair was pulled back into a ponytail, and she was quick to engage them when Kipp took a seat at the bar. Irwin was slower to sit next to his friend, glancing around the tavern twice before facing the doorway. They bought a few drinks while inquiring about a trustworthy Oracle who might perform services this late into the night.

The sweet barkeep was clearly enjoying Kipp's flirtatious banter. After a while, she asked the only other waitress to relieve her of her duties while she took the two men to a place near the southern side of the wharf.

Kipp kissed her before she left them with the Oracle, Amanus Lunas.

An older Telepath, Amanus Lunas, still presented a youthful beauty that put them at ease. She did not look ancient, but confessed that she was. Her child-like bright blue eyes held a certain innocence.

Irwin was apprehensive about being around any Telepath. He was on guard, wary of patrols or anyone else who would harm them. He kept a watchful eye on Kipp, hoping he would not forget their situation.

Once he paid for her service, Amanus invited them into her chambers. The room was large—a circular table stood stout in the center, with plush pillows all around. She instructed them to find a seat. An old bird's nest on the table held a glass ball. Aromas of cedar incense wafted throughout the room.

Amanus's hair was a soft white, as was her whimsical clothing—her fair skin was sun-kissed from head to toe. She smiled sweetly as Irwin and Kipp took their seats. It was clear that Kipp was wooed by her kindness.

The Clan-Duin handed over the wooden talisman. "We're here to speak to our friend, Nonbry. It is of the utmost importance that we converse with him tonight."

"He speaks by proxy?" She appeared troubled by the idea.

They both nodded.

She grasped the soft-wood talisman and closed her eyes. A low hum came out her nose, and she began to sway—as had the previous Oracle.

Thin curtains moved in the nighttime breeze, and the candlelight danced. Ocean waves and distant bells softly tolled from the boats along the waterfront and out at sea. They tried not to nod off while awaiting connection with Nonbry. Amanus's face and eyes twitched. There was a moment of hope when she turned toward them—her eyes opened. But then she shut them again, still searching for Nonbry.

"I hope he hasn't cut us off," Kipp whispered to Irwin. Then Amanus's face came alive.

"You better have good news!" Nonbry's voice was distinct as it came through the woman's vocal cords.

Kipp jumped at the familiar grumpy sound of the voice. Irwin sat erect.

Clearly disgruntled, Nonbry said, "I hear you haven't retrieved her yet!"

They were both taken aback that Nonbry knew what was going on. With a shaky voice, Kipp said, "No, not yet. Though we're really close. She might even be in this town."

The woman's lips smacked together. "Doubtful. She hasn't stopped moving since leaving your side," Nonbry spoke through Amanus Lunas with thick words.

"She has eluded us. She will elude you too. I had believed that Dephen was doing a kindness for Yace, and myself. But he has wronged everything the Gypsy stands for."

There was a long pause as bitterness boiled up in Nonbry. "At this point, Dana and I believe Yace is under a powerful telepathic spell. We are unable to make contact with her, but Dephen, on the other hand ...." The woman's white eyes fell on Irwin. "As you have hopefully figured out, Yace's father is from Daos and the Ishik Empire. She is a powerful Coterie and Telepath hybrid. This means, of course, that you, Kipp ..." He/she exhaled deeply, white eyes now firmly on the Clan-Duin. "... you are susceptible to Dephen and Yace. Her power can, and will, take its hold on you."

"Wish you could have told me that a few days ago," Kipp grumbled.

Nonbry spoke over him. "Alio hopes you haven't forgotten any of his lessons—the training in how to deal with Telepaths. It's important, now more than ever, that you keep yourself mentally hidden from her. That's how she can track you."

"No, Sir, I haven't forgotten all of it."

"Kipp, this is not the place to—" Nonbry persisted.

"You don't think I don't know that?" Kipp was now as irritable as the old man. "I'm the one responsible for Yace's safety. This is all my fault." He lowered his head.

"You cannot give up on Yace. She doesn't have control of her mind. And Dephen is playing a ground squirrel and hound game with me. This is all for his own personal gain. He's unrelenting about giving Yace any control." There was a long, deep breath. "Dana's dreamed of many things since our last exchange. She showed me what happened between Yace and her father. The vision she shared was vivid, meaning that you've been dwelling on it, Kipp."

"This is all my fault."

"This was never your fault," Nonbry said. "Dephen is manipulating the situation to his advantage. As I see it, Yace is now as valuable a Talented person as Irwin. Her power potential has undoubtedly been unlocked. We all know Yace has amazing abilities. She was never able to control them, but Dephen knows how to control all her telepathic and Coterie powers. All efforts should be made to retrieve her safely and extinguish Dephen in the process."

The white eyes shifted again to Irwin. "It appears, Mister Miner, that you are the only one who can bring Yace back to the living. Your power will ground Dephen's spirit out of her body. Right now, Yace's mind is in limbo. She doesn't know what's going on. And that means Dephen has all the control. Miner, only your Metalistic touch can break this Ishik spell. But Dephen has that knowledge too. And that's why he will continue to put distance between the two of you."

Kipp's voice quaked. "This is an Ishik spell?"

"Yes! And it's a Coterie spell. You need to recognize that."

"My touch," Irwin muttered while quietly staring at the Oracle. "Shit. I should have touched her back at Lord Dephen's manor when she was asleep."

Nonbry said, "Living in the past will not change it."

Irwin harrumphed, "That I know!"

Nonbry—through the Oracle—puckered his lips, and his nostrils flared. "As you speculated, Miner, during our last exchange, a powerful Telepath can take over another being's mind and reside in their body. Sometimes the two spirits can co-exist, but not for long. The more powerful will win and shove the other deep into the psyche. Although sometimes the more powerful Telepath can overtake the subservient spirit entirely. That means they can cast the manipulated spirit outside of their own body—perhaps into a dying body and cast it off. We know Yace wasn't cast out of her body. She is too powerful a spirit, but not thoughtful enough to keep Dephen from entering her mind."

The white eyes of the Oracle shifted back to Kipp. "Dana told me, showed me, that you were compromised by Yace the other night."

Amanus moved in her seat and looked at Irwin once more. "Dana also showed me how valuable you've become, Irwin. Had you not recognized your own worth, worse things would've happened to Yace and to Kipp. Now you're responsible for both of them."

This did not sound encouraging—more like a warning.

"For some reason, Dana has given you much faith. I trust that between the two of you, Yace will be retrieved safely."

Irwin said, "Why is this happening? Do you know?"

"There's speculation around the camp. Those of us who knew Dephen—we've been talking."

"Are we positive that Yace is under a spell? Maybe this is what she wants! Maybe she wants to return to Daos." Irwin wrung his hands.

"Hardly." There was a long pause. "I'm Dephen's half-brother. We share the same mother. But we are separated by nearly thirty years in age. He's the eldest son, and I'm the youngest. Our mother was a true Telepath. She was TeleCapritian. She did things with men to get footholds on trade and political influence. She took Emperor Adabashi Ishik one night, and eight years later gave him Dephen. In return, she was given permanent refuge in Daos Harbor."

"What does it mean to be TeleCapritian?" Irwin asked.

"Not all Telepaths are TeleCapritian. A true TeleCapritian has both telepathic and telekinetic abilities. They can use their mind to do almost anything, including fire making. And mixed with Coterie powers, those abilities become amplified."

7

Listen To Your Elders

The Clan-Duin interrupted. "Yace did that. I remember seeing a light, a bluish-white blinding flame rise above her head."

"You must be cautious, or you'll be manipulated again. She might steer you into a PCP Hall next time. Our mother was the same way. She manipulated people for her autonomy. After using Dephen as a pawn, she had a place to live in Daos Territory. She and her mates could sail the open seas and pillage other ships. I witnessed much of that in my life with her, as I'm sure Dephen did. We both lived with our mother until she gave us to our fathers. And we both returned to her side as adults, but not for long. She used all of her children as pawns. Some of us came from well-to-do families; some of us served her as loyal workers.

"I'll tell you this about Dephen Ishik: He's a bastard Ishik. And being a bastard of royal blood is both a blessing and a curse. When he went to live with Adabashi Ishik, he had many challenges. He had to rise through the ranks, starting at the very bottom, to prove himself worthy of the name Ishik. But his cousins and half-brother were handed great responsibilities they had not earned. As Dephen rose in the ranks, he proudly served the Ishik Empire—especially after the Empire had found a use for him.

"Before my birth, Dephen Ishik was bestowed the title of Ambassador to Daos. Once he held that title, he went back out onto the seas and toured the territories. Our mother was at the helm of his vessel. He was given a purpose, and he used his position to influence others. Our mother taught us by example.

"Dephen made friends beyond the Daos Empire. He had charisma, charm, and Talent. Much Talent! He established alliances with all the territories, though many of those have folded since his departure from ambassadorship. Once upon a time, my brother was a good person of power. He worked diligently for the Daos Empire for many decades; he helped others. But when he was banished, he set about creating heirs."

"Why was he banished?" Irwin leaned forward.

"Somer Ishik, Adabashi's son and rightful heir to the Ishik Empire, banished Dephen because of his indiscretions. Dephen has fathered at least two-hundred children, and probably more we don't know about. He took advantage of every available woman, and that's ultimately the reason he was banished from the Gypsy."

Kipp slunk back on his pillow. "Really? I don't think I ever heard that story."

"He was a philanderer. He took Yace's mother and several of her cousins from their summer retreat off the eastern shore. She was sixteen, and he was nearly eighty, when he stole those ladies-in-waiting. Yace's mother was of TeleCapritian descent, almost as pure in blood as our own mother.

"He enjoyed having his pick of women. Dephen took women like trophies and kept them until they no longer served his purpose—usually when they became pregnant. That's why he threw them away, left them behind in townships and cities. I'm sure that once Yace's mother realized she had a child with an outlaw Ishik, she knew she had to give the child away."

"Why?"

"Because at that time, all Ishik bastards were being rounded up and slaughtered, babies included. Bounty hunters toured Urthis, looking for those matching the description of Ishik lineage. All severed heads were returned to the Daosian Empire for proof and payment. And he gave those bounty hunters who brought back sacks of heads substantial treasures.

"It's been almost thirty years since a worldwide decree was sent out to kill all Ishik blood outside Daos. About a dozen years ago, I decided to protect all the abandoned children of Talent, especially those with blonde hair and blue eyes."

"Wait a moment." Kipp sat up again and leaned forward. "The twins, Elle and Eli, are they Ishik?"

"Yes. They're related to Yace by blood, but removed from her lineage by a generation. They'd be considered a distant niece and nephew."

"That's twisted." Kipp looked over at Irwin.

Irwin was more confused than ever. "Twins?"

Kipp said, "I'll tell you about them later."

Nonbry did not pause. "Yace was told by her adoptive parents that her mother sold her to repay a debt. But in fact, she was left behind because her mother knew they would be hunted and killed. After being rescued by the Gypsy, though I knew it, saw it, I never told Yace she was born from two amazing family bloodlines. I couldn't."

Irwin asked, "Why did you not tell her?"

"I recognized that she would have the power to move the world one day. We had to keep her hidden, much like the twins. When I first confided to Dephen about Yace and her growing Talents, he said he would take her in and teach her how to use her powers properly. My plan was for her to gain the knowledge she needed to tame her abilities, and then come back to us so she could teach the twins.

"Dephen, on the other hand, had his own motives. Right now, he is taking advantage of her, and his reasons are his own. She's on horseback and moving south faster than you two." He nodded and closed his eyes.

The Oracle seemed to be coming back to consciousness, but then Nonbry reappeared in her eyes. Eyebrows furrowed, voice grim, he said, "You need to be exceedingly cautious of your interactions with others. It appears there are soldiers looking for you. Go find a safe place to stay right now."

Nonbry vacated Amanus Lunas. She was slow to come back into her own mind. Kipp grunted at Irwin to toss her an extra gold piece as he grabbed the Talisman. He then pulled Irwin by the arm.

They left through the front door and crept through the shadows. They knew not to go back the way they had come. Hearing many footfalls approaching, Kipp guided Irwin toward a large warehouse half a block from the Oracle's place. The wharf's flank ran along the backside of the warehouse. Kipp held Irwin's arm, keeping contact, remaining hidden from any telepathic probing.

They waited in the shadows behind the warehouse. The PCP's footsteps swelled. Kipp pulled Irwin close, and they held their breaths as a brigade of Erthins, with the female barkeep in the lead, stormed toward Amanus Lunas's home.

Kipp sniffed as they passed. "They're the soldiers who've been following us."

They scurried between warehouses along the wharf and then raced along the seawall's edge. "I bet you Dana told Nonbry about those soldiers. She's good at seeing things Nonbry can't." They zigzagged down alleys, through city streets—doubling back a few times to hide their trail.

It was late at night when they slipped inside the meager inn. They went upstairs to their bedroom and tried to sleep before morning's first light; but the bed was so comfortable, they both slept in. They were awoken by a pounding on the door. Irwin leaped to his feet. It was one of the inn's children come to tend the room. Handing over a gold piece, Irwin requested they rent the room for that day too. He gently pushed the child out of the room. This would allow them to catch up on sleep and to purchase a few items from the local markets.

During the afternoon heat, when most of the residents were keeping cool inside buildings, Irwin took a donkey, Jenn Jenn, to the markets down near the wharf. He was not the only person using donkeys for hauling goods. He made sure not to have metal inside himself—only his knife, a satchel of gold coins, and several silver rocks were stashed here and there on his person. He bought pounds of cooked and raw, perishable and nonperishable foods, and more alcohol. They needed to be prepared for the journey that lay ahead.

He did not spot any Erthin brigades in the markets or leering close by. He could only hope they were now behind the soldiers hunting them. He looked for Yace, wondering if she too might try to restock supplies. Now, more than ever, he had to be extra cautious and attentive to everything and everyone. Eventually, he spied a brigade of Clan-Duin soldiers on foot and kept clear of them. He looked at all the female faces, but they all had light brown hair and appeared to be locals. Irwin made sure they were packed and ready to go before returning to the room, to Kipp. He found the Clan-Duin laying on the bed staring at the ceiling.

Kipp reared up when Irwin entered the room. "You know how Yace is always saying we need to look the part?" He did not wait for an answer. "Well, I've been thinking that for us to get away with being out there and overlooked, you need to be the white-skinned man you are and be selling something—something useful to the common family. Did you know there're many salesmen on the roadways trying to make silver?"

Kipp's eyes glistened. "You could sell knives! That could be your story. You could sell all different types: short, long, paring, cleavers. There's gotta be a market for those. And, yeah, these would be special knives. They never rust, or maybe they're always sharp, and you'll sell them cheaper than they go for here in town."

"I am not sure I would want to undercut the locals, Kipp. The local smith forged his knife. It took days to perfect his blades, and with much hard labor. For me, all I must do is think about what I want, and there it is; no real work involved."

"You could offer knife repair, make dull knives sharp again."

"I think you have summoned Yace for this one."

"Quite possible." Kipp rubbed the side of his head. "I couldn't sleep."

"That sounds like a great story, but they will want to know how I make the knives. Where they are from. They will ask questions."

"Your father's forge back in Kobiton, of course! We can work this to our advantage. You can say that Kobiton knives are made from the richest iron."

"I will need a lot more iron if I am to make useful blades."

"There's iron all around us."

"I know. I try not to notice."

"Don't you get it? You'll just take a little bit from here and there as we pass through town. You know, put it in the saddlebags; casually fill them with iron. And then we'll make our way out of here and head back southward. No one will be wise to us."

Irwin understood his friend meant well, but the idea soured his stomach. "I will not steal iron as we ride through the city. That would not be safe."

"You're right. Forget it."

"Let us get going then."

They ate some of their rations while riding off into the settling dusk. All night long, Irwin kept quiet; he was enjoying this metal-less time. They stopped briefly to rest, but then kept on going. They assumed that Yace probably had not stopped in Raha, meaning they were now at least a full day behind her.

Morning crept across the distant horizon. The ocean roared and crashed to their left. Fields of wheat crops wove on for days to their right. They pressed their horses onward as the dawn of a new day was upon them. Rays of bright yellow and pink light mottled the sky; a hint of blinding white light sparked from corner to corner along the watery horizon.

Irwin had never seen the ocean. It was a remarkable sight—the sun cresting the eastern sea at dawn. At night, the ocean looked like a hazy streak, mirroring the sky's remaining light. All they heard was crashing, clapping, and rolling against the shoreline. Irwin wanted to slow and watch the spectacle.

He wanted to stay and watch the sun ascend the horizon. He was hypnotized by the sight. But Kipp implored him to keep going. They would be traveling along the ocean's edge for days, he said, and once they catch Yace, they would devote a day to watching the sun rise and set.

Irwin asked, "Have you ever seen the sun set in to the ocean?"

"Yeah. That was around the time the Gypsy found Yace. She was born on the west coast, you know."

"No, I did not."

"I was too, but farther north, where it snows every winter, and the summers are short."

"Sounds like my life. It would snow three-quarters of the year and be sunny for only one-quarter. And our diet consisted of goats, rabbits, and squirrels."

They reminisced about their separate lives.

Kipp said, "My mother loved making strawberry rhubarb pie. What I wouldn't do for a bite of that right now."

"Strawberries. Yum, that sounds good!"

"Oh, it's the best type of pie. I think Patrice has made it a few times, but it's been a long while since I've tasted it." Kipp gazed off into his memories.

They continued on soundlessly until the heat of the midday sun forced them to stop. They wandered down to the ocean for a dip—a reprieve from the humidity. But there was no place for the black furred horses to avoid the pressing heat. They had not seen one tree along this stretch of road. The horses followed along willingly and seemed to enjoy themselves in the warm surf. The donkeys, however, looked on with trepidation from the beach.

8

Dephen's Sinister Side

At the next scat sighting, Kipp declared they were about a day's trek behind Yace. She probably had stopped in Raha after all, but only long enough to retrieve some food. Most likely she returned to riding southwards, taking no reprieve at an inn.

Kipp suggested they not stop anymore. So, for many days and nights, they tried to catch up with Yace and Dephen. The sandy and sometimes rocky roadway hugged the edge of the terrain away from the trees and followed along the threshold of various bays. Tall grasses hid mounds of sand that protected them from hard winds. The rutted road plowed through tiny quaint fishing villages. On they rode.

There was no sight of any PCP ahead or behind. Irwin could not, and did not, forget that they must be aware of the soldiers still searching for them. Emotions swelled like the ocean's surf and blew like the gusty winds. They had too much time to themselves, on horseback, listening to their own ruminating thoughts while following a lukewarm trail.

Kipp insisted for Irwin continue practicing his Metalistic powers. And he did, every night before falling asleep. Meanwhile, Irwin implored Kipp to meditate and run through the techniques Alio had taught him for thwarting telepathic spells.

They both were preparing to save Yace and battle Dephen.

This time spent together, and their relentless riding, was a blessing and a curse for both men. Irwin was humbled to have found himself on such a wild adventure. Even though he was completely out of his element, he was not as scared of the world as he had once been. And the inspiration of his strengthening power, as he suspected Yace's was too, made him more self-aware. He mentally and physically noticed how much he had blossomed since leaving Yace's side. Feeling proud of himself was new, even if sometimes he felt cursed by it all. His newfound abilities shocked them both. He continued to hone his extraordinary talents.

Irwin had noticed that the longer they traveled away from the city of Onj Raha, Kipp's confidence in rescuing Yace wavered. Only when he spotted her excrement was he temporarily happy. But then he would calculate how far away she was and return to wondering if they were too late to rescue her. The Clan-Duin's circular logic was not helping their situation.

"I wish I were a raven," Kipp said as they rode along.

"Why?"

"Then I could find Yace and know exactly how far ahead of us she is."

"Yesterday you said her scat was over half a day old, not one full day." Irwin knew he needed to brighten their prospects for the Clan-Duin's sake. "That means we are closing in on her. In a few more days, we will only be a few kilometers behind."

"We've been on the road for too many days already!" Kipp bemoaned. "And we're only closing the gap in tiny bits of daylight at a time. That's not fast enough for me."

"Well then, maybe we do not stop tonight."

Kipp pointed toward the animals. "They're not meant to go nonstop. Even in the wild, they only travel as much as we do during daylight. At night, most herds stop for a reprieve."

"Are you implying we should stop?"

"I think we should limit our down-time tonight. You don't need to practice; you should sleep ... or only one of us should sleep."

"Maybe you should be the one getting sleep tonight," Irwin said. "You become irrational if you have not slept enough."

"But if we don't stop, and she does, then we can close that gap and be only a quarter day behind!"

"How has your ass been doing without a saddle?"

The Clan-Duin rolled his eyes. "Oh, you know it hurts!"

"I have offered you a day in my saddle. But you say you do not need it. I think you do. Either that, or you enjoy complaining."

"Fine. Maybe we stop soon, for a short time, that is."

"Sounds good."

They rode on a bit longer across the open landscape. Their animals needed a break; they needed to eat and rest. The horses and donkeys tried to snatch bites off the longer grasses lining the road that bowed to the evening winds, practically tickling the horse's muzzles.

Once it was completely dark, they stopped. Both men sat on the hard ground eating and contemplating the situation. Later on, they both found sleep, but it was not restful. Still, they rose before the sun and got the horses and themselves warmed up by briskly walking. When daylight finally broke through the darkness, they picked up their pace.

Kipp was clearly hell-bent on finding Yace before she traveled beyond their reach.

At this point, Irwin felt as if he were merely along for the ride. He enjoyed watching the oceanic scenery—filling him with flashes of ecstasy. The warm breezes and gulls floating offshore in search of fishy meals was what he had longed to see. *A humbling sight indeed!*

Rolling on through dense wheat fields that spilled up to the edge of the wind-shaped seascape, they traveled between thickets and villages, and then the landscape shifted again into terraformed parcels. That was how they knew they were nearing a larger town or city.

⋺⋹ ⋺⋹

Very few people worked in the agricultural fields that day; most of the expansive parcels of land were filled with domesticated animals, no doubt slated for slaughter. They rode through a medium-sized town. There was one long bridge that spanned across the giant channel from the protected harbor out to the ocean. Along that exposed part of the road, the wind spit sand in their faces. On the other side of the bridge was a fisherman's market. Merchants loudly shouted their wares, eager to make a sale, but there would be no stopping. They had no need for a reprieve or to purchase more rations. Irwin made sure the animals, and they too, would be well kept for a moon's time when he had stocked up on food back in Raha.

He estimated they were eight days south of Raha, moving quickly as always. They persisted, leaving the little sea town behind. It was a rough ride along the uneven landscape as the road crept along the edge of the world.

All this time with just Kipp at his side somehow made Irwin feel complete. This was what he had craved all his life.

Someone I can get along with. Someone who respects and accepts me for me.

He had never had anything like this since his early childhood under Great Grandpa Edwin's wing. Now those feelings were reflected by someone of his own age. And feeling those emotions was overwhelming.

I know this will all end. Nothing ever stays the same. Life has a way of changing.

They were on the grand adventure they had once wanted to take after leaving Yace at her father's.

I wonder if Kipp will want to remain friends after all of this. After finding Yace. Why not?

Around the campfire at night, they shared stories about their hopes and dreams for life after they saved Yace. These chats with the Clan-Duin led Irwin to believe that Kipp could not envision a time beyond this. Kipp's thought processes were often too linear and too negative. The Clan-Duin would drone on about what should have happened or what they could have avoided had Dana or Nonbry alerted them in time. He found fault in everything, wishing aloud that he could go back in time and change things. It was disheartening to realize that Kipp could not accept the present or believe in their future.

He thinks only of himself and of what he has done wrong. What can I do? I cannot allow his negativity to affect me. We will rescue Yace. Until then, I must keep thinking of a solution, not the problem. Ugh. Maybe I missed something along the way. Think Irwin, think!

He understood that Kipp saw his time apart from Yace as drawn out and hopeless—no longer believed they would find her and rescue her.

There was nothing Irwin could say to upturn the Clan-Duin's forlorn attitude.

Until one day Irwin blurted out, "Assassin!"

"What?"

"Think about it!"

"Huh?"

"Why did someone attempt to kill Dephen?"

Kipp stared at Irwin.

"It could be jealousy. Lover's quarrel perhaps. Or maybe a bounty hunter sent to infiltrate and then assassinate. Now that last one makes perfect sense to me."

Kipp squawked, "How do you come up with this shit?"

"Nonbry said that nearly thirty years ago, bounty hunters were sent out to bring back the heads of the bastard Ishik children Dephen created. I am guessing he was at the top of that list. So, for thirty years, Dephen has eluded his brother's decree and kept on procreating. Maybe, somehow, Somer found where Dephen was living, or one of those bounty hunters did. A female bounty hunter, dressed as a servant, got all friendly with that lustful old Letch and tried to kill him.

"That was the reason for us to get to Onj Raha so quick: he had been poisoned, and Death stood at his door. Although he had friends willing to help him escape Death, he was on the edge. We saw it. And to escape Death, his powerful daughter, Yace, comes, and he uses her to save himself.

"He must have known who her mother was. He probably remembered that she was TeleCapritian. He is Coterie and TeleCapritian. He knows how to use Yace to his fullest advantage. All those spells we witnessed in Onj Raha—"

Kipp was sitting high on his mount. "You think too much."

"Dephen is trying to get us off his path because he knows we can halt what he is trying to do." Irwin paused, hoping that his friend would not lose interest.

"And that is?"

"I believe Dephen plans to assassinate his brother, Somer."

"Holy Hakra!" The Clan-Duin hooted at Irwin.

"Dephen is seeking revenge for the attempted assassination."

"Is this why you were beaten as a child?"

"What?"

"For your overactive imagination?"

"Do you not see this for what it is? What other reasons would there be for traveling southward to Daos? Dephen will use Yace to kill his brother. And unless we can stop them, it will happen."

"She's not strong enough to do that. He would've picked a male heir if he wanted to kill his brother."

"A male body might just corrupt his mind, allow him to follow temptation and procreate more. But with Yace, he cannot just give in to those desires. She could become pregnant. With him inside her, inside her psyche, he must remain focused. Her body forces him to stay on task."

"Yeah, you definitely think way too much!"

"How could you not see it?! Why else are we heading to Daos?"

"How do you know this is the way to Daos?"

"Where else is Dephen leading us?"

"You actually believe everything you just said? I think this is all just stupid luck."

"Even Nonbry said that Dephen is doing him a disfavor by keeping Yace against her will. There is too much coincidence here—too much intent behind what is going on for this all to be 'stupid dumb luck'."

"So what you're implying is that a bounty hunter, hired on as a servant, possibly more powerful than Dephen, pretended to fall in love with him to then kill him? And because of that, you believe Dephen is gonna assassinate his brother? An Ishik! Using a twenty-year-old female? What you say makes no sense!"

Irwin ignored Kipp's stubborn rudeness. "He will do so using the powers she has always possessed. By now, he has unlocked them all."

I hope I am not right. Shit, I hope I am not!

He searched his mind for a positive angle. "That story Nonbry told us about Dephen's upbringing has merit. Remember? Dephen had to work his way into the Daosian Empire. He had to earn everything: clothing, food, and most of all, acceptance. I understand that perspective. Yet someone had loyalty to him. Most likely it was his father, Adabashi. Even if he was not accepted within the larger family, Dephen was still allowed to be a part of the Ishik Empire. I am guessing here, but Somer probably felt betrayed that his bastard brother was given any ranking position within the empire that promotes incestualize cronyism.

"Who would have appointed Dephen head of anything? How do you become Ambassador to Daos? Someone must believe in you. Or he was being conned by someone, possibly his mother. Nonbry said she used her children to manipulate people of power." On they rode—both pondering Irwin's ideas.

"But Dephen was Ambassador to Daos," Irwin said finally. "With that privilege, he was given the ability to tour the world. I imagine that he pandered to and influenced many rich people during his time as an Ambassador. That is maybe how he knew of Yace's mother's summer home. Nonbry said that Dephen established alliances in all the territories ... he was known as a good person of power who wanted to help others.

"Now that bit of information coincides with what Paulur told me about Dephen being a philanthropist for the locals of Onj Raha. Perhaps because Somer oppresses his people, he could not tolerate what his brother was doing, either out in the open or secretively. Not only was Dephen establishing trading opportunities, creating harmony between Daos and other territories, but he was also having his share of women.

"Oh, the stories Dephen shared must have irritated his brother. Somer probably was not good with Dephen's negotiations or with the women he brought home. And that was why Dephen was banished from Daos. He was breeding with the common-bred. But even after being banished, Dephen carried on defying his brother's orders. Yace is a perfect example of that. Maybe this is a colossal set up."

"Your mind is sick."

"Why do you say that?"

"Do you really believe all that?"

"Hey, I am just looking at the evidence. It fits together," he said, gaining confidence in his own conclusions. "I mean, I can see an emperor ordering his bastard brother to be assassinated over watering down the bloodline. And I can also imagine that same bastard brother trying to bring about justice because of all he had endured—what he fought for. They might be Coterie, but they are not infallible!

"They have kept their purebred lineage going through inbreeding for generations. That type of proliferation must do something to the blood, to the brain. Maybe that was why Adabashi was tolerant, even proactive with Dephen and his upbringing in the Ishik Empire. It is possible that fornicating outside of the family had occurred before, but now it is not tolerated. Dephen cannot be the first Ishik bastard ... definitely not the last!"

"I get jealous of Yace all the time: when you two sleep together, or when she's walking with you ..." It looked as though Kipp's mind was wandering to different times and places. "... or flirting with other men. Even when she's dancing with other women, I get jealous."

"Where is your mind, Kipp?"

"Dephen was supposed to help Yace. Even Nonbry said that Dephen was gonna help. Why would he do this to—"

"Are you fooling me? His reasons are his own, but my gut tells me there is something far more sinister going on. Dephen took Yace, her mind and her body. And he is not planning to give her back. If you remember, Nonbry also said that Dephen is doing a disservice to the Gypsy." He reached over and grasped Kipp's forearm. "I feel like you have forgotten all that was said only a few days ago. Maybe you are under her control now."

"It's been eleven days, Irwin, and I remember what was said. I'm just skeptical, same as you usually are."

Irwin struggled to control his rising anger. "Maybe at one-point Dephen was going to help Nonbry and Yace. But once he became incapacitated, he had every reason to use Yace and her powers.

"Nonbry knew after first seeing Yace—almost ten years ago—that she could be a powerful being. He probably disclosed that to Dephen, inciting him to use her now for his own advantage."

"You've said before that you thought Yace was just going home ... that she wants to be a part of a family—be pampered. What happened to that idea?"

"What I just said makes more sense than that idea. That was my first hunch. Your thoughts are maddening sometimes, Kipp. I think you are tired. Maybe we should stop and water the animals."

"Yeah, maybe."

9

Pour Cupines Pub

They traveled swiftly from Raha to Radia—only half a moon cycle to arrive. They refrained from entering the medium-sized city until nightfall. Under the cover of shadows, Irwin and Kipp hit upon a livery with its lights still on and doors still open. Irwin paid for stabling their animals for that night. Handing over an extra coin, he asked the stableman about an inn where they might also spend the night. The young stableman gave them directions to a boarding house where, he said, there were always extra rooms and meals on hand.

They walked only a block when Kipp came upon Yace's scent on the cobbled roadway. It came to him on the breeze from the wharf. It appeared that Yace was traveling into the heart of the Talented District.

She had stopped in that spot not too long before they arrived. Her scented handprint remained undisturbed on the tall building's stone façade. She had turned that corner and went down the road before them.

Kipp stopped to smell the wall and then the breeze again.

He grabbed Irwin's arm, pulling him along.

"What is going on?"

"It's Yace!"

"Keep calm. We cannot let her know we are here."

Kipp nodded, and Irwin twisted his arm so he could now hold on to Kipp's biceps. He pushed the Clan-Duin ahead of him and they followed the scented trail.

Two blocks over and three more down, Kipp seemed hypnotically drawn toward a tavern's open doors. Irwin pulled him back.

"What are you doing, Kipp?"

"She's inside. I smell her. Her scent is fresh. She has to be inside."

Irwin held Kipp as he squirmed to peer inside the bustling establishment.

"I do not see her in there, Kipp. But I believe you. Let me go first. Keep a hand on me. I do not want her to take your mind again." He prepared himself to enter the busy tavern.

A pale skinned Erthin walked toward them from the opposite side of the street, but then he stopped and turned away.

Irwin sensed that Kipp was frantic.

The Clan-Duin whispered, "The name of this place is Pour Cupines Pub. PCP! Only those with Talents are allowed inside. Mortals are prohibited, and PCP are encouraged to flock together. You don't look the part, Irwin. You look too Mortal. I'm sure that's why that Erthin just turned around. He doesn't wanna be involved in any fights because you're a Mortal entering a tavern that caters to PCP."

Irwin was dressed richly in his calf chaps, his dirty red shirt, and red embroidered indigo pants. Indeed, he was outlandishly dressed, especially in this place. He absorbed one of his blades. "My smell will have to do."

A salty wind from the wharf blew his deathly odor into the tavern. Immediately, all the Clan-Duins were keen to his scent. All eyes turned toward him. Irwin pushed out his chest and charged forward into the noisy bar scene that fell eerily silent.

He took in all the faces, searching for a pale-skinned, blonde female, but saw only all the other shades of women. He stepped up to a U-shaped wooden bar. Several men moved away from him while others leered. Irwin smiled and nodded at the older Clan-Duin barkeep who also scowled at him. The hairy barkeep stopped helping customers, his blue eyes firm on the newcomers. They were surrounded by all types of burly men and women.

Irwin sensed the encroaching soldiers with their many blades. There were over three dozen vigilant soldiers seating throughout the busy floor. Most were Clan-Duin; he had raised many hairs just by entering.

Kipp kept close to his side but took his hand off Irwin and stepped around several men. His brown eyes scrutinized all the women, most of whom wore thick makeup and had their hair pulled up or braided alongside their faces. Even the serving wenches wore bright-colored dresses.

Women who might work elsewhere were enjoying drinks with friends but wore servant outfits dirtied from their daily toils—except for one woman. She did not appear to belong. Her clothing was fancy, tailor made, with a hint of pirate-style not common amongst land-lovers. A deep maroon, almost black, petticoat pushed up her endowed chest, covering her lavender pantsuit beneath. She appeared to be Erthin, and had long, soft red hair braided off to one side. Her eyes were bright blue, hinting at telepathic powers. She glanced at Irwin. Kipp stepped up next to him. She was trying to keep her eyes on the two soldiers at her side.

A middle-aged Erthin approached from behind. "Who let you in here?"

"You stink like Mortal," a soldier said.

"She's here," Kipp whispered.

One of the angry-eyed Clan-Duin soldiers asked, "Whatcha doin' here, whitey?"

Irwin felt many eyes staring at him and turned to look at every set. Most were brown, amber, green, and gray—only a few were blue. "I am here for a drink!" He faced the barkeep again. He did not like seeing or hearing the encroaching soldiers or feeling all their metal. "I will take a bottle of your best whiskey!" He slapped down several gold pieces onto the wooden bar. His lips barely moved as he whispered, "I do not see her."

Another soldier said, "Go back to where ya came from."

Kipp murmured, "Neither do I. What are you gonna do about this?" He glanced over his shoulder.

The bartender stared at the coins. "Bottle of whiskey?"

Irwin struggled to focus. "A bottle, yes." He reached into his pocket for more coins and again mouthed to Kipp. "Do you think she is still here? Maybe she left out the back door?"

Someone growled, "Your kind isn't allowed here."

Erthin and Clan-Duin soldiers crowded around them. They were clearly ready to do more than heckle Irwin and Kipp. "I wish I could be out the back door," muttered Kipp.

Stacking several dozen gold coins onto the bar, Irwin turned to engage the soldiers. "And I am buying a night of drinks for everyone!" He was sure he heard Kipp thinking: Have you gone mad?

The Clan-Duin soldiers were caught off guard by this gesture. Undoubtedly, no one had ever come into this bar and bought drinks for all. Several of the men quickly turned ecstatic, while others took a moment to consider what was being offered.

"We will get out of this," Irwin hissed. "I will be the distraction. You ask about Yace."

Someone shouted, "Free drinks?!"

A few yelled out, "Sure smells bad."

"Smells Mortal."

"Mortals smell better than he does."

"Like Death, I'd say."

"He must be one of those albino mutants."

"He doesn't look like a mutant, but sure smells like one."

"Smells like somethin'!"

"He bringin' free drinks, mate!"

"If yer buyin', I'll take a bottle."

The bar erupted. No one scoffed at the gift or even questioned it. At least half the patrons cheered, hooted, and hollered. Although the barkeep appeared overwhelmed by the large order, the stacks of gold coins were enough to keep things rolling.

Irwin surveyed the barroom again, thankful that the heckling Clan-Duins had softened toward him. They gave him space, filing up to the bar to refill their cups. Irwin's silvery eyes watched them all. He then turned to the lovely Erthin woman. She had been gazing at him, did not appear amused by his proposition. She looked back at the two Erthin soldiers at her side.

Irwin shouted at them, "Free drinks!" The two soldiers appeared enticed by the offer at first. But the beautiful lady they were with continued to ignore him and his offer. She made a gesture with her hands for them to follow her, and she stepped back from the table.

That is odd. Why would they not take me up on my offer? Somewhere to go? But it is late, and everything is closed. Besides, people who enjoy drinking appreciate it when their libations are free. Their behavior is odd indeed.

The distraction was working. All the soldiers, and even the servers, were enjoying the free alcohol. They pushed up to the bar, trying to get their mugs refilled. Irwin put his hand on Kipp's shoulder. He wanted him to notice that the two Erthin soldiers and the woman were leaving the barroom.

Maybe they have somewhere to be.

But Kipp's eyes were already trained on the female and the two soldiers with her.

"Here's your bottle of whiskey," the barkeep said, setting two small ceramic cups onto the bar top.

Irwin poured himself a shot.

"What's the occasion?" The Clan-Duin barkeep asked as he continued to refill drinks.

The chorus of metal around Irwin sung to him and through him. "I just finished a long, drawn-out journey. It paid quite well!" He chugged the shot. Then he poured Kipp and himself another.

He grabbed his friend's forearm and leaned toward his ear. "Stop being sentry. I need you to be engaging. Ask about Yace." Irwin then lifted his shot glass up high. "To Radia!" He would make himself the center of all attention so Kipp could do what needed to be done.

"Yace," Kipp shouted, after everyone else yelled 'Radia' back at Irwin.

Irwin scowled at his Clan-Duin companion.

He watched the Erthin beauty and her soldier friends move around the crowd. The two men looked back toward the bar, but she was clearly cautious of the enticing drinks being offered. Irwin restrained himself from eyeing her. Most people who frequent saloons and taverns were there to have a good time; they overindulged; they were egocentric and used one another for their own gain by goading, heckling, baiting, and trapping each other. He had seen all of it under his father's rule—the games men played to get what they wanted. The Erthin woman who was walking out of the bar intended to do something just as menacing with those somewhat older Erthin soldiers. He noticed it in how she moved, and how she pretended to ignore everyone in the barroom.

He knew not to pay too much attention to her. Kipp would do that work, even though he had been asked not to. Irwin must keep the ruse going. He turned to the closest soldier and engaged him in small talk. He asked about where the Hall was and when was a good time to report for reassignment. The soldier's posture changed immediately. He asked simple questions about Irwin, but nothing specific. Irwin lied, speaking casually about nothing in particular. He then poured his 'new friend' a shot of whiskey.

He felt Kipp trying to remain calm. He, too, had turned to a soldier on his left. "Have you seen a gorgeous blonde-haired blue-eyed goddess of a Telepath come in here, maybe earlier tonight?"

The soldier, a Clan-Duin a few years older than Kipp, said, "Na, why ya ask?"

"I am looking for a Lady Dephen. She has eluded her father's requests to return home. Her scent led me to this bar." He looked around. "Maybe if I can speak to a Commanding Officer, a Telepath?" His voice shriveled. "Then I don't have to bother you." Kipp showed his nervousness to be asking for a Telepath, let alone a Commanding Officer.

"The Commanders ...." The soldier looked around the room. He was trying to find the two men who had followed the Erthin woman out the back door. "They were with that pretty pirate. Looks like they left."

"The female Erthin pirate who sat there? How long was she here for?"

"She was here when we arrived. And we showed up just before ya did."

Yace's scent was fading from the barroom. "Well then, I should really speak to those Commanding Officers, preferably now."

Kipp jabbed his elbow into Irwin's arm. "I am gonna go talk to those commanders." His eyes insisted the Metalist follow.

Irwin took one more shot of whiskey and handed the bottle to his new soldier friend.

"Let me go with you," Irwin said and turned back to the soldier. "Hold on to that for me, please. We should be back soon." He followed Kipp away from the bar, pretending to stumble—to be drunk. But as they walked up to the closed backdoor, he sobered up.

Kipp stepped out into the wide alleyway where the commanders were taking advantage of the pretty Erthin woman. Were those Yace's blue eyes staring at them?

"Her scent ... it goes this way. Follow me." Kipp did not wait for Irwin and took off running.

The woman closed her blue eyes and repeatedly screamed out, "Yes!"

Irwin averted attention, repulsed by what the two men were doing with her. But the blue eyes opened once more and stared at Irwin. She was laughing and screaming as the men ravaged her voluptuous body.

Kipp was leaving him behind.

While Irwin was glad to be out of the thick throng of soldiers, he was also happy that Kipp was back in Yace's scent.

She must have slipped out right before we arrived. Dang it, Kipp, slow down.

10

THOSE DAMN PIRATES

Irwin dashed after Kipp and away from Pour Cupines Pub, further into Talented territory. Although they had not passed anyone on the roadway, there were PCP up ahead, gathered under a streetlight. He knew that Kipp's impulses were keen, and hurried to catch his friend before they were spotted, stopped, and questioned. They were not walking as they should be. His cool touch brought Kipp back to reality.

Yace's scent was nowhere.

Kipp appeared disoriented, and Irwin knew what had transpired. "Are you fooling me? Kipp, it happened again! That was her! Back there in that alley, I am sure of it." Irwin guided them both from the middle of the roadway. "Yace was that female Erthin pirate in that PCP Saloon. We should have known! She was the only well-dressed woman of the bunch. I know you smelled her. She was right under your nose!"

"Are you sure?"

"Coterie have the ability to shapeshift." He pulled Kipp along the road. "Shit! Dephen knows how to shapeshift her body. This is no good."

Keeping to the shadows, he led them toward the tavern's back alley.

"We can't go back," Kipp balked and pulled Irwin to stop. "I'm a liability at this point. Nonbry said it himself. I can't be trusted. I'm bonded to her. She has my mind and heart. And she'll always have it. She can do what she wants to me anytime I'm close to her. Every time we get near her, she will know."

"I bet she is still there," Irwin yanked on Kipp to follow. "We are going back!"

"Are you crazed? Had we not left when we did, we wouldn't be .... Well, I mean, I wouldn't be alive."

"Nothing would have happened to us." He pulled the Clan-Duin close. "I will never let anything happen to you, Kipp. You are my best friend. I cannot imagine my life without you. I will always keep you safe. Please trust me."

"I trust you. But you're not taking us back. They'll be looking for us."

"Why? What have we done?" Irwin wanted an honest answer.

Oh, right, I killed hundreds of men and women. But not lately.

Removed by nearly a moon's cycle from the horrific circumstances in Onj Raha, they had almost forgotten. Almost. It was possible that no one here in Radia knew of the incident. They had seen no more brigades on the roadway searching for Irwin, the mass murderer.

Kipp ruminated, "Alio warned me about my thoughts, Irwin. We've had many lessons about Telepaths. Even Nonbry warned me. Dang it, I should've remembered. Every time I go anywhere ... and I know what Telepaths are capable of, I have to be thoughtful about being thoughtless. I give away my position to someone I'm bonded to—to Yace, every time."

"I thought you were practicing what Alio taught you!"

"I have!"

"You have?"

"Yeah, I have. Not every night, but I do it while we're riding."

"I wish you were not so easy to manipulate."

"This is all my fault," Kipp grumbled. "I bonded with her a long time ago and have been dealing with the consequences ever since. I should've never allowed her to have my heart and soul. Ever since then, she's used me. Nonbry's right. You're the one who has to be responsible for all of us.

"Even then .... I looked straight into her eyes before we left that bar. That moment gave her access to me. Without you, I'd probably have gone and given myself to the Hall. Or worse. She might have drowned me."

"Kipp, stop thinking about what could have happened. Focus on what needs to happen."

"Of course, she'd be the well-dressed woman in a saloon—flaunting herself, getting soldiers to be hers. She was bonding with those Erthins in the alley! She was making them hers to control. That's how Telepaths do it. That's how they can have absolute power over anyone—through a psychic bond. She can see through eyes, hear thoughts, twist minds. Dang me! Now she's bonded to Erthins! And she has access to my mind, too."

"You cannot let her power over you paralyze you. If you do, she ... her father, wins. Besides, as long as I am close—and can touch you—she cannot control you."

"You can't protect me from her," Kipp whined. "She can enter my mind at any time. Hear my thoughts any time. When I look at her, she controls me! You witnessed it the first night we met!"

"Your bond does not sound fair. What do you get from having a bond so deep with Yace?"

"In a Clan-Duin's world, you get ultimate loyalty and commitment. I feel her and she feels me. We know each other's emotional state—how we feel toward any given situation at any given time. We have a soulful connection. We have that same connection with our cubs too—I mean children. And if she were to die at the hands of someone, I would see his face when she dies. Then I'd seek revenge."

"But you do not have that now?"

"No. Not since she left Onj Raha. I haven't felt her since the night she met her father."

Are those tears on his cheek?

"When were you going to tell me this?"

"Why does it matter? I can't reconnect with her. That's how I regain the bond, through her trust, her loyalty, by being with her. The bond has been manipulated. Cut somehow. She can still feel me, but I-I .... It's the same feeling, like when a family member dies. That's what makes death hard to accept sometimes."

"And you think I am mentally messed up?!" Irwin pulled Kipp along. "We are going back whether you want to or not."

"Why?"

"Although I am enjoying the adventure, we need to save Yace—right now." He tightened his grip. "As long as I have contact with you, she will not know where you are."

"How do you know that for sure?"

"It has worked all the other times."

"And if she's not there?"

"Then we will have you follow her scent. We were just there. She had sex with those men. That should be an easy trail to follow, correct?"

Kipp fell silent, and Irwin drew him back toward the alleyway beside the PCP Saloon. There was a congregation of soldiers along the way, but thankfully no one bothered them. Irwin maintained his regal position. Kipp was three strides behind, practicing what Alio had taught. The Clan-Duin caught her scent again, but now it was a menage with those two men—an easy stench to follow. They hustled down the alley to the next roadway.

As they turned the corner, Irwin placed his hand on Kipp's shoulder. He nodded and took up a quick stride. Yace had crossed the street, walked down a block, and then took the next crossing. They slunk together through the shadows. As often as he could, Irwin kept a hand on Kipp's arm. He knew Yace could be watching them through Kipp's eyes. They followed her scent, which curved through a gated doorway. Irwin tightened his grip on Kipp, holding him back. They had found Radia's PCP Hall—similar in size to the one in Raha.

There were no soldiers standing guard, but a conglomeration of at least ten men dressed in dark attire strode toward them. Holding his grip, Irwin led them up a dark stairwell beyond the Hall. They hid in a closed doorway across from the foreboding building. He held tight to Kipp. They waited in the shadows for the footfalls to fade.

"I cannot believe she went into the Hall!" Kipp hissed into Irwin's ear.

Irwin felt the metal gates closing. "How brazen of Dephen."

"Maybe he's hoping we'll walk right in, not noticing it's the Hall."

"Ha." His lips twisted with amusement. "Maybe we should stay here and wait her out. There is only one other way out that I can feel except for the front door on the other side of the Hall. I believe I will feel those gates moving."

"We're gonna wait her out!?"

"What else should we do?"

"I don't know." The Clan-Duin's face wrinkled with concern. "Keep moving. We can't stay here in Radia tonight. The closer to her I am, the more susceptible I'm to her powers. Let's keep moving."

"Keep moving? Where are we going to keep moving to? She is here! In that building! Why are you being like this?" He squeezed Kipp's forearm tighter. "I am right here. She cannot hear you while I have contact."

"If she's been eluding Nonbry and Dana, she'll elude us too," Kipp said, reiterating Nonbry's words. "She's not gonna stay there. Not in the Hall. Besides, women are prohibited in there."

"Then why did she come here? Were you actually smelling Yace, or just her scent on those two soldiers?"

"I smelled her and the soldiers. They all came here."

"Is there a Hall for women?"

A breeze moved a stray hair into Kipp's eye, and he angrily batted it away. "No, only brothels or saloons. But if they're Erthin, then there's the Healer's Hall, or a Bath House. But you're right, I might not have smelled her. It might have been just those men. Their scents are intertwined. It's disgusting. No, Yace might have already left Radia. She knows we're looking for her, and she—Dephen—wants to put more distance between us. Isn't that what Nonbry said?"

Irwin rubbed his eyes.

Kipp, you hurt my head.

He had to keep them both focused. "We should continue to hunt her trail!"

"The only scented trail I smelled led to the Hall, Irwin. I don't know what you want me to do. But we shouldn't stay here. We need to keep moving."

"Where should we go then?"

"Back to the stables. We should saddle your horse and leave."

"You are being irrational, Kipp. We need rations at the very least."

"Rations? Why? I can hunt!"

"Your hunting takes up valuable traveling and sleeping time. We need rations. The animals need rations. We need water. And we need sleep."

"I don't wanna stay here."

"I said nothing about staying here." He pointed at their boots, tired and not knowing where else to go—he knew he did not want to stand around waiting for something bad to happen.

"Maybe we sleep in the stables."

They were both tired. Irwin yawned. "If that suits you, I am alright with it. Sleeping on hay will be the best bed we have had in half a moons' time."

"You might have to pay more."

"Or I could slit the stableman's throat," he said with a straight face, but was joking.

Kipp's brown eyes stared at Irwin. "Or you could do that."

"Do not worry, that is not my plan," a smile drew up his lips, Kipp's too. "We will go to the stables. And tomorrow, first thing, I will restock our supplies. And you will sleep."

Irwin used his silver-filled baggage as a beacon back to the stables. The two slipped between buildings, around intersections, and into the backside of the barnyard. Not once did they spot any more brigades.

After a night filled with restful slumber, Irwin woke at first light. He took his Jennies and left Kipp behind in the barn where he would be out of sight.

Irwin looked around the markets and down by the wharf for Yace. He needed to know that continuing their journey was what they must do. Kipp had insisted that she had already moved on from Radia. But Irwin held out hope that Yace would take a reprieve even if it was for only a day. As it was, they both could use a few days on two legs and comfortable beds to sleep on.

He bought all they would need and more, surprising his friend with a saddle, saddle pad, and leather bridle. Kipp hugged him several times, jumping up and down like a child. He saddled his mount and was ready in no time.

Now he cannot complain about his aches.

He felt happy in these moments when Kipp seemed pleased. But there were other feelings too. Sometimes his emotions regarding Kipp were a jumble of confusion. He could not put his finger on it, but he could not imagine a happy life without his Clan-Duin friend.

11

TWO AND FOUR MAKE SIX

Kipp resumed his complaining. "I'm done with this ground squirrel and hound game."

"Yes."

Please Kipp, do not start again.

"And I'm done with all this riding!"

"Yes."

This is all for naught. We are being led along. For what? Give us hope, Yace, Dephen, whoever you are. At this rate, we will never catch up.

His eyes were trained on the green and brown horizon.

I do not think we will see her again. This is a ground squirrel and hound game indeed.

At this point, their travels were not as much fun as they had once been—riding all day, hoping to catch up to Yace. Their hopes of thwarting Dephen had wavered.

They passed through a small fishing village not long after the daily catch had been brought into port. Fresh fish smells lingered, and Kipp sniffed at the breeze. "Are we gonna have more overly salty dried food?"

"Yes. There is no time for hunting."

"What I wouldn't do for a live meal," Kipp lamented. "The blood! The heart. Mm, warm meal."

"You are gross."

"I'm Clan-Duin." Kipp looked longingly at the small marketplace with four vendors displaying various fruits and vegetables for sale. "Do we need anything at the market?"

"No. Keep focused, Kipp, please."

"Can we stop for just a moment?"

Irwin snapped back, "Do you think Yace stopped?"

"No." Kipp stared wistfully over his shoulder as they departed the village.

I want to stop too, but we cannot. We must keep going. Just think of the goal. Goal. Task. It will be a task. Stay positive. Kipp needs me to think positively. When was the last time we smelled her? Do not ask that question. He will never shut up if you do. Breathe. We will catch her. Stay positive. Every day we push harder than she does, we gain ground. But she has a pathway into Kipp's mind. She knows where we are. Stay positive. We will catch Yace and free her from Dephen's evil plot.

Will we?

They rode on; weary and worn out. Too much time had been wasted.

Kipp was right about when Yace left Radia—in the middle of the night after we found her at Pour Cupines Pub. We have been chasing an elusive trail. And now she is with two other riders.

Both of them had noticed that Yace and her soldiers hadn't bothered to hide their camps along the roadway, nor their scat.

Her scent was always old by the time they caught up to it.

On they rode.

Kipp said, "I feel like we're back where we started after I found her scent the first time south of Onj Raha. And we're as far behind now as we were back then."

Irwin did not respond. He had to believe they were closing the gap every day. As long as they rode longer than she did, and rested less, they would catch up.

He rigged a timer using metal and the medium-grained sandy dirt he found all around. Every night he fashioned the timer, and well before morning's first light, they began their day in the dark. Irwin was finished honing his Metalistic skills. He was ready to rescue Yace.

This game has gone on long enough. We must catch Dephen and save Yace.

Every time they found a trace of her, and Kipp calculated how far ahead of them she and her soldiers were, again their hopes were dashed. Kipp's nerves were wearing thin.

This time Kipp said, "There's substantial moisture, which is good, but she's still half a day south. I hate to say it, but it seems she's right on our riding schedule."

"How is that possible? I was hoping those soldiers would slow her down."

"Nothing has changed, Irwin. She's still the same distance away. You do know, soldiers are trained to sleep very little—to be ready for anything."

"Much like us at this point."

"We're never gonna catch her."

Unless he was constantly touching Kipp, he knew Yace could tap into the Clan-Duin's mind. She could see through his eyes, hear their conversations. She would know what Kipp was thinking, would know what Irwin was saying.

From now on, we will hold back our talk unless I am touching him.

They were stuck in a vicious cycle.

But then one night ....

Kipp! Kipp! Please hear me. I'm at Pirate's Cove Pub. Kipp, please save me! Yace sobbed. *He's getting four more soldiers. We already have two. They will wreck me, Kipp. Please, save me! Kipp, Kipp, please, Pirate's Cove Pub!*

⋺⋲ ⋺⋲

Kipp awoke from what he believed was a nightmare. He told Irwin about the dream, told him everything Yace had said—repeating the story over and over.

Irwin was hesitant to fall for the ploy. Nevertheless, he said, "We should ride."

The Clan-Duin rubbed his head. "All I hear is: 'Kipp, please save me'. Dang me, ground it out!"

Irwin placed his hand on Kipp's arm. "You really believe the validity of those words?"

"Throughout my soul. That was our bonded connection. That was not Telepathy."

"Talking to you without being physically present, that is the definition of Telepathy, Kipp."

"We need to go."

"Yes, we do, and fast with the wind. But caution is needed."

Kipp rolled his eyes. "Duh!"

This telepathic call is a trap. There is no way Dephen ever allows Yace any space within her psyche. That old man is too calculative. He is a Telepath. He wants to control this situation. How could this not be a trap? We will not fall for it.

That night, they slept close to Ahradah. If not for the reprieve, they would have arrived early in the morning and well before anything was open—a time when only PCP soldiers would see them. As it was, they would arrive by the time most people would be up and working.

"I think we should dress like soldiers and ride straight for the Talented District." Kipp said, eyes wild.

"We will be stopped, Kipp."

"Not if we have a mission."

"Are you sure about that?"

"We can always ask to talk to a commanding officer, like before, and then give them the slip."

Are you fooling me?

"How about this? You allow me to do all the talking." Again, Kipp rolled his brown eyes at Irwin.

Without further discussion, they donned their roles, wearing identical uniforms, then raced off into the dawn.

I am glad we will arrive during the light of day. We must remain transparent. Keep calm.

As they rode, Irwin randomly reached out and grabbed Kipp's arm to keep him grounded in the here and now.

I wonder how he can tell the difference between reality and a contrived dream.

∋∈ ∋∈

They arrived in the busy city of Ahradah by mid-morning with little sleep and empty stomachs. Luckily, they were not too out-of-character in this place. Even though Irwin did not feel the role, he tried his best to act like a PCP soldier; he sat tall on his mount, scanning their surroundings.

Nonetheless, their uniforms were dirty and not detailed, nothing like what the soldiers this far south would wear. They were looking for Pirate's Cove Pub, most likely in the heart of the Talented District, and most likely close to the local Hall.

They soon learned there were two Talented Districts—a northern district, located in the richer part of the city, and a southern working-class district twice as large as the northern. They rode alongside the vast wharf. Ships with large and small canvases were setting sail, smaller crabbing boats remained on the near side of the long seawall. Gulls soared on the ever-present wind. There were many small horses and donkeys being used to haul up heavier loads from the large ships docked along stone wharfs. Irwin supposed that if Jenn Jenn and Nee Nee had been born down here along the eastern seaboard, they too would have been hauling heavy loads of imports and exports every day, a mundane existence.

They had many more city blocks to cover than they had planned. Side by side, they trotted along wider streets. The donkeys marched cooperatively behind Kipp's horse. The Clan-Duin's nose was ever keen. He sniffed every street crossing, swiveling his head back and forth like an owl. The further into Ahradah they ventured, the more heated the Clan-Duin became. Keen to find her, Kipp yearned to catch a whiff of her or a glimpse of Pirate Cove's Pub.

After a while, Irwin insisted, "I think we should board the animals and go by foot. There are many narrow side streets here. We and the horses will not fit, especially with the donkeys in tow."

"But we need to be ready to ride!"

"We must find her first," he snapped.

Kipp is ready to be done with this mission, and so am I.

The city of Ahradah went on and on. There were many tight streets and towering buildings, and it was just as filled with loud noises and ringing and singing metal as Onj Raha had been.

Keep calm. Keep focused.

Kipp hates not having any control over the circumstances. So do I. It is becoming more and more a sore subject. At least he realizes I am trying to keep us safe. He listens to me, but there is that attitude.

They found an overnight boarding stable in the working-class Talented District. A long and narrow building, it extended from the street to an alleyway behind. There were many empty stalls. Irwin bought four—three for the animals, and one for their belongings—that way, if they did not find a place to slumber, they could take refuge in the extra stall.

Footsteps echoed on the cobbled streets as people moved to and fro. Walking side by side, they followed a narrow avenue for several blocks down a side street, then Kipp led them toward the wharf, toward the salty and fishy odors. It was easier to find both Talented Districts—both intricate in building and street layout—from the water's edge.

It took them a while to locate Pirate Cove's Pub and Saloon. And though the doors were open, there were no patrons inside, only ladies cleaning.

Kipp strode ahead of Irwin over to the bar. A female barkeep was polishing and stacking glasses. "Were there any well-dressed women in here last night? The lady we're looking for has two Erthin soldiers with her, but possibly six."

"What breed?" She put her hand forward, no doubt hoping to get paid for what she knew and shared.

Kipp elbowed Irwin to supply the cash. The barkeep was a thick Clan-Duin woman, but she was more muscle than fat. Her dark hair was pulled back into a tight bun. The tattoos on her face highlighted her dark feline eyes and thick eyebrows. There were more intricate tattoos drawn along her exposed arms. She had several piercings in each ear and on her lip, nose, and eyebrows. Though she appeared to be Clan-Duin, her skin tone was lighter than most. Her grayish-blue eyes suggested she might also be telepathic. Her eyes shined on Irwin and remained on him.

He did not know if she was asking about his background or of the woman in question. He handed over a silver piece. "Coterie." He watched her reaction, curious about how others felt about Coterie. He made sure his elbow touched Kipp's who was gazing at the ladies busily cleaning the giant barroom.

The barkeep's fingers fondled the silver coin as she studied Irwin. "A pretty little ashen-blond Telepath in a swanky purple dress, no older than the two of you, came in last night with two guards."

"How'd you know she's a Telepath?"

The look the barkeep gave him implied he should already know the answer. "Blonde hair. Blue eyes. But a quiet mind—most unusual for a Telepath, if you ask me." She hummed as she contemplated the situation. "All she did was watch the shows, eat, and drink. But those Erthin men with her, they were another story.

"They ignored her but seemed to expect her to pay for everything. And they ordered a lot! Those two were busy carousing with other soldiers, buying them drinks and such. They were here all night. And then at the end they—along with four other soldiers—they all left together. They all swarmed that pretty lady like bees on a flower. It was odd, even for around here."

Kipp looked at Irwin. "Two and four make six." He signaled for another silver piece.

A question he had wished he had asked at the last place occurred to Irwin. "How did she pay? Gold or silver?"

Kipp interrupted, "Why do you care?"

"Gold." She cocked her head slightly, considering Kipp. "It was a small satchel, and probably a little light on weight for how much those men of hers drank and ate."

Irwin paused and then handed over another silver. "Did you happen to overhear any of the soldier's conversations?"

She took the coin. "A bunch of cocky banter. They were goaders, that's for sure. Would you two like a drink?"

Kipp said, "No, thank you," and spun around and grabbed Irwin by his sleeve. "She was here!"

"I will agree with that assumption," Irwin said out of earshot of the barkeep. "And the bartender's accounting lines up with the timing of Yace's telepathic call to you."

The Clan-Duin dragged Irwin out the door. "I know she was here last night! We're so close. The barkeep described Yace to the point. She's gotta be close. We have to find her. We have to find her and save her from Dephen. Nonbry said it; you've said it. We have to!"

"Where are we going to start? Do you smell her now?"

They stopped and gazed at the people streaming past. Kipp looked up at the fast-moving clouds overhead. He said nothing.

"Maybe she has moved on again. With six soldiers at her side, she could do almost anything she wants. She could buy a boat, or a team of—"

"She's not getting on a boat!"

"Says you." Irwin was tired and hungry and in need of a reprieve.

The Clan-Duin said, "Maybe we go around to the stable-yards and ask if any horses have been bought recently."

"Soldiers get their mounts from the Hall, Kipp—you know that."

"And if they are traveling on horseback, they'll need a few extra horses for rations. Your logic confuses me sometimes, Irwin."

My logic?

Irwin glared at his companion. "We know nothing more than the facts. She was here last night. That has been confirmed. That, and she went from having two soldiers at her side to six. Confirmed as well. But we know nothing else. We cannot make assumptions about her location without more facts. For all we know, she continued riding—but now with a larger brigade."

"No! She's here in the city. I know it."

"I thought you said you were unable to feel her."

"It's weak, but I can feel her."

Irwin placed a hand on Kipp's forearm. "Do you feel her now?"

"Not when we're touching. She was probing. I felt it. But when we touch, I feel nothing. That means she's here! We need to find her today. Right now!"

Irwin raked his hand through his gritty hair. "What we need to do is regroup. Find a room, get cleaned up ... have a nap and get food in our gullets. We also need to gather information around the docks and go past the stable yards, like you said. We need rations. We need to be mentally and physically ready for whatever comes next."

The lack of sleep and too many days on horseback were wearing Kipp down. Irwin softened. "You and I both know running around, hopelessly searching for something we cannot find, is not a good idea—especially in a big city like Ahradah. If we are seen out of context, things will escalate out of control. You know this. We need to be smart about our tactics right now. Dephen is waiting for us to slip up. He is hoping to expose us. Or exploit us. We must be on our best behavior." He watched the anger wash across Kipp's face—the flexing of his jaw muscles. "Come on, Kipp, you know better than to be outright foolish—unless she has your mind." He tightened his grip on his friend's forearm.

"Well, we *are* in the Talented District. Might as well find some food and a bathhouse."

"Maybe there is an inn between here and the stable yard. Something centrally located so that if we must move fast, we can."

"I don't wanna be tied down."

"Kipp!" Irwin was tired too. He wanted to stop, if only for a little while. "Maybe we only rent a room for the day. You know, get cleaned up, sleep on an actual bed—do what we need to do to keep searching for Yace."

The Clan-Duin chewed his lower-lip. Irwin had hit that nerve again.

Kipp conceded through gritted teeth.

There were more residences than rentable rooms along the avenues. They marched around several blocks looking for an inn or a hostel. The streets were crowded. The smell of people was almost as overwhelming as the ringing of metal. Children played around their mother's legs while they washed clothing at a communal well. Kipp reached for Irwin's arm.

"I found her scent! She was just here. She's close." He sniffed the air noisily. "And she's with those guards."

Now they were looking for at least a threesome, if not six soldiers surrounding one dainty female. They turned, peering through the sea of faces. Being in the Talented District made it harder to find Yace and her Erthin soldiers. There were many shades and shapes of people of color. Irwin deepened his grasp, and Kipp continued to sniff at the air. Like the hound he was, the Clan-Duin located a tendril of her odor. He pulled Irwin along. With all the people on the roadway, the scent was muffled, but her odor was distinct—straight ahead. Her stench led them through several intersections. They went downslope toward the primary avenue that hugged the wharf.

Kipp's nose led them to a tall narrow building labeled Beverly's Bed and Breakfast, located just past a quiet intersection. The stone-made abode looked like something you would find along a grand wharf. The surrounding buildings were similarly constructed. Kipp stopped in the middle of the road, several feet from the stoop. They were at the edge of the Talented District.

Waves crashed against the wharfs' thick wall and seagull-calls were loud on the wind.

Irwin leaned toward Kipp. "What is going on?"

"Her scent leads into there."

They stood looking at the four-story residence. There were many windows, all small but perfectly lined with square stones. Irwin felt a large sum of gold on the third floor. He could tell how far from the front windows it was hidden. Indeed, Yace was inside the building. Another satchel of gold, only half a pound, was fixed on a person who was going up the stairs. He pointed at the front door. "A vacancy sign. Maybe we should ask for rooms!"

The Clan-Duin held still, perhaps trying to summon the courage to move up to the wooden door. Irwin did not move until his counterpart took a step. To keep Kipp from being noticed, they had to maintain contact—neither was ready for a confrontation. But they were ready for their journey to come to an end, so they marched together up the front steps. Kipp thrust his hand forward and banged on the thick wooden door.

A kind-looking older Mortal man opened the door—it creaked loudly. His wife appeared into view behind him, wiping her hands on a small linen. "If you are lookin' for rooms, we're filled up."

Kipp pointed at the hanging wooden board with painted words. "But the sign says—"

"I know. I know." The old man said and shook his head. "These Clan-Duin gentlemen came in last night. I haven't gotten around to taking down the vacancy sign."

"Well, we do have one room," the wife chimed in, "preferably for the Clan-Duin." She looked at Irwin as she moved past her husband and into the doorway. "Are you Mortal or Talented, young man?"

Irwin replied, "I am Mortal."

"Are you *good* friends?" She appeared to be hinting at something neither man understood at first.

Kipp said, "Yeah, we are. We've been through a lot." He glanced at Irwin. "We're really good friends at this point."

"Oh, really good friends? I see. You two prefer to share a bed?" She raised her left eyebrow, and Irwin nodded. "We don't accept your kind either."

Irwin did not understand. "Our kind?"

"Oh, no, it's nothing like that." Kipp now understood what the woman was implying. "We are just good friends traveling together. We're here trying to locate my sister. She sails on one of the boats, but we just arrived and aren't ready to find her yet."

Irwin kept his arm against Kipp's.

"You are just good friends?" She eyed Irwin.

"Yes, just good friends in search of employment on his sister's ship."

They both peered into the front room, and the woman continued, "If I had two rooms to rent to you, I would. Our rooms are tiny, large enough only for a single bed—except the suite, and that has been rented for a few days. We prefer each guest to have their own room; that way, they have their own space." There were two Clan-Duins sitting in the front room. They were large-bodied and muscular in build. The cushioned chairs where they sat looked like children's seats—ready to break. Both men stared at Irwin and Kipp.

The older couple huddled in the doorway, as if protecting the inhabitants from prying eyes. Irwin persisted. "This is a large residence. How many rentable rooms do you have?"

"There are eight rentable rooms. We prefer to cater to Clan-Duin clientele—or Mortals. Anyone with any other Talent need not enter. We don't accept any type of crossbreed either. Unless you are a Clan-Duin, crossed with Mortal blood, such as yourself." She looked at Kipp. "Erthins, Telepaths, or any other type of *Vol*—well, there are other hospices where they can sleep. We don't want any *Vol* trouble. We pride ourselves on being flexible for our guests—amenities and such.

"Now we don't want to sound judgmental. It's just that we have learned over the years which type of *Vol* we can trust." She smiled and nodded, as if convincing herself. "But just because we aren't *Vol*, doesn't mean my daughter and I can't do it all. We can do overnight laundry, cleaning, and mending. We also have a bathing tub in the cellar. You can have it hot or cold. And Luanne, our daughter, gives great massages.

"Oh, and if there is anything you need from the markets or a specific shop, my hubby Huck here knows all the people and best places to buy anything you might need—including hard-to-find items. We try to make it easy for Clan-Duins who pass through on ships and such." She paused, but then percolated with excitement once more. "Oh, oh, and you can stay for as long as you want. We can do rates for multiple days and multiple rooms. Like I said, we try to make things convenient for visiting Clan-Duins."

Irwin felt Kipp tense and grasped his wrist, hoping to cool him down. "How late in the evening do you accept clients?"

"Oh, well, you two can stop past at any point—that is, once a second room comes available. We always accept those in need of respite."

Feeling the Clan-Duin readying for an attack, Irwin squeezed him again. The Metalist asked, "And when do you think that will be?"

"In a few days, I suppose."

"Well, thank you for your time. You might see us later."

12

WE'RE ALL VOLATILE

They peered into the front room again before stepping off the stoop. Irwin was hesitant to leave the area. He sensed all the weaponry inside the manor, some on people; some had been set aside. He wanted to go back, but knew not to be brash.

Kipp grumbled as they walked away, "Vols. They smelled like Vols! I'm not so sure that they are full-blooded Mortals.

"I did smell Yace in there. Though, I'm not sure she's still there—at least not in the front room. But her scent was everywhere."

Kipp appeared hypnotized, even with Irwin making contact.

"And there were several others." His eyes came back to focus. "You saw those Clan-Duins. They're soldiers. They have that look. Even if they wear different clothing, a soldier's always a soldier, no matter what they wear." Kipp looked back to the windows above the entrance to the bed-and-breakfast.

Irwin also glanced up. "How many scents, total, did you smell?" All the windows were drawn closed by curtains of various colors, of teal, purple, and grass green. He hoped to see someone peering through an opening—see the curtains move while someone tried to catch sight of them.

That will not happen while I am looking at the window.

His eyes drifted toward the harbor—a serene view. Small and medium-sized boats moved with the rolling tide—some sailing, some rowing. Others were tethered to one another, conglomerating around wooden poles and docks. Gulls called from above, and the ringing of bells and whistles was tranquil to behold.

The Clan-Duin said, "Nine ... no ten. The mother and daughter smell similar. But how obscene do you have to be? I mean, they don't allow anyone other than Clan-Duins to take up residence? Out of any species, I wouldn't allow Clan-Duins access to a Mortal home. We're animals! How can they defend against a Clan-Duin if one decides to eat them? They can't! I mean, I can understand why no Erthins or Telepaths. Erthins are far more volatile. And Telepaths, they've no rationale. But I can't believe Mortals are being hypocritical of every other person of Talent except Clan-Duins. We're heathens!"

They moved down the street and then looked back.

"So they should only cater to Mortals? Kipp, it is likely those two were under Dephen's influence. I definitely would not take their words personally if I were you. I think they were meant to provoke."

Kipp grumbled.

Irwin studied his friend.

What should we do? Should I ask? No, I will tell Kipp what to do. No, that will not work. I must think things through.

I should go in there. Go in there and what? If I leave Kipp behind, she will know he is here. She can sense him as he senses her. I will have to take Kipp. But he is a liability. If I do go in with Kipp and retrieve Yace, it is possible I will have to drop his hand to take hers. And if I am not fast enough, she will have his mind. She knows how to use him.

Ugh!

How will I get to Yace without bringing Kipp? I cannot. No matter what, if I leave him behind, she will have him. If I go in and there is too much fighting, and I lose touch with Kipp, again she has him. I do not want to go in and lay to waste everyone. No more death, please.

There is always death. It cannot be avoided.

He snorted at his thoughts.

Get over the fact that you are a mass murderer; Kipp has.

UGH!

I need to be smart about this. Can I be selective? Am I that strong? I must be. Take Kipp with me, hold on, and hope to keep him safe as I turn Erthins into dust, slaughter Clan-Duins, and hope the Mortals do not retaliate. They will. At this point, they are Dephen's puppets. He will do with them as he wishes.

How do I get Yace if there is a confrontation? What if there is a back door? What if she uses her telekinesis? What about other PCP in the vicinity? Or at the Hall? She could contact them as a Telepath in distress. I can see that happening.

Maybe Kipp is correct, I do think too much.

"What do you think we should do, Kipp?"

The Clan-Duin was still staring at the bed-and-breakfast's front door. He reached for Irwin's forearm. "I smell her again." Kipp then led the way down a barren side street.

"Are you sure about this?"

She cannot have his mind if he makes contact with me. But how sure am I of that?

"We might not want to go too far. She probably knows we are here, and that we know where she is. I guarantee she is going to flee. We need to stay close. She will get away if we do not."

"Her scent might've been strong in that house, Irwin, but it was dissipating. It wasn't really really fresh. It was like she walked in, went around the house, and then left."

Irwin peered back at the intersection. "I felt coins moving up to the top floor. But now they sit idle. I believe she is still inside, hiding up on the fourth floor."

"I don't think she's there anymore."

"Really? Where do you think she went?"

Kipp shrugged.

"Are you sure you want to leave her behind?"

"I don't think she's back there, Irwin. I know what I smell."

He is acting on instinct again.

"Are you sure you smelled her?" He planted a hand on Kipp's arm again and held it there.

"Yeah. Her scent took us to Beverley's, but it didn't linger. It wasn't strong. She went in and out. I'm sure she exited out a side door."

Kipp stayed close as they walked away from Beverley's Bed and Breakfast. They were both hungry, tired, and frustrated.

We cannot leave. There is more to this than we see or feel. Why is Yace here? Why is she now stationary after all this time? Tired? Plotting something? So many options in a big city like this. We must be cautious. We will come back after Kipp blows off some steam. At least I know what to feel for. That is a lot of gold they are carrying.

"What does Vols mean?"

"Vols. Vols. Oh, Vols. That's short for Volatiles," Kipp said.

"Volatiles?"

"That's what we are, Irwin. In some places we are called Talented; in others, we are Volatile." He squinted back over his shoulder again, back toward the bed-and-breakfast. "We're all Volatile, but especially you!" The side street on which they walked ended at a T intersection several blocks from the bed-and-breakfast. Large wooden warehouses surrounded them. Kipp stopped and sniffed the air. "That way," he pointed to the left.

They zigzagged around warehouses, and Kipp caught a whiff of her again.

I hope he is not telepathically possessed, leading us to our death.

Irwin randomly reached out and touched his friend's arm and then let go. It was almost a game now. Then Kipp picked up her scent again, and Irwin placed his hand back on his arm. If they were close to Yace—and Dephen—he did not want Kipp to give away their position.

They passed several large stone and mortar warehouses, casting shadows over a wide break in the buildings. A well-kept wooden fence separated the roadway from a cobbled yard. An enormous corral was filled with idle wagons, carriages, carts, and other vehicles lined up in rows. Some were more ornate than others, inscribed and carved, lacquered, stained, or painted in bright colors. Some were inlaid with glass and metals or gilded emblems. From flashy to plain, it was an amazing sight.

"Slow down. Yace's scent is strong here." Kipp sniffed as they walked toward an open set of large metal gates.

"We must stop." Irwin felt surrounded by metals. Some were being melted together in vats, soldered, or standing idle. As they walked through this section of Ahradah, he felt more and more magnetized; the harmony was maddening. "I cannot go in there."

His grip on Kipp's arm tightened.

"Are you alright, Irwin?"

"No. I feel like I might go Onj Raha."

"That bad?"

Breathe. Keep calm. Mountain meadows. Open oceans. Forests and rivers. Stay calm.

His mind throbbed; his body shook. "I cannot go in there."

"Fine. Then I will."

"No. That is not safe."

"But I have to go."

I hate feeling weak. Breathe. But the metal wants me to let go. No. I must keep calm.

"Then I will go too."

"But you're gonna go Onj Raha!"

"And if you leave my side, she will have your mind." Gold swirled around his irises. "I will go in with you." They passed through the gated entrance to Wild Willie's Wagon Corral. He dropped his grasp but stayed close to Kipp, arm to arm.

"What are you doing?"

"Maintaining contact."

Three lot attendants approached them, all Mortal, elderly, and greedy for a sale—but obviously cautious as they strode toward Irwin and Kipp.

"I'm hoping you'll do all the talking," Kipp muttered softly.

Irwin was surrounded by a dozen different types of metal all ringing their own melody. Some of the songs were in tune, but some were not, and he longed to fix them—to make them flow freely, together. He wanted to scream out in pain but suffered through it.

Calm down. Breathe.

"You do the talking, Kipp. My head hurts. I cannot think."

Kipp slowed and then stopped. The Mortals met them halfway. "Hello, Sirs!" Kipp called out. "We're here to find out if a female with a brigade of soldiers came through here recently."

Irwin stared at the ground. Meanwhile, he used his Metalistic powers, tried to locate Yace and her side kicks. A lot of metal was moving, but only in a few places. Everything else stood idle. He was concentrating so hard he barely listened to the conversation.

A balding, potbellied, white-skinned man with a thick mustache said, "We've had no customers today."

"I don't think she came through to look at your wares," Kipp said. "She's been avoiding her father's request to return home."

"Sorry to say, but we haven't been visited at all today by anyone other than you."

"We've been following them, and their trail leads here. You don't need to keep quiet about the brigade. The Hall will not punish you."

"You can check if you feel it's necessary," the older man said with a sweeping hand gesture.

Kipp stepped forward, wide eyed, and surveyed the giant wagon corral.

Irwin's pinky tickled Kipp's arm. He needed to leave the corral. He was feeling weak and holding back all desires to let his power take over. Kipp's nose could still track Yace even if she ran into a neighboring warehouse.

"Thank you." Kipp pushed Irwin. "Let's go." As soon as they were outside the corral, Kipp said, "She went in there. But once again, she didn't stay. Her scent is getting fresher. I bet she stood in the very same place we were standing. Her scent drifts toward that warehouse." He pointed. "They must have slipped by just as we walked in."

Dephen was keeping up his game of ground squirrel and hound. "I wonder why she went to Wild Willie's out of all the places to hide?"

"She's trying to escape us. I'm guessing she can't hear me because of you. But it's obvious they know we are following. And that probably angers Dephen."

Irwin's nerves were shot, and his head hurt. He heard Kipp's stomach growl. "We need to eat."

And I need to stop moving.

Irwin added, "We need to bathe and clean our clothes. Maybe we locate an inn. Have some time off our feet and hot baths." He strode away from Wild Willie's Wagon Corral.

"But her scent leads this way!" The Clan-Duin attempted to pull him.

Irwin was bone tired. He had his own wants but gave in to Kipp's demands. He took ahold of his friend's forearm. "Fine. Continue."

13

NO ONE LIKES TO WAIT

They followed the perimeter of the building where Kipp had picked up her fresh scent. They were a block away from Wild Willie's Wagon Corral when her distinctive fragrance emerged again from a set of doors on the other side of the roadway. She was sweating, as were the four men with her. The congregation of five was easy to track for Kipp, but Yace and her men were still nowhere to be seen. With several blocks between them, the road now traveled along the contours of the land and the buildings.

Irwin was not sure he wanted to follow the Clan-Duin's impulsive nose any longer. This was just too convenient for Yace to be so close, yet not close enough to be seen or touched. Dephen was taunting them. The old soul was up to something devious, and Irwin wanted to know what that was.

We need to plan for retrieval and escape with minimal casualties. We know where she is hiding out. Right now, she has no gold on her, no beacon. We must be smart about our approach.

Kipp was going on impulse and willing to expose himself while trying to save Yace. Dephen was trying to use the Clan-Duin's lack of thoughtfulness to his advantage ... trying to play them both and put them into harm's way. Irwin saw all of this for what it was: a ruse. But they knew where Yace and her men were staying.

Dephen is brewing up something evil. I know it. He is being tactical, staying at Beverly's, and using Mortals as his front. Provoking Kipp with Yace's scent. He is trying to lead us somewhere. How could we be so close and still not have her? Dephen is using us. He is going to use those soldiers too, but for what? His own opportunities. To stifle us. Well, hopefully having that many to feed, house, and clothe will make for easy tracking.

Kipp persisted in his hound-ish pursuit of Yace. She did not stop from district to district. Dephen did not avoid places where their kind were not allowed—left a scented trail without regard for the order of things. Yace could act regal, even look it—especially with a brigade of soldiers surrounding her. Irwin and Kipp, on the other hand, had to play their roles.

Irwin wore a sleeveless tunic under his dark blue, long-sleeved PCP shirt. He took off his over-shirt, rolled it up, and secured it around his waist like a belt. To do that, he had to release his contact with Kipp. He had to act like he too was Mortal. The laws dictated Mortals were allowed to go everywhere, as were their servants, assuming they followed proper etiquette.

Despite Irwin's reservations, he too could not stop tracking Yace. They were close. He paced three steps ahead of Kipp, hoping his friend would not become hypnotized by Dephen.

They passed intersection after intersection, and now their lack of contact unsettled Irwin. He peered at their reflections on passing windows to make sure Kipp was still three strides behind. The Clan-Duin appeared to be still fully aware of himself and his surroundings. Seeing Irwin's eyes in the windows allowed Kipp to communicate through hand signals. He indicated that her scent, and her soldiers, had turned down the next intersecting street.

They took a right turn and followed the flow of people into a partially covered marketplace. Once her flock entered the markets, their scents were drowned out—no way to follow. That was what Dephen had hoped, no doubt.

They moved into the fresh food section where there were both small and large open stalls. Children walked about with baskets of bread rolls and assorted fruits, calling out their sales. Elaborately patterned tapestries lined fresh food buffets. It was a smorgasbord: dozens of open tables laden with large carved bowls and woven baskets filled with all different types of fresh vegetables and meats. The displays were dazzling, and they were both famished.

There were fresh or prepared foods to be had. Erthins would cook a meal for you on small stoves or grills—food was practically given away. Nearing supper time, meals were served in ceramic bowls or on wooden skewers; there were cabbage or seaweed wraps dished up right into one's hands. Irwin indulged Kipp in a small feast.

Soon enough they were back on the street, Irwin in the lead once more. He routed them down and around side-streets, keeping away from the main roads. Her scent was lost to them. They saw many brigades of PCP standing around at intersections watching people move about.

Please, let us not be seen!

Surely they had not forgotten about his treachery back in Onj Raha. The two stepped into and out of shops. They went down quiet alleys, avoiding mounted soldiers. When they stepped out into an immense cobbled city square, there was suddenly no place to hide from PCP eyes. Now they had to walk with purpose.

They had found Ahradah's City Center. There were platforms on either side of the center street—one a stockade, and the other held gallows. Beyond the platforms, fountains spewed gallons of water into perfectly chiseled ponds. Grand halls towered above entire city blocks. This was where the people of Ahradah were protected—the sick and hurt came here to be healed. Commerce, justice, and public safety were a powerful influence on the Datzarian culture, giving those who needed it peace of mind and protection.

Thousands of city folk milled around, busy with their daily activities, bustling here and there. The streets were thick with people and vehicles. Irwin followed the ringing of *his* metal. He knew exactly where the stables were. Kipp, on the other hand, was surprised they had found the barn so easily—several blocks from the square, and just as far from the wharf. They retrieved some personal belongings, and then sought an inn. They searched between the wharf and the stables, hoping to find something close to both. A few blocks away, they found an available room and at this particular inn they could share.

The bed was large enough for two people, but Kipp offered it to Irwin and claimed the floor. After a brief nap, they left and crossed the street to a laundering facility. The female Erthin at the counter promised a two-hour turnaround. A large bathing pool in the basement was free to use for paying customers. But Kipp made a fuss about sitting in tepid water and being around people they didn't know. So Irwin paid extra for a private bathing room.

The cost of things mattered little to Irwin, and it baffled Kipp how much money he seemed to magically create.

"It's always interesting, Irwin, to watch you come up with exact change every time and for every transaction."

Irwin smiled and felt a growing sense of warmness for his friend.

They enjoyed the private bathing room with a window and a view. They had two hours to relax and enjoy an Erthin-heated bath. Off and on, a young woman came to refresh their bath water and helped scrub their backs.

Irwin wanted them to enjoy a good soaking. Along their hard journey, they had no time for such frivolous treats. They both needed it. Once cleaned, Irwin shaved and watched Kipp push and pull his hair to suit his appearance. The Clan-Duin gave himself a close facial cut. Then he pulled his clean hair into a ponytail away from his brown eyes. It was humid in Ahradah, and they both wanted to keep cool.

Kipp helped Irwin trim his shaggy hair. By the time the sky dimmed, they and their clothes were clean and folded.

They would use the rented room mostly to keep their belongings closer to the wharf than the stable yard. Feeling refreshed and rested, they took off toward the tavern adjacent to their inn and waited for a nighttime meal. There was free cheese-tasting that night, probably to draw patrons into the establishment to drink and eat. The tavern was busy.

Irwin placed his hand again on Kipp's forearm. "What are we going to do tonight?"

"Go back to Pirate's Cove Pub and wait for Yace."

"I do not think she will return there."

"Maybe her soldiers will."

"I think we should go and watch Beverly's for a while."

"If we go, we might as well save Yace!"

"I have a bad feeling about confronting Yace, Dephen, and his soldiers at Beverly's." Irwin looked around the busy tavern. "Things will not go the way we want."

"What do you mean?"

I will kill too many. No, I cannot kill anymore.

"There must be another way, Kipp."

"Which way is that?"

"I cannot guarantee anyone's safety if we just go in and save Yace. Dephen is much too keen. He might use us against one another if I lose contact with you." He leaned in close and spoke in hushed tones. "I do not want anything to happen to you. There are so many unknown factors I must think about."

"You know what you need to do? You need to stop thinking so much."

"Yes, I know."

They gorged on five different cheeses while awaiting their pre-purchased evening meal. Unfortunately, the cheese and bread tasted better than the overly spiced meaty dish. Neither said anything to their hosts about the meal.

The tavern soon filled with patrons. The two slipped out the door. Between Kipp's nose and Irwin's ringing head, they found Pirate's Cove Pub and Saloon in a short time. The barkeep they had talked to earlier was now dressed up and waiting tables. They found a booth near the corner of the room and looked out over the large wooden barroom from the shadows.

"Yace and her soldiers will appear, I just know it," Kipp said, as if to himself. But the night was young.

Irwin wanted to talk to Kipp, but the Tavern was noisy, so he spoke loudly. "Why do you think Yace went to Wild Willie's?"

"She knew we were following her. That was a good place to lose us. You couldn't enter, remember, it would've set you off."

Irwin took a drink off his whiskey. "Why do you think she has stopped in Ahradah?"

"Probably tired of constantly going just like we are."

"Possible."

Kipp took a swig of his ale—already drunk and punchy. "It's obvious you're thinking something, Irwin; what is it?"

Irwin glanced around and took in the surge of patrons stepping through the front door. He made sure he was touching Kipp. "She probably is tired of all the constant riding, like you said. She is female. I cannot imagine how it affects her. But if you remember Beverly—I am guessing here—she said the suite room was rented for a few days. That means Dephen is here on purpose." They stared at each other and took sips from their drinks. "I believe that Dephen might be looking for another route. Maybe this is where he takes passage on a ship to Daos."

Kipp snapped, "Yace isn't getting on a ship."

"Or maybe she is going to buy a cart? Or maybe a wagon? With that many men, they would have to buy a string of horses to carry all their supplies unless they buy a vehicle."

"You're thinking too much again." A nearby table of card players tossed their cards up. The boisterousness caught their attention. "Take another drink and relax for a moment, will you?" Kipp said.

They stayed close to one another throughout the long night—kept their conversations short and to the point. They tried card games. Kipp's timing was off, but Irwin's was not. He made sure to win enough hands to break even for the two of them, but not win too many as he didn't want to draw attention to his card counting.

They waited and waited. They didn't know what those soldiers looked like, but Kipp would know them by stench alone. Their wait was long, but they were enjoying their time off horseback.

It was much later when Kipp drunkenly spat, "I think we should go look for her."

"Are you up for that?"

"Either her or a whore. And I'd much prefer a woman I know than one I don't!"

He is sloshed!

"We should just go, and you can just get her," Kipp said, slurring his words.

They moved from their darkened seats across the barroom. Irwin held Kipp's arm to steady him, to maintain the connection so important to keep him safe from intrusion. They left through the front door into the night air. From Pirate's Cove Pub, the walk to Beverley's Bed and Breakfast was only seven blocks. They held back in the shadows of a neighboring building and watched the lights turn on and off in the bedroom windows along the avenue.

"You still smell her?"

Kipp's eyes were closed. "Yeah, I smell her," he slurred and hiccupped. "I smell my lovely Yace. Maybe we should go get her now."

"Is that your plan? We just go in and get her? Forget the fact that there are six soldiers guarding her and three Mortals inside that residence."

"Yeah!"

"You are drunk."

"Yeah!"

"Alright, I will humor you. So I go in and rescue her and—"

"I wanna rescue my beloved!" Kipp radiated a dopy smile. "Place a kiss on her tender lips and break the curse."

"I did not think you had that much to drink! I am the only one who can break the Ishik spell, not you."

"You're not allowed to kiss her."

"I do not want to kiss Yace."

Kipp made kissing sounds, closing his eyes, following his own fantasy. "I love you Yace."

"Alright, you disgusting canine!" Irwin shifted his position for a better view of the darkened rooms. He too closed his eyes and allowed his senses to feel the metal, but not touch it. There was metal all around them, and he, too, was tipsy from alcohol. "I think you are too drunk for either of us to rescue her."

"Whatcha doing?"

The metal was singing, calling, wanting to be touched. He tried not to reach out for it, but the *want* was powerful. And then he located her gold. The large cache was still there—in the same spot he had felt it earlier that day. The weight had not changed either. There was another smaller amount—a satchel of gold in another room. He wanted to put it with the rest but resisted that urge too. He took several deep breaths. The alcohol helped him loosen his Metalistic grasp. There were too many other metallic items buzzing and humming to maintain his focus for very long.

He opened his eyes. "I am trying not to fall asleep."

"We gonna rescue her?"

"She is inside, along with everyone else. We will come back here before first light and watch for her. Then we should do more investigating. We need to find out why Dephen is staying here—and what his next move is."

Kipp's drunken voice raised yet another decibel. "She's not gonna ride on a boat!"

"Alright! Alright! She will not ride on a boat. We can go to the stable yards." Then he added in a hushed tone, "Maybe we will find Blacky. If we do, we can track her."

"Only if I can have a whore tonight."

Irwin saw the look of lust in Kipp's eyes. "Do you want to go back to Pirate's Cove Pub?"

"Yeah!"

They returned to the pub in time for the last show. Kipp was ecstatic to see a dance before he picked out his wench. He was beyond drunk but wanted to embrace a female—insisted that Irwin stay in the room and watch. But by the time Kipp was ready to perform, he had nearly passed out—definitely blacked-out. The whore only took half of Irwin's money and helped him get Kipp down the stairs to the barroom. Afterwards, a kind elderly Erthin man, walking in the same direction, helped Irwin navigate his drunken Clan-Duin friend down the avenue toward the inn.

Never had Kipp drank that much in all the time Irwin had spent with him. He tried not to see a correlation, but not having Yace with them was beginning to devastate Kipp. And now she was so close, yet so far away.

He managed Kipp up the stairs to their room, gave his friend the bed, and found a spot on the floor. The bedrolls of wool added some cushion to the hard wooden surface.

It was the middle of the night when Kipp rose from the bed and spewed puke out the window. The Clan-Duin cursed and collapsed across the bed again, nearly missing Irwin's head with his feet.

14

FOLLOWING THE CORRECT PATH

Kipp was worse off by morning. Irwin had not slept as long as he wanted. He left his friend with two bowls: one for bodily refuse, and the other for cleaning up. He hoped Kipp would remember the difference.

Although he did not want to, he had to leave him behind. To ensure that Kipp would not leave, he locked him inside their rented room. They had things that needed to get done, and only Irwin was sober enough to accomplish those tasks.

He returned to the wharf and found a cozy spot a block past Beverley's Bed and Breakfast. There was an old driftwood bench where Irwin sat and watched. He was not alone on that bench. Two young boys were trying to catch breakfast with a hook and line. They took turns tossing and reeling up, hand over hand. Irwin noticed small fishing and crabbing boats taking off from the docks on their way to troll in the large bay. Others were on their way out to sea.

Nothing had changed at the bed-and-breakfast since the previous night. The large cache of gold and the smaller satchel, along with all the other metal pieces he felt earlier, were still in their positions throughout the house. He remained on the bench until his stomach would not quiet. The husband, Huck, was the only one who had gone and come back with a basket of fresh morning treats. Irwin was sure Yace and her companions would still be there upon his return. Until then, he needed to feed himself, retrieve the donkeys, locate the markets, and buy supplies.

As he traveled back up the avenue, he noticed a long line at the bakery.

They must be waiting for sweetbread. Smells good.

He thought about stopping there on his walk down to the wharf, but did not. Now the bakery was beyond capacity. He went to retrieve the donkeys before going to the markets where he would find a meal.

The marketplace was situated on a long, wide street. Hundreds of shops and open-air booths lined the boulevard, creating a grid of narrow alleys filled with shaded stalls and eager merchants. The markets commenced at the center of the largest wharf and spanned toward the city square. Peddlers were still stacking their wares. He found a small booth where they were making flat bread sprinkled with cinnamon. He had never heard of, or ever tasted, cinnamon before. He delighted in his quick meal.

As Irwin perused the markets making purchases, he felt more inconspicuous with both donkeys at his side. There were many other men with multiple animals on a tether clogging up the aisleways too. It seemed a common theme and put Irwin at ease to see so many small animals thriving, albeit in a cityscape-lifestyle. And their masters, usually men, all wore dirtied clothing—were about as unkempt as Irwin. For now, he was in a heavier set of pants from his mining days, and a sleeveless tunic to keep him cool. His calf chaps made him look a bit out of the ordinary. But he was dressed as he preferred. And he did not look to be Talented or Volatile—just eccentric. He figured the stares came because he did not dress like a local. For now, at least, he looked and smelled normal, albeit ashen pale. He hoped his exposed flesh would turn a warmer color, like Kipp's soft brown skin, but all it became was a bright crimson.

He pulled his Jennies along at a slow pace as he shopped. Their only detour was around an area where they sold pots, pans, and metal utensils of all types. They hung and swung and were precariously stacked; they all sang their songs to him. He averted his eyes and attention when he passed sword dealers, tin tenders, and copper peddlers. He took his time and was thoughtful as he gathered rations. He also bought many pounds of feed for the animals. By the time he found everything on his list, the bags were heavy, and the donkeys were weighed down.

It was mid-morning when he bought himself a quick seafood delicacy from a local Erthin vendor near the piers. He made small talk while awaiting his meal. "How often do large ships come to port here?"

Frying up small pieces of flour-dipped calamari, the vendor replied, "All the time. There are many ships that stop here with trade, though most come from Al Lieur Isles, northern Datzar, and Arisham Territory. We do see ships from Oceans of Brauf. They come from far beyond the Al Lieur Isles more often than those traveling from Ar Var Harbor. Most of those big ships follow the trade winds. We had one ship leave for Ajihya before the full moon. Another arrived a day later from Gustin."

"Gustin, where is that?"

"Half a world away, my friend." The merchant handed over a skewered piece of calamari.

Irwin paid a silver over the cost. "Do ships from Daos come here?"

"Daos?" The vendor made a sour face. "No one trades with them."

Irwin took a chewy bite of the hot treat. "Yum, thanks. This is really good!"

He walked on, back into the mass of merchants and patrons. Amongst all the clatter and racket of the markets, Irwin found a mapmaker. The man was old and appeared wise; he was tutoring a child in the art of mapmaking. The child sat quietly, mostly hidden from view, allowing the approaching patrons to see the artful displays. Both the mapmaker and child looked Mortal, but not related.

Numerous maps were exhibited along that stall's walls. Some were intricately designed; others were merely a few lines on a canvas. The larger maps had been tied open for better presentation. One giant map of Urthis, with all the major city names, hung like a tapestry behind the old mapmaker. His small cubicle was filled with many worldly maps and nautical charts. There were dozens of images of each territory, amazingly detailed. All the landscapes showed major rivers, lakes, villages, towns, cities, and roadways. This shop was a visual wonderland. There were also individual city maps from Alnabaldu to Gustin and everywhere in between. Many were very detailed to help outlanders navigate those cities. There were more stacks near the old man's feet.

Irwin asked for a map of the Daos territory; the mapmaker pulled him in close. "South is a terrible place. Not a place to travel."

"Okay, I get it. Terrible! But do you have one?" He pressed. "Do you have a map of Daos Territory?"

The brown-eyed man looked down at the piles of cut canvas; they were all the same size and of many different locations around the globe. His old fingers popped a few times as they sifted through a stack of maps. He peered warily up at Irwin and hurried as he thumbed through the pile. There were only a few of Daos Territory, and the old mapmaker knew exactly where everything was, but bumbled through the piles, nonetheless.

Again, the old man said, "No good come from south." He looked through a second pile. "They kidnap Mortal and behead PCP. Slave trade and worse happens there." He pointed at Irwin. "You look smart. Go north instead." The mapmaker pointed to the enormous map of Urthis behind him. "North to Onj Raha. North good! Many women. Many jobs!" He nodded, probably hoping that Irwin would understand what he was insinuating. "I have maps of Onj Raha city, other cities too. They show districts, street names; some pinpoint only the best saloons!" They both saw the word DAOS in the corner of a small square canvas piece. The man's hand shook as he pulled it loose from the rest of the bunch. He said nothing and continued to study Irwin. Clearly, he did not want to hand it over.

Irwin smiled, nodded, and then pointed to a larger flattened canvas, more intricate in design of Urthis. He said, "I will take that map of Urthis and this Daos map. Please and thank you."

The mapmaker thrust his hand out for payment before he would pass off the Urthis canvas. "That be thirty-five silvers."

Not sure if it was a good deal, Irwin did not want to haggle for a map that might get him too much unwanted attention. He paid the mapmaker and hustled away from the small cubicle.

He felt accomplished for the day.

He had wanted a map of Urthis for some time. And now, he also had a map of Daos Territory. He would have something to study when he was bored with the scenery. He rolled the maps together, stuffed them into one of his satchels, and continued wandering through the markets.

As he meandered, donkeys in tow, Irwin could not quiet his mind. He was listing probable outcomes if they did not catch Yace here in Ahradah.

I must stay positive. But I cannot control Kipp, or anyone else for that matter.

Dephen was brewing up a change for them. As Irwin saw it, for that old telepathic man to be idle in a city, this long meant something was going to happen. He could not envision Dephen pausing in his journey and retrieving more soldiers as mere coincidence.

Why would a Coterie need guards? They could be used as camouflage, or for their bruit strength and prowess. It is possible that old Telepath is tired from constantly moving. Even if he has a fresh, youthful body? Maybe he is readying for a confrontation. Now that we are so close, the probabilities of a conflict are astronomical. I must keep a level head and all options open. It is possible the old man is waiting for something to happen, opposed to initiating. Maybe Dephen is hoping Kipp will act on impulses in a city full of PCP. Either way, I must be prepared.

Pulling his mind away from all this worrying, he breathed a deep sigh. He was glad to be done with the markets' crowds. The amassing shoppers grew more dense as the morning progressed.

It was a short walk from the markets back to the inn. Even though they had only been there one day, Irwin was beginning to recognize Ahradah's city streets—all the best routes. His mind and his body were glad when he returned to the inn at last. Kipp was awake and furious.

"Why'd you lock the door?!"

"Because I did not want Yace to take you from me. I figured you could not slip out that window and survive the three-story fall."

"You left me behind!"

The room smelled of all types of human waste.

"You were too hungover. Besides, it would have taken us longer to do everything together. You were in no state to do anything but sleep. As of right now, we are all set with rations." He grasped Kipp's forearm before speaking again. "I bought enough for three people. It amounts to about half a moon's rations for the three of us and all the animals. And the donkeys are below at the hitch post. I was hoping you would be ready to go by now. We do not need to stay here any longer. Like you said last night, we should walk around the city—hit up the stable yards and such. Look for Blacky.

"Oh! And you should know that I went to Beverley's this morning. I sat around for a while, but only Huck came and went."

"Was Yace still there?"

While he sat there on the bench in front of Beverly's, Irwin had not felt the gold leave the residence. The same two amounts were in separate locations inside the house as before. There was one larger reserve on the third floor, and he was sure the other stash moved around with Yace. He knew that Dephen, nor Yace, would leave the larger cache of money behind.

How else would Dephen support the lifestyles of six soldiers and himself?

"She was when I left. And that was well past sunup. I arrived as the sun hit the water. And I stayed for a long time before going to the markets. We can go back to Beverley's if you want. Or we can look around the stables and the wharfs. What do you want to do, Kipp?"

Kipp looked brokenhearted. His lower lip quivered, and his eyes were full of water.

"I'm really sorry about last night, Irwin. I didn't mean to get that drunk. Not to say that I didn't want a night off to forget all this horseshit. I did! I know we need to visit the stables, but what we really need is an Oracle. We need to talk to Nonbry. We need to tell him what's going on—see if he and Dana can help us."

There was trepidation in Kipp's voice. Irwin recalled walking past an Oracle workshop several streets up from the markets. "I saw one along my way this morning. It is between here and where the horses are—down a block. Should we go tack up and be ready to ride? Or do we leave the animals at the stable?

Either way, we need to be inconspicuous. We should also toss those nasty smelling bowls." He pointed at the mess Kipp made.

"I think we should take the horses," Kipp said, disregarding the stinky refuse. "That way, we can move in a hurry if we have to. Hopefully, talking to Nonbry won't take too long."

"It might be too early. We might be barked at for interrupting his drive."

"Don't get me started."

Irwin changed out of his heavy hemp pants. The warm day called for lighter attire. He was dressed for his part in his red shirt, tanned vest, and wide-legged pants tucked into his dark brown calf-chaps. Kipp wore his dark and bland uniform. They went from the inn to the livery, donkeys in tow. Both were pros when it came to saddling their horses. But they did not ride through the city streets; they walked, not wanting to draw attention.

They maneuvered down a busy avenue. Irwin only had one animal to deal with in the crowded streets. Whereas Kipp and the remaining three animals caused traffic snarls, clogging intersections, as they tried to get through. It was a busy part of the day. Thankfully, there were hitch posts along the wider avenues. Half a block down from the shop they were looking for, they hitched their horses and sought the help they needed.

The Oracle's workshop was just opening for the day as they stepped up to the door. A young, voluptuous telepathic woman greeted them with a smile. "Good day, sirs," she flirted with Kipp, tossing a coy smile his direction. This twenty-something woman appeared to be all Telepath—glowing golden shoulder length hair, slightly curled, and dark blue, almost violet eyes. She held the door open, urging them inside. They entered a small waiting room next to an opened office door. She motioned for them to follow her into her private room. Once inside, Irwin noticed that there were no other openings in the cozy fortune telling room—no windows or doors. It would soon be stuffy in there.

"Take a seat." The cramped little room was only wide enough for a narrow table and a dozen pillows of various sizes and materials. The space smelled of lavender. From ceiling to floor, the walls were covered with elaborately woven fabrics. Though well-kept, one tapestry had a tear exposing the wooden wall behind.

"What exactly are you two here for today?"

"Contacting a loved one," Kipp rummaged for the talisman in his pocket.

"Dead or living?"

"Living."

"Oh, okay. That'll be three silvers."

Kipp jabbed Irwin who handed her the coins; she slipped them between her cleavage.

Irwin could not help but look around the small, sultry room. He tried not to watch too closely as Kipp surrendered the talisman. They had been in this situation several times before. As he took in the familiar environment, he found it odd that the room looked like every other Oracle's place. He did not ask any questions.

The young woman grasped the talisman. There was a long silence while she summoned Nonbry who took no time to step forth into the female Telepath's body. She coughed; Nonbry grumbled through her. "About time we talk! When will you rescue her?"

Kipp glanced over at Irwin who was opening his mouth to speak.

Irwin ignored Nonbry's outburst. He knew it was only meant to rile them up. What they needed was an update and to receive suggestions on how to proceed. "We are in Ahradah. We have located Yace. She is staying at a bed-and-breakfast along the wharf. This is the first time she has stopped for a reprieve since the chase began. We have learned that she has mastered her shapeshifting abilities. And because of that, she now has six soldiers guarding her."

"You're in Ahradah already?"

"And she has six guards!" Kipp burst out.

"Yes." Irwin was unrelenting in his dialogue with Nonbry and tossed a glare at Kipp for speaking out of turn. "As you stated last time we spoke, Dephen is doing something sinister with Yace. I truly believe that Master Ishik is planning on returning to Daos. That is why we are here in Ahradah."

The Oracle frowned. "You believe he is returning to Daos?"

"We know he is not just running away from us. There is purpose in what Dephen is doing. You hinted at that before." He put his hands up, hoping not to offend Nonbry. "And I know I am just speculating here, but all signs point to Dephen returning to Daos to assassinate his brother." He struggled not to avert eye contact, but staring at all-white eyes was unsettling. Irwin wanted to be heard. He truly believed that Dephen was far more threatening than Nonbry had first alluded to.

"Hm. Dana has seen much since our last meeting." He sat back, reserved in telling them what he knew. "Extreme caution must be taken when making decisions. Consequences will follow and may take you two down a nightmarish road."

Kipp could not hold back. "Did Dana see Yace being raped by soldiers? Did she see Dephen taking them as his mindless slaves?"

The white eyes of the Oracle settled on Kipp. "Yes. She did."

Kipp visibly flinched.

Irwin wanted an answer to his pressing question. "Does Dana see Yace being used as an assassin?"

The Telepath replied, "Yace's future is foggy, at best. What we know is that Dephen is constantly plotting, and that is why there are so many outcomes to your predicament."

15

Observant Oracle

Snuggled close inside her lair, Irwin tilted toward the Oracle—toward Nonbry. "Does Dana see Yace going by boat to Daos?"

The Oracle's head nodded. "By horseback, by ship, and by carriage—Yace has been seen in Dana's mind over and over. And each time she follows you two toward horrific outcomes. Of course, the same happens for herself too. Dana has seen Death take Yace one night, and the next night she's Death doling out waves of panic and terror."

Irwin whispered, "I am amazed Dana is not afraid to sleep." Nonbry's expression told Irwin that Yace's mother did fear closing her eyes at night. But she did, nonetheless. She needed to stay in contact with her only daughter.

"Dana fears for Yace and what will happen to her and to both of you. There is no denying that this is a bastard stunt taking Yace's body, as Dephen has. And if you cannot find a way to touch her, she will slip away. Unless ..." His eyes never left Irwin's. "... unless another Telepath sees the charade. If you two could prove what Dephen is doing, somehow show another Telepath ...." he paused. "The problem is that Dephen is powerful. He's hidden Yace. No one can hear her crying or screaming. No one can see what Yace is going through except Dana.

"If I could be there, I'd call him out. It takes a well-trained Telepath to see what's going on. But you won't find any in Ahradah. It's too laid back a place." He paused again. "Some of the best trained Telepaths live farther south. But you don't want to go that far.

"It seems that you're learning how well Dephen uses his Coterie Talent. And being in Yace's body, he's a chameleon. He's well-trained in manipulating situations to his advantage. He's had a lifetime to master his powers. But now that he's in a much younger vessel, Dephen will grow more powerful." The white eyes studied Irwin. "That's why you, Irwin, need to rescue her—today! This hour! You're the only one who can save Yace. And you must be willing to give your life to save her. If Dephen continues to elude you and draw you south ...." Nonbry shook his head as he trailed off.

Irwin clenched his fists. "I have heard enough about Daos to understand how terrible a place it can be for anyone, Talented or not. We will stop her before then. We will stop her today. We know where she is, but we have been hesitant to advance. She has six PCP soldiers at her side. Four of them are Erthin and of various powers. The others are Clan-Duin mixes. And as of this morning, they were still residing with a family of Mortals."

The old man chided Irwin. "There are places just as bad as Daos."

Kipp asked, "Should we cause a scene?"

Nonbry scoffed again at the impulsive Clan-Duin. "Do not think that if you rescue her, you two will be out of the wolf's den. If you call too much attention to yourselves, your ability to complete your mission will be nil. And you'll be put into service of the PCP." Nonbry looked back at Irwin. "Or worse! You must stop her now in Ahradah. If you don't save her there, your capacity to save her farther down the road dwindles. As I've said, Dana has seen many unfortunate hardships in your path. You need to rescue Yace, posthaste!"

"Sir, I fear saving Yace. I worry Kipp will die in the process. In fact, I cannot guarantee anyone's safety if I go save her. There are trained soldiers accompanying them, and I know Yace/Dephen can take Kipp's mind at any time."

"Fear is what'll kill you both. You cannot balk at what needs to happen."

"I asked around the wharf about ships voyaging south, and I was told that one left several days ago before any of us arrived. And it did not sound like there were any that traveled directly to Daos. Though there are ships that head in that direction, they are far and few between. Do you think it is possible they missed their ship? That maybe they are trying to hideout until another one comes along?"

"It is possible. But the reason he acquired the six guards was for protection against you." A finger pointed at Irwin. "You've already shown Dephen you are relentless and dangerous. You've also displayed a knack for not being manipulated by him. And your unique power keeps you in the shadows of all Telepaths. Use your knowledge and retrieve Yace at once.

"You must know there'll be bloodshed, no matter what path you take. Don't hesitate or falter." Nonbry snarled and snorted. "The fact that you know where they're staying and haven't attempted a rescue is a disservice to Yace."

"I plan on saving her, Sir."

I had not counted on giving my life. Or thought of how to do it without Kipp being another casualty.

"We will save her, Sir. That is our plan. We wanted to make sure that she has no other escape route you would know of. After we are done here, we plan on locating Blacky and having him ready for departure when we retrieve Yace."

"Do not wait! If indeed you suspect Dephen is returning home to assassinate his brother, you can't allow him any more time in Yace's body."

Irwin reflected on what he knew about how Emperor Somer Ishik treats his people. "But would it not be a good thing if he assassinated his brother? I mean, if the current Emperor abhors those with Talents and represses his people for no other reason than his own personal gain, I think killing him would be a good thing for the people of Daos."

"Repercussions from an assassination would be catastrophic. We can't allow that to happen."

"Alright then. We will rescue her posthaste." Irwin was not as trusting in himself as everyone else wanted him to be. He was also wary of Kipp being controlled by some Telepath if something were to go wrong in their rescue mission. "But I know Dephen will put up a fight. I believe he will sacrifice those soldiers—and probably the Mortals he is living with. He will sacrifice everyone around him, compromise Kipp, and negate my ability to save her—even if I do give my life."

"Doubting yourself will not help."

Irwin nodded. "We will do everything in our power to save Yace, but what if Dephen still eludes us?"

The white eyes in the Oracles shifted back to violet. Her own smile drew across her face as though nothing had happened. "Is that all you need me for?" She blinked again, and her eyes changed back to white. "Dephen's an arrogant man with a large ego."

Kipp groaned, "Holy Hakra, here we go with another story!"

Nonbry went on, and his voice rose above Kipp's. "As I confessed last time, we harbored Dephen as a fugitive. He lived with us Gypsy for several years. Back then, he was full of anger for being banished from Daos. He thought that being from Ishik blood gave him family rights. But he's a bastard! He's never had any rights to his Ishik name.

"While he traveled with us, he cursed his father's name, wishing he hadn't been born to him. During that time Dephen drank heavily." The white eyes persisted, but now they stared off between both men, back and forth. "I recall one drunken time he confessed to me that he wanted to kill them all—every one of his family members. Even then, I saw his malicious intentions. This was around the time Yace would have been an infant. I believe he was plotting revenge against his brother back then. I'd hate to think that this was all planned out, but ....

"I have always known Dephen as a man of word. He had always been effective at commanding attention and articulating ideas. He could suck the air out of a room—much like Yace. There are too many striking resemblances between those two ...." He trailed off.

Nonbry blinked. "Dephen can concoct outrageous plans. He's the one who instigated Tamera's freedom. I know you've heard that story at least a dozen times, Kipp."

The Clan-Duin was staring off, not listening to the old man.

"Even back then, he had plans for the Gypsy. He saw how things—in his mind—should be, and he tried to manipulate our way of life in his favor. I saw through his trickery, but I had to make the others aware of this chicanery. And once Captain Hari saw it, he didn't hesitate to broadcast Dephen's lies."

Nonbry's voice rose. "Everyone knows I'm the one who started the underground Gypsy movement on land. It was our mother who began the liberations from the sea. But I digress; Dephen is Coterie. He has powers that are above mine. Even if I am a more powerful Telepath, he's capable of outsmarting the best of us. Let caution be with you.

"I can see Dephen casting into motion a horrific set of events, using Yace as the catalyst." Another long pause took hold. No one spoke until Nonbry said, "In any case, rescuing her today is your only option."

Irwin's mind raced. "What if she claims to be Ishik? What if she uses that name to some advantage? —to obtain immunity or to slip away unseen? What would happen then?"

"To be Ishik outside of Daos Territory is a death sentence. But not everyone knows that. For many years, the Ishik family haven't allowed voyages outside the territory, let alone across Urthis. At one point, there were several distant relatives who lived outside Daos Territory. But I'm certain they're all dead by now.

"Besides, Emperor Somer Ishik put out a bounty on all those who call themselves Ishik. Even those who had Ishik blood, not knowing they were descendants of the emperor, were sought out. His half-brother, Somer, also put a halt on most types of trade into and out of Daos. It's been like that for over three decades."

They all sat quietly, soaking it all in.

Nonbry added, "But there are ships that trade with Daos. They trade anything from food to narcotics and people. Daos Territory isn't a place you want to be."

His eyes settled on Irwin. "Unfortunately, Dana has seen it otherwise." The white eyes never shifted away from Irwin. "She has seen Yace in Daos City. She has seen her on both small and large ocean-going vessels—and in the Jungle of Datzar. She saw Yace working in a whorehouse in Arenu Village. In another dream, Dana saw exact duplicates of Yace everywhere." They sat quietly while that information sank in.

"What this means for the two of you is that Dephen's constantly plotting, and you must be on guard. He's smart. But Dana gets the sense he's still trying to figure things out, and that's why her dreams are erratic." He pointed at Irwin. "And then you imply that Dephen is up to something deadly. What makes you believe he is gonna assassinate his brother?"

"An assassin tried to extinguish him. That assassin was a servant, one he had taken to bed before committing the act. Only a well-trained bounty hunter would be so bold."

Kipp was now paying attention. "Or a jealous woman."

The white eyes were still trained on Irwin. "No matter what happens, Dephen will make use of Yace's skills. Be prepared for anything."

Kipp sounded as if he had just woken up. "Wait, you said Arenu Village! Isn't that the place where they put the worst of the worse?"

"Nuaki Village is the place where the worst of the worst live. But both are places you need to avoid."

"We will retrieve her before then—before sundown."

If we can.

Irwin tried not to show Nonbry his true thoughts.

We just need a foolproof plan.

They must be tactical—a simple hope. But he was not sure he could guarantee no lives would be lost, especially if he must give his own.

The Oracle's body began to squirm. "Don't contact me again until you have her." And just like that, Nonbry left his telepathic hostess.

Her eyes dwindled from white to violet, and the Oracle returned to her body. Clearly winded from this ordeal, she asked, "Is that all you need?" She gripped her sides and swayed for a moment.

They nodded their heads in unison.

"I hope your communications went well." She handed the talisman back to Kipp.

It was all over.

Yet when her hand touched Kipp's, the Oracle's body stiffened. She grasped his hands, and her eyes shifted from violet to white again. She leaned forward, her voice rattled. "Kipp! They have me. They're going to kill me. I'm in the square. I don't want to die! Please help me!"

Was Yace trying to communicate with them through the Oracle? Kipp sat forward, clutching the woman's hands as tight as he dared.

Her eyes receded again from white back to violet.

Kipp gasped, "Yace? Yace! I'll be there! We've gotta go."

The Oracle reached up as Kipp released her hands. She stood to face them. "That female is in grave danger. Those who have her will kill her if given the opportunity."

The woman's words of unwanted advice shook Kipp at his core. Irwin knew for certain that his friend would not, could not, stop in his frantic pursuit any longer.

Kipp rushed to the door.

Irwin followed close behind, aware he could no longer control the Clan Duin. They tore down the street and climbed onto their horses. Kipp was in the lead, and Irwin sensed the danger this implied.

Kipp was first to get his horse trotting; donkeys were yanked forward. People in their path parted ways for them to pass.

Irwin kicked his horse to a lope and fell in stride alongside Kipp's massive, black-furred mount. They rode shoulder to shoulder; the crowds stood watching in their wake. Irwin should have been leading, scanning everything, looking for brigades on foot and on horseback, but most importantly, for Yace.

They located the ornately cobbled square again, this time from the northern side. Merchants stood alongside their kiosks shouting their wears above the murmurs of shoppers. Scores of local children ran here and there, screaming and playing in the water fountains on either side of the rectangular square. Between the watering fountains, the large wooden stockades and gallows loomed ominously.

They rode on past the Healers Hall. Promenades above connected to the Sanatorium, another extensive building. Both buildings were several stories tall, and two city blocks long. They slowed their horses to a fast walk along the House of Datzarian Government, heading straight toward the Building of Civilities across from the gallows and the stockade. They passed the Headquarters of Peacekeeping. The PCP Hall sat at the far end of the great square. There were soldiers everywhere. Irwin's heart raced. They were not riding as they should, and only he seemed to care.

Yace's scent lingered in the air. Kipp signaled for Irwin to stay at his side.

Irwin reached out and grabbed the Clan-Duin's arm, in an attempt to bring Kipp back into this moment. They stood out. Kipp was wearing a PCP uniform, but Irwin was not. And they rode side by side, not as they should.

Someone parked a large carriage on the wide roadway at the corner of the House of Datzarian Government. As they approached, the opulent vehicle rolled forward toward the Building of Civilities. They followed, shielded by that carriage from another PCP brigade crossing the square on horseback. Four well-dressed soldiers on horseback surrounded the grand coach. Irwin and Kipp persisted in following. The horses and carriage took a right turn; the mounted soldiers turned too. They did not look back, unaware that Irwin and Kipp were trailing. Yace was apparently sweating heavily—her scent was thick.

"I can smell her ... practically taste her!" Then Kipp caught sight of her.

She was being shoved into the stockade—her hands bound by large steel balls. Her mouth was gagged, and a thick helmet was thrown over her head. The front of her purple dress was discolored with blood splatter, and her blonde hair was matted to her head; she disappeared beneath the helmet. There was no way Yace would be able to free herself.

Kipp slapped Irwin's shoulder. "Did you see that?! It's Yace!" They rode past, glancing back over their shoulders at the horrific scene.

The Clan-Duin rerouted their horses around the courtyard. People were staring at the spectacle surrounding the stockade.

Soldiers stood vigilant next to door fronts; some walked the avenues in pairs and quads. There looked to be a hundred or more out and about. Any of those soldiers could walk up and halt Irwin and Kipp at any time, but none did. Anxiety tightened Irwin's throat and heightened his senses.

Four Erthin soldiers stood guard at the corners of the stockade. They looked haggard from a lack of sleep, and they were being rough with the young woman in the purple dress. They pushed and pulled her and thrust her into the enclosure, slapping her around as they did.

Kipp didn't witness the roughness, but Irwin had. The Clan-Duin grumbled at him for staring too long at the scene.

Irwin said nothing, not wanting to further rile his partner.

"Looks like we'll be staying in Ahradah at least another night," Kipp said.

They rode back toward the stables and the inn they had left behind earlier. Kipp stayed close to Irwin's side.

This all seems too good to be true, and too much of a coincidence for Yace to speak through that Telepath. It is their link. She has Kipp every time. He admitted it. I hate to think that I have to keep contact with him all the time. But maybe I do. And then she summons us out into the open plaza where there are hundreds of soldiers afoot. The fact that this happened right after Nonbry revealed Dephen's past as a manipulator ....

How is it possible that Dephen/Yace got caught? Nonbry said there are no other powerful Telepaths in Ahradah. Dephen is too smart to get caught. This was all calculated.

Irwin had noticed the young blonde woman before she was helmeted. What he had seen was a younger version of Yace—her face rounder, more childlike—the look in her eyes was more naïve, more innocent.

And though he trusted Kipp, he kept touching his friend's arm, trying to ensure that he was not being possessed. "You really believe that is Yace in the stockades?"

"Of course that's her!" The sight of Yace being shackled, helmeted, and left out in the midday sun was more than Kipp could tolerate. Irwin understood this.

He too had seen Yace, or someone who looked exactly like her, being dreadfully mistreated. He held his tongue and remained at Kipp's side while his friend chewed on his thoughts all the way to a stable yard.

They went to a different barn than before, but they rented the same number of stalls. This time, Kipp did all the unpacking and setting up the animals with feed and water. Irwin stood as the master figure, watching people move along the street outside the barn. He was making sure they had not been followed. He made sure they were quiet with their interactions. There were several stable boys and a young owner who were watchful of their tenants. It was good role-playing practice.

He waited calmly for Kipp to be done. Then they went in search of and then found an inn with several rooms available. Irwin rented two for the night, but was fairly certain they would only need one for the day. He did not want anyone to suspect anything. They needed to blend in.

⋺⋹ ⋺⋹

Irwin went to the Clan-Duin's room, closed and locked the door. Although they had followed Kipp's nose before, it felt as though they were going down the same telepathically laced route again. As he used his power to lock the door,

Irwin watched Kipp take a seat on the bed. "Nonbry told us to be cautious—that anything could happen."

Turmoil washed across Kipp's dark face. He barked, "Nonbry isn't here to help us."

"How positive are you that the woman in the stockades was Yace?" As soon as he asked, he regretted it.

"You saw her!" Kipp snarled. "You saw her with that gag in her mouth and the helmet crammed onto her head. That was Yace! The dress was just like the one that barkeep described yesterday. And I smelled her. Holy Hakra, I smelled her. THAT'S YACE!"

"I am sorry for second-guessing your nose, Kipp, but Nonbry mentioned Dana seeing many outcomes for Yace's future—for our future. That includes duplicates or twins of Yace. We cannot just jump forward blindly. This could be a trick. Nonbry made it clear that Dephen enjoys trickery. I do not want to get us into a situation we cannot get out of."

"I don't see how this can be a trick," Kipp growled. "Isn't that why we're back here? To plan what to do next?"

"Do you not think that this is all a little coincidental?"

"How could it be coincidental?"

"That we were ... that you were contacted immediately following our conversation with Nonbry. Yace knew you were with a Telepath, and so did Dephen." He reprimanded himself for his own lack of thoughtful action. "I should have had contact with you the whole time."

"You can't protect me, Irwin!"

"Kipp, I do not want us to fall into a larger trap than what has already befallen us."

"That was Yace out there!" Kipp was livid and pointed to the window. "She's in those stockades locked away for who knows what type of crime. How can that be a trick?"

"We both know that Yace is too smart to get locked up. Besides, Dephen has had a lifetime of manipulating others. Do you actually think he would have slipped up and exposed himself? Nonbry said there is no one here in Ahradah powerful enough to see what Dephen is doing, remember?"

"Dephen's old! And in a foreign body. Imagine yourself being trapped in a female's body." Kipp stared off and hummed to himself. "As you've said before, they're Coterie; they're not infallible!"

"And as Nonbry said, there are no powerful Telepaths here in Ahradah."

"That he knows of. Is he here? No! Did he see her? No! I'm not gonna listen to anything Nonbry has to say, especially his long-drawn-out stories that go nowhere."

"They are indeed long, but his stories have value."

"And he never gives a direct answer. I hate that."

"A lot of the answers he gives are in his stories. He is trying to get us to pay attention to all the details. Nonbry knows a lot. You know that. He is trying to share all the information he has in a way that makes sense to us."

"Couldn't he just give us actual answers, like yes, and no, and this is how and when to free Yace?"

"So much more is at stake here than simply running in and rescuing her."

"Oh, I know that! But Nonbry can't help. And neither can I. Only you, Irwin. Only you."

16

IT'S YACE!

Irwin did not want to take on the burden of rescuing Yace by himself. "You know I cannot do this alone, Kipp; I need your help."

"We can't walk right up to her, Irwin. There'll be guards all around her—all day and all night. They'll watch everyone who approaches. And because she looks like a Telepath, there'll be a lot of eyes watching." Kipp stared at Irwin. His lower left eyelid twitched. "This isn't something I can do. We already know this. This'll be all you. You'll have to melt all the metal that's hung up around her. And once she's free, sees that it's us come to rescue, I'm sure she'll help us fight the soldiers."

Silence hung thick, and worry and doubt filled the air around them. Irwin was not convinced they should do anything drastic right now. "What if Dephen is still within her? If he is, and we go to the rescue and he harnesses Yace's powers, the outcome could be disastrous." He waited, hoping he had made his point. "Besides, how do we know that was her?" His eyes never left Kipp's. "Nonbry said many things we need to think about before acting. He wanted us to free her as soon as possible. But then he also alluded to Dephen's enjoyment in plotting scenarios to his advantage. What if this is all a ruse? What if he is trying to get us incarcerated by the PCP? What is the story behind Tamera's rescue?"

"Tamera's rescue? Why does that matter?"

It matters!

"How was she rescued?"

Kipp shrugged. "It took something like ten days to convince a town to give her to Nonbry."

"That is not a story. Nonbry said you have heard the story a dozen times."

"I don't understand why her rescue matters."

"Dephen was the one who executed it."

"Oh. OH!" Kipp's eyes bulged. "The story goes something like; he convinced a whole town to allow her and two dozen other servants and Talented slaves to leave with the Gypsy. And the PCP never tried to stop them. In fact, a few soldiers went along. No one was ever stopped. That never happens, Irwin! It's usually the other way around. Dang me!" The Clan-Duin blinked, as though coming from a dream. "Dephen did that. Not Nonbry, Dephen. Double dang."

"Indeed, Dephen is a master manipulator." He waited again for what he said to sink in. "See, for me, Yace being in those stockades seems too coincidental. She is smarter than that. And so is Dephen. He would not get caught unless he could work it to his advantage."

Kipp pointed toward the square. "That is Yace, Irwin! I smelled her. We both saw her. We both know that's Yace. She's trapped against her will. And there's nothing I can do about it. But you! You can do everything." His eyes lit. "That Oracle said Yace was in danger. She said Yace would be killed by those who have her. We saw how many soldiers are guarding her. Any one of them could kill her at any time."

This was all just too convenient. Irwin could not imagine Yace or Dephen allowing themselves to be placed in restraints. He wanted to believe Kipp's ideas. But he saw the flaws in Kipp's thought process. "What if Dephen is still within Yace? Maybe that was what Nonbry was alluding to—that Dephen is the one who will kill Yace. We need to remember that Nonbry told me to touch Yace. Touching her will get rid of Dephen. Only I can bring her back. I need to make physical contact with Yace's flesh in order to set her free. If Dephen is still within her, he could smite us while we are trying to free her."

Kipp shook his head again. "Did you not hear me? She'll be guarded. And no one is allowed to walk up to the guilty. Only her guards, and those higher up in the PCP, are allowed anywhere close. It's the law. Unless ... unless the person offended calls a Gathering. It's only when there is a Gathering that anyone is allowed to be close to a criminal. Like spitting close."

Irwin raised an eyebrow. "Then what must we do to have a Gathering?" He watched as thoughts rolled around behind the Clan-Duin's eyes—the emotion boiled across his face.

"You've never seen anyone in a stockade before, have you, Irwin?" Kipp's expression turned solemn. "What your father and grandfather did to you as a child is comparable to what they do to people in stockades. But what we would have to do—we'd have to stone her. We would have to know the crime she committed and call her on it—then initiate the stoning of her." Grief filled his words. "That usually happens around midday. And usually it's the person who was wronged, or family of, who initiates. Since I look the way I do, and I'm in love with Yace, I can't do it. You'd have to. You'd have to berate her and then beat her."

"I cannot do that."

"That's why you need to free her. Only you can do this, Irwin. But I'll be there right by your side."

"What if she is being stoned right now?"

"There's a process for these types of things."

"Enlighten me."

"Well, from what I understand, the guilty are found and brought to the Peace Keeping Building. They are interrogated and then put in the stockade, unless they pose a threat to others; then they are put in a hole which is usually covered by the stockade. They're usually in the stockade a full day before any stoning happens. Sometimes it takes two or three days. The idea is for those who are guilty to be seen, berated, and punished before their peers.

"But don't think that it's always the Vols that get put in there. Mortals are shut away just as often for stealing or being violent. It's a way of bringing reality to everyday life and can be a humbling sight to witness a female, especially, being shackled in the heat of the day."

Irwin's silvery stare made the Clan-Duin cower. "You do realize that if we go and save Yace, I just might be committing one of those violent acts."

"This is different. This is Yace. We need to protect her. We need to save her. Nonbry said so!"

The Clan-Duin was trying everything to convince Irwin to just go out and rescue Yace. But Irwin knew they could not be so brazen. They must remain painstakingly cautious. "What about those six soldiers of hers? Why are they not with her?"

"Huh? Oh, you mean what happened to them?"

Irwin nodded.

"Well, it's possible Yace was caught performing her telepathic magic. She might have been trying to steal something or do something sinister, like you keep hinting."

"Why? She has more than enough gold with her. She does not need to steal." Irwin paced across the room and grabbed onto the bedpost. "Besides, there is no way Dephen would resort to stealing. A man of such wealth and power would not commit robbery. He is a Telepath. He could just will people to give him things."

Kipp wrung his hands. "Stealing is what Yace used to do all the time."

"We must remember that Dephen is in control, not Yace. I am fairly sure that he would never steal. And if Yace did need to steal for some reason, there are those soldiers at her side who would do that for her. They would be the ones pillaging.

That way, if they were caught, Yace—Dephen—could walk away and not be taken to the Hall of Justice."

"Maybe that's what happened. But then they were all caught. And that was how she was found guilty. They probably excused those soldiers of any wrongdoing; seen as how they were under her control. I'm guessing here, but either way, those six soldiers are probably being debriefed and reassigned missions inside that PCP Hall right now." The Clan-Duin's eyes glazed over. "Waiting until nightfall will be better for us."

Irwin did not like the idea that they should wait so long. At the very least, they should go back to the square with Kipp's nose and have him take another whiff. He wanted to know for certain that it was Yace who was shackled.

Maybe I can get close enough to touch her.

None of this feels right. Too contrived, too deliberate. But Kipp is positive that is Yace. Then maybe ... maybe we take the horses and just free her. Shit. Now I am starting to sound like Kipp. I cannot allow myself to act on irrational thoughts. That will get people killed! I must think more abstractly. Dephen surely is.

Kipp asked, "Did you buy any more merchant-style clothing while you were out?"

"I did not. I was focused on purchasing enough food for three people and five animals." Irwin tapped his fingers against his thigh. "We should not stay here any longer than necessary. We will not do ourselves any good staying idle."

"I'm not going out there."

"Why not?"

"I'll wanna rescue Yace."

"Is that not the point? Nonbry said we need to. Today! This hour, if possible. Do you not remember? We need to observe and survey what we can ... strategize the best route to and from the square. I am not going to rescue Yace without a good exit strategy. Being impulsive will only hinder our ability to rescue. We should go on foot—do that stupid master-servant walk and gain a clear understanding of our problem. Maybe we will see an easier solution than your run-in-and-rescue option."

"And if we're seen?"

"You were not so worried about being seen by the PCP when we were on horseback. This time, we will be on the ground. And you will be walking your three strides behind."

"No." Kipp shook his head violently. "We should stay here."

"But Nonbry said—"

"Holy Hakra, are you in love with Nonbry? We can't go out there!"

"Why not?"

"If we went to make sure it was Yace, I'd wanna free her right then. No! We're better off here for now."

Waiting for time to pass, they fiddled with this and that, tapping fingers, grumbling, and coughing. Irwin went over and over the conversation with Nonbry.

"How far away from Ahradah is Arenu Village, Kipp? You said it was a place that the worst of the worst go."

"It's south of here. And that's why we need to save Yace and return north …." His eyes darted around the room; then he peered out the window. "Back to the Gypsy. I'm done with all this." He turned back to look at Irwin. "Further south is bad."

Irwin was worn down and weary by all this repeating. "The mapmaker was hesitant to sell me this map of Daos Territory. But he did. I also bought a world map, for which he kept pointing to the north; Onj Raha, he said." He could never return to Onj Raha, of that, Irwin was certain.

"You bought a map of Daos? Why?"

"Knowledge."

"Can I see those maps?"

They rolled them out flat on the bed.

He studied the map of Urthis while Kipp perused Daos Territory, surveying its many rivers and villages. After a while the Clan-Duin grumbled and asked for the other map. Irwin was reluctant to hand off the picture of a world he was learning so much about. He had traveled far from Kobiton to Ahradah. Yet, as far as the map showed, that distance paled in comparison to Urthis's circumference.

There were words of warning on the map of Daos. Above the most northern city of Vidigen, and just below the text 'Datzar Jungle,' read 'Enter at your own risk'. "Kipp, what do you know of the Datzar Jungle?"

The Clan-Duin lifted the world map. "Everything below this line," he pointed at the equator, "is very bad. There are man-eating apes and waterways filled with alligators and man-eating fish. Every vicious creature you could imagine lives in that jungle. It's considered protected. Let's just say it keeps Vols like us from heading south and keeps the Daosian natives from wandering north."

"I dislike the word Vols, Kipp. I prefer Talented because that is what we are. We are not Volatile like some people would want us to believe."

Kipp laughed. "Oh, there's some out-right Volatile people out there, Irwin. Arenu Village is a great example, from what I understand. They only host

Volatiles. And from what I've heard, most of those people are assassins, mercenaries, and thieves. They slave trade and deal in black market stuff. I've been told some of the most powerful people on Urthis live there. It might be the perfect place for you to visit at some point. You'd probably fit right in."

Irwin closed his eyes and wished once again he had never lost control in Onj Raha. All the carnage! He could still feel all those Erthins his body had assimilated. Behind closed eyes, he could still see flashes of the blood and the bodies, male and female, strewn every which way—his metallic twisters twirling around and dealing out death. That would be forever etched into his mind.

"It's alright to be Volatile, Irwin," Kipp softened. "Besides, we might need you to cause a distraction tonight."

Irwin did not want to be like his father. He did not want the wrath or the singing metal to consume him. It was hard to keep control. "That is an irrational thought right there. Nonbry said that causing a distraction might void our mission. And we would not want to do that. I would like to think that even though he is an old man with his own issues, he is trying to help us. Remember, Nonbry's mission in life is to help those with Talents. Dephen, too, was a humanitarian until recently. Now he is doing a disservice to the Gypsy by using Yace for something ulterior. We do not want to be like Dephen."

"You're choosing to believe what Nonbry has to say. He's not here with us. He's not helping us make these choices we have to make."

"I can always refuse to be Volatile." Irwin replied, frost on the edge of his words.

Kipp's brown eyes pleaded. "Irwin, I need you to do what needs to be done to save Yace. Nonbry hinted at that too—you need to be willing to give your life. We know there'll be PCP in our way. You need to be comfortable in dealing with them."

Irwin wanted to do good by and for others. And yet he knew he had the capacity to maim anyone without any initial regret. "What about you? What if you are compromised by Erthin crossfire? What if I think I have control, but it reels out of control? What if I get you killed?"

"At least you'll have rescued Yace."

"And how will your death help? I am the one who is supposed to be sacrificed, not you." Although Irwin did not want to die for Yace, Nonbry insisted that might happen.

"Look, Irwin, if we're gonna do this, I need you to do whatever needs to be done. Don't worry about anyone else except Yace. Hopefully, if everything works out, she'll keep me safe. All you need to do is get rid of that metal around her head and hands." He tapped his chin. "Oh, and touch her. Maybe do what you did in Onj Raha. You know, with the metal and all those bodies? That way, we have time to escape."

"If we do this later tonight, we will not need a distraction."

"Most likely there'll be Erthin guards surrounding her. They'll have to be taken down first." Kipp wasn't listening. "And there might be others hiding. You'll need to get rid of them too."

"So let me get this straight. You want me to melt the metal attached to Yace without touching her first—unlike what Nonbry suggested? And if there are any Erthins or Clan-Duins in our way, you want me to snap them out of existence?"

"Yeah, something like that. Look Irwin, I wouldn't be upset about killing a few Erthins. They're scum. But most likely it won't come to that if we do this late tonight. If it makes you feel any better, you can touch her after we release her from the stockades."

Though Kipp seemed to be himself, Irwin was not sure. "You sound out of your mind."

"What? Me? Why?"

"We would be going against everything that old man told us to do. And Nonbry said you were more susceptible to Yace's powers. Maybe she has your mind right now!" He reached forward to touch Kipp's hand. "Do you feel any different?"

"No. I'm in my right mind, not my left. And I know what needs to be done, as do you. Don't worry over things that have yet to happen."

Those were words Irwin had spoken to Kipp on several occasions and now tossed back at him.

"Are we still waiting for the sun to set?"

Kipp nodded.

17

There Are Always Options

Silence hung over the room.

Irwin returned to looking at the maps while Kipp slumped onto the bed, staring up at the wooden ceiling. "I hate waiting."

Intrigued by the maps, Irwin gazed at them for a long time before his mind returned to the problem at hand. "What if ... what if I bought a wagon?"

"What? Why would you do that?"

"I am assuming that Blacky is long gone by now. So, we would have to buy a horse for Yace and all the tack and such." He paused long enough for Kipp to follow. "But what if ... what if she cannot ride because of being in the stockades? You saw how those men were treating her. She looked bruised up even before they pushed her into the stockade. Her wrists had those heavy metal devices on them that would cause bruises. And the shackles around her ankles have probably left welts too. That will make boot wearing uncomfortable at the very least. Not only that, Yace might have pains we cannot even comprehend.

"We will need to transport her without issue, Kipp. And if the donkeys are weighed down with all our stuff, they will slow us even more. At this point, the horses can do a steady pace for many kilometers, as can the donkeys if they are not weighted down. Pulling a wagon with what, three hundred pounds of grain, eighty pounds of food, plus you, me, and Yace, and a barrel of water—that maybe equals a thousand pounds total. Pulling that across even land will be a fairly simple task with a wagon. And before we know it, we will be heading back north."

Kipp gave Irwin a look of repulse.

"Besides, with a wagon, I can ensure your safety."

"Is that what this is about? Keeping me safe?"

"I can and I will. Like you hinted before, I have an entire city at my disposal. All the metal I could ever want is out there waiting for me to summon it. We could go to Wild Willie's and get a basic wagon. The cost is probably comparable to buying a horse with all the tack.

"If Yace is unable to ride a horse," he continued, "we need a better plan than tying her to the saddle. Besides, we already have the perfect pulling horses. With a wagon, it will be easier to keep moving." He stopped to think it through. "Maybe I buy a smaller set of harnesses so that the Jennies can help with the driving too. They have experience pulling carts of coal up from the mines. They know how to work as a team."

"Those donkeys pull a wagon! Ha!" Kipp cackled and slapped his thigh. "We're better off trading the donkeys for a horse and tack for Yace."

"Did you not see how much food I bought? Besides, I am not selling them—ever."

Kipp kept on laughing, wiping tears from his eyes. "You have such an alliance with those Jennies of yours. It's ridiculous!"

"As ridiculous as your undying love for Yace and her unacceptance of you?"

Kipp drew his hand into a fist.

Irwin readied himself to be hit, but continued to speak his mind, "You too have an amazing alliance to Yace, yet she pushes you away every chance she gets. And I have seen how jealous you become when anyone tosses a glance her way. We both know she does not feel the same as you feel towards her."

Kipp looked down.

"Please do not make fun of my loyalty to my animals. Beyond you and Yace, they are my only family. And though they may not seem necessary to you, I will not throw them away."

Kipp looked as if he had just been slapped. His fisted hand fell flat onto the bed. The Clan-Duin averted his eyes; they sat in silence once more. A few throat clearings and the shuffling of bodies ended the quiet that had fallen over their room.

Kipp spoke first. "Maybe a walk is a good idea."

"Should we take an animal or two?"

"If we show up with animals at a wagon corral, we might appear desperate." Kipp replied. "Okay, maybe we just take Jenn Jenn. Maybe steal some metal along the way." A grin of greed stretched his dark lips. "And you can practice your blacksmith story. Maybe we can steal enough metal to make blades and daggers. You know, have something to show as proof of your goods. Maybe you can use a blade or two in trade for a wagon."

Is he egging me on?

"We would have to go past a forge or two to find all the types of metal necessary to complete that task. But I suppose that could be part of the plan."

"How much metal were you thinking of getting?"

"I would need about a hundred pounds."

"A hundred pounds?!"

"If I am making up an inventory, proof that I am who I say I am, I need a lot of metal. Do you know how much metal is in a typical blade?" Irwin pointed at Kipp's short knife. "That blade of yours is nearly a pound and a half. It contains iron and steel, nickel, and a touch of chromium. It's a good blade and made by a well-versed smith. On the other hand, a long blade—the type we see the PCP carrying around—is five or six pounds, sometimes up to eight depending on the length and hilt. Pots and pans are two to five pounds, sometimes more, depending on how much tin or iron is used in the making. I can make my products lighter, but that would compromise their integrity. Be it a pot or a knife, I will not be making shoddy items like the ones Yace bought."

"Stole!"

"Stole? No wonder her pan was warped. It was probably used to smack someone on the head as it was stolen."

"I think it was." Kipp laughed.

"And it was poorly made, but that is beside the point. The things I make will have my signature. I will not make shitty items to sell—if I must sell at all."

"If you're not gonna sell, then why get a hundred pounds?"

To keep you safe, you stupid Clan-Duin.

"I would rather have too much than not enough." If he had a hundred pounds of metal, he could encase Kipp and completely protect the Clan-Duin from any Erthin onslaught or telepathic possession. "Let us go for that walk."

"Maybe you should ask for your money back since we're not staying here."

"We do not know if we might need a place of refuge later this evening. I think it would be best if we left a few trails to follow, too, like Dephen has. Besides, if we are still being followed—"

Kipp rolled his eyes. "We're not being followed anymore!"

"—we do not want to lead a path straight to us."

They left the inn with Irwin in the lead. It was several blocks to the stables, and along their walk they crossed the path of a mounted band of PCP. The gang of four darkly dressed soldiers did not look twice at the two young men. Kipp had assumed his position, as had Irwin who strode ahead confidently and looked forward with purpose. Even though his clothing was bright, he did not call more attention to himself than any other merchantman.

Back at the stables, Kipp retrieved Jenn Jenn while Irwin waited at the main doorway and listened to the stable boys being lectured on how to hot-shoe their horses and not get kicked. Women walked in groups, giggling with one another and glancing at men who looked their way. Merchants stood near their storefronts, waiting for patrons, setting up new displays. It was a typical afternoon in Ahradah, as Irwin saw it. And when Kipp finally came out of the stables, they set off.

Irwin did not take a direct route.

"Where are we going?" Kipp was already anxious and annoyed.

Irwin said nothing. He wanted to return to the stockades so Kipp could take a whiff to confirm it was Yace. He knew what avenues to take to the city square. From the stables, it was six blocks down and two over. But he took a roundabout way, turning every two blocks and meandering around the heart of the city. The street on which they entered the square paralleled the stockades and gallows, then continued on across the square toward the Sanatorium and Headquarters of Peace Keeping. That same road would lead them almost straight to Wild Willie's Wagons, perhaps a kilometer away.

They were about thirty feet from Yace as they walked past. Irwin kept his eyes forward, but his ability to feel the surrounding metal was constantly tuned in. Those who stood studiously near the gallows had multiple blades on them; most were visible. People walking or riding horses possessed coins, teeth, jewelry, and every other metal item imaginable. It all sang to Irwin.

It was the busiest part of the day. He had to stay mindful and ignore every urge to summon the metal. He reminded himself to slow his pace. He glanced back at Kipp. "Smell her."

Kipp held his position three feet back, and Irwin never fully stopped, but took shortened strides. Only after exiting the open square did their pace pick up. They walked down and around several more blocks, taking another roundabout way toward Wild Willie's. Kipp signaled to Irwin, wanting to talk, but there was nowhere they could sneak away without being seen by soldiers or curious merchants.

Irwin doubled back, crisscrossing several streets. They did not return to the square. Instead, they proceeded a few more blocks and doubled around again.

Soon they turned down the street that ended in front of Wild Willie's Wagon Corral.

They stopped in front of the wide-open metal corral gates. The three men who were there yesterday, plus one more, moved toward them. They had little time to talk.

Irwin whispered, "Was that her?"

"Yes, Sir."

The four salespeople stopped a distance from the front gates. Only one older man broke off from the group.

Irwin hurried to add, "I noticed she had urinated. There was a lot of it. Were you able to smell that?"

Kipp nodded. "It was all really confusing. I smelled several masculine and female types of urine and Yace's sweat. There was the smell of blood and manly scents of copulation too. And I smelled another female scent. It was also pungent. My nose is really confused."

The salesman called out, "Good afternoon, Sir!"

"Yes. Hauss, just stand and enjoy the afternoon air. I will be in here a while." Irwin turned to engage the approaching sales associate. He walked into the large, fenced area, leaving Kipp, who he would now refer to as Hauss, behind.

Slapping his hands together, the older salesman said, "Good afternoon, Sir. What can I do for ya today?" He was a large man with balding hair and a wrinkled smile. He had seen much sun in his life and was pure Mortal, as were the other sales attendants who returned to their seats on a covered porch.

Irwin slowed his stride. He could not help but glance back at Kipp for suggestions, but remembered that Kipp was not supposed to be there to help. He found his focus. "Ah, yes, I was hoping to look at wagons."

"What type of wagon are ya thinking? We've got all types here, from one axel and wooden wheels to three axels and steel rims. We've got buckboards, springboards, two seaters, four, six, and more. We've got short beds, long beds, wide beds, two sides, three sides, or four sides. We also have flat-bed wagons and ones with drop sides and tailgates. We could go tall or short. Your pick is here—I guarantee it, Sir!"

Again, he glanced back at Kipp, overwhelmed by all the choices.

I feel like I just filled my boots with coal and jumped into a river. What type of wagon do we need? Is this what adults do—make important decisions like this?

"We would ... I would, like .... What I am looking for is something I can use as my portable shop."

"Portable shop? What is it that ya do, my good man?"

He mustn't hesitate. "Blade, knife and swords repairman." The words all came so fast they had no meaning until the salesman asked again. Irwin figured out exactly what to say this time. "Cutlery Repairman. I mostly sell, but I can repair knives and blades. I also have many already forged."

"A cutlery repairman, don't ya need a forge for that?"

This is where Irwin could be creative with his lie. "Many of my blades were made back at my home forge. And all my supplies and tools are back in the room I rented. What I need is something that can carry my tools. I decided a while ago to tour the globe, selling my wares by ship. But now I want to take to the land and see the sights of the eastern seaboard."

"Ah ha, I didn't peg ya as a local. Your tongue's too flat to be from around here." The salesman chortled and pointed to Irwin's clothing. He stepped closer. "Ya take the ship from Ajihya?"

"You mean the one going to Ajihya?" He tried to act nonchalant.

"Ah, yeah, that trade ship! Many people come by boat to Ahradah from the other world. Noble women and peasant men alike travel to our city for our bountiful landscape, our imports and exports, and our food. Yes, Ahradah has much to offer the world traveler.

"In fact, the Princess of Daos visited us today. She said she arrived by ship not too long ago. Came here to take in our land—there's so many places and things to see here in Ahradah, and of course up north too. She probably came to find a mate. I mean, I saw no Prince by her side." He licked his lips with far-off eyes. "I must say, what an exquisite take on the female body. She encapsulated everything I would imagine a Princess to be. She and her entourage—definitely a menacing group of Volatile men—came here this morning and bought our top-of-the-line carriage. It had originally been commissioned by an older nobleman, but we got word he passed away recently. So, it was never used ... must have been sitting in the warehouse waiting to be driven away for half a year." The man was looking Irwin up and down.

"And those mates out back, it took them nearly a year to complete that vessel. But what a grandiose carriage it is! Built-in cabinets, built-in bed, an ice chest, large trunk space, and seating for eight inside with tables. It also has ornately stained-glass windows on all sides—even the roof! And everything inside has gold inlays, bronze features, and amazing carvings. It is immaculate!" He made a kissing sound. "The epitome of extravagance, if ya ask me. And that carriage, fully loaded—fully loaded—everything a Princess would need to tour the land without giving up any comforts. There're even lantern hangers at each corner. Truly one of our masterpieces."

Again, Irwin resisted the impulse to glance at Kipp. He hoped his friend was listening in. "Oh, yes, the Princess of Daos." He went along with it, if only because he was curious. "Yes. Yes, she was on the ship I traveled on. And I agree she is quite beautiful. Her hair is so ...." He waited for the salesperson to fill in the silence.

The older man nodded. "She is very exotic with those almond shaped blue eyes, that midnight black hair, and her golden Daosian features." The salesman's mind drifted off. "Like a goddess! But then again, we don't get very many princesses around here."

Was he trying to get a rise?

"I was impressed at how young she appeared—maybe twenty years old. I wouldn't have believed the Emperor of Daos would allow such a beauty to go off and venture across this land of ours. We do have heathens here." He glanced toward Kipp.

Irwin tried to ignore how insensitive the salesman was being toward Talented people. But he continued to goad the sales associate for information. "Those soldiers she had with her were a gruesome bunch. They heckled a couple of the sailors on the boat, us too, many times."

"Holy Hakra! And you lived through it? What a ghastly bunch!" He dabbed his sweaty face with a handkerchief. "I know Clan-Duins are the lowest of the soldiers—a gruesome lot. But the sight of those Clan-Duin/Erthins following her was quite intimidating. I couldn't even look at them while they were here. Although, she seemed calm having them follow her around. I imagine being in Ahradah she needs the protection—you know—to ward off potential predators and thieves."

Irwin tried to include Kipp. "Anyone who has pounds of money or merchandise must have a guard." He pointed with his thumb over his shoulder toward his Clan-Duin friend. When he looked back, Kipp was staring off at the clouds, smelling the breeze.

"These were smarter than yours." The salesman chuckled and encouraged Irwin to follow him. "But I understand. You need yours because of your wares. He looks like he's got some strength to him."

"Yes, Hauss is very strong. I keep him around for intimidation purposes. As we both know, one cannot trust the common man either."

The sales associate snorted; possibly perturbed by what Irwin had insinuated. "So, you're selling your wares across the mainland? That must be exciting. Where're ya from?"

Irwin paused, trying to brew up a lie. "Goshee. It is a small town on the west coast, near Gustin. We have absolutely the most beautiful sunsets there."

The salesman, partially bald and overweight, hummed for a moment before looking again at the Clan-Duin and donkey. "Is that your only mode of transportation?" He was pointing at Jenn-Jenn. "Because if you're looking for something your animal can pull, ya might as well find something tossed into the wharf."

This salesman was trying to antagonize. "I plan on purchasing a horse or two," he said. "For the moment, I would like to see what you have that suits my purposes." Irwin urged the salesman on. "Maybe we can look at something for two horses to pull and go from there."

They walked down a line of maybe three dozen wagons. "Did ya know we're the leading wagon dealer ever? We make a wagon every half-moon and export them across the entire world. Of course, what we sell across the oceans are only basic frames with nothing extra, much like these models here. Now if ya want water barrels, that'll be extra. If ya want ration boxes, extra. Cushioned seat, extra. We also have wagons ya can take apart and add to. Those are tongue and groove. That means ya can purchase more slats and extend the back if ya want. And there's others that are securely nailed into the frame, if that's what ya desire." They looked at a few of those wagons. Less metal hummed along the tongue-and-groove wagons, but they had a narrower-shaped bed. Those that had nails holding the bed together were wider. A few had wheel wells converted into interior seats. The metal in those models made them sing like an orchestra. Irwin was not seeing anything that completely thrilled him.

"What would you recommend?"

"Well, for what ya want to do, it sounds like you'll need a lockbox. On some models, it's under the seat. We make them all shapes and sizes."

They looked at one wagon with a springy bench seat. It flipped up to display a lockable wooden box nailed into the wooden frame below. "I recommend getting a few of the water barrels and the ration boxes. They come in handy. The ration boxes are all the same size and are twenty silvers each. But the barrels, now we've two sizes to choose from: twenty gallons and fifty gallons. The twenty gallon is an extra pound of silver; the fifty is two pounds. If ya ask me, fifty gallons is a much better deal.

"Now, if ya want a canvas cover, the poles alone are a pound of silver. And that strong type of canvas, perfect for keeping out them hard winds and rains, is usually only found down in the markets, and they'll make ya pay for it. Pretty steep by our standards. But here at Wild Willie's, we can have one made up by this time tomorrow. And we'll throw in that canvas if ya buy the ten poles necessary to erect it. Most models have the capability to install support poles here," he pointed at one of the corners. "Or ya can always extend the wooden sidewalls upward and build your own wooden roof. We can also put on a tailgate so none of your supplies fall out the backside while rattlin' down those roads. But that'll cost extra too."

Irwin felt Kipp's eyes boring a hole into the back of his head. He was almost afraid to turn around, but he did.

"How much?"

"Well, my good man, if ya be looking to make a deal, we might be able to cut a better one." The salesperson moved away from the wagon they were looking at and over toward a used vehicle. "See, this wagon has that lockable box and a tailgate already. The wheels are practically new, and the chassis works well. The frame on the backside suffered some wear from pulling a herd of animals. But other than a few flaws, this vehicle is better than that one over there and we'll give it to ya for ..." The salesman glanced back at his peers "... twenty pounds of silver."

Kipp gasped loudly, "Twenty pounds!"

The sales associate clearly did not like the Clan-Duin's outburst. He shot a disapproving look at Kipp and then returned his attention to Irwin. Through grit teeth he insisted, "Twenty pounds and it must be retrieved today."

Irwin looked at Kipp, then at the vehicle. "How much for that other wagon?"

"Oh, that one's much too expensive for ya, I'm sure. It costs thirty pounds, and that's without the tailgate and lockbox."

The fact of the matter was that Irwin could afford both. He did not appreciate this sales associate. He eyeballed the well-used wagon and felt the imperfections, saw them as well. "The axle is rusted, and the hinges are broken on the tailpiece. These boards here need to be replaced." He noticed Kipp smiling at him.

"The lockbox under the seat is not secure. It is just set in place." Irwin pushed at the box and continued to walk around the wagon. "I do not think it even locks." He stepped up onto the bench and glanced at the locking mechanism. "Yes. It is broken." He jumped down and kicked the wooden wheels' spokes. "And those look ready to break." He stood before the salesman. "How about twelve pounds?" He did not wait for a reply. "I will be back with some horses."

18
Understanding The Signs

"I know she was here," Kipp whispered as Irwin stepped up to him and Jenn Jenn. "I smell her. It's not fresh, but it's not from yesterday either. That scent is long gone. But she was here today. She came here a while ago."

"Yes. I know she was here."

"What? How'd you know?"

"I thought you were listening in?"

"I could only hear half of what was being said. I was too busy smelling her and her men."

"Indeed Yace, Dephen, and their men were here this morning. She claimed to be a Princess from Daos. And with that claim, and probably all of Dephen's gold, she purchased a top-of-the-line carriage. The salesperson boasted about pull outs, beds, seating for eight, and more. It even has an ice chest, whatever that is." His stride was long and fast. Kipp was hustling behind him to get Jenn Jenn jogging.

"Why would she purchase a carriage?"

Irwin did not respond.

"What's going on, Irwin?"

"We are going to retrieve the horses and buy a wagon."

"You're going through with it? I didn't think you were actually gonna buy one of those things. Don't you think it'll get in the way of escaping?"

"It is the safest way to rescue Yace." He was on automatic pilot, using his metal as a guide back to the barnyard. As they hustled along, he went over in his mind everything he had seen and heard today.

Why would she buy a carriage? Is that how she was captured, posing as a Daosian Princess? An Ishik? Dephen is smarter than any of this. He would not get caught. None of this makes any sense. But Dana has seen something like this occurring. Yace in a carriage? How would they have been captured? Think ... think! I am missing something; I know it!

By the time they reached the barnyard, Kipp was visibly angry.

Caution needs to be with us now. I cannot show my hand to Kipp, or Dephen will know. He is watching me through Kipp; I know it. Dephen is playing us. This is a game, and I must end it. But how? What is his next move? Maybe he bought the carriage as a getaway vehicle, much like us. He must know using his Ishik name will call attention to him. Maybe that is the reason he is in the stockades. But I know Dephen is smarter than this. He would not allow himself to be captured. Think!

What does Kipp know?

He approached his friend in the shadows of the donkeys in the stall at the end of the row. "What was so confusing about the scents you smelled on Yace?"

"Huh, what?"

"You said you smelled many scents on Yace before I went into Wild Willie's." Irwin softened his tone.

"Are we gonna rescue her now? I thought we'd wait until dark, late dark, right?" Kipp was still growly.

"Where are your thoughts, Kipp? I need you to stay focused. We are not freeing her right now. We are purchasing a wagon." He saw the fear in the Clan-Duin's eyes. "You said her scent was confusing. What do you mean by that?"

"It was just confusing, Irwin. I think those soldiers peed on her. She reeked of urine. I could smell Yace's body odor, her sweat, but there were other pungent female scents on her too. They almost drowned out her personal stench like they rolled around together or something. And then there was the blood of others on her dress."

"Maybe she got into a fight?" Irwin winced. "But why would Dephen, or Yace, fight when she could use her soldiers or telekinetic power to defend against an attack? Something does not fit here."

"What?"

"I am trying to figure out the why. How Yace and Dephen would have messed up enough to wind up sealed in the stockade?" He scanned the barn and realized they were alone. "Especially after buying such an elaborate carriage!"

"Maybe she spoke to someone the wrong way and got into a fight. Maybe she killed them, along with several others, and got their blood all over the front of her dress. Someone must've witnessed it ... maybe another Telepath. Or maybe she was fighting with a Telepath. Who knows? It doesn't really matter now, does it? All we gotta do is save her without killing ourselves."

That is a lot of maybes.

Several voices echoed from outside the barn. Irwin traipsed around his horse. He took up the other horse's lead while Kipp attached the donkeys. He whispered, "You want to walk past her again?"

"No," Kipp hissed.

Irwin nodded, understanding that the loyal Clan-Duin would want to rescue Yace then and there. Kipp was noticeably anxious about waiting until nightfall. There was that agitated look in his friend's eyes again.

We are so ready to be done with this escapade.

Once outside the barn, Kipp insisted Irwin ride while he walked alongside with their animals behind—look the part.

Irwin would play along until the time came to rescue Yace. Only then would he, could he, be himself.

With no deviation from their route, he led them back to Wild Willie's. By the time they arrived, it was late afternoon, and the shadows were beginning to grow long. As they approached the front gates of the gigantic corral, there were only two sales attendants on the porch.

The younger of the two walked over to Irwin. "Good day, sir."

"Yes, it is a good day. I am here to pick up my wagon."

"Your wagon, Sir?"

Irwin looked around for the salesman he had spoken to earlier. Sitting atop the large warhorse gave him the ability to see across most of the vehicles. "I spoke to an older man earlier. I was here a while ago. I know you two saw me. And he knew I would be back."

"Oh, that's right! You spoke to Enrik. He's out for the afternoon, but I can help you." There was a bit of pompousness in the man's reply.

"I came to purchase the wagon around the corner of that building." Irwin pointed. The two sales associates were waiting for him to dismount, but he ignored them. His horse stepped toward the corner of the building.

The younger of the two salesmen moved in front of the dark horse. "Did Enrik have you sign an agreement? A proof of purchase?"

Tempted to look back at Kipp for help, he shook his head. "Look. I am here to purchase a wagon. Enrik and I agreed upon twelve pounds of silver for the wagon around the corner."

"Was that in writing?" The salesman's face was scruffy, maybe from sitting around all day playing cards.

"No."

"Why don't you dismount, my friend? Leave your horse with your servant and follow us."

Irwin held his emotions. He slithered off his tall horse and motioned for Kipp to come and take the animal. The salesperson was assessing him. All the salesmen appeared Mortal, but Irwin knew appearances could be deceiving. This man appeared mostly clean-cut and kindly, but stank as though he had been wearing the same clothing for days.

Once he was at the sales associate's level, the man became more engaging. "We've many models of wagons to choose from."

"The one Enrik and I agreed on was used. It is around that corner." Irwin pointed and led the way.

Kipp followed the salesmen, but kept his eyes to himself. Although he did look around when no one was paying attention.

The wagon Enrik had agreed to sell Irwin was no longer there ... only more rows of wagons and carts. "Where did it go?"

"We've got many other wagons to choose from," the salesman said. "Anything you could want, we have. We've many attachments and specialty items in stock. Or we can have our men make something specific for you."

"The wagon should be here. He told me to come and pick it up today."

"Well, it's not here. And if you want a wagon today, you'll have to find it here in our lot. We're the only wagon dealer in Ahradah." The salesman grinned. He had sandy brown hair with gray highlights. His face was tanned from years of sun exposure. "You can look, but I'll have to ask that your servant take the animals outside the front gate. We prefer to keep this place as clean as possible. Not everyone is used to walking through manure."

He looked directly at Kipp, but the Clan-Duin stood aloof; he basked in the glare of the man's eyes. "Oh, you mean me. See you soon, Master Smith."

"Yes, Hauss. See you soon." Irwin waved his hand, then turned to study the parked wagons again. This was not how he wanted to spend this waning afternoon, but he had no choice. The salesman lingered by his side—grinning and watching Irwin the whole time.

Irwin wanted to find the best wagon for a cheap price. He strolled around each vehicle before heading on to the next, hoping to find that used vehicle he had wanted. All the fixes on that wagon would have been easy to mend. And he would have learned more about his own skill set. He wanted to know how to make hinges and locking mechanisms. They might be items he could sell too. Now that Kipp had dared him with the idea that he could use his powers to create everyday items, he continued to brew up even more ideas. And all these wagons sent his imagination soaring.

It was dusk by the time he figured out what he did not want. In the end, Irwin selected the plainest model. The salesman wanted twenty-five pounds of silver for this most basic of wagons. But it came with a barrel and two ration boxes already attached to the exterior frame. This was above the price Irwin and Enrik had agreed to. And yet, the wagon he agreed to purchase was brand new—no dents, no issues to fix, a better get-away vehicle.

The two horse hitches did not come with any leather driving items, making it impossible to connect the horses to the wagon. So he negotiated for those tack items too. Another eighty-five silvers for each horse's leather harness, strappings, headstall, and thirty-foot reins. Thankfully, the wagon fit all their packed items, and there was still space for a raised bed—freeing the donkeys of their burdens.

∋∈ ∋∈

It was dark by the time Irwin and Kipp had the horses hitched up and drove away from Wild Willie's Wagon Corral. The donkeys towed easily behind. In all, Irwin had spent almost thirty pounds of silver to ensure he had everything necessary for traveling with a wagon—more than he had wanted to spend.

Kipp was happy to be in the driver's seat—he knew how to steer the horses, one of his specialties he had said. He sat proudly on the bench.

"I thought twelve pounds in silver was too good to be true," Irwin slumped next to Kipp. "But thirty?"

"Thirty? I thought it was twenty-five!"

"I had to buy the horse's leather tack, and I also bought two more ration boxes and another fifty-gallon barrel for water. I feel conned."

"And this was the most basic of wagons?"

"I did get two fifty-gallon barrels out of the deal. But those ration boxes on the sides are so small not even the animals' grain sacks will fit."

"I can't imagine how much the carriage Yace purchased must have cost. I think they gouged you."

"Dephen probably used Telepathy to get that carriage for free." Irwin leaned back against the wooden seat.

Kipp clucked to the horses to speed up.

Sitting forward, Irwin put his hand on Kipp. "Go slow."

"Why?"

"It is nighttime, and I feel like pillaging."

Kipp nodded, mimicking Irwin's coy smile.

He rolled up his red blouse sleeve and put forward his palm toward Wild Willie's Wagon Corral lot. They drove down the street paralleling the rows of vehicles in the corral where there was much ornate and gilded metal on the fancier vehicles. It all oozed off the carts and carriages, straight into Irwin's outstretched hand.

There were iron, copper, silver, gold, lead, and other trace elements that melted from the rows of vehicles. His tap on the metal was acute. He had practiced so much that now he could control how much was sucked into his skin. He did not take much from any one cart or wagon—only pieces from all of them. But all that metal still had to float through the air with precision into Irwin's outstretched hand.

The metal flew into his right hand—his left hand behind them and their wooden-backed seat. The liquid metal poured out his left hand and formed a solid rock nestled between bags in the back of the wagon. The amount of metal grew. He channeled a steady stream in through one hand and out the other, forcing it to conglomerate into one big metallic mess.

By the time they were done driving through the warehouse district, Irwin had channeled sixty pounds of metal. A gleeful smile stretched across his face. He looked at Kipp and giggled. "Now drive down that road. This is fun." He was getting high off stealing the metal as they then drove through the industrial district. Shops, warehouses, and storage yards were closed and easy to steal from. Irwin could summon a gate or door to open and then the liquid alloy would stream through the air, unbeknownst to anyone in the vicinity.

They drove around, mildly robbing the local businesses. In all, Irwin collected over two hundred pounds of metal. He kept them congealed, making it harder for others to steal. He giggled like a child.

"Are you about done?" Kipp demanded.

"Well, we could go through the residential districts now."

"Or we could be done and go eat."

"You and your stomach."

19

DUPLICATES OF YACE

Kipp's brown eyes sparkled as they pulled up to a saloon. They parked the wagon outside the bustling establishment where they could keep watch on it and their belongings.

Irwin pulled out a few blankets and covered his newfound wealth. "This was a good investment."

"Yeah, for as bare bones as it is. You should've negotiated for more features," the Clan-Duin chastised. "At least larger ration boxes—maybe another barrel. They took advantage of you."

Irwin saw the wagon as a sound asset, regardless of how Kipp felt about it. They could make additions as needed. "Negotiating for anything else would have taken much longer. We did good, my friend!" He patted Kipp's shoulder.

Dressed in his fancy attire, though he was not seen as a man of Talent, he still stepped with confidence into the Talent-filled tavern. This was a place of upper scale wealth and tastes, and yet it looked as though it catered to those who worked for the wealthy. There were a few noblemen with no Talent carousing around. Their pale features stood out amongst the sea of darker-skinned faces. The two took a table next to a window with a view of the wagon.

Kipp said, "We could make a cover for it with your tent. And building a lock box should be simple enough for you." He was looking at reflections in the window—watching a Clan-Duin server dart around between the tables.

"The wagon my family owns was built and rebuilt several times. Several years ago, Flinn got chickens. She wanted cages for her chickens. So, we made cages and attached them to the sides of the wagon right where those ration boxes are.

"And then Dinill wanted to enclose it, so we did. We built up the sidewalls and made a sloped roof. But she had to concede her plans to completely close off the wagon bed. Our mother wanted the front and back to remain open." Kipp kept on watching the patrons in the window's reflection. "We usually made provisions with what we found or had on hand. The chicken boxes were basically bamboo shoots tied together with vines. The walls were made from sticks woven together, then muddied and coated with moss. And the roof was made of grasses and sticks, mud, and moss too. We put sod up there and made an herb garden." His brown eyes followed the servers, probably wondering when they would be waited on. "We'll make that wagon unique."

Irwin smiled as his friend carried on about the Gypsy wagon.

"Good day, sirs." A partial Erthin server stepped up and greeted them. Her black and white attire matched the other servers in the room. She beamed a wide smile; her teeth were large and straight. Her auburn hair curled around her face, and her green eyes were as bright as her attitude. "We have many choices tonight! Roasted pig with potatoes, a fresh seafood bisque, or baked fish with fresh vegies. And we serve sourdough rolls with all our meals."

They both ordered the roasted pig and potatoes with a pint of ale and a glass of whiskey. Irwin settled back into his seat and watched people move around the saloon—some stepping into and out of the gaming room. "You know what bothers me? Why did the PCP stop chasing us?"

"Resources probably. I've noticed a lot less PCP on this side of the mountains than anywhere else. Most of these people here, you can tell they work for well-to-do households or merchant ships. They're all at ease with everything. On the other side of the mountains, in every tavern where Talented are accepted, you'll only see brigades. Servants don't carouse like this. And if they do, it's done in private—dark cellars and such. On the other side of the mountains, people like us are constantly on guard—always looking over our shoulders. But here, all I see are relaxed people. It's kinda nice."

The Clan-Duin hesitated but added, "You know what I believe? I believe the PCP gave up on us." He leaned back in his seat. "So what if you've killed over a hundred. New recruits are born every day—Clan-Duins being the highest procreators of all ... besides Mortals that is. You extinguishing so many lives allows them to fill necessary jobs with cheap and stupid labor."

He leaned into the square tabletop; eyes firm on Irwin. "If you knew how it all works on the other side of those mountains, we would have been caught and brought to judgment already. We wouldn't have made it past the edge of Onj Raha's gardens. They would've killed me and taken you in."

Irwin could see that the Clan-Duin did not really care if they were still being followed. His priorities had changed. His mind was on other things, especially the reflections in the window. Kipp continued, "And yet if they are still looking for us, here we sit in plain sight. Just like last night.

"I don't think they're looking for us anymore, Irwin. They don't know who we are. We're just normal people at this point. Besides, this isn't a PCP promoted place like Pirate's Cove Pub. Not that we won't see them here. If they didn't get us in that place, they won't find us here. Yeah, they probably lost interest in us." Kipp's eye caught sight of something, and he turned away from their conversation.

"With how many I killed?" Irwin whispered. "I think not. It is foolish to believe they have given up looking for us."

Kipp's attention shifted across the saloon's busy floor. His smile grew when he spotted their server coming with their drinks. The moment she placed them on the table, they both took a drink. The Clan-Duin downed half his stein of ale before turning his eyes back to the window.

They sipped their drinks and watched patrons stream around their wagon toward the saloon's doors.

A young, dark-skinned male Clan-Duin came in with a younger, meeker-looking, pale-skinned friend. They stepped just inside the open door and stopped, forcing other patrons to file around. They looked out across the large barroom, and then the pale-skinned man was pushed forward by his taller Clan-Duin companion. They moved toward a small empty table next to Irwin and Kipp.

The dark-haired Clan-Duin grumbled at his younger counterpart, "Hold your tongue while we're here."

The older Clan-Duin's dark-brown eyes scanned all the faces, checking out the saloon. Then he left his friend and slunk toward the gaming room. The younger man was pale skinned with medium-long platinum-blonde hair pulled back into a ponytail. His high cheekbones and small rose lips made him look like he could be related to Yace. His features were as striking as hers—down to the same light blue eyes. He could be of Ishik descent but appeared worse for wear—reddened eyes and messy hair. Dark clothing torn in a few spots, he appeared nervous, and he kept glancing over at Irwin and Kipp.

"Rondee said I'm not supposed to talk to anyone." The young man was clearly more naïve than Irwin had first guessed. His eyes looked almost white they were so light blue—an eerie sight. He almost looked possessed.

"Then don't engage us," Kipp scoffed at the young albino and raised his right hand as if to hide what his left hand was doing—pointing at the young man. He whispered, "Is it just my imagination, or could this boy be a long-lost cousin of Yace?"

Irwin studied Kipp for a few seconds and then turned to engage the white-skinned boy. "Hi, I am Samuel." He thrust out a hand toward the boy.

The white-skinned lad bent forward and shook Irwin's hand. "Antzel." During that moment of contact, the miner hoped that something would happen. But the boy's eyes and demeanor never changed.

He looked back at Kipp. "He does not appear possessed or spellbound, but I concur with your suspicions."

Antzel said, "Rondee says he can find an Erthin who can melt metal here, but I'm wary of places like this." His pale bloodshot eyes went back and forth, taking in the room like a scared creature.

Irwin replied, "It is good to be cautious, especially in a saloon."

Kipp whispered, "Did I hear that right?"

Irwin nodded, cocking an eyebrow and replying softly. "Yes. This young man is looking for an Erthin who can melt metal." He turned to engage the young man again. "Why would you need an Erthin who can melt metal?"

"My beloved, my sweet Avarian—her life is in peril. I must save her."

Kipp turned to Antzel. "What happened to your sweet Avarian?"

Antzel's lower lip quivered. "She's betrothed to a wealthy mogul. He sent his maid yesterday to check her virtue. She found out Avarian's no longer a virgin. Oh, my sweet Avarian." His eyes swelled with tears. "We've known each other since birth. Our birthdays are only a day apart. And our mothers are best friends. I am an only child while Avarian has several sisters. We grew up together in one huge family. She and I are the oldest and have always watched over her younger sisters together. Avarian's mother is poor. She sold her to a wealthy man in northern Datzar in order to keep our home.

"Poor Avarian, she didn't have a choice—even if she loves me. She was going to leave yesterday for his manor with the maid." He was almost hyperventilating. "But then the maid found she is with child." A tear dropped from his eye and dribbled into his mouth. "We already knew. It's our child. She confessed it to me several nights ago. We both knew it before the maid came ... but now, now ...."

Antzel again scanned the barroom; the murmuring of voices grew louder. "Our parents don't understand our love. Avarian and I are meant to be together. She is my sun, sky, and everything that makes me, me! I can't live without her."

"But if she is betrothed to another, it sounds like you're gonna have to let her go," Kipp said and took a sip of his ale. "Besides, you look like a Vol. Maybe her mother didn't want your 'sweet' to get involved with a Vol."

"Avarian is Vol too," Antzel's face flushed. "We are both Talented in the same ways. We have the same likes and dislikes. We do everything together ... even look alike. That's how we know we're meant to be together."

Kipp continued to poke. "Let me get this straight. You impregnated a betrothed girl."

Antzel nodded. "But she wasn't betrothed until after!"

"Then why do you need an Erthin who can melt metal?"

Irwin could see where this was going. "Wait a moment. Avarian looks like you?"

The young man hunched forth and lowered his voice. "My Avarian is in the stockades! She's been convicted of murder." He continued to drum his fingers on the table and look around. "It's a horrible tragedy, and it makes no sense. They say she killed her mother and siblings this morning after I left for work at the wharf—that she confessed it all to the Elders in the Building of Civilities."

Irwin and Kipp exchanged glances.

"I know in my heart that Avarian would never kill anyone. It's not in her nature to kill. And her sisters! She loves them. She's always been highly protective of them." He lowered his head and then raised his eyes, tears dripping down his white cheeks. "She's been wrongly convicted, I tell you, but I have no proof. And I won't be able to get any proof by midday tomorrow!

"I know many of the people who will stone her. Everyone we lived around loved her mother and those girls. They will make Avarian pay for their deaths. She didn't kill them. She couldn't! I know her innocence in my heart."

It was noisy in the saloon, voices kept raising.

Antzel wiped his nose and gazed again around the rowdy room. Then his voice rose. "Rondee says he will help me free her. That's why we are looking for an Erthin who can melt metal—a metal Erthin ... I've never heard of one. I always thought that was someone who worked at a forge."

Irwin recalled sitting on the driftwood bench outside Beverly's, watching the local boys throwing their fishing line over the seawall and reeling it back, trying to hook breakfast. Now he saw it all clearly.

Dephen instigated this!

The old man had known of his offspring living in Ahradah. They were timid and less powerful children—easily manipulated. Dephen was using Avarian.

Antzel's Avarian was Dephen's distraction to escape Ahradah without their being any the wiser. She was for certain a much younger-looking Yace. And that was exactly what Dana had seen. She just did not understand what her vision really meant. Irwin stared at Kipp with a look of disdain. "Dana saw all of this happening. And Nonbry tried to warn us." He did not want to point out that his initial hunch about the female in the stockades was correct.

Kipp apparently had not heard everything that was just said. "Do you believe this guy? Looking for a metal yielding Erthin!"

Agitated, Irwin kept his cool. He chuckled and leaned back in his seat. "Our day just keeps getting better and better." He glanced over at the timid young man. He needed to confirm what Antzel was implying. "Avarian. Is she the blonde female in the stockades? The one with the purple dress?" He looked at Kipp who was staring across the barroom at some pretty ladies.

"And her eyes are so blue, and her lips are so soft." The albino gazed off. "I hope Rondee can find an Erthin who can melt metal without melting skin. We've been to four places now. I've never heard of anyone having that power. Have you? Sounds like a very powerful Erthin. Someone I sure wouldn't want to anger."

There was a sudden and loud clanging from the kitchen, catching most of the patron's attention. There was a pause, and then the commotion in the saloon resumed.

The server returned and placed their hearty meals on the table. "Would you two like anything else? More drinks perhaps?" Kipp pushed his glass forward.

Irwin said, "I'll take a bottle of whiskey for the road, please." He smiled at the woman and added, "Thank you." He bent over his hot meal and grumbled at Kipp, "This is a Dephen trap if I've ever seen one."

Kipp cut bites with the side of his fork. "This looks good! Aren't you glad we came here for supper?"

"You and your stomach." Though Irwin seethed, he was also smug in knowing that he had been right about the female in the stockades not being Yace.

Kipp, on the other hand, either was not paying attention or appeared to have forgotten everything they had just heard. His stomach had taken over. "Tastes good!" He chewed loudly on a thick slice of pork.

The Clan-Duin looked again over at the albino who was staring at them. After swallowing, he said, "Sorry, friend. Wish we could help you out." He looked at Irwin with another mouthful, chewing and asking, "Do you think this guy's story is for real?"

"Yes, I do."

20

TELEPATHIC SPELLS UNFOLD

Irwin tasted contempt mixed with his meat and potatoes. He was increasingly aware that all of Dana's dreams about Yace were coming true. They should have heeded Nonbry's words of warning at the beginning of the day. Had they been more aware, they would have seen the illusion being cast. But the trails Dephen had created for them to follow were irresistible to Kipp.

Gnawing on a large bite, Kipp asked, "We eat and go?"

"Where are we going?"

"Well, if that's not Yace in the stockade, then she must be at the bed-and-breakfast. We still need to save her." He shoveled more bites.

She will not be there.

Irwin pointed at Kipp with a bite of pork on the end of his fork. "You remember what the salesmen at Wild Willie's said?" He waited for Kipp to respond, but the Clan-Duin was busy eating. "A Daosian Princess bought a carriage."

Kipp kept on shoveling and chewing.

Not sure if he had been heard, Irwin resumed eating the pork and potatoes.

We are being led along. Dephen does not want us to know what he is up to, where he is going to go next. Indeed, a ruse.

He stared at two partial Erthin/Clan-Duin mixes, male and female, who were eating at the table behind Kipp. The man's pale hazel eyes were a lovely contrast to their darker Clan-Duin skin. He was handsome—his eyes met Irwin's every time he glanced at him. And every time they made contact, Irwin looked away. "I need you to do something for me when you are done eating. And then we will leave."

Kipp set his mug of ale down after taking a long swig. "Sure, what is it?"

Irwin handed over a few silvers he had quickly made up. "I need you to find out if there are any ships heading south in the upcoming days. Use the city of Tresdahla as a point of reference unless you feel like asking specifically about Daos."

"Tresdahalala?"

"Tresdahla. It's south of Ajihya."

"Why-why a ship? Why Tresdahalala?"

Irwin stared at Kipp, repeating the city's name. "Tres dah la." He glanced over at the albino man sitting next to them. "Because Dana saw duplicates of Yace. She also saw her on a ship."

"But you just said she bought a carriage. Didn't Nonbry also say that Dana saw her in a whorehouse in Arenu Village?"

"Yes." Irwin took a sip of whiskey. "Yes, he did. She also saw her going by carriage and horseback. And she has been riding on horseback until today. She could be in a carriage, or she could be using it as a ruse until she gets on a ship." He watched Kipp get worked up about Yace's disdain over sailing. "We cannot second-guess Nonbry and Dana's observations. We must follow through. I need you to do this for me. Please."

Kipp returned to his food.

They fell silent and ate their last few bites of meat and potatoes. The server brought Irwin his bottle of whiskey. He created eight gold coins as payment and handed them to her.

"Thank you very much. Will that be all for you, gentlemen?"

"Come back in a little while and we will see." Irwin smiled at her. She turned to speak to Antzel, but he sent her away. Irwin pushed the silver pieces toward Kipp. "I need you to go and do that. I will sit here and watch your seat."

"Yace doesn't like the ocean."

"Yes, I know. But remember, Dephen's mother was a sailor, and so was he. And if Yace has no control .... We owe it to Nonbry to check out all our options. Ask about ships voyaging long distances." He knew not to disclose too much and motioned for Kipp to be off.

Once Kipp left, Antzel leaned toward Irwin. "You guys are going on a ship?"

"No."

I hope not.

He watched Kipp step into the gaming room.

Poor guy. He is like a lost canine without Yace and would do anything to save her, including acting without thought.

Irwin knew to always think things through. He did not want to be like his father, brash with his intentions. But finding out that they were being duped again, ground on his nerves. He wanted to react but knew not to. He could see the conspiracy floating around, but could not quite catch all of it.

Dephen was clearly trying to keep Yace out of their grasp. He flaunted her scent for Kipp to follow. And yet, she consistently eluded them.

Dephen knows I could ground out the old entity and bring Yace back to the living. And because of that, he is using her powers, and her connection to Kipp, to his advantage. So far, it is working.

Irwin did not believe that Dephen would still be at Beverly's.

If Dephen has a carriage at his disposal, he is as good as gone.

Irwin churned over the day's events—replaying everything he had seen, heard, and felt. It was obvious that the old Coterie had used his time off horseback to contrive a plan to bring him and Kipp into the grasp of Ahradah's PCP. And the scheme almost worked, but the love-struck Antzel was insistent on saving his so-called beloved.

I feel bad for Antzel and Avarian. Neither of them knows a master Coterie has manipulated them.

He snorted and sipped his whiskey.

I cannot believe that Dephen is as destructive as my own father. And he is their father! I can see it in that young man's eyes. Yet they will never know. Maybe that is better than my situation. Maybe it is better they do not know of the evil their blood might possess. They surely do not need to be a part of Dephen's sick and twisted game.

He was beginning to understand Dephen's mindset. The old Coterie would use anyone and everyone to his advantage. Irwin was all too familiar with that type of arrogance. He had lived under manipulative rule all his life. He had been around men who masterminded grand plots against one another. His grandfather and father had goaded him, turning him into their pawn, using him to be cruel to one another. They manipulated him to do—to be a part of things that were inhumane. He knew the terror.

A small part of Irwin missed the feeling of constantly being terrified. It had been a long time since he had pondered how he would be beaten or tortured. Nowadays, he did not fear his father. Nor did he fear the people he met, Talented or not. It was the metal that sang all around him—that is what Irwin feared.

It is all about deception. My father did it. Jebadia did it. And now, Dephen. Is this how manipulative men are? Or is this what type of people I attract? No, Kipp is not like any of them. Nor is Yace, for the most part. I am a victim of circumstance. I must remember that all this bad stuff shall pass. I must be patient.

He looked again at the male Clan-Duin/Erthin sitting at the table behind Kipp's seat. The man was gazing out the window. Irwin looked out the window too, and then closed his eyes. He could feel what type of Erthin powers he held: Wind. And this counterpart was a water possessing Erthin.

Suddenly, he could feel the other twenty-nine Erthins in the establishment. This was a newer sensation—being able to feel Erthins' powers. He had been aware of it for a while but had few chances to just sit with it and understand this newfound power without interruption. He could feel what made each Erthin different—identify what types of molecules resided within each. He understood the part of their power that allowed each Erthin to harness water, or fire, or air, or earth, or even healing powers. This ability to feel Erthins, their proximity and power types, was new and unique.

Every day I amaze myself.

As he sat in silence with his eyes closed, he felt their server walk up and take the barren plates. "Will there be anything else?"

He knew not to float coins, but his Metalistic power wanted to. He opened his silvery eyes and handed her some freshly minted coins. "The extra two are for you and the cook. Thank you for feeding us. The meal was wonderful." He smiled at her; she reciprocated and bowed her head.

"Thank you. No one has ever complimented before," she whispered and leaned in to kiss his cheek.

He was not expecting this contact. But when a spark flew between her lips and his cheek, she giggled and scurried away.

She is a Fire Erthin.

Irwin blushed and poured himself another half-cup of whiskey—he needed the alcohol to calm his nerves.

Antzel was studying him, so he acknowledged the young man. "Would you like a drink?"

"Oh, no I'm too young."

"If you are going to free your beloved, you just might need some liquid encouragement. That is what my father called whiskey."

Albert also called it night-night water. I am so glad I am not with him any longer. What an asshole.

Rondee came out of the gaming room looking irritated. "No one here can help us," the gruff Clan-Duin told his companion as he sat down across from Antzel. "I was told that no Erthin can melt metal without making hot fire. And I've heard that Erthin fire kills on contact. So, we can't do that." He thundered. "The next best thing is metal cutters, but they aren't guaranteed to cut those types of chains or bolts."

"Where do we get those?"

"A forge."

"Now we're going to a forge?" Antzel groaned. His voice squeaked. "How will we free Avari before tomorrow? She will be denounced and hung by the end of the day. They might not stone her. They might just hang her, no questions asked." He lowered his voice to a whisper. "I know she didn't kill her family."

The Clan-Duin looked around and then back at his albino friend. "I was told there were no Earth Erthins here. One of the other Erthins suggested I find one. Said they might be able to help. Let's stop at that tavern two blocks over. I don't want to stay here."

Irwin felt three earth yielding Erthins in the building. They obviously did not want to help the young Clan-Duin. He took another sip of his whiskey, hiding a coy smile. He watched Antzel stand up and caught his forearm. "If you don't find any Earth Erthins, come back. I might know of someone who can help." He was aware that his eyes gleamed with silver.

Rondee sniffed at him. "I wouldn't trust you."

"I get that a lot from Clan-Duins. But I am quite trustworthy. I will be here for a while, so go and look for someone to help. But if you do not find help," he shrugged, "come back and look for me."

Rondee grumbled and grabbed Antzel's shirt. He pulled his young partner out of the saloon.

Irwin watched them walk past the window and on to the next establishment. He continued sipping his whiskey, watching people buzz around. All this time alone allowed him too much time to think.

How could Kipp have smelled Yace on Avarian? This is Dephen's doing. That old man has too much access to Kipp. But I touched him many times along our ride-around. Ugh, what did I miss?

He replayed everything, once again, he had witnessed since the prior night after leaving Pirate's Cove Pub and Saloon. His thoughts churned around what Nonbry had told them and what he had learned on his own.

A true Princess of Daos would never be permitted to venture outside of Daos. And if she truly were, she would not be flaunting it. But Dephen is trapped in a young body, and with all his guards he is fine with showing off his wealth. Must be part of the ruse. Driving around in a glamorous carriage. Manipulating bastard children. Not caring about anyone but himself.

He could not help but see the correlations between Dana's dreams and the reality in which they wandered like lost cows.

"The carriage!" The one parked by the House of Datzarian Government! It all made sense now.

It was quite warm by midday, and the windows on that carriage were open. That is what allowed Yace's sweaty scent to escape. And when the carriage began moving, it drew her pungent odor along. There were four soldiers riding behind that grandiose vehicle. There had to be at least one driver, if not two.

"Of course," he spoke out loud to no one but himself. He gulped down the rest of his cup of whiskey.

His mind turned and turned while Kipp's mouth moved. Soon the Clan-Duin was back, down on money but up on knowledge about the local ships. He had quit after losing his last piece of silver. Irwin's bottle of whiskey was half consumed by the time Kipp was back.

"You look ready for bed."

Irwin perked up and snapped out of his daze. He extended his hand to touch Kipp's. He did not want Dephen to hear their conversation. "What is the word about those ships?"

"There will be a ship bound for Tresdahla, with a brief stop in Daos, due here by the new moon. That's about a dozen days away."

"Anything going back north?"

"I didn't ask about the north. But they said that most of the trade ships revolve around Tresdahla, Nandrues, or the Al Lieur Isles routes. Why north? You never said anything about northbound ships."

"Options. But I am quite certain that Yace is not on a ship."

"And you had to send me away to figure that out yourself? Are you alright Irwin? You have that far-off look."

"I am alright," Irwin drunkenly replied. "I have been thinking, that is all."

Kipp leaned in close. "About what?"

"You did smell her."

"I smelled her! I know I smelled her." Kipp's fists hit the tabletop.

Now there were eyes on them. "I know you smelled her." Irwin spoke in hushed tones, hoping Kipp would do the same. He grabbed Kipp's forearm. "And we both believed we saw her. Dephen is that conniving."

Kipp blinked, his mouth agape.

"The carriage, Kipp, the carriage."

"What carriage?"

"The carriage the Princess of Daos bought." Irwin took another sip from his glass of whiskey. "That was her carriage right in front of us."

Kipp still looked confused.

"When we rode through the square—do you recall the carriage that was in front of us? It began moving as we entered the square, then it turned southwest between the House of Datzarian Government and the Building of Civilities. I am sure her odor trailed from those open windows.

"Do you remember seeing the four soldiers on horseback riding as escort?" He watched Kipp try to remember. "Who knows how many were sitting as driver. There was at least one driver, but maybe even two."

"You think that was ...?" Kipp's face wrinkled as he tried to understand Irwin's insinuations.

"That was Yace! That was Yace and Dephen, and they left Ahradah at midday. They are heading south, just as they have been—Nonbry even hinted to it. He said we needed to rescue her right then. Only then could we save her, he said. But now ..." He paused to draw a breath and take another sip. "... now Dephen is heading to Daos. That has been his plan all along. We are simply an unexpected hiccough in his plot. So he schemed to get rid of us here in Ahradah."

Irwin leaned closer to Kipp's ear.

"Nonbry did not understand all the signs, nor did Dana. But he knows Dephen has animosity toward his family. This relentless journey south is about revenge. Dephen is going to assassinate his brother. And we missed our window of opportunity to save Yace from that brutality."

Kipp's eyebrows furrowed so deep they looked like a unibrow. "How do you know all that?"

"For being Clan-Duin, you are not as observant as you should be."

"What? I'm observant! I just hate Nonbry's stories."

"No. That is not it. You dislike him. And you ignore his stories because of it. I do not know what he did to you, but he is trying to help us. He does not want Yace, or you or me, to die."

"Ha! He said he wanted you to give your life for Yace. He doesn't care if you die."

"He was making a point. He was telling me to do whatever it takes, just like you have been saying. So, you do listen! Just not very well. Nonbry's stories are his way of keeping us from making the same mistakes he has. He is trying to teach us."

"Nonbry's never been a good teacher."

Irwin narrowed his eyes. "We must learn from the mistakes of others and those we ourselves make. If we do not, we are doomed to repeat those same mistakes."

"Let me understand this. You believe that Yace left the city earlier today using the carriage as cover—and used the female in the stockades as bait for us?"

"You did not really believe that Dephen or Yace would have gotten themselves into a bloody match? He is not that stupid—not with six soldiers at his disposal. Besides, what else would Yace or Dephen do with a grand carriage fit for a Daosian Princess? Sit idle with it at a bed-and-breakfast?"

Kipp's eyes dilated. "Oh, I get it, her scent!"

"Yes, her scent. You were too hooked on what you were smelling to see what was really going on around us. I was the only one paying attention to everything."

"Then why didn't you say something?"

"Because I was reacting to your reactions and did not have enough time to process what all was going on. You summon your inner animal too much. Maybe you should work on being a man and use the intelligence you have instead of allowing your Clan-Duin instincts to get in the way. You need to think things through a little more."

Kipp reached for the half-empty bottle of whiskey and pulled out the cork with his teeth. "Dang it." He took a drink from the bottle and then made a long-winded sound. "Ugh! How do you drink this stuff?"

"My father had me drinking this since I was a babe."

"Your father is so messed up! I don't know how you survived. I would have killed myself."

"Trust me, I tried many times. But in the end, I always healed." They sat in silence while he finished his glass. As he downed the last sip, he smiled at Kipp. "I might have offered to help Antzel and his friend."

"You're fooling me, right?"

Irwin shook his head.

"Dang me? Really? Why'd you do that?"

"I figured we would be leaving town no matter what. So we steal some metal as we go."

"She's not our problem."

"We were going to free her before we found out she was not really Yace."

"What does that have to do with any of it?"

"Antzel and Avarian are both victims of our circumstance."

"They're the victims?"

"We need to right this wrong, Kipp."

"But we know it's a trap! I think we should stay away from the courtyard."

"Before that young man entered here, we would have saved that young woman and found out the truth later."

"Do you think saving that girl will make you feel better about killing, how many Erthins again? One hundred-seventy, was it?"

"One hundred seventeen. But this is not about how I feel. This is about righting a wrong. We will drive through the courtyard. I will summon the metal. And Antzel and Rondee will do the rest of the work."

"You're serious!"

"Avarian is the actual victim here." Irwin did not falter. "Dephen is using his offspring, manipulating them to serve his own needs. He does not care who he hurts or kills."

"We're the victims, Irwin!" Kipp reached for and drank another mouthful from the whiskey bottle and slammed it down. "I think you've gone crazy."

"Sure, maybe I feel remorse for those affected by Dephen. No one, including us, deserves to be taken advantage of by such a Coterie. Dephen will keep doing as he has done. He does not care about anyone but himself and the prize ahead of him."

"You're gonna get us killed. I'm thinking that's what Dephen wants! You said we need to be cautious. This isn't being cautious!"

"We will be cautious. I will not allow you to be killed. You will drive. And I will do what needs to be done. No one will see anything until it is too late."

"Being cautious means that since this is not Yace, we don't need to save some poor girl."

"I thought the Gypsy are all about rescuing people of Talent."

"Last time we rescued someone, I lost my mother. And the guy we rescued was wily and unkind; we should've let him rot in those stockades."

"Avarian happens to be in the stockades only because of Dephen. He used her situation to his advantage and turned her into a decoy for us to follow. For all we know, Yace was the maid who came and checked her virtue. Who knows, he might have a hand in the carriage too. It had been commissioned by an older nobleman who passed away recently. This all seems very suspicious to me. And the description made it sound like a chariot built for a princess. Everything is too coincidental for us not to intervene. We need to right this wrong, Kipp. Avarian does not deserve to meet Death for something we know she did not do."

"We? How'd this suddenly become We? And how do we know what she did and didn't do? It's possible she murdered her family. Women are not above murdering!"

"If she is as young as Antzel, and as innocent, she could not kill without good cause. If Avarian is like any Hakran follower, they know the rules, just as you do. She wants to be with Antzel ... not sold to some old letch." Irwin watched Kipp's annoyance boil again. "We need to right this wrong!"

Kipp shook his head no and flung his hand, trying to toss the conversation aside.

"Before we knew that female was not Yace, we believed she was. Why should our plans change now? We purchased the wagon for a quick getaway. We should aid in the rescue of Avarian." He paused, hoping to convince Kipp. The Clan-Duin was huffing and puffing, fluttering his cheeks. "Besides, her friends will do most of the work saving her. We will only be the distraction." Irwin wanted to right the wrong he believed Dephen had created.

"This is horseshit, Irwin. Not our problem."

"Kipp, she does not deserve to be shackled any more than Yace does."

"Maybe she does!" Kipp's hard brown eyes met with Irwin's silvery stare. "I thought Nonbry said no distractions."

Irwin held back the urge to rebuke.

Kipp's nostrils flared. "If I decide to do this, what'll you do about the lights around the square?"

"I can extinguish them." Irwin snapped his fingers and pulled the fire from the copper candle sconce on the wall into his hand.

"Don't do that here." Kipp looked around.

"That was an Erthin trick, nothing more." Irwin frowned at Kipp. He too scanned the room, but was not really frightened of any wrongdoing. Although he did wonder if anyone noticed him do the trick.

Kipp took another swig from the whiskey bottle. "I don't get you sometimes, Irwin."

"I think I am easier to understand than you and your emotional state."

"Emotional state? I run on instinct."

"And your instincts are based on your emotions." Irwin tapped his fingers on the table. "We should not be fighting over this. We need to keep our focus."

"I agree. But our focus is to rescue Yace." Kipp's eyes tightened. "If you've chosen to help someone else, that's your choice. Not mine. I'm going after Yace."

"Come on Kipp, we do not separate. I will kill no one—unless I must. And you can have contact with me so that your mind stays yours."

The Clan-Duin's frown deepened, his steely brown eyes darkened. "Why are we doing this again?"

"Because Avarian nor Antzel, or Rondee for that matter, do not deserve to be hostages to our problem." Irwin downed the last bit of whiskey in his glass.

"They'll already have enough to deal with once we free her—PCP chasing them and all."

"I would like to think they can start anew once reunited."

Kipp smirked and poured a small amount of whiskey into Irwin's cup, tapping the nearly empty bottle against the glass in salute. "To Yace."

21

Escaping Ahradah

They left the saloon before the evening's first show. Kipp was ready to leave, ready to find Yace. And Irwin definitely did not want to watch another procession of women denigrating themselves. They got into the wagon and took off. Roper and Bodi made a good driving team, especially when Kipp held the reins. Only Irwin believed Dephen/Yace had left Ahradah, Kipp insisted they return to the wharf. For the Clan-Duin's sanity, Irwin agreed.

The wagon rattled down the dimly lit avenue along the water's edge. They went slowly past Beverley's Bed and Breakfast before turning around beyond the benches where Irwin had sat early that morning. Kipp said her scent barely lingered. Same for the stench of soldiers that surrounded her. Her trail was going cold. Irwin felt for the gold as they passed Beverly's. As he suspected, all the gold was gone. They did not waste any more time driving in circles around city blocks. Kipp routed them down a wider avenue and back toward the saloon.

"So, if she's not at Beverly's anymore, then where is she?"

"They are heading south, toward Daos. Nonbry said so, remember?"

Kipp chewed on the sides of his lip, his angry eyes forward. They were both bitter from this outcome.

Further down the avenue, they spotted Antzel standing outside a small shop. The young man noticed the wagon driving toward him.

Irwin instructed Kipp to slow down. "Do you and your friend still need help?"

Antzel looked up at Irwin as if he were sent by Hakra himself. "Yes. Yes, we need help."

"Go get your friend Rondee. Tell him that someone will free your sweet Avarian momentarily." Kipp's eyes warmed the side of Irwin's face. "Stay hidden until the lights go out. After that, she will be free."

The Clan-Duin heaved a hot breath out of his nostrils. "How are *we* gonna do this again?"

Antzel called up to them, "I remember you. You were at the Wise Guys Burlesque Bar. Thank you so very much, kind sir. I'll get Rondee right now. We'll follow you." Irwin motioned for Kipp to get going.

"Go around this block," he said, "and then over three more. At that point, we will turn right and take the road south. That should bring us alongside the gallows and stockade. That is also the same avenue Yace's carriage took to exit the square. Once we are on that road, we will drive straight across. Do not deviate from the route." He held Kipp's hairy arm. "I cannot tell you the entire plan, just in case."

"Just in case of what?"

"There are others listening." He refrained from saying anything else about the matter. Kipp drove the wagon. They made a good team—even when Kipp was disgruntled. They communicated without words, using hand gestures and sideways glances.

Irwin maintained contact with Kipp. As they rolled along the quiet city streets, he summoned his cache of metal to seal the wagon's bed, wheels, and seat. He had to keep their possessions from catching fire, and Kipp too. The heavily loaded wagon squeaked and bounced as it rumbled across the cobbles. The donkey's quick hoofbeats trailed behind.

Once they entered the large square, their racket echoed. He sensed Kipp glancing at him nervously. The Clan-Duin could smell how many men were in the courtyard, and Irwin could feel the metal and the powers some of the people possessed. There seemed to be more PCP than he had originally estimated. Beyond those of Talent, he was also aware that Kipp knew of the mutable animals hidden in shadows—his eyes scanned rooftops and alleyways.

Side by side, the two were quiet amongst the loud grinding of metal against metal and the clopping of hooves. "Do not slow," Irwin whispered as they neared the halfway point in the square—swiftly approaching the stockade and gallows.

The street crossed the middle of the enormous square, closer than Irwin would have liked. Being there in the center of it all, they were susceptible to an attack. There would be no easy escape route if anything treacherous were to happen. The four Erthin soldiers standing guard around the stockade watched the wagon roll past. Irwin exhaled, trying to keep calm.

After they rolled past the stockade, Irwin stood. One foot on the bench, the other secured to the metal-coated wagon flooring below, he was grounded to the wagon's structure. Nothing could move him from his stance. He snapped his fingers, and all the lights in the square shut down. Flames from all the lights streamed toward him like lightning strikes. The sudden darkness startled everyone in the square.

He knew that now, Kipp could barely see—that his Clan-Duin eyes would need a moment to adjust to the sudden blackout.

"Irwin?"

"Go faster and keep straight."

Irwin channeled his power, taking metal from the soldiers first. Their swords, knives, and notched arrow heads—and all the metal possessed by others—flew into his hands. He pulled from the stockade—fetching all the metal wrapped around Avarian's limbs and head and summoned it to surround Kipp.

The Clan-Duin jumped, startled by what was growing around him.

Irwin had a solid grasp on *all* the metal, but was only channeling selected portions, even though all of it wanted to be summoned. But he restrained himself. There were lightning rods on rooftops and steel art structures in front of the Hall of Civilities. Hinges, latches, doorknobs, and knockers—the list of what he could summon was endless. Metal liquefied and flew into his raised hand. And at the same time, the metal poured out of his other hand. He was unrelenting in creating a protective barrier around Kipp.

The soldiers were caught off-guard when the lights flickered off. Even the Erthins, who surrounded the stockade, were bewildered by the sudden darkness. The soldiers guarding the stockades were the first to assault them.

Those few Erthins harnessed their fire powers, tossing burning globes at the swiftly moving wagon. There were other Erthins posted in hidden positions around the yard. Many more than Irwin imagined, were guarding Avarian. But none of them dared to harness their own awesome powers. They were still assessing the situation.

Before the fiery onslaught, Irwin had coated himself in metal. His red shirt, dark pants, and boots glimmered as flames radiated into his flesh. His magnetic power pulled for and grounded out all the fire. The wagon glistened as fiery balls flew over it and into Irwin's silvery hands.

A burst of fire lit up the sky. It was now as bright as day!

While many of the Fire Erthins began showering the moving wagon, Irwin's magnetic power held strong and then grew even stronger. His power asked for more fire and more metal. It was a struggle to keep it all from overwhelming him. Yet he never deviated from crafting a high-backed metal seat for Kipp. All that metal curled around the Clan-Duin, forming a ceiling and walls. He wanted Kipp to feel safe while they drove further into Volatile PCP territory.

"Irwin!"

He knew his friend was scared and overwhelmed by what was happening, and so were the horses. Though they knew to follow orders and not question, they tried to alert Kipp of the Erthin fire. Tossing their heads and itching to speed up, the horses were thankfully kept at an even pace.

Kipp was now almost fully encapsulated by metal. "Dang it," he grumbled forcefully.

Irwin ignored him. With both feet on the bench now, he felt the melodic symphony all around and did not want it to cease. The metal-coated seat bounced up and down, as did the wagon, but Irwin held firm—himself magnetized to the metal coated bench.

He let the fiery balls and metal melt into his flesh and churn throughout him. It was easy to ground out the Erthin powers through his feet and out through the wheels. But the metal he continued to absorb was now pouring out of him, like water all across the wagon's body, making it much heavier.

The soldiers kept on struggling to use their powers. As the wagon rolled on, they all witnessed the metallic-encased man suckling upon their Talents. The PCP of Ahradah were learning that Irwin was unlike any other man of Talent. No one could stop the moving vehicle.

A burst of Erthins ran toward the wagon from all directions. There were at least fifty soldiers in indigo uniforms streaming like a rush of water. More poured out from hidden doorways and alleys.

A few air Erthins tried to stop the horses by using whipping winds but failed. Windy whirls flew into tiny spirals and were sucked into Irwin's outstretched hands. Water Erthins attempted to drown the animals, or Kipp, but Irwin's awesome powers prohibited that from happening. Instead, the water poured out of his flesh. Water dribbled off the bench and the metal encased wagon spilling onto the cobbles below, leaving a trail to follow.

There were eighty-seven Erthins that Irwin could feel, and most of them were fire and water yielders. Those who tried to use their powers against Irwin and his curious entourage were grounded out and left helpless or dead. And when the winds strove to whip around the wagon several times, they died down to a breeze just as fast. Irwin was able to contain outrageous Erthin acts by summoning them into his hands, dissipating the forces trying to bring them down, trying to stop this ensuing nightmare.

Three Earth Erthins who made an effort to harness their powers against Irwin were disintegrated and instantly absorbed. Had they held back the urge to join in the fight, Irwin could have ignored the metal in their blood. But the moment those Earth Erthins tried to tap into their power, Irwin's own power assimilated them into his flesh. There was nothing he could do to counteract the reaction of his own power. He was not experienced enough with these newfound Talents to understand how not to absorb an Earth Erthin.

He did not stop. The distraction went on long enough for Antzel and Rondee to run in and rescue the young Yace look-a-like, Avarian. It was a heartwarming sight for Irwin to witness as he continued to lure the PCP away. With all eyes on Irwin and his metal-covered wagon, no one saw the rescue happening behind them.

"Irwin?"

"Do not question me." He sounded like his father as he chastised Kipp. But he was trying to keep focused, to keep them safe. Irwin was their only lookout. From his tall perch, he could see what was ahead. He knew of the dangers here within the tight walls of the city streets.

They were now across the square and dashing down the wide avenue. Up on the rooftops of tall buildings, countless intimidating Clan-Duins waited to ambush the luminous wagon. Dozens of felines, canines, and raptors raced and flew along the rooftops and through the lit sky in pursuit of the wagon as it rattled and clattered down the cobbled avenue.

As Nonbry had predicted, being a decoy was working against them. Growls, howls, and bird calls echoed through the once dark and once quiet streets. It sounded like hundreds of Clan-Duins were ready to pounce. He didn't want to think that all the soldiers in Ahradah were chasing, but it surely looked like it. Irwin remained aware of it all. He hoped his stench and the sight of him gleaming in the streetlights would refrain the vicious Clan-Duins from pursuit. He was certain that they innately knew what he was and what he could do.

Irwin took the opportunity to use their intrinsic Clan-Duin fear to his advantage. He seized his metallic façade and his pose for countless kilometers—his silvery eyes always scanning. He was keenly aware of all that was going on all around them. He never let down the protective metallic bubble surrounding Kipp. He did not trust anyone or anything. He hoped that with Kipp inside his Metalistic barrier, he would be impervious to telepathic control.

Irwin was also aware that Kipp was feeling claustrophobic, and that the shield of metal muffled his senses. They had many more blocks to navigate before escaping Ahradah, heading south. He held tight to his perch on the metal seat, surveying each crossing street and the throng of soldiers following on foot and on horseback. He was positive that none of the beings chasing them would, or could, harm him or Kipp. He believed these soldiers were as wary of him as the PCP had been in Onj Raha.

He employed his keen night vision in order to see the shadows of animals flying overhead and running in pursuit along rooftops, down alleys, and at each cross street. He heard and felt shod horses clamoring along the cobbled roadways, shadowing their escape. They would be pursued. There were scores of Erthins on horseback and Clan-Duins in their animalistic state, relentlessly chasing. Hunting them like wild animals. It appeared the PCP were not going to allow Irwin and Kipp to leave. But Irwin would have his way. He did not want to have to kill any more of them, but he would keep his animals, belongings, and his best friend safe—at all costs.

The PCP soldiers who continued to keep up with the wagon did not let up as they pursued the vehicle, even as the end of the city neared, and the last block of buildings fell away. There were no walls surrounding the city of Ahradah—only fields.

While it appeared that they were free to go, the soldiers on horseback continued to chase at a serious pace. The Clan-Duins who had been on the rooftops were now on the ground or flying overhead. They did not let up either. PCP followed them all night long without incident, without catching them—long after leaving Ahradah and heading south.

They rolled on, never letting up. The horses and the donkeys had not been harmed that Irwin could see. He allowed the metal capsule around Kipp to open up to some extent. Now they both could look back at the dozens of riders, along with dozens of Clan-Duin canines and felines still in pursuit. Clan-Duin vultures spiraled overhead. Irwin's attention on all the Clan-Duin animals remained unfaltering. He had to make sure he understood their true intentions. Thankfully, no one implemented an attack, but those who were following were surveilling them with the same intensity. It was war, and it was confusing to all in pursuit of Irwin.

Finally, after several kilometers had passed, Irwin settled into his seat.

I feel empowered. The PCP fears me.

He smiled, happy in knowing they would be safe.

Kipp's jaw was clenched tight. His eyes and body were rigid, and he stared forward. "That was the second most stupid thing you've done!"

"Stupid? Are you fooling me? I have done many good deeds tonight. I only killed three Earth Erthins. Everyone else, I spared."

Kipp looked over his shoulder at those still in pursuit. "You spared, Ha! You got the attention of all of Ahradah's PCP. They're gonna follow us. Then they'll kill us. We ... You shouldn't have done that."

"Follow us where? The map shows no major towns or cities until Datzar Jungle. I believe they are chasing us to make sure we do not return, like they did after Onj Raha."

"Dephen has won, that's for sure." Kipp groaned loudly into the night. "We'll never see Yace again."

"I held back, Kipp, I held back. I spared many lives! I could have let loose and killed them all. What I did, all that I did, was purposeful. The fire, the water, and the wind were easy to manipulate this time. If there had been any Healer Erthins .... I do not know what would have happened. But the Earth yielding Erthins would have caused destruction. Mayhem. I could not allow them to channel. And when they tried, I absorbed them. I was good about everything else. I summoned the hydrogen and oxygen molecules the water and fire yielders would have used to ignite us and drown us. None of the animals, or you, were ever in danger."

He needed Kipp to understand.

"I had possession of every Erthin within a two-block radius, the whole time. I still could kill them, but I will not. I could have decimated Ahradah's Erthin PCP. But I did not! And that act, in my mind, makes all the difference."

"That doesn't matter to them, Irwin. They've seen you! All those PCP are attached to at least one Telepath," Kipp shouted. "Telepaths talk!"

"You were never this worried about PCP before."

"You should've killed them all. Knowledge of your powers will spread like wildfire. They don't care how many you did or didn't kill. But they now know about you. Even if you killed them now, Telepaths across Urthis know about you. You've doomed us."

"I did not show much of my powers other than the fact that I can absorb all Erthin powers and channel metal. But even so, all those Erthins know what I could have done. I am sure they all felt my hold on them. And if any were near those Earth Erthins, what they witnessed will keep them up at night." The nightmares of all those he had assimilated back in Onj Raha endlessly haunted him.

"You're crazed!"

"And all those Clan-Duins will be wary of us, thanks to my stench, so there is not much to worry about with them."

Kipp kept on shaking his head.

"As for the Telepaths," Irwin continued, "they can only speculate what all I can do. They cannot get into my mind. And with me constantly touching you, they cannot take yours either."

"Captain Hari crazy."

"Because of all of this, I understand the powers Erthins yield so much more—especially after that exchange in the square." He glimpsed over his shoulder to see the pack of soldiers still in pursuit. "Those Fire Erthins only have carbon and hydrogen to play with. That is why there are so many of them. Fire is easy to master. There is already carbon and hydrogen in every living thing, so using those elements is easy. But those Fire Erthins have more of it inside them, and that is how they make fire."

He wiped sweat from his forehead.

"I thought Fire Erthins were the most powerful, but they are not. Not even Water Erthins have that great of a Talent. All they do is summon hydrogen and oxygen molecules to make water. As for Wind Erthins, I think what they do is pretty boring too. Exciting nitrogen and oxygen molecules to create wind, well, any Erthin should be able to do that with a flick of their finger." He paused to remember. "But Earth Erthins ... they harness all that and much more."

He looked to see if Kipp was listening. The Clan-Duin's jaw was still clenched tight.

"I mean, pulling land up and down is akin to levitating an object, but easier because soil can become a liquid state, unless you want it to remain solid. And Soil is made up of the same elements as water, fire, and air, coupled with many base elements. Manipulating soil for them is like my ability to transform metal from a solid into a liquid! And Kipp, I noticed that Earth Erthins have large amounts of minerals in their blood—that is how they do it—they pull for those elements in the same way I use my magnetic field."

The wagon bounced noisily for a short bit, and then Irwin mused aloud, "I wonder if they can make things out of the soil like I can with my metal. I know they cannot manipulate metal like I can. I mean, I have not met any other Metalists beyond the ones I am related to. But who is to say they do not exist? If I am here, there must be others. But those Earth Erthins do have more metal in them than any other being I have ever encountered. I felt large amounts of iron, lead, zinc, copper, carbon, calcium, and magnesium in their blood. There are so many similarities between a Metalist and an Earth Erthin."

"You're truly crazed. I don't even know what you're talking about, Irwin. You need to stop this madness," Kipp snorted. "Any normal Clan-Duin would run from you, but here I sit, driving your wagon."

"I would not have let them hurt you, Kipp. You must know that by now."

"That's beside the point," Kipp gasped. "We've drawn too much attention to ourselves. If they didn't know about you back in Onj Raha, Telepaths will definitely know about you now. They'll speak to others across the world. They'll share the images of what happened back there in the square. It might seem like we are safe for now, but we're not ... you're not. You'll never be safe, Irwin. Never."

Irwin heard horses only a few hundred feet behind, pursuing at the same pace. They pushed forward into the cloudless night. A sliver of a moon hung in the sky, barely lighting the way.

Kipp continued to vent. "Maybe that's why they haven't really been pursuing us in the first place. Maybe they have known about us since Onj Raha. Maybe Dephen told the Telepaths, back then, that he would deliver us to those in Arenu Village."

Kipp adjusted himself on the seat. "Maybe that's why Dephen is heading south, drawing us into their den—delivering you to them. He knows what you are." The Clan-Duin looked to be ready to cry or howl. "Yace's memories told him what you can do, and maybe he decided to take it upon himself to have you incarcerated, or worse. We're heading into the land of true Volatiles, Irwin. This is the place where the worst of the worst live, remember?" He peered at the Metalist. "And those PCP are herding us that way like sheep to a slaughterhouse."

Irwin glanced again over his shoulder and considered the legion following, the dust billowing behind the wagon. "You really think that?"

Kipp pursed his lips. "Dang it, Irwin, didn't you look at that map? Everything south of Ahradah is bad," he snarled and ran his long fingers through his dark and messy hair, trying to remove stray strands from his eyelashes.

"I understand your anger, Kipp."

"I don't think you do!"

The wagon felt heavier as it rattled on down the now graveled road.

A long time passed before either Irwin or Kipp said anything.

"Where we're heading," Kipp said finally, "is considered no-man's-land. And I mean that no man without Talent will ever be found in this land." His voice shook.

"I'm warning you as I was warned. This isn't a place we want to be, let alone die in. If we're truly a team, I need you to tell me all your plans: no holding back, no lying, and no mischief-making. Oh, and you can't use the excuse 'a Telepath will take my mind' either."

Irwin still felt high from the night's experience. "I kept you safe, Kipp. I am not sure you even realize what I did."

"What you did was call more attention to us," Kipp spat. "Didn't Nonbry say we shouldn't do that? Didn't you even say it? They wouldn't be following if they didn't know about us. Dang it! If you hadn't volunteered to help save someone, someone who we had decided not to. What we should have done was left after supper. We didn't need to go back to the wharf. We should've just drove on. We'd be that much closer to Yace by now. As it is, we're not."

Irwin tried not to take Kipp's words to heart. He had felt right in helping those who had been taken advantage of by Dephen. Besides, had they not found out about Avarian, they would have been liberating a fake Yace. And either way, Kipp would have been just as livid.

He understood Kipp's anger about the lack of trust with valuable information; that could be the only weak link in their friendship. He really wanted to trust Kipp completely and fully. But with the Clan-Duin's bond to Yace, and ultimately Dephen, he knows he could not.

"You need to be on your best behavior, Irwin. This means you let me do all the talking if we're ever approached by anyone of Talent from here on out. I've grown up with these types. I know what to expect and how to act. We must keep peace if we're gonna have any chance of stopping Dephen and Yace."

"Why are you acting like I am a bad person, Kipp? I only did what I believed was right."

"We didn't have to help them! They will not help us. No one can help us." Kipp wagged his thumb back toward the horde of PCP, still in pursuit. "I think we both know that was a trap Dephen created so we'd reveal ourselves to the PCP and die at their hands. We knew it and still we fell for it! Well, you did at least. And now we'll be escorted to Arenu Village to be tried and hung."

Irwin tried to be patient with Kipp—he had just been through an ordeal. "Dephen is diabolical, but I do not think he saw any of this happening. Indeed, I believe he was hoping we would be killed back there. And that would be it! So what if we have PCP following us? Dephen could not have planned for that. And if they are following us, and we are chasing him, do you not think things will become heated when we do catch up with Yace? Dephen probably hoped we would be eradicated in Ahradah, but we were not. We are still here, Kipp. And the PCP still has not attacked us. They are only following us. Maybe we can use them to help reach Yace and Dephen."

"They're following us because they're looking for a weakness, Irwin. They're studying us."

"Our only weakness is Yace. We need to have them see her and what is happening to her; maybe there is a Telepath amongst them powerful enough."

"That'll never happen."

"Then we use them. As we get closer to Dephen and his crew, our pursuers will see them. He might be intimidated to see us with a legion of PCP in tow. And if Dephen tries anything diabolical, the PCP will see it. Maybe we can shed some light on the fact that the Princess of Daos is here in Datzar. Or maybe the soldiers will approach Dephen and his men for us. Think about it. Why would a carriage, as impressive as that one, be intentionally heading south into no-man's-land? And we could have gone any direction, but we picked south too. That cannot be perceived as mere coincidence."

"You've definitely gone crazed!" Kipp looked ahead down the dark road. "The PCP isn't gonna help us. What they're gonna do is escort us to Arenu Village. And from there, most likely, they'll take you to Nuaki Village—a place you'll never escape from."

22

LINGERING HOSTILITY

The road heading south from Ahradah was now lined on both sides with tall, man-made rock walls. Only between three to four feet tall, anyone could see that on the other side of the walls were hundreds of heads of cattle, goats, bison, and horses. The herds were segregated from one another, and the animals were all grazing on low-lying grass. Irwin observed some of the livestock being moved to other pastures by wranglers on horseback. There was much open space between each farm, and every acre was utilized. Enormous fields were fenced and cross-fenced, with wooden gates separating the pastures to help promote grass growth for grazing. There were no crossroads. And beyond an occasional wooden gate leading into a settlement, the wide stone fencing appeared to go on and on in all directions except to the east. The ocean would be their buffer, possibly for the first few days. He wished there was more time to study the maps again.

The wranglers most likely lived in the meager abodes along the road's edge. And those places were as rugged looking as the men and women working the land. None of the drab buildings stood over two stories tall. The outbuildings and barns blended into the scenery. This was all different than the road from the north where they had traveled from Onj Raha into Ahradah. The further they traveled, farther and farther away from the plantations north of Ahradah, the stucco houses in the settlements became less colorful, usually dreary shades of brown and orange. And it became increasingly hotter the further south they went. All the mud and stone houses were much smaller in comparison to the wood and stone homes up north. Most had reddish-brown roof tiles and large, covered porches. The gardens were also smaller but looked to be as bountiful as those farther north.

As they traveled on, there were more stone barns and outbuildings. That first long driving day, south of Ahradah, there were smaller plots of fenced land filled to near capacity with chickens and pigs. The scents were foul smelling, but not as harsh on the senses as their relentless drive.

The soldiers at their backs never let up. They pushed onward, not allowing any reprieve. While the PCP soldiers seemed to be rotating their horses, possibly trading them for local stock, Irwin and Kipp, or their four-legged friends, were allowed to rest. It was the soldier's way to herd them southeastward, showing them that they were caught, and that their punishment had begun.

"This is not fair to them," Irwin pointed at the horses. "Even the soldiers who chased us from Onj Raha stopped for the night."

Kipp nodded. "But those soldiers didn't know much about you. These ones do. These are trying to kill our animals." His dark face now held a permanent grimace, and he kept his eyes on the road.

"It will not work," Irwin said. "Our animals are conditioned for long rides."

"The heat will kill them. If our horses can't stop to stand and sleep, they won't last more than half a moon's cycle, if that. The donkeys might last longer ... but probably not."

Irwin was quick to rebuke. "Do you not remember that first night out of Onj Raha? We raced for hours. And though they have tried to prevent us, we have found time to feed and water the animals."

"Once a day isn't often enough," Kipp scoffed. "You know animals prefer to graze. And drinking while walking is impossible for horses. They'll choke! We can't keep up like this." He too glanced again back at the soldiers. "But they will. They've been rotating horses and soldiers. Alio told me once about this tactic." He glared at Irwin. "They're waiting for our animals to fall over dead."

"And what do you think will happen to us, then?" Irwin was not buying all this.

"They'll either kill us or escort us to Arenu Village!" Kipp's eyes were on the straight roadway ahead. "At this point, it looks like we're willing participants. We haven't even tried to get out of this situation. But trust me, if we put up a fight, I'll be dead, and you'll be captured and taken to Arenu Village."

"You and I both know that we will not be captured. Nor are we going to Arenu Village. We are going to rescue Yace before then."

"Do you see her on the horizon?"

"I cannot see more than a few kilometers ahead. The horizon shimmers with images that are not yet real." Irwin pointed southeast. "But what we do know is that she is ahead of us by half a day. And with this marching push the PCP is giving us, we might catch up."

The Clan-Duin groaned, "We're right where we were when we left Onj Raha."

"Please, Kipp, do not ruminate about the past. It does not serve you any good to think about what could have been. We can only change our future."

"Hey! We wouldn't be in this position if you didn't have such a soft heart."

Irwin fell silent.

Kipp is right; I do have a soft heart. That is what made my grandfather and father dislike me. Yes, another terrible mistake on my part. I wish I could die.

He moved closer to the edge of the bench, away from Kipp. He felt the anger radiating off his friend. The Clan-Duin wanted his space.

The gritty natives did not look like people to socialize with. They looked angry to be working, to be chasing after animals in the day's heat. But apparently this was life south of Ahradah. It was obvious from the stares and glares that no one ever drove this far south, especially with a PCP escort. They were watched intently by everyone they passed.

Night descended, but the soldiers did not let up. They rotated horses and riders. Irwin was aware of it. The two weary men yearned to allow their animals a reprieve from this constant push. But that would not happen as long as there were soldiers on horseback in pursuit. At least the two of them could rotate laying down in the back of the wagon to catch a nap, bouncy as that was. But that was a luxury the horses and donkeys would not get.

Once again, just before morning light shone upon the landscape, they found time for a quick watering and feeding along a canal. The soldiers never had been seen stopping; they just sustained their relentless march. For three more days, their journey went on like this. The horses and donkeys sweated until white lather coated them during the day, but they were rehydrated by the next morning. Luckily, there was always a shared aqueduct along the way where they could pause for a short time.

The grazing herds disappeared when the last bits of civilization transitioned to barren wasteland. The road was still lined with the rock walls, but the hundreds of kilometers of free-range land were now barren of life. Green grass was sparse—most of dried and dead—and there were fewer and fewer trees on the horizon. They found no local water sources. The air became a dry heat. It was amazing that anything would, or could, live in this parched and desolate landscape.

It was on the sixth morning when Kipp observed that the riding soldiers had parted ways. There were, nevertheless, still packs of wild dogs following on the ground; dozens of vultures circled above. It had been two days since sighting any buildings, and they were now a day's ride from the last maintained watering hole.

There were no breaks in the rock wall, no spot large enough for their wagon, or a glamorous carriage, to turn around. Because the landscape was so formidable, they did not fear that Yace and her men had deviated from the roadway. Still, they were bewildered that they had not yet spotted the carriage on the flattened horizon.

Yace and her soldiers were still heading south. The last few days, they had spotted fresh camping spots with litter and excrement in the middle of the roadway. Irwin and Kipp had hoped to catch up with them by now, and they would not stop until they did.

By day seven, the escort of canines had spanned out beyond the rocky walls. They were no longer seen on the road and were likely camouflaged among the dried panorama. Irwin was aware that Clan-Duin dogs and vultures shadowed the wagon but were not following as close as before.

Now they could allow their animals daily reprieves, especially during the day's heat. Kipp's anger toward Irwin was as hot as the air they breathed. He kept to himself and maintained his stoic demeanor and silence. All around them the reddish-brown land sweltered, distant mirages glimmered; cactus and scrub brush were a common sight. The occasional plateau or taller tree stands were the only places that offered a reprieve from the overhead sun.

There was nothing but the brutal heat, and the banging of the wagon wheels, and the animals' hoof beats on the gravelly dirt road. The winds whipped them, slapping exposed skin with tiny bits of grit. Billows of dust covered the wagon bed. They were all choking from it, but on they went, hell bent on saving Yace.

When they stopped, Irwin made modifications to the wagon. Using his tent frame and canvas, he constructed a cover for the wagon bed. This minor alteration helped keep the perishables cool and provided a shady respite for the animals. He re-used some of the extra metal to create a semi-portable canopy over the driver's seat. It was built to rotate off the left side of the wagon, offering more shade than what the canvas canopy gave the animals during the heat of the day. Other parts of his newfound metal were used to craft a sleeping-bed frame, a lockbox, and numerous blades that could be sold if the need arose.

As they journeyed further away from civilization, they traded turns sleeping and driving—except during their daily reprieve. After the mid-day nap, Kipp would take up his driving position and Irwin sat alongside or sometimes hid inside the wagon, working on his metal manipulations or playing with his Erthin powers.

)-( )-(

On the afternoon of the eighth day, Kipp said, "I see a dust tendril."

"You do?" Irwin perked up from the makeshift bed. He pushed through the portal and out onto the bench—squinted in the late afternoon sunshine; he stood tall, trying to get a good look at the dusty trail. "I think I see it too ... I cannot tell."

With the afternoon light, the wisp of wind and dust was just barely a tone darker than the rest of the drab landscape. Kipp's face and attitude had not changed during this leg of their journey. "Take the reins."

Irwin sat and drove as Kipp held steady at Irwin's side. "Yeah, just barely," he said with a touch of excitement. "But that's them alright."

"How many kilometers separate us, do you think?"

Kipp sounded optimistic for the first time in a while. "I don't know. All I know is that we're close enough to see them!"

With the heat of the day melting the horizon, seeing clearly into the distance was difficult.

"I don't think we should stop until we reach them." Kipp's nostrils flared, and his jaw muscles flexed; he was clearly biting back emotions. The Clan-Duin was ready to pounce, but still must wait.

Irwin knew to go along without question. They had already argued enough in the past days about every aspect of this predicament. Nothing could be done to change their dreary situation until Yace was caught and Dephen ground out of her.

They followed the dust twister until it became too dark to see. The wagon rolled on and they kept on trying to catch up with Yace. They stopped well into the night—only long enough for the animals to sleep—and once the waning moon ascended the starry sky, they used that light to hitch up the horses and move on.

)-( )-(

For the next two days, it felt as though Dephen was watching them, driving on their schedule. The gap between their position and the carriage never shortened. Perhaps Dephen was using his own Clan-Duin soldiers as scouts—his eyes and ears. The carriage stayed well ahead of their wagon.

By day ten, the stone walls were gone. This had happened during the night's drive. The roadway was rougher than before. Now, the larger rocks were thrown to the wayside instead of piled up neatly as fences. On the bright side, their drive was decently maintained, with access points to watering holes and stands of scrub oak and pine for shade.

The first watering hole was dried to mere cracks. At first, it didn't seem like a deliberate act, until they came to the second watering hole. It too was nothing but dried mud.

It was obvious Yace/Dephen's carriage had camped there during the previous night. Their horses had drunk from the pool; fresh hoof imprints could be seen all along the water hole. They had camped there long enough for the soldiers and Yace to leave plenty of bodily refuse behind.

Irwin assessed the situation. "We have enough water for another two days, maybe three, if we ration carefully."

"The horses need eight gallons each, minimum, a day. That barrel carries fifty, and it's less than half full. Now I'm not very good with math, but I think I can count on one hand how many days that gets us. There better be a full watering hole by tomorrow, or we might face more trouble than we bargained for."

They stood side by side next to the dry and cracked hole.

Irwin added, "Or we could pick up the pace–"

"Are you fooling me? These conditions are worse than they were five days ago. We can't keep going without stopping. The horses need time to cool down. And they need water to do that."

"I know that!"

"Maybe you use your Erthin powers you speak so highly about and summon us a rainstorm."

"How about a cool breeze?" He believed he could, at the very least, summon cooler air. Unfortunately, he did not know how to manipulate air molecules for cooling. Trying to practice, all Irwin was able to do was send sand and dust particles flying every which way. The horses put their heads down, and the donkeys hid their faces behind the back of the wagon.

Kipp put his hands up to protect his face and shouted, "Alright, enough!"

The dirt, dust, and grit fell around them. Irwin said, "That did not work the way I wanted it to."

"No, it didn't."

"I need to practice."

"Yeah, you do." Kipp climbed up into the back of the wagon bed. With a partially filled flask in hand, he jumped back down and secured the tailgate. "Maybe you should work on summoning water before we run out of it."

Irwin was still staring at the mud.

Finally, he whispered, "I think Yace did this."

"You think she did it?" Kipp slapped the flask into Irwin's hands.

"Her Erthins did it." He was still trying to be patient.

"Get to making water." Kipp marched off.

Irwin was tired of all of it. "I will work on it later tonight. You cannot be left alone."

Kipp called back, "Don't you say it!"

Irwin thought the words Kipp did not want to hear.

You are acting possessed again.

"We are getting closer to them. Our efforts are paying off. And I need to be by your side when the time comes. We will save Yace."

Kipp stepped up onto the wagon. Irwin, five strides behind, caught up and jumped on. They sat side by side, ready to watch the arid scenery drift by. Their horses and donkeys had been watered with what small amount they carried and were allowed a momentary pause. They walked on much slower than before. They were all baking in the heat.

After a long silence, Irwin said, "I feel like they stopped."

"Who stopped?"

"The PCP. I have not seen any flying Clan-Duins since daybreak."

"I saw a flock earlier. But they're probably off eating a carcass right now."

The road was long, straight, and without reprieve. There were no trees, and the shrubs were barely tall enough to hide jackrabbits. Never had Irwin envisioned a place so sparse of life.

When I said I wanted to go somewhere warmer, I did not mean this.

"I did not know it could get this hot anywhere."

"Oh yeah, it does. Summer in central Hakara is just as relentless."

"Really?"

"You know, I think it was hotter in Onj Raha with all that humidity."

"That was a moist hot, not a need to find shade or a watering hole *hot*."

"Says the man who comes from mountain tops. Everything will be hotter than you're used to."

Irwin daydreamed of the cool autumn breezes and the luscious spring and summer greenery. Being surrounded by such drab flatness and deadened colors was depressing. He did not know that the world could be like this.

The road went on and on like a sharp arrow pointing southward, allowing for good visibility even though the horizon wavered in the heat. They saw dust storms heading toward them, and when a wall of dirt and sandy debris came pushing their way, they had barely enough time to turn the wagon sideways and use it as a shield against the gritty onslaught.

The horses and donkeys were unhitched and brought to the protected awning on the side. Kipp held the animals' heads close to his body as the wind whipped around the wagon. Meanwhile, Irwin braved the elements to harness his metal and create a protective barrier that funneled the sand around the wagon and its inhabitants.

The sand blew endlessly at them like shards of glass. When done with his chores, Irwin sought the safety of his shield and sat quietly and among the comfort of his two-legged and four-legged friends. Kipp, too, would sit still, his eyes closed, gripping the lead lines until the wind died. Once the cloud of sand had passed, they hitched the horses and donkeys to the wagon and headed out again. Windstorms would not stop their forward progress.

Irwin could tell that these sandstorms had been Erthin-created, but Mother Nature had aided in spreading the cloud of sand, dirt, and dust across the harsh landscape. He tried to ground out the Erthin energy, but he could not. He did not want to tell Kipp the storm had been created by Dephen's goons. Instead, he spent his quiet time pondering how to end this ruthless escapade.

Dephen was trying to maintain space between them. But the wagon was closing in on his carriage. Beyond suckling all the watering holes dry and causing windstorms, there was not much the old Coterie could do except create more distractions. Irwin kept close contact with Kipp; there would be no room for error concerning the devious old man. This meant that Dephen was forced to trust his extra sets of eyes to watch out, to see what Irwin and Kipp were up to.

23

Conned One More Time

The wagon stopped late into the night. The lack of motion summoned Irwin from a weary sleep. He got up from the bed and climbed out to the front seat to find Kipp squatting off the side of the road. "Hey, when you are done, would you like to change positions?" Although he was not fully awake, Irwin wanted to be.

"Yeah, sure, sounds good."

Irwin retrieved one of the last apples and cut it up into pieces for each animal. He jumped off the back of the wagon and fed the donkeys. Then he walked around toward the horses. By the time he gave the horses their treats, Kipp had already climbed into the enclosed wagon. It swayed as he moved to the makeshift bed. With the overhead lamp lit and shining the way forward, Irwin cued the horses on.

Crickets and cicadas sang a final song as the wagon rolled past. Soon he noticed they were going up a slight incline. And as they neared the top, he slowed the vehicle. Off in the distance, near the base of the next basin, he could faintly detect a metallic melody. It had been days since he had heard such a song. Even though there were pieces of iron everywhere across the barren landscape, they had a dull tune. This melody was a combination of many metals, but a cache of gold resonated the loudest. Although the singing was muffled, he could hear it, The carriage! With a quick snap of his fingers, the lantern light extinguished. He pulled the horses to a halt and scanned the vastness for a campfire.

He closed his eyes, and the melody grew louder; he focused his mind and his power. But once his eyes opened, the song dwindled. From this distance, Irwin could do nothing more than hear the song. He could not summon the metal, nor could he feel the Erthins in that camp. From where the wagon was stopped, he knew they were about two kilometers away from freeing Yace. This was the closest they had been since Ahradah.

This is our chance. Under the cover of darkness, perfect timing. Everyone will be asleep.

Kipp snored loudly inside the wagon.

Good, he is sound asleep. He cannot know what I am about to do. Be quiet. Be tactful.

Irwin gently tied the reins to the brake. He slipped across the wooden seat. He waited with deep meditative breathing before jumping off the wagon.

He made contact with the ground, but still held his breath. He listened for Kipp to move, to notice that the wagon had halted, but only more snoring ensued.

Good. Sleep well, my friend. I shall have Yace with me upon my return.

He waited, nuzzling the horses, and then took up a quick stride. He did not want to leave Kipp behind, but he believed that this was his only chance.

I must be precise. Take out the Erthins. Just absorb them. Do not worry about the Clan-Duins. They are casualties. I know Dephen will try to harm me. I must keep Yace protected. I am thankful that old man cannot hear me coming.

He chuckled to himself as he took off running.

Only the sound of the toes of his boots making contact with the gravelly road disturbed the still night. He was careful, yet suddenly the insistent nightlife quieted. It was an eerie silence. Once Irwin realized he was the only one making any sounds, he stopped.

Although the carriage had not begun moving, the surrounding land was. He did not want to give away his position, but he wanted to know what else was out there. With a snap of his fingers to create a spark, he spied several sets of eyes reflecting in the glow. They all paused too and stared back at him from a distance. Once the spark of light disappeared, he wanted to ignite it again to see if those eyes and bodies were still moving. It felt as if a horde of beastly animals were closing in on him.

He snapped his fingers again, but the landscape was now barren of the iridescent eyes. This took his breath away, and he turned to look behind. Again, he snapped his fingers—looking for those glistening eyes. He was hit head on.

From out of nowhere, an angered beast growled and lunged at him from the darkness. Whatever or whomever had disregarded his smell and taste, it wanted to fight with him. A large hairy animal threw him onto the hard ground. The canine took a large bite out of Irwin's forearm, down to his bone, as he protected his face.

The frothing mouth grasped Irwin's forearm, ripping more flesh. Kipp's canine body faded into his two-legged form. Kipp became himself, transforming into his human form, and rolled off Irwin, possibly disoriented and confused. Then he returned to the vicious state Dephen wanted him in. The Clan-Duin threw himself toward Irwin again, but Irwin deflected the blow. He felt the carriage begin to move off in the distance.

"Dang it, Kipp." Irwin's opportunity to save Yace was gone, racing off into the night.

From behind him, the Clan-Duin's voice boomed. But it was not Kipp. "You silly child! You believe you can outsmart me." Dephen was in control. "You and your Clan-Duin will die out here. I will see to it."

Angered that Dephen was using Kipp, Irwin turned on his heels. "I have had enough of you, old man." He raced toward and tackled his friend, landing atop Kipp with a hard blow.

Their foreheads knocked together, and Kipp awoke from his trance. "Oh, ouch … what the … what are you doing?"

They both rubbed their bruised foreheads. Out of breath, Irwin stared at Kipp. He had nothing to say. He did not want to admit what he had been trying to do. "I was saving you."

"Saving me?"

"Dephen took your mind."

"What? But I thought I was asleep."

"You were!"

"Dang me." Kipp put his hand on Irwin's shoulder. "I guess I should thank you then!"

"We need to get back."

"Get back? Get back where?

"The wagon. It is behind us by about a kilometer."

"Dang me! I ran that far before you were able to stop me?" Kipp bowed his head. "I'm sorry Irwin."

"It is not your fault, Kipp." He did not want the Clan-Duin to ruminate over this small disaster. "But we need to hurry." Irwin turned to walk away.

"Why?"

"The carriage," Irwin said, and wished he could withdraw those words that instant.

"What about the carriage?" Kipp grasped Irwin's forearm, the bloody open bites taken out of his flesh that were closing. "Woah, wait. What happened to you?"

Wincing from the pain, Irwin said, "Do not worry, I will heal."

The Clan-Duin was obviously confused. "Was that from me?"

"Kipp, do not worry about it."

"Did I bite you?"

"Like I said, do not worry about it. It will heal soon."

There was a brief pause before Kipp questioned Irwin again. "What about the carriage?"

Irwin had no answer.

"Are we close to it?"

"No."

"Did Dephen send me north? Is he trying to distract us again? This means we're close to them, right?"

Not wanting to tell another lie, Irwin fell mute. He picked up a rigorous pace and did not let up until they could hear the horses snort and stomp. With a snap of his fingers, the lamp secured to the corner of the wagon ignited, shedding light across the darkness.

"I went south?" The Clan-Duin was visibly confused. "Why would I go south?" Kipp reached inside the wagon for his pants, shimmied into them, and took his seat on the bench alongside the Metalist. "Tell me what really happened, Irwin."

Irwin kissed at the horses to walk on. He stared forward, disgruntled by it all.

For days Kipp had been on edge, angered by everything. Now it was Irwin who spoke through tight lips. "Dephen knows what really happened." Yace and Dephen had gotten away. He had been so close! He was bitter about being stopped short of his goal. He wanted this chase to be over. He could have rescued Yace had Dephen not been so keen. There was no animosity toward Kipp for assaulting him, only guilt for trying to free Yace without his help, without him knowing what was going on.

"I don't care what Dephen knows," said Kipp. "All I know is he keeps taking things from me that I'll never get back."

Irwin's lips remained tight. He would not confess what he had attempted to accomplish. Kipp would be angry either way, so it did not matter. All he wanted to do now was make up for lost time. For the rest of the night, he drove and Kipp dozed on and off in the back of the wagon. Later, after much jostling about in the bumpy wagon, they switched places, and Irwin managed a long nap before the day's heat overtook them and Kipp stopped the vehicle.

Irwin was slow to rise until he heard Kipp cursing, "Dang it! You gotta be fooling me!"

"What is it?"

"There's no water."

"Another dried watering hole?"

"No. Worse. The barrel is dry."

"What? No. There should be—"

"Well, there isn't any!"

Irwin jumped from the bed. "That is not possible. I know there was water in there last night."

"Yeah, it can be empty, and it is!"

He buttoned his pants but left his shirt behind. "Last night there was about four gallons, maybe five."

"Now there's none."

"That is not possible."

"Do you know how to make water yet?"

"We have water. My traveling flasks are still full," Irwin said as he jumped off the wagon's end.

"That's not enough water for all of us to survive more than two or three days in this heat ... especially if every watering hole we come to is empty."

Irwin moved around the corner of the wagon. Kipp, too, was shirtless. They stared at one another, and Irwin said, "This is part of Dephen's plan."

"You and your fukin' plans."

"Kipp, do not get heated. That is what Dephen wants. He wants us to fight. He wants to cause a rift between us. He knows we cannot survive without each other. He wants us to die out here. Do not buy into Dephen's horseshit, Kipp."

"You need to learn how to make water."

Irwin leaped back on the wagon, standing tall on the driver's seat looking south. "We need to find the next watering hole."

"And if that one is dry, just like all the rest, what will you do then? Will you make water?"

"I will have to."

Kipp pointed toward the west. "Why don't you just go and practice now?"

"I am not leaving you."

"The animals and I are not going anywhere. We'll be napping." The Clan-Duin spoke bitterly. "You're gonna go practice. Don't go too far off, though. If you do, Dephen might take hold of my mind again and send me after you."

Had Kipp figured out the lie?

Irwin took the subtle hint and a half-full flask. He jumped down, leaving Kipp and the animals in the midday heat. They needed time apart. Dephen was trying to manipulate their situation to his advantage, more-so now than ever.

He trudged away from the road and the shade of the wagon. He went about five-hundred feet and sat against a large boulder trying to enjoy its shade. A snake slithered by, and the wind stirred the dusty ground. He took a sip from the flask and examined the hide-covered bladder.

Make water—the most difficult of the Erthin powers. Make water. What pressure. If he could not make water, they would have to abandon the wagon. The animals would not make it. And with their steeds dead, any positive outcome for survival would dwindle to nothing. He could still hear Dephen's voice: You and your Clan-Duin friend will die out here. I will see to it.

"Being an Erthin is easy," Irwin mocked himself, "molecules interconnecting, and hydrogen, and carbon. Dang it, I sound like an idiot. Kipp was right. I do not know what I am doing. We are going to die out here."

After being found out by Dephen, and having his best friend used against him, Irwin felt defeated.

I wish I could die, but I cannot. Only time kills a miner.

He was ready to rehash the reasons why he left the safety of the mountain tops, then stopped himself.

You cannot allow things from your past to keep you there. Be in the here and now. Easier said than done, Papa Edwin.

"Why did I agree to any of this?" He covered his face with his hands, feeling hopelessly stuck. The flask slipped from his hand and some of the water seeped out onto the dry ground. "Fuk! I cannot do anything right." He scooped up the flask and corked it.

He watched the water fizz and then be absorbed into the reddish-tan dirt. He stared at that spot, watching as some of the water molecules moved around and combusted into steam and then evaporated. For a long time, he dozed off, almost meditating, but not really. When he noticed Kipp moving toward him later that afternoon, he pulled himself up from the hard and dusty ground.

The Clan-Duin called to him, "You figure it out?"

Irwin shook his head, walking toward his friend.

Kipp turned back toward the wagon, climbed onboard, and took up the reins. With a loud kiss, the rested horses walked on.

Irwin had to sprint to catch up. He jumped onto the step-up and grasped the seatback to steady himself.

Why was Kipp not willing to wait for him? "Are you alright?"

"We're gonna die out here, and it's your fault!"

"You want to move over? I would like to take a seat."

"No! If you hadn't shown your power back in Ahradah, none of this would've happened!"

"You think this is all because of me?"

"We could've caught up to Yace and saved her by now."

"They had a half day lead before we even found out they left." He placed his hand on Kipp's shoulder. "You are not acting like yourself."

"Are you fooling me? I haven't had any issues with my memory or hearing voices for a long time until last night. You're the one not acting like himself. You're the one keeping things from me. You promised you wouldn't do that anymore, remember?"

"I am caught in a bind, Kipp. I am the only one who can save Yace. Dephen knows that." He gazed at his friend. Kipp continued to watch the roadway, ignoring him. "Last night we were so close to them. I decided to leave you behind. I thought you would be safe. I did not think Dephen would sense me coming. And if I had woken you, he would have known my plan. I thought I could be quick. My plan was simple—decimate everyone but her. But he used you against me. And that was how they escaped. And now they have put more distance between us." He dropped his eyes. "I am sorry Kipp. I should have told you the truth."

"There's moments when I believe you're smarter than me, and then you go and do that type of shit!" Kipp was once again bursting with anger. "He has Clan-Duins. We're stealth in the night. My vision is ten times better than yours, even if you are a miner! And my hearing, I could hear your breathing from the wagon back there. I thought you were asleep against that rock. Who knows, he's probably been watching us since we arrived in this desolate place." Kipp's dark finger poked Irwin's chest. "You should've woken me."

"I am very sorry Kipp."

The Clan-Duin's face flushed red with rage. "I don't want you here." His angered eyes glared at Irwin. "You need to make water. Or don't return."

Holding onto the less-than-half-full flask, Irwin's head lowered. "I deserve that. And I will make water." He pointed to the broiling horses. "I have to do it for them."

Kipp pulled the wagon to a stop, and Irwin leaped to the ground. He stood at the edge of the gravelly road and watched Kipp convince the animals to leave him behind. He began to amble down the road, flask in hand.

24

Molecules And Murder

Irwin walked and thought. When it came to creating water molecules, there was a staggering amount of concentration needed. And pulling it out of the hot air was nearly impossible. After a while of following behind the wagon, Irwin believed that if he sat in the presence of water, perhaps he could figure out how to make it. He stood still.

In these moments of meditation, eyes closed, he could see every particle that created everything. Every living thing from soil and gravel, to trees, air, and water was of a common descent. From the jackrabbits to Irwin himself, they were all composed of these infinitely tiny specks. And he could see in his mind's eye all those atoms. He could see how these miniscule specks came together to create all of existence. Everything around him consisted of billions of molecules, each coded for higher purposes.

During his meditation, Irwin pulled from the organic life that surrounded him. Although they were far and few, there were plants that held water in their roots. He also took water from the air, summoning it from the breeze. Though the coastline was far away, there were water droplets that floated across the arid landscape. He even pulled water from himself to see how it felt to have hydrogen particles extracted. He had to understand the process. This would help him create more water. Irwin knew he could accidentally pull too much water from himself. Yet at the same time, he wanted to fill his flask and show Kipp his bounty.

He stood in the same place until he felt the sun disappear beyond the western horizon. It was then that he came to. The slightly cooler evening air was a welcome reprieve. Slowly, he awoke from his meditational daze and realized that Kipp was nowhere in sight. He felt silly for not paying attention and recalled chiding Kipp for the same blunder a while ago. He moved his flask strap across his shoulder and felt the fullness within. He had done it! He had made water. Feeling depleted, Irwin replenished his thirst. He drank but a quarter of his flask.

Feeling happy for the first time in a long time, Irwin strung the flask across his shoulder and began to jog. Shades of dark purple and orange glistened in the final moments of daylight. Then the night sky grew around him. The first few stars sparkled; tonight there would be no moon. In the distance, cloud formations hugged the coastline. The stars slowly presented themselves, and then Irwin was surrounded by this miracle of existence. Overhead, the sky looked like a river of twinkling light and reminded him of his tranquil mountaintop home. He kept on at a medium pace along the dusty, iron-riddled road. He knew where his wagon was. He could feel his metal off in the distance still traveling away from him.

There was a lone howl. Concern rippled down his spine. Then he heard several other howls call back from his right and left and from behind. It sounded like a pack closing in on him, attempting to surround him. He hoped they were wary of his scent. A soft wind blew, and although he knew not to, Irwin began to run.

In the stories Alio had told Kipp, he had mentioned packs of Clan-Duins who roamed freely across this portion of barren land. Kipp had shared those stories with Irwin, telling him that these animals were PCP rejects. And it was here, in the desolate desert, that those Clan-Duins were allowed to live out their days as the beasts they truly were.

For the first time in a long while, Irwin felt vulnerable. He had less than a pound of metal within him, but iron flecks and rocks surrounded him on the ground. Again, the canines called to each other. They barked to one another from behind him and along his flanks. He did not slow his pace.

And then a howl came from ahead. A large canine's silhouette against the starlit sky blocked his passage. He slowed his stride and glanced around and saw more closing in. Several dozen wolves encircled him. Most of these dogs were less than curious about Irwin, probably more angered by his presence.

He stopped. His legs wanted to move, but the countless eyes around him did not. He was wary of making any sudden movements. They growled as they sniffed at Irwin and barked amongst themselves. Then that lone canine walked up to him—a bold alpha with a thick scar from above his left eye to his jaw. His body grew larger; his hackles rose.

The other canines watched their alpha as he sniffed at Irwin's hands. The alpha tried to bite at his flesh, but metal flushed across Irwin's face, forearms, and hands. He only wanted to intimidate. He did not want any actions taken, but he would defend himself if necessary. He had hoped his stench would be more than enough to keep these wild dogs at bay.

"I mean you no harm." He did not want to show his fear, but he was certain they could smell it.

Again, the alpha snarled at Irwin. The wolf wanted to fight. Sharp canine teeth came into contact with him again. He kept his fists clenched, but to his side. The alpha was testing his resolve, but he showed his patience and his will to endure.

On the fourth snap, Irwin struck back. He hit the alpha. "I mean you no harm. But I will keep myself safe." He had to establish that boundary.

Once more, the dog snarled and snapped at Irwin. This time, he did not withhold his wrath or his abilities. All his metal flushed around his left hand and with a hard whack, he hit the wolf when the animal tempted fate again. The hardened metal hand made contact against the canine's skull. Irwin did not mean to use so much force, but he had. The Clan-Duin's head crumpled, and the enormous beast fell over dead. Although Irwin could not see it, he and the other animals could smell the blood soaking across the Alpha's gray fur.

Irwin had crossed a line. He had not meant to kill—knew the imminent danger he had put himself in and so did the ravaging dogs. They were ready to pounce on him, regardless of his smell. They were going to tear him apart. Irwin put his fists up, standing his ground as the wolves lunged for his flesh.

Armed with the metal inside him, along with the pieces of iron felt all around, Irwin allowed his power to surge and rotate out of control. For the moment, he had to ignore his regard for life. These animals were going to tear him apart. He had to kill them first. He knew he could not get away from their assault. He had to face them head on. Churning the metal, with a touch of Erthin wind, iron pieces lifted and swarmed all around him. The particles were hard and piercing as they flew through the sky, ripping through the Clan-Duin canine's flesh.

The angry animals were trying to kill him, biting and tearing at his body. Even though he was in pain, he still had control over all the metal within a hundred feet. Irwin would protect himself from the onslaught of teeth pulling on him, ripping him apart. He dropped into a ball, his head between his legs and his arms, as the dogs viciously tore into him. He didn't stop summoning the metal. Thousands of metallic pieces bore through the flesh of the frenzied canines. Pointed flecks of iron tore through all the animal's bodies, leaving pieces of skin and hair everywhere. Bone and cartilage were sliced through too, and each dog bled out.

A moment after they began their attack, all those wolves were howling loudly, painfully. Many fell over dead. The howling intensified as the oscillating iron flew away from him, riddling those trying to escape with holes. The teeth stopped tearing into his flesh, and the commotion stopped.

Irwin shook uncontrollably.

He huddled there, listening to the nightlife. The few dogs who remained had been far enough away to survive. They ran off in all directions, escaping the swirling jagged metal that continued to oscillate around him, protecting him from certain death.

Once he had calmed down and felt ready, he sat up. His whole body throbbed with pain. Bleeding from many bites, the agony was intense at first, but then it subsided. The broken bones, some had been shattered while others were pulled out of him, corrected themselves back into place. It was incredibly painful. The copious bite marks would heal quick enough. His blood dribbled and then dried, staining his flesh and tattered clothing. It was difficult to assess all his bodily injuries, but he could tell that his pants were ripped. He pulled off pieces of his torn clothing to reveal his pale legs that were riddled with bloody marks. His back stung; he had sustained claw and teeth marks all over his body.

This reminded him of being beaten by his father and grandfather. Irwin missed that sensation of fearing for his life. He took another drink off the flask, allowing the water to rejuvenate the parts of his body that had been punctured during the fight. He sat there for a while, allowing himself to heal more before he was ready to be on his feet again.

After a long reprieve, Irwin jogged away from the bloody scene. He was tired, vaguely scared of the darkness all around, but alive. He wanted nothing more than to be at Kipp's side, sitting on the wagon, watching the night sky pass by. His run was long-winded. He was wary to slow down, fearing that another clan of canines would pick up his trail and get to him before he found Kipp.

The wagon was making good time. Irwin did not catch up with Kipp until the first spark of morning light. Kipp had found the next watering hole; the wagon sat idle. There were trees sporadically growing in a horse-shoe shape around the large pool. Off in the distance, more trees followed the dried riverbed to the west. The horses and donkeys were tied to the backside of the wagon, resting peacefully. They perked up upon seeing his approach.

The dried-up pond was being guarded by several clans of felines. In all colors, from light flaxen to deep brown, the felines ranged in size and age. They lounged lazily, keeping guard of the muddied watering hole. Some of the wild cats looked more intimidating than others as they watched him approach. They were obviously all thirsty, conglomerating around the deepest spot of the waterless pool.

Kipp stood protectively between the wildcats and the horses, apparently waiting for him.

With arms folded across his chest, the Clan-Duin glared at Irwin. "I told you to keep up."

A few patrolling cats followed Irwin. He noticed them as he stepped up to his donkeys who bellowed when he patted their butts. He went over to Kipp. "What is going on here?"

There was a momentary look of relief in Kipp's eyes as Irwin stepped by his side.

Irwin's clothing was tattered and stained with blood. Kipp sniffed. His jaw stiffened. "I won't ask where you've been or whose blood is on you besides your own." He sniffed again. "Did you figure out how to make water?"

Irwin watched all the feline eyes staring at him. "It took me a while, but yes, I did." He offered his flask. "What is going on here?"

"That muddied hole is the only reservoir within many days' walk of here. And as you can see, it is dry. I hope you can make a lot of water."

Irwin smiled while looking down at his flask. "I can make water. Although it is not as easy as making fire."

"I'm not sure if you see the dilemma here." Kipp motioned toward the cats. "I had to make an agreement with them. And since it looks like you can perform the task, get to it. If you make water, they'll allow us to live. If you can't refill their watering hole, we won't have to worry about dying of thirst."

Irwin looked over at the dozens of eyes watching his interaction with Kipp. "You hoped I would just figure out how to make water?"

"Of course I did. I didn't really want to see you again if you couldn't."

Even though the Clan-Duin was being critical, Irwin had missed being around Kipp in those few hours they were apart. "I would have enjoyed your help with the scuffle I was in. Of course, you might have been killed in that battle."

Although Irwin's scars had healed, Kipp stopped to take in his friend. "You'll have to share the details later."

Two large female felines approached. They pranced up the small embankment toward the two men. Kipp stepped forward and engaged them with their unique Clan-Duin vision-scent oriented speech.

Irwin remained close to Kipp's side, happy to be by his friend once more. It startled him to see the many felines congregating there along the edge of the muddied pool. He counted fifty-three of varying ages and colors lying around—a few playing with one another. Many of them seemed to be entranced by the two-legged men and watched their subtle interactions. Unexpectedly, the donkeys bellowed loudly; Irwin jumped. Several more felines approached.

"Seriously Irwin, you need to get to making water. I bought us all the time we could get. But they're gonna kill us if we can't follow through."

"Pressure is the one thing I do not need right now, Kipp. And if they get anywhere near you, they will be the ones to die. Trust me; they do not want to push me. I was shoved around earlier, and that did not end well. I know you can smell the blood." He felt a sense of bitterness about what he had to do during the night to stay alive.

Stepping ahead of Kipp, Irwin went straight to the two alpha felines. They turned and escorted him to the muddied puddle that was once their watering hole. He wanted to look back at Kipp for support, wary to see all the felines watching intently. Dozens of lives were counting on him, and he did not like this type of pressure.

And then he saw how it happened. The Erthin magic still lingered in the air. "Yace's men did this," he said, seeing water molecules thick in the sky. And as the warm day ascended, all that water-vapor would evaporate. "But I can fix it." The Erthins had been careless in extracting the water and making it into vapor. They had not stolen the water, only changed the basic composition of it. Irwin put his hands into the air, moved them around enough to summon the water vapor that hung low in the sky. His Talent was now undoing the dubious spell the Erthins had created.

All the water that had been taken away from the large pond began to brew inside clouds Irwin created above their heads. Every drop of air-bound moisture within a half kilometer was then drawn around Irwin, Kipp, and all the animals, turning into a very thick low-lying fog—very cool to the flesh. Irwin pulled all that water vapor in the air to conglomerate in front of them in the once-filled pond.

It was the first time they had felt such chilly yet thick humidity in a long time. All the moisture pulled together, swirling around, wringing itself into the deep pool and turning back into water. For a long time, as the lightening sky brewed above, the fog occluded everyone's view of their surroundings. And then the last puff of condensed water vapor was pulled into the muddied hole, leaving a large pond of clear, drinkable water.

"Holy Hakra!" Kipp watched the event unfold.

Catcalls radiated from the watering hole. Some of the young ones dared to jump into the cool liquid. Others moved slowly to retrieve a drink.

Irwin burst with excitement. "I did it! I cannot believe I actually did it! I get it now, Kipp! I understand how the particles fit; how to conglomerate them. Making water needs the right conditions. Out here, nighttime is the best time. That is when the cool air descends and allows the water vapor to stay close to the ground. When there is water vapor, there is drinkable water; learning how to condense it or extract it from the air is the hard part."

Kipp watched the feline Clan-Duins gathering along the pool's edges. "Good job, Irwin. I wasn't sure how this would turn out. Thanks for saving us." He motioned for Irwin to follow him back to the wagon, where they retrieved all their empty flasks and jugs.

"And you're right! Dephen, Yace, they were here. Those goon Erthins of theirs drained this watering hole. And they did it right in front of our newfound friends." Kipp pointed at the distant morning clouds that were changing now to brilliant shades of pink and orange. "Looks like another one of those sandstorms is coming."

"Well, it's far enough away that we can prepare for it." Irwin stepped up to the first barrel. He poured a little bit of water from the flask inside before moving his hand around to create more water from the existing molecules.

"Our feline friends said the carriage passed by around sunset last night, so we're back to being half a day behind—if not more."

"Hey, at least I can make water!" Irwin cackled, pointing at the barrel.

25
TRUE INTENTIONS

There were more distractions in the days to come. Winds from the ocean swooped across the flattened orangish-tan landscape, from east to west at daybreak, and Dephen's Erthins took advantage of this phenomenon. They would summon dust and sand to form a wall, and Mother Nature would take it from there. Sandstorms, hundreds of feet tall and many more kilometers long, would persist for hours. And though it was easy to spot them approaching, they were difficult to defend against.

Once again, the wagon was used as a shield. Irwin used the placement of the wagon, along with all his metal, to form a protective bubble-like barrier around the animals and Kipp. He was exasperated that he could not ground out the Erthin-created tempests. Dephen wanted to put more space between them, but the young men were dedicated to saving Yace before it was too late. They took their daily reprieve when the explosions of wind and sand hit, allowing the horses and donkeys time to stand or lay. The animals would have time to eat and drink and remain undisturbed for a long period. But for the rest of their day and night, the horses and donkeys walked through the sweltering heat and then chilly night air. As long as they got their daily rest, they were revived enough to continue on and on through the torturous and treacherous journey.

The mostly flattened roadway was leading them closer to lands' end where plentiful and soothing moist winds blew. Beyond the annoying sandstorms, a half dozen Clan-Duin felines decided to follow the wagon. They trailed only a few hundred feet behind for several days. Though they always stayed close enough to study the two travelers, none of the wild cats ever advanced into their camps or the wagon while the men were driving. But without a close water source, the felines had to turn in other directions.

Although they now saw or felt no eyes upon them, Irwin and Kipp knew they were still being watched. There were Clan-Duins abound and throughout the dry landscape. Occasionally, they saw swirling shadows from large vultures spiraling overhead—hunting, hoping for a fresh carcass. The weary travelers were deep within Volatile Territory, and they knew it. No matter where they rode, they would meet up with packs of Clan-Duins.

On the sixth day after leaving the reservoir, they found the ocean. It brought a cooler, but swifter, breeze. Although it was still hot, the moisture in the air, and an occasional cloud, bolstered their spirits. The few clumps of grass found along the way were eaten by their hungry animals as they walked past. They still had not seen any dusty tendrils, and the camps they found were a day old. Now there was a considerable distance between them and the carriage.

Morale was low. It did not seem that they would catch up with Yace, Dephen, and the soldiers before arriving in Arenu Village. Every day that passed only confirmed that prospect. Kipp continued to warn Irwin of what type of place they were approaching. He retold Alio's stories about Arenu Village. Each storyline repeated the same theme: people who reside in Arenu Village are soldiers and warriors. They do not fear death, and they are not to be tested or interfered with. Everyone in that village can and will defend themselves to the death—from the baker to the laundry attendant. It is a place where horrible people with amazing powers are accepted and allowed to coexist.

One afternoon while bumping along, Kipp said, "I imagine your father would have fit right in."

"No, he would not. He hates women. And he has never respected anyone, ever!"

More of Kipp's stories told of an underlying acceptance of all those with power in Arenu Village. And because of that acceptance, all types of trade happen there—not just food, clothing, liquor, and other commodities. People were sold and bought. Pedophiles, thieves, and murderers walked among the soldiers and the common man without worry—an honored agreement for all who entered the village. Respect and be respected; eradicate and be eradicated. Anyone living within Arenu Village could challenge another to fight if the cause was just—and those duels were usually 'til death. Brutality, servitude, and suffering were common in Arenu Village, as in any other place on Urthis. It was also true, according to lore, that the Village was not a completely desolate place where one was doomed upon entering. There were ways to survive if you were the right type. Kipp shared all this with Irwin as they bounced and bobbed along in their wagon.

Good or bad, Irwin and Kipp were not keen about arriving at Arenu Village. And the likelihood they could catch up with Yace, Dephen, and his goons was waning. Irwin could feel defeat brewing in Kipp's heart, so he tried to find the lighter side of life, as usual, for his friend's sake.

"Take it easy Kipp! Had I not been able to make water, we both would be dead by now ... our animals too."

"Had you woken me that one night, we could've rescued her and been done with all this! I really wish you trusted me."

Irwin rolled his eyes. "I do trust you. It is you who does not trust me."

"Says the man who never tells me his true intentions!"

Irwin made notches on the seatback to count how many days they had traveled since leaving Ahradah. Thirty-two days had passed, and most of their rations were near empty—but they had water! On the morning of the thirty-third day, the wind shifted, pushing against them head-on. A rainstorm was brewing offshore. Thick, heavy clouds rumbled above the sea. Humidity was rising, but only at the shore's edge. Those farther inland would not feel any respite from the dryness and the heat.

Their horses walked slowly, heads down, pulling the wagon into the wind. The only reprieve from the hard southerly winds came when they rolled into a bay. Some bays were shallower than others, but the road continued to follow the lay of the land along the edge of the world.

As they neared the crest of a small hill, Kipp said, "Do you think this is Erthin created? Or is it an actual storm?"

"None of this feels Erthin." Irwin pointed at the amassing cloud formations. "This is *all* Mother Nature."

On this day, the air was cooler and filled with ocean spray. It felt good, but the hard wind never let up. Violent waves crashed against outcroppings of rocks and along bluffs. Sitting side by side, the two men tried to enjoy the blustery day.

As the road wound across the land that stretched into the ocean, Kipp said he had detected an intense scent. He handed the reins to Irwin. Then he stood on the seat and sniffed the air. With his hand on Irwin's head, he inhaled deeply many times as the wagon rattled along.

Irwin kept his eyes on the landscape, hoping to catch sight of what Kipp smelled.

"Sourdough! I smell sourdough." Kipp drew in another few large sniffs. "Oh sourdough. It's freshly baked. Oh, yum." He gripped Irwin's shoulder. "That means we must be close to civilization." He sat back down.

Irwin fondled the reins.

"Dang it, I didn't think we'd come to Arenu Village so soon!"

"Hold tight, Kipp." Irwin did not believe they had driven that far in so many days. From looking at the maps, he had estimated Arenu Village to be at least fifty days southeast of Ahradah. "Are there any other scents?"

"Trees."

"You smell trees?"

"Yeah. I see them too." Kipp pointed.

Irwin slowed the horses. "Do you actually believe we are coming up on Arenu Village? I know we have traveled fast, but we could not have traveled that far in so many days. The map of Urthis shows Arenu Village as a dot against a river, and rivers are usually marked by mass vegetation, by more trees than I see." He pointed at the scattered trees on the horizon and then westward at the lack of vegetation. "I am sure that if we were approaching Arenu Village, we would see more manicured land and groves of trees. There would be acres of cultivated crops."

"Dang it, Irwin! I don't know what to think. All I know is that we should've rescued Yace by now."

"Do not get ahead of yourself, Kipp. I do not think this is Arenu Village. I believe we are still several days away. Maybe a trading post?"

Kipp kept sniffing. "I smell sheep and goats."

"Good. Anything else?"

"Yeah! Pigs and chickens too."

"Maybe we are approaching a farm!"

The wagon labored on and then rolled out of another bay, up a small incline. That was when they spotted a long stone fence. It spanned from the west for many kilometers along the hip of the next hill they were approaching and spilled down the other side, where the stone wall disappeared into the ocean. Oak trees blocked their view of everything southwest, but they could both smell the animals now. As they crested the next bluff, the road slithered down into a wide, protected bay. They shifted in their seats, anticipating what was coming up. Trees clustered along a creek's edge down toward the ocean and then fanned up and out along the topside of the bay's bluff, hiding the animals they smelled. What little water the creek contained, dribbled down the carved valley and out into the ocean.

Perched on an upcoming hillside facing north was a small dwelling. It was built into the hillside with a sod roof and protruding stone and mortar facade. Wooden shuttered windows were opened to the day's breeze, as was the doorway. The little abode had a view of every direction, except south. At the base of the bay, before the sandy beach, grass grew abundantly and was tall enough to satiate a few four-legged animals. The trees up-slope offered ample amounts of shade for animals and people. This was a perfect place to take a break.

There were two parallel rocky walls, one taller than the other ... a perimeter wall that sloped westward for many kilometers. The inner wall was not as long and followed the rise in the land from beyond the trees and created a corridor for herding animals onto ferrying boats waiting in the small bay. Presently, wooden gates were latched closed across the roadway. The wagon would have to stop while a herd of pigs were being funneled down the chute and onto a small boat.

Two other boats, already leaving the shore, were filled with animals—rowing toward a grand ocean-bound ship anchored outside the bay. They watched shipmates moving frantically across the main deck, probably readying the vessel. Facing southward, the ship hoisted up the first ferryboat filled with livestock.

Three dirty and unshaven Clan-Duin/Erthin men on horseback manned the chute. Irwin watched as these men focused on the task at hand. They did not seem to notice the wagon. But other Clan-Duin/Erthins, who stood on the far hillside in the shade, just down from the little house, were watching their approach. They pointed and conversed amongst themselves. From beyond the trees, dogs barked, and several came running toward the wagon. Thank goodness the gates were closed. But now this small community was alerted to their presence.

Irwin gripped the reins.

Kipp said, "You get to practice your act!"

"Cutlery Specialist." He repeated the name a few times.

"That's right. Maybe you should look the part."

"Look the part, yes, I know." He handed off the reins and climbed back into the covered wagon. He had one clean change of clothing but felt too dirty to wear the pants and the red blouse. In all their drive along the ocean's edge, they had not bothered to stop longer than to sleep. Cleaning themselves was but a luxury. And stopping for anything other than the horses seemed absurd, so they took no time for themselves—too intent on saving Yace before she made it to Arenu Village.

A middle-aged woman stepped out of the little house built snug into the bluff and walked toward the gates. She appeared all Clan-Duin—dark skin, tanned and wrinkled by sun and time. Her brownish-gray hair and bland mud-colored dress whipped around her face and legs in the wind.

"We're being approached." Kipp alerted Irwin by whispering back into the covered wagon.

"I am almost done," Irwin said as he moved around, rocking the wagon slightly.

"Good day, Ma'am," Kipp obliged with a loud voice. The woman was still hundreds of feet off, but near enough to hear his greeting. The scent of sourdough was thick in the air.

"Good day, Clan-Duin," she called back.

Irwin saw her summoning two of her men to come with her to open the gates.

"I assume you would like passage?"

Kipp hit the seat and glanced back into the wagon.

Irwin muttered, "Yes, almost done."

Kipp continued to engage the woman. "Yes, please. Master Samuel will pay for passage."

Irwin jumped down from the backside of the wagon. He patted his Jennies lovingly and then ambled toward the front of the wagon. "Good day, Ma'am."

"Good day, Master Samuel." She smiled. "Passage costs ten silvers, unless you have something to trade." Her brown eyes gleamed. "And because I've been hosting all morning, chicken soup and sourdough bread has been made. I still have a few meals left. You two are more than welcome to join me."

The wranglers on horseback were soon through with guiding the pigs onboard the last rowboat. They turned their horses around and galloped past the gates before they were opened for the wagon's passage. The two Clan-Duin/Erthins that walked with the woman unlocked the gates and stood aside.

Irwin stepped ahead of the wagon, past the stone walls and wooden gates, the haggard-looking men, and across the lightly flowing creek toward the woman. "I have knives for trade," he said. "If you are farming animals, as I can see, a good butchering blade is essential."

Her dark brown eyes scrutinized Irwin, while a warm smile stretched across her dry, cracked lips. "You sell blades?"

"Yes. That is my trade."

"I would enjoy seeing some of your work. Maybe we can make a trade for passage. As I said, you and your Clan-Duin are more than welcome to join me for an afternoon meal. You've traveled through the harshest of lands, and if you seek Arenu Village, there are still three days separating you from your destination.

Come and take some time off. Allow your horses some time in the shade and grass to eat. Enjoy a warm meal and a serene view." It all sounded tempting.

Kipp parked the wagon and jumped down. He approached Irwin, bowing his head. "Samuel, Sir, I would like to water the animals."

The woman tossed her hand toward the wranglers. "Oh, my men will do that for you."

"Thank you, Ma'am, for your kindness." Irwin nodded his head.

"Lady Gretchen, please. You two have come a long way, and formalities are unnecessary here." She waved at her Erthin men. "Bring water pails for the horses and donkeys." The older of the two men stepped up and took the lead reins. The horses pulled the wagon up the slope and into the shade. The other man retrieved wooden buckets for water. "Please, come, join me," Lady Gretchen said before she turned toward her house and walked away from her visitors.

Irwin raised an eyebrow—curious about this woman. He did not want to assume anything, but she was being almost too nice, so he followed with caution. She continued ambling toward her house, glancing back at them and smiling. She looked devious somehow. Irwin couldn't quite figure out why, and wanted to ask her many questions. He didn't know what to ask first. "You said you have been hosting all morning?"

"It seems like my day should be through, but the sun is still high," she said with a light laugh. "Much time has passed since anyone has visited, and then I am met by land and sea in one day. I don't mind though. I enjoy the company, and hearing everyone's stories, of course. We get little action here, as you can probably imagine. Raising goats and pigs and chickens is hard work with no proper reward." She looked at Irwin. "My reward is meeting new people and hearing of their adventures." She turned away again and continued to climb up the hill.

He wanted to ask about the carriage, but knew to make idle small talk before asking anything pointed. "How often do you get visitors?"

A few short steps from her front door, she paused and turned to Irwin. "Well, ships usually come after the new moon, depending on the season, of course. It's rare that we see people come by roadway. Soldiers will come by horseback, occasionally. Very few people purposefully drive this direction. But when they do, they're usually searching for immunity in Arenu Village. All who come here are accepted, even Mortals who have lost their way." Her smile never faltered as she swerved toward the door.

Kipp stepped up along Irwin's side—still sniffing the sourdough scent. Irwin touched his friend's arm. The Clan-Duin's demeanor never changed, and with an enormous smile Kipp said, "Chicken soup. I can't remember the last time I had chicken anything!"

The idea of a warm meal, not overly dried or salted as they had endured for so long, was very tempting. Lady Gretchen entered the darkened dwelling first and kept the door open wide for Irwin and Kipp.

26

Lady Gretchen

The woman's house was not large, and it was oblong in design. A stone and clay fireplace took up most of the space at the dark end of the room—embers still glowing. A small wooden table and three chairs had been placed under a set of windows looking out onto the bay. A narrow bed was situated opposite the kitchenette area and had been made to resemble a couch with pillows that rested against the wall. Irwin was sure that only Lady Gretchen lived here in this homestead. He surveyed the one room home.

Where do the wranglers sleep?

She went toward her kitchen cupboards and opened them. Pulling out two large ceramic bowls, she handed the first one to Kipp. He grasped the bowl and Lady Gretchen's hands in the process. She smiled at him as he cheerfully stepped toward the cast iron cauldron that had been removed from the dying fire.

Irwin accepted the mug she presented to him. He nodded with a slight bow. "Thank you once again for your hospitality, Lady Gretchen."

She grinned as he took the bowl. "It's always my pleasure to meet new people." Her brown eyes followed Kipp as he stepped over to the hot cauldron and ladled up enough soup to fill his bowl.

Irwin waited. His mind was racing.

What to ask next? I really want to know.

"When did the carriage arrive?"

"The carriage? Oh, yes, the carriage. It arrived just as the ship pulled into view. And since I knew the ship was coming, I tended to the captain and his requests before allowing the carriage passage through the gates."

They arrived when the ship did. But we were at least a day behind.

Kipp passed by Irwin as he asked the next question. Their eyes locked momentarily. "Did they stay long?"

"For just a short while, yes," she shrugged. "They watered their horses and traded for some fresh food. That is my business. If you'd like, we can talk about trading for a chicken or a pig. You two look as if you have eaten very little during your journey. I've more than enough food to spare."

"It's hard to calculate how much food you really need on a journey like that," Kipp said. He turned toward the table and took a seat near the door. Without hesitating, he reached for two large slices of sourdough bread. Inserting one into his soup, he stuffed the other into his mouth.

"That is very true." Irwin agreed with Kipp. "Had I known, I would have packed more fruit and oats." He ladled up a medium-sized portion of soup.

Lady Gretchen stood behind him, keeping that same cheerful smile. "I hope you like it."

"Thank you. It smells good." Irwin passed off the ladle to Lady Gretchen and then went to the table.

He sat next to Kipp and smiled at his friend. They were both glad to enjoy a moment of relaxation and actual food. Lady Gretchen was the nicest hostess they had met in a long time. She sat next to Irwin, opposite Kipp, smiling and nodding at the men as she, too, reached for a piece of bread. Placing the piece of bread next to her bowl of soup, her hand moved next to Irwin's, and then atop it.

In that moment of contact, his whole body felt as if needles were piercing every inch of his skin. Everything hurt! He wanted to retaliate, but he could not.

I cannot move! What is happening?

"Kipp, dear," pointing as she commanded, "would you please retrieve the blue vial from the cupboard? And bring that wooden funnel."

And then she began laughing.

Shit!

Irwin tried to move his eyes but could not. From his periphery, he saw Lady Gretchen's dark complexion and mostly brunette hair slip away. All her hair turned white, her skin lightened and appeared more wrinkled—brown eyes turned blue.

Watching Kipp climb up on her counter to reach the blue vial, she said, "I do appreciate the younger Clan-Duin body. This one has good tone and sturdy structure. Most of the Clan-Duins who arrive here are starved, homeless, family-less, stupid, no good, lazy Clan-Duins who have no incentive, no reason to live. They aren't even PCP worthy." Again, she cackled, "So they're brought to me. They come and I mold them into more acceptable creations." She goaded Irwin. "But he is acceptable as he is, isn't he, Master Samuel?" Her eyes lingered on Kipp as he climbed down and brought her the vial.

How are we going to get out of this?

"Good boy, Kipp. Now open it, and ..." She peered into Irwin's bowl to see how much soup was left in it. "... pour all of that into this cup." She watched him obey. "Now stir it. Make sure it's all mixed in." Her eyes darted from Kipp to Irwin.

She told Irwin, who could hear her in his mind: *I do not wish to be seen as the only bad person here.* And then she ordered, "Kipp, give me the funnel." She turned to Irwin, *Open your mouth.* And though he did not want to, his body followed her telepathic order. "Kipp, now pour his soup into the funnel. Do not touch him. He will burn you. His flesh is hot." Her words and eyes commanded, and Kipp somehow followed.

Irwin wanted to move—wanted to scream—to summon his power and make the metal in the room kill this wicked woman. He wished to have some under his flesh, a way to heal from this death knell. But all he could do was sit and listen and obey. Her hand never left his. Lady Gretchen carried on laughing aloud, and also in Irwin's mind.

He mentally pleaded, *Please do not do this.*

They both watched Kipp stand back far enough not to come into contact with Irwin. The Clan-Duin then raised the cup and began force-feeding Irwin who choked and sputtered, but the warm meal made its way down his throat and into his stomach. Lady Gretchen cackled as she watched. She was a force to be reckoned with.

"Dephen couldn't get rid of either of you. Ha! What a fool he is!"

You know Dephen?

Her tortuous laughter never subsided. "We're cousins. Though I'm smarter. Obviously!" Her hand grasped Irwin's again. "You don't feel it yet, but you will. Your beloved Kipp has dosed you with a lethal amount of poison."

You are cousins? And I thought my family was messed up! Using poison to kill? That is a weak way to kill. But maybe that is the only way your family can dispatch death!

Lady Gretchen continued to cackle out loud and in his mind.

And I thought Dephen was evil.

"Dephen *is* evil! Ignorant to a fault at times," she said. "He told me all about you, Samuel Irwin Miner. He said you were powerful, but I don't see it. I only see a boy marked by defeat, beaten by chaos.

"You're stupid to believe that you and your Clan-Duin friend here could actually save that beauty Dephen inhabits." She shook her head and let out another hideous screech. "He didn't believe I could rid him of you. But you're male. And all men are weak." She lightened her grasp, but not her contact with his hand.

Kipp stood idle, awaiting another command. His eyes stared out the window at the ship that was now hoisting up its sails. "Wave, Kipp," Lady Gretchen ordered of him, and he complied.

Irwin yearned to resist the power that was holding him down, but he could not. He was immobilized by her telepathic control. "Would you enjoy seeing a trick, Master Samuel?"

He held his mind calm.

"Did you know that your partner here is the perfect type of pet? He's very loyal, almost to a fault. That's why I promised Dephen I would destroy him. Although I'd appreciate having a specimen such as him. To watch him work all day ...." She inhaled deeply and hummed to herself while gazing at Kipp.

Whimpering on the inside, Irwin was fearful of what she would do to his beloved friend. Then her telepathic voice echoed in his mind. *Oh, how cute. You don't want him to die. I'm sorry, but I don't break my promises.* "Your best friend here just happens to be one of those special types of Clan-Duins," she giggled. "I'm seeing more and more of these tri-tribe Clan-Duins. They're usually crossbred with Mortal blood. It taints their blood, but in a good way."

Irwin felt the urge to vomit.

"Of course, crossbreeding within a pure Clan-Duin community also forces this mutation to happen. These types of traits are coveted in the PCP world, usually because of their fluid shape-shifting abilities. He might have made a nice soldier, or servant, had you two made it to Arenu Village." She paused and nodded. "Perhaps they would've seen his potential and trained him to be a Hakran Guard. He's better kept than most I've seen, including the sloths Dephen has taken." Her hungry eyes studied Kipp.

"But since he's in hot pursuit of his precious sweetheart, and refusing to give up his pursuit, Dephen says I must get rid of him." Her lustful glare was still on the young Clan-Duin. "Besides, you and Kipp can't continue to believe that you will be triumphant in saving her. Your Yace is now Dephen. And there's nothing either of you can do about that. Especially now," she crowed wildly.

"Watch this!" Lady Gretchen looked Kipp up and down one more time. "Kipp Hauler, you're such a pig ... yes, you are. You are no longer a man; you are a pig. You're a filthy, disgusting rolls-around-in-your-own-excrement pig. You swine; you disgust me, you're nothing but filth and wallow. You *are* a pig, you dirty, dirty pig ... you piggy pig. You *are* a PIG!" She used her words to cast the spell, and Irwin could not comprehend how she accomplished the task. She still had contact with him, but right before his frozen eyes, Kipp began to change. His clothing loosened, his body morphed, and then his tunic and shorts fell around him. Kipp had mutated into a pig!

What the ...? No! No, you cannot do this! You cannot take him away from me. No! Not Kipp!

Frantic, his stomach began to move. At first the ache was slight, but then the pain grew.

What did you poison me with?

The pain swelled, but Irwin did not want to give in.

I must save Kipp.

A burp of chicken soup and a garlicky taste surfaced in his mouth.

Arsenic?!

His stomach churned again; agony shot throughout his body.

I must be here for Kipp.

He tried to stay positive in his thoughts. But the telepathy and arsenic were having their effect. He wanted to close his eyes and crumple into a ball.

Boys! She attempted to command her men. *Come and get this filthy pig out of my house. Oh, that's right ....* Lady Gretchen had to let go of Irwin's hand to telepathically command her men who were somewhere outside the domicile.

The stinging Irwin felt now flushed tenfold. His head slumped forward and hit the table. His blood stirred violently, and his body expelled what little metal it held, dripping out of him like water. His insides boiled. He wanted to scream, but taking a breath was painful. Everything hurt. He could not think; he was in too much agony and grief. And though there was metal everywhere in the room, the arsenic soured the metallic notes. He did not want to pull for the metal. Just thinking about it made his stomach twist more.

I do not want to die!

"I think it's funny how much you covet Kipp—how much you want him to lust after you as you do for him. But that'll never happen. Kipp will never be yours. He's always been a ladies' man, not a man's man." Lady Gretchen made a sound of distaste. "He will never reciprocate the love you have for him. That's easy to see. This whole time you've been with him, hoping to help, hoping to make him happy—it's a farce. You can't even make yourself happy, Samuel Irwin Miner. You chide yourself every day for lusting after him. Why? Maybe you should just die!" She cackled as Irwin rolled off the chair and onto the floor.

"And Dephen thought it would be harder for me to kill you than this. HA! Females are the superior beings. Always remember that!" She kicked Irwin's leg. "We give birth. We adapt our lives. We give our time. And all you stupid children ever give us is horseshit!" She stepped around Irwin and goaded the pig, Kipp, out the door. He had been smelling around the table, like a dog, hoping for another piece of sourdough bread. He was close to Irwin, but she kicked him viciously in the gut, and he squealed. "All you ever do is take and take and take." The pig moved away from her swinging foot and scurried toward the open doorway.

Horse hooves rumbled toward the house. Two wranglers Irwin had seen in the chute earlier climbed down from their mounts. Their clothing was muddier than before. The two large, brown-skinned men with dark auburn scruffy hair wasted no time escorting Kipp away from the front of the house and up the hill.

"I must make sure he gets on a Daos bound boat as a token to Dephen," she muttered as she stepped back inside. "Are you dead yet?" She chuckled and moved toward Irwin, her skirt rustling as she moved. "Now, what will I do with your body?" She knelt close to his face.

His eyes rolled back in his head and his body jerked uncontrollably as it rolled and cramped into the fetal position. Every muscle was flexing and contracting. It hurt beyond remembering. Irwin was in terror for his life and for Kipp's.

"Oh! You're still alive. Well, you won't remain like that for much longer." She was cool. "The PCP will be saddened to know that Death found you first. They were quite curious to know more about you after you showed up on their telepathic radar in Ahradah."

She stood up. "From what I understand, your people. Your relatives haven't been seen for over half a century. And what records there are about your family members are vague at best," she sighed. "I could send your body along after you're dead. But they'll want to test your blood, and then they would find out that you were poisoned."

She placed her hands on her hips; her eyes glared like a wild boar in heat.

"No. That won't work well for me. They would question me, and I hate being cross-examined." Lady Gretchen frowned. "But had you remained alive ...." She sighed and stepped around him. "Had you remained alive, which you won't, they would want your memories. They'd want to know all your dirty little secrets, Samuel Irwin Miner."

She sauntered over to the window and gazed across her realm.

"Lucky for you, only a few people know everything about you. And I do mean *everything*." Lady Gretchen hinted that she knew what Yace had seen upon first meeting Irwin. "No! It must look like you never arrived in Arenu Village ... that somewhere along the way, Death found you and your friend. Whether it be the lions and jackals of the hot zone, or thirst, it won't matter. They won't know anything more than what we allow."

Irwin's intestines twisted, and his head pounded like a drum. Every muscle in his body was tight, and he still couldn't move. He lay below the table between the chairs and was on the verge of passing out. He struggled to stay awake, to stay alive. Lady Gretchen had moved to her kitchen area. She poured herself a mug of wine and sipped it and watched Irwin writhe in pain. His agony amused her.

"Maybe I should have a taste of your blood before you go. I can tell much about a person through their blood. That's my specialty! If it's not clear what type of creature you are, someone like myself can discern your breeding." She retrieved the knife she used to cut the sourdough and pressed it against his arm—cutting Irwin open. He did not flinch. Nor did his flesh absorb the blade. His body was preoccupied with the copious amount of arsenic he had ingested. Blood seeped out of the fresh wound, but momentarily healed where she had cut the skin.

Lady Gretchen licked the blade and took a seat at the table. She kicked her feet up onto Irwin's hunched body. "I can ingest only small amounts of arsenic." She continued to taste his blood before spitting it out. "You have a strong metal lineage. But your family has been watered down by Mortal blood." She paused with thought, her tongue still discerning his blood—slapping the roof of her mouth. "But there's something peculiar about the taste. Oh, oh! I sense ... I sense Coterie. I see it now." With dilated eyes, she gasped, "We're related! Huh, very interesting."

She lingered in thought and then kicked at Irwin's ribs.

"I sense that your Coterie powers are weakened by an extra generation of Mortal blood. A bastard child indeed, and because of your Metalist abilities you'll never be able to use telekinesis or mutation." She looked up at the ceiling, then back down at Irwin. "Oh, but you can do other things with the Coterie Talent that I've only dreamed of. How fascinating!" She kept on clucking her tongue against the roof of her mouth. "Your blood would mix very well with Erthins. Now those offspring would be very powerful!" She put her feet back on the ground and strode off.

"You have an interesting combination of traits to breed. Had they found you on the other side of Kruluver, they would have numbed your mind and put you into a breeding program. But you're here with me, and the women I have here aren't desirable crosses.

"Clan-Duin blood would sour your Metalist traits, my dear. Those offspring would be irritable at best. I happen to know that metal and animals do not mix." He heard Lady Gretchen move across the room and pour herself more wine. She droned on, "Which is probably what has preserved your species. Yes, you're very special indeed. Too bad Dephen ordered your death. I could've traded you to the west for a thousand Clan-Duins." She approached Irwin again. He did not move and lay crumbled up on the floor.

He was no longer conscious.

Yet from deep inside, Irwin was aware that Lady Gretchen telepathically summoned her men. After some time had passed, the thundering hooves returned. He felt the same riders step inside, awaiting her orders.

"Take him to the manure pile and bury him."

The walnut trees blocked the view from the roadway. Up-slope from Lady Gretchen's place, there were three dozen half-acre sized pens surrounded by rock wall fencing. Paired together in quad formations, all the pastures were finished with stone walls that stood about a foot wide and four-feet high. Only a few had wooden gates. Not all the pastures were being used, but many of them stunk from animal refuse. Goats, pigs, sheep, chickens, and turkeys were all segregated and were being watched after by a montage of half-blooded Erthin/Clan-Duin men. There were no other women on the property other than Lady Gretchen, the matriarch.

Irwin was dragged out of the house by ropes hung from horses, then yanked uphill between the pastures and beyond the trees and the dogs. His head bounced over rocks and tree roots. Guard dogs barked and chased after the mostly dead body as it was heaved past them. The three wranglers on horseback hauled Irwin's lifeless body beyond the last set of pens. They stopped at a pile of manure. Their horses stood still while the wranglers began digging his grave.

Mostly dry on top, once the men churned up the well-composted manure, small and large worms emerged. Soon, small flies surrounded them, flying into open mouths, crawling across them. The bugs also landed on Irwin. The wranglers ignored the flying pests and dug a hole many feet deep into the fertilized ground, then shoved Irwin's body into it, kicking the loosened soil across him, leaving him to die and decompose.

The men did not check Irwin's vitals before tossing him into the grave. They were unaware they were burying a live person. They were only doing what was commanded, nothing more. They did not think independently. Lady Gretchen would not allow it, never allowed it.

If any of these Erthin/Clan-Duins had forethought, they might have listened for a heartbeat. Had they stopped to observe Irwin's body, they might have seen him breathing.

It began to rain, and these men wanted to be done with it.

27

NOT DEAD YET

As Lady Gretchen had boasted, Irwin's Metalist and Coterie abilities worked very well together to keep him alive. While he lay four feet deep, Irwin's powers manipulated his metabolism and encouraged the processing of the harsh arsenic element. Deep within the ground, his body worked at removing the poison from his system. And being encompassed by churned compost, sand, gravel, selenium, and other organic materials and minerals aided in his body's work at recovery. The organic soil against his skin also helped extract the arsenic that coursed inside him. Moisture filtered through the freshly churned ground, nourishing him, and aiding in his regeneration.

He lay there all night, numb to his pain and surroundings. By early morning his body had purged the arsenic into the soil. His powers worked hard, keeping Irwin from going with Death. The surrounding dirt reeked of arsenic and manure. The stench woke him finally, and the lack of air startled him.

Weighed down by soil, Irwin's head lay downward, and his feet were upward. Although he was buried deep, there was a small pocket of air around his head. But as he moved, it vanished. He tried not to panic. He knew to stay calm and thoughtful. As a child, he had been tossed into a hole and sealed in. He had also once been trapped in a small passage between caverns for two days. Back then, as well as now, Irwin had felt the weight of the world. He knew not to panic, but as a child he had. Back then, the young miner had to talk himself down from his fear; now he knew to relax. Holding his last breath, Irwin used his senses to find the surface. He sent up a rod of his metal.

The rod was slender and pushed through several feet of soil before finding the surface. Breaching the churned ground, he used all his focus to extract more metal from the soil, pulling it into the rod and expanding it into a cylinder. As the cylinder widened, Irwin kicked his feet, loosening the soil. He tried to move around just enough so that he could rotate upwards and catch a breath.

As the hole grew, morning light filtered down upon him. The stench of manure was overpowering, but he inhaled many times—trying not to cough. Wispy white clouds floated overhead and began to block the sunshine. He was happy to be alive, and at the same time, he was befuddled by his predicament.

Is this real?

He saw a seagull fly past hundreds of feet up in the morning sky.

Where am I?

His brain began to work faster as he swam out of the hole.

What happened?

He looked around and saw a rocky wall straight ahead and open land behind him. Dried grass rattled against itself, crickets and occasional finches made sounds; close by, pigs and goats and chickens oinked and grumbled and clucked.

Thirsty and alert, he was still somewhat disoriented. The sights and sounds were off, as were the colors. Luscious dark-green trees lined a creek north of where he lay and rolled off westward as far as he could see. A swath of green grass trailed that creek, but all the grassy sprigs further out and away were yellow and brown. The sound of the ocean seemed distant now. The only thing he recalled seeing before was the ocean and trees. Then his memories came flooding back. He remembered everything that had happened with Lady Gretchen.

He was haunted to the core now. The feeling of immobilization and being taken mentally hostage drove a shiver down his spine. But worse, recalling Kipp being used by yet another Telepath. And this time, the Clan-Duin had been puppeteer'd into poisoning him.

Lady Gretchen had telepathically seen how Irwin disliked Kipp's mental pliability and used that to her advantage. He cried softly there in his hole. He did not want to remember.

Out of his grave, he rested against the stone wall, helpless, wondering what else had happened to him after he lost consciousness. He was not sure if what he was experiencing was real or something telepathically conjured. The sounds of frogs, crickets, goats, sheep, pigs, chickens, turkeys, horses, dogs, and the murmurs of men in the distance was surreal. For many days, all Irwin had heard was the wind in his ears, Kipp, the horses, and the donkeys.

Huddled against the stone wall, out of sight of anyone, Irwin was recovering mentally and physically.

How is it I am still alive?

He looked at the hole from where he had just emerged. His eyes scoured the landscape north, west, and south. Beyond the mounds of composted manure, all he could see was vacant land with small nubs of brownish-green grass. But there was also a creek, trees, and a rock wall that spanned to the west and beyond the horizon.

He smelled of soil and animal excrement. He removed his dirtied clothing. The stench would call attention to his whereabouts, and so would the trace amounts of minerals in his flesh. He did not want to throw away his red blouse—but he did—and his pants too. He threw his soiled clothes into the hole, and then he recovered it back over with the smelly dirt. No one needed to know he had just escaped from his grave. Not yet. He would cover his tracks and keep a low profile.

Assessing his environment, Irwin sat up just enough to peer over the wall. He saw pigs in a pen.

Pigs! Kipp turned into a pig!

Again, he sat back against the cold stone wall.

What type of farm is this?

'He is the right type of Clan-Duin.' Irwin remembered Lady Gretchen saying right before she told Kipp he was a pig, and he mutated into one.

What kind of Volatile is this Lady Gretchen? To have such power over myself and Kipp.

Her voice echoed in his head, 'We're related!' Irwin's heart pounded, and he took a few deep breaths to calm himself.

Related, meaning what? How can I be related to her?

He did not want to believe her revelations.

It does not matter how we are related. Lady Gretchen is as evil as Dephen. She must be stopped.

The morning sky darkened as a storm pushed ashore. Crouching, Irwin sat up high enough to peer over the tall stone fence again. He looked to the east and took in a conglomeration of pastures. He saw a long stone and wooden barn-like structure with a wooden corral attached to it.

Fifteen or so wranglers sat around a campfire watching as one of their peers stirred an enormous cauldron. None of them noticed Irwin; they were all just waking up. Half of the dogs beyond the wranglers were tied to trees. The others lazily lie around—none of them alerted to Irwin's presence.

He knew to stay downwind, out of the wranglers' smell. Now that he knew the layout of the mostly flat land, he began to edge himself down the side of the stone wall. When he came to the first lane crossing, he sat for a bit and surveyed the pens with the pigs, sheep, goats, chickens, and even a few turkeys. He was careful not to stand too tall and crawled in order to keep out of view until he could come up with a plan. Until then, he was gathering more information about this place.

Each pen he passed, he examined and counted. He surmised that there were five-hundred pigs, three-hundred sheep, eight-hundred goats, and about two-hundred chickens and turkeys.

Could they all be Clan-Duins? Or were some real animals?

He came to the last set of pens. Goats bleated, trying to munch up the few small pieces of grass available.

Irwin reached over and touched a coarse-haired goat—a daring move. He felt the hair change to flesh beneath his hand, revealing an older man.

He held his breath.

Clan-Duin!

Irwin sat back down and heard the man make a noise. The freshly changed Clan-Duin screamed. It was only a peep of a sound, not bold enough to catch anyone's attention. And just like that, the old man ceased to exist, eaten by hungry goats who had an affinity for flesh.

Are you fooling me, man-eating goats? How will I find Kipp without getting mauled?

He stood tall enough to see the wranglers moving away from their morning camp and commence with their daily routines. He could feel the horses being tacked up; metal bits and stirrups clattered and clanked.

Shit. I guess it is time for a distraction.

He moved into position before using a touch of his Earth Erthin power, summoning a section of rocky wall to open.

I hope this works!

The goats were quick to see the breach in the wall and began to go toward it. At first, only a few moved from the small pasture. Irwin touched the goats as they passed through the opening. Then the herd realized what was going on, and they all pushed toward the breach. He changed as many as he could back into two-legged men and women.

Four-legged bodies morphed into two-legged ones. Naked, disoriented, and scared, Irwin yelled at them. "GO!" He pointed to the west, hoping the bewildered Clan-Duins would listen and heed his words.

Several goats got past Irwin, but there was nothing he could do about that. In fact, that added to the chaos he was trying to create.

Plan; must make a plan. Find Kipp!

He did what he could and touched the backs of numerous goats. All the while, he watched as the wranglers were alerted to the commotion at the southwest side of the property.

Yes. Good. Come this way.

He allowed a few more goats to pass by. The pen was nearly empty before Irwin scurried down the fence line toward the next pasture. Thundering hooves raced around.

Jumping over the fence into the next goat yard, he heard a wrangler spot him the moment a goat sprang at him to bite his shoulder. He put up a hand to defend himself against the hungry herd. All the while, he was transforming goats into men and women. While they tried to bite Irwin, he made contact with them, and they were repulsed by his taste. The goats metamorphosed into Clan-Duins and were now aware of their surroundings. They too had to beat back the other goats who charged forth with hungry intentions. Irwin never stopped touching and changing every goat he encountered.

He shouted at the people as they became aware of themselves and the situation. "Jump the fence. Run away!"

But a telepathic command was sent out to all the refugee Clan-Duins. All those standing upright on two legs, naked and scared, were abruptly frozen where they stood.

When Irwin realized what was happening, he began retouching those he had already changed. "Go! Run! Get out of here!"

Then he felt the first of the three mounted wranglers arrive. The first man readied to send fire toward Irwin who stopped in mid-motion and looked at the rider. With a wave of his finger and a coy smile, Irwin's eyes shimmered silver with his power. In one swift motion, his hand rose and that Fire Erthin was vaporized. Nothing was left of him. That wrangler's startled horse whinnied and watched, awaiting the rest of his band to arrive. And they did!

Again, another telepathic command was cast, and those few Clan-Duins running away stopped in mid-motion; a few fell over. The wranglers began harnessing their powers, throwing fireballs, and whipping up dirt and dust. Without any hesitation, Irwin assimilated them. His hands then went back to touching all the crowding goats around him. He did not want to stop, but the sight of more wranglers approaching scared him into action, and he jumped up onto the nearest wall. He did not want an all-out war. His fight was with Lady Gretchen.

Maybe if I kill her, all the Clan-Duins will become normal again.

The remaining men on horseback and the few running on foot pressed forward with their advance. One large Clan-Duin/Erthin-powered man rode ahead of the others. He pulled his steed roughly to a halt. The dirty gray animal reared up.

Her voice boomed out of the large man. "How's it you still live, Metalist? You were dead on my floor."

"The only thing that can kill a miner is time."

Lady Gretchen stared at Irwin through her wrangler whose body she inhabited. "Everyone dies. You cannot stop the inevitable." He recognized these words. She used Albert's familiar vengeance against him, sneering at him. It was clear to Irwin that Lady Gretchen knew far too much about him, and she taunted him unrelentingly with that knowledge. "I'm sure we've got something around here that will kill you." Several of the Erthin wranglers metamorphosed into their ferocious feline forms.

Irwin was finished with Lady Gretchen and her malicious games.

He knew what he had to do. It would take only an instant. He closed his eyes and felt a cool wind on his neck. It began to rain. He could hear all the metal around him singing. There were countless objects in the barn made from metal: picks, shovels, axes, horseshoes, nails, and many others singing sweetly to him. Irwin's wagon was three-hundred feet beyond the barn and held all his personal metal. If he wished, all that metal could surround him in a flash. It merely awaited his command. He could just let go and decimate hundreds of attackers, absorb all the rest of the Erthin/Clan-Duins and eradicate Lady Gretchen. But that was not Irwin, and he was not foolish. He only wanted her dead. He believed he knew who were friend and who were foe.

Inside Lady Gretchen's house there were many more objects, heavy and light, and consisting of different types of metal. He felt her moving a knife back and forth, using it to cut something. The cauldron, silverware, jewelry, and other items inside her farmhouse were all at his disposal now. Those metallic pieces allowed him to locate Lady Gretchen's location inside her house. The instant he had a grasp on all those pieces of metal, Irwin let his power surge.

Within that brief moment, metal from the wagon liquefied and flew toward the house's exterior. The entire façade, windows and doors included, were sealed up tight. Lady Gretchen would not be able to escape his wrath. Then a tornado of metal inside her living room began to move and soon reeled out of control. For special effect, Irwin goaded the fire to roar, flash-heating the room. No one could hear her screams.

In her last moment of life, Lady Gretchen tried one last telepathic trick; after sending out that command, she was burned and torn to bits.

The morphed feral felines sprang toward Irwin, claws outstretched, mouths open and exposing sharp, pointed teeth. He felt the half-breeds coming after him, but they were all assimilated before they could do any damage. Those left standing and those on horseback were shocked and astonished by what they had just witnessed.

Irwin looked down into the pens and did not see any change. Those he had already touched remained two-legged. And all the goats in the next field were still animals. "What the shit! What type of spell is this?" He carried on scrutinizing the heads of the four-legged animals that he could see.

"Who be you?" The wrangler, whom Lady Gretchen had spoken through moments before, asked of him. He was trying to sound assertive, but there was a tone of fear in the wrangler's voice and eyes.

Looking out across the fields of goats and the eight remaining Erthin/Clan-Duin wranglers, Irwin replied, "I am Samuel."

"Are you our owner now?"

Shaking his head, Irwin said, "No. No one owns you. You are all free." He looked at the others, watching him intently. "Before now, you were all in servitude to a witch of a woman named Lady Gretchen. She was a Telepath." *And Coterie, I think.* "I just killed her. You are all free of her tyranny."

The Clan-Duins who stood on two legs, and the others watching from down the lanes, heard Irwin's words. Slowly, cautiously, they moved toward him.

"Master Samuel." The last Clan-Duin he had touched stood witness to the power Irwin had yielded. "Thank you for saving me. I pledge my life to you, Sir."

"No, please. I am no Master. You are all free. Please, go, be free!" He pointed off to the west.

Those Clan-Duins who were already changed echoed their gratitude. "Thank you!"

"I give my life to you, Master Samuel."

"I pledge to you!" A female voice cried and was drowned out by other voices calling to Irwin from inside the pen and behind him.

He turned around and saw everyone he had urged to go and run standing there watching him. No one moved to go.

Shit, this is not what I wanted. Well, maybe I can use this momentum to find Kipp.

"Thank you." He turned to take in all those who he had already transformed. The two pastures he had rescued, probably two hundred goats, were now back to being Clan-Duin. "I," he gasped, not knowing exactly what to say, "I need your help. Everyone here, every animal, I suspect, they are all Clan-Duins. That means I need to get everyone changed back, and ..." They all stared at him in awe. "... and I will need your help, all of you." He nodded toward them.

"How can I help?"

"What can we do?"

"Yes, let us help you!" They all began to scream at him at once.

His first thought came out of his mouth before he could bring it back. "Do not eat any of the animals in any of the pastures until we know for sure they can be saved by my power." He was fearful for Kipp's life and felt the sting and terror of this emotional roller-coaster.

What Irwin really needed was a moment to sit down and organize his thoughts. He was parched and famished—drained physically and mentally. He needed to recharge his power and his stamina. Although he believed his life had been training him for this, he was overwhelmed by the outpouring of kindness and support. He did not know what to do with all the beaming eyes staring, smiling, and idolizing him.

He jumped down from the wall and began walking amongst the people he had changed. Although he smelled like metal, they were not repulsed. A few cringed as he passed by, but no one stepped back; no one showed much fear or hostility. They all understood that Irwin was there to help—to liberate these lost Clan-Duins.

Many had been sent to Lady Gretchen's to be changed into a meat product. Children as young as ten, and men and women as old as fifty, stood filthy and naked. They smelled of excrement. Many were skinny and malnourished. But they could smell their former selves on their dirtied bodies. Many of them remembered what they had been before being brought back. It was uncertain how many of these Clan-Duins recalled how they arrived here at this horrible place. But it was obvious that none of them remembered Lady Gretchen, including the wranglers.

They are clean slates, ready to start anew.

He walked toward his wagon and realized that many of the naked Clan-Duins were following him. "Make sure to round up the goats that might have strayed." He hoped someone would rise to the task. "The donkeys and the two draft horses are my animals, but they can be ridden and used to help locate the goats."

Even though these Caln-Duins did not appear ready to cause him harm, Irwin knew to be careful about what he said. Who was to say that there would not be another Telepath in the mix? "Oh, and please do not let any other animals out of here. We need to keep them contained so I can change them back. I believe they are all Clan-Duins, like all of you. It will take time, but I am sure I can change them all back."

I feel anxious with this many around, naked at that. Breathe, be calm. I am helping them. They know this.

His innate fear of being around so many at once kicked in. He wanted to be by himself and calm down.

With a fast pace that most of them could not keep, Irwin crested the slope and walked past Lady Gretchen's house. He moved his hand and all the metal on the abode's façade flew between trees and around the wagon's exterior, encasing it. He climbed in, slipping past the sheet of metal wrapped around the canvas covering. The wagon was now impervious to everyone. Inside it was incredibly quiet. No one could see him.

He quenched his thirst and drank half a flask before eating one of the last pieces of smoked salmon—only half, and left the rest for Kipp. His friend would be hungry once rescued. In the meantime, he had to keep his thoughts positive. Transforming so many would be overwhelming.

He clothed himself in a tattered tunic and cut-off pants. Then he jumped off the back of the wagon and resealed the opening. The metallic wagon looked to be invincible.

A young female greeted him, "Master Samuel!" She smiled through missing teeth. "Let me know if there's any other need that no one else can give you." Irwin stepped back from her.

She might be a Telepath in disguise.

He spoke with a touch of venom in his voice. "Thank you. I will let you know." The woman shrank away from this coarseness.

It was raining, and he wanted to get the day of grounding out telepathic spells over and done with. Many of those he had saved held close to the trees, watching him walk toward the first pen—a chicken yard. And though he wanted to go straight to the pigpens, he felt obligated to save each and every Clan-Duin. They had all been two-legged at one time and had been transformed and incarcerated here on Lady Gretchen's property. Their lives were just as valuable as Kipp's.

He was disgusted to know a new truth about meat he had possibly purchased at the markets along their way.

I would hate to think that we have been eating Clan-Duin meat this whole time.

That idea rattled him as he summoned an opening into the chicken and turkey yards.

The poultry huddled together, trying to ignore the rain. But when they saw him create an opening in the fence line, a few perked up and began to move. He knelt, waiting for a long time for other chickens to follow the few he had just transformed. None of them moved toward him, so Irwin stomped through the muck and over to a small conglomeration of animals. His hands touched the heads and backs of the birds. Nearly all morphed back into their two-legged form. Only ten remained fowl.

Maybe there are actual chickens intermixed with Clan-Duins.

He moved on to the next yard, filled with just as many birds. Only a third of them transformed into two-legged Clan-Duins.

Huh, more chickens in this pen than Clan-Duins.

In the next pen, none of the birds mutated.

The lead wrangler joined Irwin at the fence line. He was on a fat draft horse. The older Clan-Duin/Erthin stared down at him. They both watched chickens and turkeys return to their laying. The birds were trying to weather the storm. He approached the perched wrangler.

"They are not changing like the others. Do you know if Lady Gretchen had real chickens and turkeys here?"

"The thing I know about Clan-Duins, Master Samuel, is that over time, if we maintain a specific totem, like a chicken or goat, or a dog even, we become them. We can't transform back. Our mind turns animalistic."

Irwin recalled Kipp mentioning something about that Clan-Duin trait. "So those chickens and turkeys were once Clan-Duins, but since they have been chickens and turkeys so long ...."

"Yup, they're no longer Clan-Duin."

From triumphant to heartbreak, Irwin's emotions were taking him on a ride. "How long does it take?"

"How long does what take?"

"To transform? To forget?"

"With each Clan-Duin, it's different, I imagine."

Irwin grumbled to himself. "Dang it, Kipp, please do not forget who you are before I find you." He removed himself from the last poultry pen and headed for the pig pens.

28

RUNAWAY PIGS

It was raining, but several of the most loyal Clan-Duins stepped out from beneath the cover of trees and followed Irwin. As he opened the next pen, several pigs came squealing through the exit. His hands touched pig's backs, and the animals went from running on four legs to pushing themselves up into two. Each one who was transformed was greeted by another Clan-Duin and ushered away. Some of the able-bodied Clan-Duins stepped in to help keep the animals contained, but pigs being pigs, they wiggled and bit and pushed their way around one another. Several by-passed Irwin's hands and raced for freedom.

Hoping they would be caught and brought back to him, he did not stop touching those who were right before him, transforming each one. Every pigpen held pigs that were more ravaging and violent than the last, and they pushed past the handlers. Many of the Clan-Duins who had pledged their lives to Irwin, along with two of the riding wranglers, tried to corral the runaways. It was a muddy chaos, with pigs squealing and racing away from their naked biped counterparts.

There were not enough Erthins to help make the weather cooperate. The storm was moving swiftly across the terrain. The wind pushed and the rain pummeled, but Irwin managed to touch every last one of the animals. It took all day to transform so many from penned animals back into semi-thoughtful Clan-Duins. But not all of them changed. Some had already accepted that they were a goat, or sheep, or pig. There was nothing Irwin could do to change them back. He was not a Telepath. He could not change thoughts.

It is hard enough trying to persuade them.

The weather continued to turn, and so did Irwin's hope of finding Kipp. There were still loose animals. But they were caught and roped or herded back to Irwin. He had to believe that his friend was on the property somewhere, eluding those on foot and on horseback. He hoped Kipp had not forgotten who he was. He tried not to fret that Kipp might have already accepted being a pig. How Lady

Gretchen had talked to Kipp had gotten the Clan-Duin motivated enough to change into one.

Irwin worked hard all day long. One woman found an old blanket to keep him warm and dry when the rain and wind picked up, but he shrugged it off. They offered water and food, but he turned it down. There was nothing for him now but the thought of Kipp. His emotional turmoil was ready to boil over.

When he ran, none of them could keep up. That was one of the downfalls with being kept in pens. None of those Clan-Duins had maintained endurance during their capture. They had lost muscle and gained fat—perfect for selling as meat in the markets at major ports of call. Only those on horseback could keep up with him.

Along the roadway, south of Lady Gretchen's property, seven goats had been roped and awaited Irwin's touch. He rushed to them and shed away more telepathic spells. Although none of the goats would be Kipp, that did not stop him from filling with anger and sadness. The telepathic spells he had been melting all day had wasted his energy. He was beyond tired. He was irritable. He hoped Kipp was still Kipp, but his doubts lingered and grew with the storm.

Another wrangler on horseback called to Irwin. He had spotted a few pigs heading south down the roadway. Those animals were just up ahead around a bend. From desperate to ecstatic, Irwin rolled with his emotions. His belly and his heart ached. He wanted nothing more than to have his only confidant back at his side. He wanted to be done with this emotional day and leave this nightmare of a farm far behind.

Clan-Duins on horseback drove the plump hogs back the way they had come. Irwin raced toward the pigs, but they scattered upon seeing him. Each animal went in different directions and away from those in pursuit. Finally, after more frantic running and roping of the agitated pigs, they were all caught.

Tired from running, and cold from the rain, Irwin went to each pig and placed his hand upon the animal's belly or backside. Each transformed back into their original body, revealing everyone but Kipp. It was not until he transformed the very last pig that Irwin faced the man he wept to see.

Naked, confused, and startled, Kipp came to and stood up.

Irwin was crying, and the rain was coming down just as hard. He embraced Kipp. "YOU ARE ALIVE! You are alive! Oh, I am so glad you are alive, Kipp. I am so sorry. I am so sorry about everything that happened back there." There was a spark of indescribable energy that happened between them.

The rain hacked at them, dousing them. Kipp looked around, gawking in confusion at the three other nude Clan-Duin men and the dressed wranglers on horseback. Those on horseback signaled the startled men on foot to follow them into the harsh and darkening landscape northward. They all appeared to have just awoken with foggy minds.

Kipp remembered nothing. "What happened?"

Irwin stepped back from Kipp, allowing his friend some personal space. He looked down at his own hands. They were gritty with dirt and animal dirt and dander. He used the falling rain to wash himself. He had touched many beings today, peeling off layers of telepathic spells that were many moon cycles old. He let the rain moisten his mouth. "We damn near died today. They were fixing to make you into food! And I-I was buried and left for Death!"

Kipp wiped his face. "What?" He rubbed his head. "How? All I remember is the smell of sourdough?"

Irwin's smile was filled with love. He stared at his best friend in a way he had seen Kipp stare at Yace. In a flash, he withdrew. He did not want Kipp to see this emotion. "Let me just say this: I am as guilty of gluttony as you. And our hostess was guilty of much more. Luckily, she is no longer with us."

"Dang me. I wish I could remember."

"Be glad you do not. What was done to us was horrific. If you do not recall it, that is good for you."

"Wasn't there a lady?"

"Yes. Lady Gretchen."

"Lady Gretchen?" His expression changed as he was remembering. "Ah, a young brunette woman with brown eyes; I didn't think she was telepathic. She appeared Clan-Duin. Her place reeked of feline pheromones, so I just guessed she was Clan-Duin."

"Young? She was an old woman with white hair." Irwin looked at Kipp in an attempt to confirm what he was coming to understand. "She must have had your mind from the beginning. But then I touched you. And then you touched her hands when she gave you the bowl. How devious. Lady Gretchen admitted to me that she was Dephen's cousin. Now, I am not fully sure of her lineage, but I am leaning toward Coterie. And a powerful one at that!"

But maybe she is related to Nonbry? What she did with her powers was ....

"You're usually cautious. How could you ...? I mean, how did it happen? How did this Lady Gretchen get—"

"I let my guard down. I let her get too close." He shrugged. "I did not think she was telepathic. She acted like a Clan-Duin, slightly coy, slightly aloof. And she seemed nice until she was not. There was no way for me to know! Not until it was too late." He would have a hard time forgetting everything that had happened.

The vacant look in Kipp's eyes while he was telepathically used would haunt him the most. That, and being poisoned by his best friend at Lady Gretchen's cue, disturbed Irwin to his core. And then there were Lady Gretchen's observations about his true feelings for Kipp—those words lingered in his mind too.

Irwin had never acknowledged how he really felt about Kipp—not until this crisis. And now he knew exactly how much he loved Kipp. He could not ignore these feelings toward his two-legged friend. He would do anything for his partner. The Clan-Duin made him feel safe and appreciated. And those were two feelings Irwin had yearned to feel long before meeting Kipp. Only when they were together did Irwin feel complete. Never in his life had he felt that way about anyone. And now he would have to work to keep those feelings contained.

"Actually, that Lady Gretchen reminded me of the Clan-Duin women in Uer' Bin Territory." Kipp was smiling, remembering. "Most of them have soft brown hair. And their eyes are every shade of brown, but usually dark ... sultry. She looked nice, you know, pleasant, fun to sit with and listen to. To tell ya the truth, I was jealous that she was flirting with you and not me."

"Let us walk, Kipp," he motioned for them to follow those on horseback. "You know how I am with strangers. I was cautious about her, but she caught me off-guard. She was being smart, sweet, and kind, and then she reached for a piece of that sourdough bread. When her hand touched mine, as if by accident, her powers surged through me. She immobilized me in that moment."

"You allowed her to get that close?"

"You were there! We were having some chicken soup. Do you not remember commenting about not eating chicken anything in a while, and how happy you were?" Irwin stared at Kipp as he shook his head. "What do you remember?"

"Sourdough bread. Smelling it; and the pretty lady."

"I should have kept my guard up." Irwin's shoulders slumped. "But how often have we met people on this road? The last house we saw was over thirty days ago. I would hate to think that everyone we meet will be ruefully evil."

"Nearly all the Talented people I've ever met have had personal intentions, Irwin. So, yeah, most of the time you should be suspicious."

"You know my intentions are always to keep you safe while helping you save Yace."

In that moment, Kipp's eyes glowed golden, "Good, 'cause that's what I want too!" He patted Irwin's back, and water splashed off his soaked tunic.

He gazed at Kipp, feeling lustful.

And to stay with you for as long as you will have me. Hopefully you will not cast me away like father did.

They walked quietly side by side, warm rain running down them. A smile of satisfaction drew across Irwin's face. He could hardly believe Kipp was really alive. He placed his arm across Kipp's shoulder. The naked Clan-Duin leaned in. "And now, because of all this crazy crap, Yace is at least a day and a half, if not two days, ahead of us."

Kipp stopped. "Are you fooling me? How's that possible?"

"We have been here for over a day."

One of the men on horseback approached and halted before them. "Is there anything else you wish of me, Master Samuel?"

"Thank you for the offer, but no. As long as I have touched all the animals, then my work here is done. Thank you for all your help. You have all fulfilled any obligation to me. You are free to go."

"Master Samuel? Touch animals? What are you talking about?" Kipp turned to Irwin, his mouth hanging open.

"You will see soon enough." They left the roadway and ventured up a rise, taking a short-cut back to Lady Gretchen's property.

It turned out that all who resided on Lady Gretchen's plot of land were hesitant to leave. This was the only place they knew. And if they remembered their lives before meeting her, it was now inconsequential. They were all stuck here against the edge of the world and surrounded by desert land. At least there was livestock to eat, and fresh water to drink. Even so, it was a desolate place to start anew.

Any Clan-Duin still on Lady Gretchen's property when the next ship arrived would be caught in a bind. The best situation for the remaining men, women, and children would be to join the desert Clans, head west for the rigid Kruluver slopes, follow the road south to Arenu Village, or set out north on the road and take the hard walk back to civilization.

As Irwin and Kipp crested a hillside, they saw numerous fires burning under the protection of the trees. An enormous camp of Clan-Duins, who had not run off, had gathered as if a tribe were forming. There were at least eight times as many men as there were women and children. Young and old were making friends, establishing clans, and finding order in the chaos they now shared. A few of the Clan-Duins took it upon themselves to make food from the spare animals. They did not care if it was cannibalism; they were all ravenous. Meat was cooking upon spits over fire pits. No one would go hungry tonight.

Irwin and Kipp stopped to take in the sight. Hundreds of naked Clan-Duins were sitting, walking, making conversation, tending fires, and roasting food. Kipp gasped, "Dang me! What happened here?"

Irwin chuckled light-heartedly. "I think I have made up for all those I killed ... and then some!" The sight of it all was mesmerizing. "It looks like I saved over a thousand Clan-Duins, Kipp."

Kipp's jaw dropped again as he took in the crowded hillside. There were well over a thousand Clan-Duin men, women, children, and teenagers—all different colors and sizes. They were mingling around the stone pens and along the distant creek. Campfires spotted the grounds, and the boisterous buzzing of conversations was vibrant. "This looks more like ten-hundred Clan-Duin's, Irwin. Dang me, I don't remember any of this."

"You would not. Well, you might. They were the animals you smelled, but we could not see them from the roadway. Like I said, Lady Gretchen turned you into one of them—a pig!"

Many of the men and women Irwin had freed rose from their seats. They began shouting and chanting, "Master Samuel!"

"Dang it, Irwin." Kipp leaned in toward Irwin's ear. "At least you didn't tell them your real name."

The rain had lightened. A moment of evening sunshine drew across the land. The mass of humble Clan-Duins chanted as Irwin and Kipp walked past. Other Clan-Duins moved toward him. It startled both men, seeing so many wanting to be around the Metalist. He understood the loyalty he had created, so he led the way into the horde of naked humans, toward the barn, the trees, and Lady Gretchen's bungalow.

Kipp was clearly impressed. "Wow! How?"

Hands reached out, wanting to touch Irwin.

Being shy all his life, and now having so much attention focused on him was almost as overwhelming as feeling all the metal in a city. He did not want to show his fear of the hundreds who stood before him and hoped his Metalistic scent masked his panic. He scanned the sea of mesmerized eyes. All these people basked in his presence, wanting a moment of his time. "Master Samuel!" They called out his name, trying to turn his attention away from Kipp.

He wanted Kipp to understand what had happened. "All of these people were under some sort of telepathic thought control initiated by Lady Gretchen. She had turned them all into goats and sheep, turkeys, chickens, and pigs. And she has been doing this for a while; long enough that she had ships she traded with on a regular basis."

Kipp stopped moving and took it all in. Irwin understood that he should be careful and patient with his friend.

"Do you recall those pigs we saw being funneled down the chute onto the boat? They were Clan-Duins. Those boats we saw rowing to the big ship, they transported probably a hundred head of livestock total. All those animals were normal Clan-Duins until Lady Gretchen used her telepathic powers to change them all for her benefit."

"How's that possible?"

"Sadly, not everyone I touched changed back. There are about three hundred Clan-Duins that now believe they are the animal they are. Most of those are chickens and turkeys. And those dogs over there believe they are dogs, too. Only two of them turned back. And the vultures ..." He pointed to the darkening night sky. "... have not yet landed, so I am not sure about them either."

"Dang me!" Kipp looked around in awe. "What did you say I was turned into?"

"You can probably smell it on you," Irwin said with a chuckle. "I know I can." He started walking again.

Kipp lifted his arms and took a whiff of his armpits. He was more than dirty. "I was a pig? But-but how's that possible? What kind of spell did she put me under?"

It became increasingly difficult for Irwin to describe what all happened. "She said you were a tri-tribe, a special type of Clan-Duin. I am not sure how else to explain it, Kipp, but she told you to become a pig. Over and over, she repeated the meanest of words to you, ordering you to become a pig. And then, just like that ..." He snapped his fingers. "... you mutated into a pig!"

Kipp laughed. He gasped, held his stomach, and wiped a tear from his eye. "What type of creature was she?"

"She confessed she was Dephen's cousin."

"Cousins?"

"Yes."

"That's gotta be one amazing spell. There's no way I could just morph into a pig because she said to."

Irwin was stone cold sober when he said, "The amazing part is that she said it while touching me! It did not seem that her spell was telepathically created, even though somehow it might have been." He paused in thought before exploding with exuberance. "But I am not fooling you, Kipp. You mutated into a pig! You turned before my eyes! I saw it happen. You were a pig. And she did not coat you with any tincture. All she did was speak to you, which makes me think it was telepathic. But how it all transpired, I am not sure because she was touching me." He paused again, watching Kipp try to comprehend what he was telling him. "It was the craziest thing I have ever witnessed."

The smile fell from Kipp's face. "That's not possible. My totem is canine. I can't change into anything but a canine."

Irwin threw up his hands. "Hey, I am just telling you what I saw. You might not believe it, but know it is true. All these Clan-Duins are just like you. That was how they became goats and pigs and sheep. Well, most of them were. There are some true Clan-Duin canines and raptors that were long ago tricked into believing they are vultures and dogs. And I am fairly sure all the wranglers are felines."

"That's not possible," Kipp muttered to himself as they found their way further into the horde of newly changed Clan-Duins. He looked at his hands, then at all the other dirty faces.

One of the females stepped up to Irwin. "What shall we do for you, Master Samuel?"

Another, who was standing next to Kipp, said to Irwin, "Yes, please tell us what to do."

"How may we serve you, Master Samuel?" another called out.

His name continued to echo on many lips. "Master Samuel."

Samuel Irwin Miner did not want any of these people to do anything for him. They had already done enough by helping him rescue Kipp. He turned away from his friend and climbed up onto the stone fence. He raised his hands, calling attention to himself, calling for silence. But once all the eyes were upon him, he was shy to be the focus of so many. He swallowed that fear. The sight of so many people who had suffered at the hands of Lady Gretchen disturbed him, yet thrilled him at the same time.

He shouted, "You are all free now! No one owns your lives but you. Go. Go now! This is your time to live; go and live. Live the best lives you can. I will tell you not to be here when the next ship arrives. I am sure there will be Telepaths on that boat. Those with blue eyes and blonde or white hair, you should avoid at all costs. If they see you, they will convert you all back into livestock. That is why I tell you all to leave! Head west, or north, or south, but leave now before the next ship arrives!"

An older man hollered, "We want to follow you, Master Samuel!" Many of his fellows agreed, hooting and howling.

"We want to serve you!" Several women cried out in unison.

Kipp came to Irwin's side. He put his hand on Irwin's pant leg. Irwin leaned down and listened to Kipp. "Clan-Duins prefer to have something or someone to follow, someone to serve. It's obvious these want to follow you, even if their instincts tell them to run. You saved them, Irwin, and now they're indebted to you."

Irwin could hardly believe that so many were so willing to be loyal—not yet knowing anything other than his kindness. He was obligated to do what was right for them. He did not want them to feel indebted to him. He wanted these men and women to take responsibility for their lives. What he really wanted was for them to not be so susceptible to telepathic influences—to survive for themselves and their loved ones and no one else.

Staring at so many people, all waiting for him to say something inspiring, made his stomach turn. He was on the verge of getting sick. He had to swallow his fear.

Calm down and breathe. I do not fear these people. I have compassion for them. I have given them another chance at life. This is their time. They need to seize it!

Innately, Irwin knew what to tell these loyal Clan-Duins—in part because of his childhood under Albert's cruel rule. He hoped they would heed his words. "I ask you all to make an agreement with yourself—today, here and now.

"You will be accountable for your own livelihood. Do not allow others to rule you." His words echoed under the high canopy. "Do not dedicate yourself to anyone but yourself and your loved ones. Do not follow me or any zealot. Follow your heart. Follow your dreams. You all have your own purpose on this plane of existence. Do not let anyone take that from you. You are your own creatures; you can do for yourselves regardless of your age or sex."

He wobbled for a second or two on the stone wall. The crowd was beginning to murmur.

"Remember, you have this one life! This is your life to live, not mine. Do not give your life up to anyone, including me. Live it for yourself and those you love. We are all equal, regardless of skin or skill. No one person is above another. And if someone says they have more power, remember you have power too." He held still, looking out at the sea of naked, dark-skinned bodies.

He could not help but think about his father. The truth he had just spoken were words he had yearned to hear his whole life. He wondered how his father was living without his help. Then he glanced down at Kipp who was watching the mass of Clan-Duins gaze up at Irwin in adoration.

I only care about Kipp now. My father is dead to me.

He looked back at the conglomeration of Clan-Duins and shouted as loud as he could, “You are all free beings! Now, go and be free!”

29

THE LINE BETWEEN LOVE AND HATE

Wasting no time, Irwin and Kipp retrieved their donkeys and horses, hitched them to the wagon, and left Lady Gretchen's behind without so much as a backward glance. They were out of that hellhole and had to make up for lost time ... to find Yace before she arrived in Arenu Village. But hopes of that were slim now. They drove and talked late into the rainy night.

"You know," Kipp said as they took off, "having a legion of Clan-Duins following you might be a good thing. I mean, if they're gonna be loyal to you, wouldn't it make sense to have their help? Think about it. We could have them find Yace for us."

"We do not need to bring others into our problems, Kipp."

"But they're loyal. You could use them as an arsenal. They could be the distraction this time. You wouldn't even have to use your powers. Think about it—a display of a thousand Clan-Duin men and women marching along with us. That show of loyalty just might intimidate the soldiers in Arenu Village."

"We do not want to invite more undue attention. Besides, a Telepath could use those Clan-Duins against us. They would tear you apart. And they would turn against me." Irwin shook his head at the thought of all of this. "No. Not after saving them from deaths unbefitting your people. If I had to kill them all after saving them ...." He drifted off. It was bad enough that Kipp was so easily influenced by Telepaths. And if the Clan-Duins followed, they could compromise their mission.

He changed the subject. "Maybe you could practice mutating into a bird."

"A bird?"

"I know you said your totem is canine. And I know you have mutated into different sizes of canine. What is to stop you from trying that with a bird—any type of bird, mind you?"

"I don't think you understand how this works, Irwin. I cannot mutate into anything other than a dog."

"But you were a pig not long ago!"

Kipp huffed. "I know how to change into a dog; it's easy. Maybe since a pig is close to a dog, in some ways, and maybe that's how Lady Gretchen had me change into a pig. Changing into a bird—that's just impossible."

"I do not think that the word 'impossible' works in this situation. Your Clan-Duin power can be more fluid than you think. Lady Gretchen said you were special." He wanted Kipp to at least try. But first he had to help him open his mind to the possibility. "How about this ... how do you become a wolf?"

"I just do it."

"Is there not a process? When I call for the metal—it is already calling for me. It sings. And each type of metal has its own tone. I can define what I want when it comes to pulling for it, such as how much and of what type. So, when I ask for the metal, it has already accepted me. It wants me to be its new host before I even take it as mine. It is a magnetic type of attraction, but more intense. And when my body summons it, the metal knows to turn liquid. There is never hesitation for the metal, even if it is embedded deep within a rock or wall. It flows into me like water."

"I just become a wolf. I think 'be wolf' and it's done."

"Is it that simple?"

"Yeah. When I was younger, when I first started understanding the transformation, it hurt. But that was because I had to let go of my two-legged form. Now it's easy. I enjoy being a canine, so becoming one is easy."

Night had fallen, but Irwin had lit the lantern that swung from a hook on the front of the wagon. The rain had lightened up, and the clouds in the distance parted. A beam of moonlight cast its light on the edge of the land and the rough ocean surf beyond. The wagon hardly rattled as it rolled on into the moist night. Only when it hit a hard rock did it make a sound. All the modifications Irwin had made on the bare-bones wagon made it homey inside and smooth sailing along the endless road.

"Did you ever want to become another animal?"

"No." There was a long silent pause between them before Kipp spoke again. "Although I was jealous when I found that there were Clan-Duins who could mutate into birds. The only types of Clan-Duins who lived with the Gypsy were canines and felines until we rescued Alio, Olei, Leola, and Koloto. They can mutate into anything, and I mean anything!

"I thought that would be a fun totem to have—being a bird ... able to soar in the sky." He sighed and stared off toward the moon. "Flying hundreds of kilometers in a day or two instead of walking or riding that same span in a moon's time is fun to imagine."

"So Olei and Alio never told you that you could cross-mutate?"

"No."

"Huh. I have seen dozens of different types of birds, but only a few types of dogs," Irwin said. "You could have more advantages being a raptor Clan-Duin."

"I've always liked owls." Kipp jiggled the draw reins, keeping the horses on the road.

Irwin was tired—exhausted. "Maybe you should try that when we stop."

"I don't wanna stop. If we stop ...." Kipp's jaw muscles flexed.

"Most likely Dephen and his goons will arrive in Arenu Village by tomorrow. There is no way we can go that far in so little time. We must accept the fact that we will not catch her out here. Unless you can turn into a bird and—"

Kipp glared at Irwin. "I can't stop Yace. Last time I tried to stop Yace, Dephen used her power against me. You and I both know you're the one that saves her. And you can do it without my help."

"Last time I tried without you, you attacked me."

"Well, you should've told me what you were gonna do!"

The tensions rose, and they fell silent.

After a while, Irwin muttered, "I cannot fly."

"Neither can I!"

"Kipp, I know what I saw you do. I know you have amazing abilities. I have seen you change. I believe in you. Not only can you become a dog, but you became a pig. You can become an owl, or deer, or even a squirrel. You can change into anything you want!"

Kipp sneered.

"If you tried to mutate, if you did change into a bird, you could fly ahead and survey the land. You could locate the carriage. You could go and watch Yace. Practice that quiet mind stuff, and just watch her. She does not know that you can turn into a bird. Not yet."

"If Lady Gretchen knew, then Dephen knows. You said it yourself—she was a powerful woman. By the way, how did you get rid of her?"

Irwin blushed and smiled and looked away. "Lady Gretchen's mistake was not making sure I was completely dead. Like I said, I was buried alive. When I came to, I dug myself out of the grave. Then I caused enough of a distraction that when it came to dealing with her, it was easy." Irwin was not too sure he wanted to go into the gory details.

"Oh! What'd you do? Slit her throat?"

"No; death by metallic twister."

Kipp cackled, "You're devious! So, did she make you think you were dead or something?"

"No. She poisoned me with arsenic."

"Dang! That's devious."

"It is straight up evil." Irwin took in a few deep, calming breaths.

"Are you gonna be alright?"

He would not admit how he was poisoned, even though the thought of it boiled his blood. "Yes, I am alright. Although Lady Gretchen did confess much while I was writhing in pain after being poisoned, and after she changed you into a pig. She spoke of the PCP. She admitted that they know about me, but only after exposing myself in Ahradah."

Kipp sniggered.

"Quiet you! I know what I should and should not have done in that situation. But she said nothing about Onj Raha, which might be good. Although she confessed the PCP has known about my family for fifty years."

"Fifty years? That's creepy!"

"Yes. But what is really creepy is that Telepaths talk, even from long distances."

"I've been trying to tell you that."

"You said they were not very organized."

"On the other side of the mountains they are."

"Yace told me the same. I just did not understand to what extent. But it is unnerving to know they have known about my family for so long. Why do they care?"

"Dang it, I don't know. Maybe it's all part of Hakra's plan." Kipp rolled his eyes. "What do you think will happen when Yace arrives in Arenu Village?"

"Hopefully she will not be whoring in a saloon like Dana mentioned."

A grimace was plastered on Kipp's face. "I remember Nonbry mentioning powerful Telepaths living there. Maybe they'll see Dephen inside Yace. Maybe they'll save her!"

Irwin shrugged. "That would be nice if it happened. If you changed into a bird, maybe you could go off and find out."

"I can't do that!"

Irwin huffed and waited until their angst calmed before speaking again. "What I am sure of is this, Kipp: the PCP knows we are coming. They are awaiting our arrival in Arenu Village. They might think the carriage is us. Hopefully they will stop it. Maybe even question those soldiers. I do not know what the future holds for Yace's carriage, or Yace and Dephen. I am not too sure about our future either. But I am sure they will stop us in Arenu Village when we do arrive. We will ask to continue on, but they might not allow that. Until then, everything is speculative. At least we are still alive." He glanced over at Kipp.

The wagon rolled on.

Finally, Irwin said, "You know, I have not seen any roads westward. I think we should look for one, just in case. We need to know if that carriage takes a detour. A lot can happen between here and Arenu Village. Yace and Dephen are probably happy to have so many kilometers between us. At this point, our time at Lady Gretchen's house is just a rough hiccough on this journey of ours. We should use this time to prepare for the inevitable."

"What future do you see happening? What do you think's inevitable?"

Irwin stared forward. "Well, there are several outcomes I can imagine. But they are all speculative. Hopefully I will not have to use my powers. Had I known back then what I know now ...." He trailed off.

I would have tried harder.

Irwin was having doubts about all his choices—the decisions he had made and would be making. He started to think about his hectic life—all that had brought him here on this road with this Clan-Duin who meant so much to him.

Living in a mine was never this challenging.

Compared to his life now, Irwin was almost willing to hear Albert's negativity over the unknown future in store for them. "We can hope that they will allow us to purchase rations, see an Oracle, and continue on."

"And if they don't?" Irwin said nothing.

They rolled on a while longer and then Kipp said, "You said Lady Gretchen and Dephen were cousins. Did Lady Gretchen say anything else about Dephen? Or Yace?"

Irwin was quiet for a time. "Yes."

"And?"

"She said that the carriage had stopped yesterday morning, arriving about the same time as the ship. They stayed long enough to water their horses and trade for some food. Which might be true. But the bed was made up like a settee, and there were three chairs at the table. All that, and the prepared food. Chicken soup takes time to cook, as does making and baking sourdough bread. She had a medium-sized cauldron of soup, enough to feed a dozen people."

Yace, her six goons, us, and Lady Gretchen, makes ten.

"She did not seem like the type who would go to such great lengths to feed just a captain and maybe a few shipmates. That ship came for one purpose. They came to purchase livestock, not engage in lengthy conversations. So why would she have gone to all that trouble, if not to entertain Dephen and his men?"

"You remember all that?"

"Even though I was frozen by her power, my senses still worked. I had time to take in her homely features. That was how I was able to kill her."

"Do you think Lady Gretchen could be related to Nonbry too?"

"Perhaps. It might be something we ask him when we are in Arenu Village, when we find an Oracle."

"I think it's a bad idea to probe into Nonbry's life. He'll be heated enough when he finds out we're in Arenu Village—and without Yace. Who's saying that he wouldn't use the Oracle against us?" He looked at Irwin. "I fear that man's wrath."

Irwin smiled and put his hand on Kipp's shoulder. "You have nothing to worry about. You have me. He cannot harm you while I am around."

Kipp was palpably nervous about Arenu Village. "What happens if you're taken away? You know, for crimes committed!"

"Let us suspect that I will. You will not let me forget what I did to the Hall of PCP in Onj Raha, and if the Telepaths invade your mind .... And if they find out about that ...." He heaved a deep sigh. "If I am taken away, then you will have to find Yace without me. Maybe it is good that we are going to Arenu Village. Nonbry hinted that they have Telepaths who would be able to see what Dephen is doing to Yace. We need to use that place and those people to our advantage." He felt Kipp squirming. The Clan-Duin plainly did not want to arrive in Arenu Village.

"Remember, the PCP wants to know about me, not you. They used Telepathy to spread word about me, not you. I suspect many already know what I have the capacity to do, especially after what the soldiers saw of me in Ahradah." He paused to scratch his itchy head. "But you, Kipp! You are immune to them. You could even say I have been controlling you through fear and intimidation. Use me as a scapegoat if you must." He was trying to give Kipp ideas on how to spin their predicament. "Maybe Dephen is a friend of mine who took her mind. I mean, Yace and Dephen think you are aloof, and yes you play it up sometimes. But he would never suspect you to ask for help in Arenu Village."

"I'm not gonna ask for help from any Telepath in Arenu Village."

"Why not? Nonbry said—"

"It doesn't work that way, Irwin."

"It works the way we make it work."

"You and your wild imagination."

Irwin chuckled at himself and stared off into the distance. "Lady Gretchen was quite smug to have found me before the PCP got hold of us," he sighed and continued to think out loud. "Though, she made it sound like they are looking forward to our arrival. She also made it sound like she was going to make it appear as if we never arrived at her hovel. That way, she would not have been accountable for her actions."

He looked at Kipp to see if he was taking this all in.

"Lady Gretchen was a woman with many secrets. But if she is family with Dephen, they would have talked about us. They probably devised how to kill us! Who knows what all was said? They are Telepaths. For all we know, they were talking and scheming long before their carriage arrived—before we arrived. It is even possible that Dephen already knows I killed Lady Gretchen. It was spooky how much she knew about me, about us. She used our weaknesses to her advantage. Dephen has exploited us several times now. I can guarantee it will happen again, and most likely it will happen in Arenu Village. Do you remember Nonbry saying that Dana saw Yace as a whore who is working in Arenu Village? That could still happen. Dephen is a master manipulator. He can do whatever he wants, whatever suits his schemes."

Irwin stared off at the looming horizon. "The power Dephen has within Yace's body is unimaginable. To be an all-powerful Coterie—they possess all the powers, including mine. Yace and Nonbry have told us how powerful Coterie can be. And those powers of hers will grow stronger."

Silence again. To their left, the moon's light reflected amidst the choppy ocean swells.

"I can only speculate." He wagged his head and tried to figure out what to do next. "But I am certain Dephen is planning on using Yace's body for his own debauchery. He already has in Radia and Ahradah." Irwin's thoughts kept on churning.

After a while, he said, "I hope that the PCP in Arenu Village can see what is happening inside Yace before we get there. I hope they will see Dephen for what he is and what he is doing to her. Maybe they will free her before we get there.

"I know you do not want to go to Arenu Village," Irwin said in an attempt to put Kipp at ease. "Neither do I! But if the carriage has persisted southward, they will reach Arenu Village long before we do. Let us hope Dephen will stop, take another reprieve for a day or two. And they will have to refill their rations before they journey on to Daos."

Kipp said nothing.

"You know, I can almost see Lady Gretchen talking to Dephen. They probably talked all the way up until her death. I can even see her telling him that I was killing her. And if that is the case, Dephen might already know where we are and that we are coming." Irwin glanced at Kipp again. "I hope you are practicing that mindlessness."

Kipp gazed at the dark and slick roadway ahead. "I'm not thinking anything."

"If they know we are coming, they might not stay idle. Another reason to keep quiet and not stop." Irwin adjusted his footing, re-situated himself on the wagon seat.

"I'm glad I'm on your side," said Kipp, glancing sideways at Irwin. "What if Dephen manages to talk to a PCP officer first? What if he tells the PCP more about us, more about you? What if he tells them you killed Lady Gretchen?"

"Why would he? Dephen will play it safe. He would not speak to anyone who can see through the mask he is hiding behind."

Kipp snorted. "Playing it safe would be not going into Arenu Village at all."

Those words triggered a memory for Irwin. He looked over his shoulder to the north. He recalled the large ocean-voyaging vessel sitting beyond the bay at the edge of Lady Gretchen's place. The ship had been pointed southward, waiting for the smaller ferry boats to return with more livestock. Those small boats had been filled to capacity with Clan-Duin meat. There had been five people rowing toward the ship in each boat. Except for that last boat of pigs, there were eight people on that boat. Irwin had taken careful note of their movements and the numbers. He had, over the course of this journey, come to understand the value of observation, of memory, and the importance of both.

Eight, why would there be eight? I would hate to think that was Dephen 'playing it safe'.

Irwin stretched his arms and yawned several times. The wagon rattled on; then it hit several large rocks.

"Hey, Irwin, why don't you go lay down? You've done a lot today. You saved hundreds of lives, including mine."

"Yes." Irwin yawned again. "I do need to lie down, but only for a little while." His whole body was tired to the bone. The wagon did not slow when he stood to step over the bench.

"Hey," Kipp grabbed Irwin's forearm, "Thank you for saving me. I owe you more than my life." His eyes glowed golden again, and an earnest smile lifted his lips.

"It is what a friend does."

30

Arenu Village

A sort of awkwardness had developed between them. Irwin could not help but look at Kipp with adoration from time to time. He often found himself comparing his own pasty-gray flesh to Kipp's soft, warm, brown skin, sometimes wanting to caress it—to hold it. He loved how it glowed golden in the midday sun, like the beaches where they had swum along the way. The darker shaded creases in Kipp's skin were black caverns that he wanted to explore. But then he felt embarrassed by his own thoughts. He would never act on any of these impulses. And when the Clan-Duin caught him staring a few times, he asked Irwin why. Irwin held back his true reason, kept his responses vague. Kipp did not need to know Irwin's true feelings. Irwin knew where Kipp's heart lay. He loved Yace, and they were trying to save her. They had a mission. Lust and love would only get in the way.

The two men had run the gambit of emotions during their time apart from Yace. For many moons now, they had been living on adrenaline and fear. Though their time together had sharpened their skills and Talents, it also had revealed the holes in their relationship. During these last few days, heading toward Arenu Village, they started to argue again.

While they did not disagree often, when they did it was tempestuous.

Irwin was not even sure they were following Yace anymore. He had made a mental note about the horses' hoofprints before reaching Lady Gretchen's, and then again after fleeing. But things had changed. There appeared to be more horse tracks on the roadway. He was positive that some of the horses they were following were not being ridden anymore—they were being pulled. Their tracks swerved back and forth atop the wheel marks. And the carriage ruts appeared lighter; probably because of a lack of rations and the extra weight they had left behind at Lady Gretchen's. Irwin's hunch was simple: Yace and two of her soldiers took passage onboard the ship they had been harbored in the bay at Lady Gretchen's.

Kipp did not support Irwin's belief. For when they found the first days' old camp, Yace's scent still lingered. Kipp found her excrement near a tree. So he discouraged Irwin's opinions. He argued again that Yace would never sail on a ship. He clearly held onto the hope that Yace and Dephen would be stopped in Arenu Village—that Dephen would slip up—as Irwin had suggested earlier, and that Yace would become free through their help or on her own. He also hoped, Irwin knew, that one of the Telepaths in Arenu Village would see Dephen's grip upon her mind and take action.

Irwin felt deep frustration; he was sure none of that would happen. Dephen was too smart for any of those maneuvers or outcomes.

Because of their disagreements, their desire and their quest to reach Arenu Village turned into a love-hate situation. Kipp was headstrong about saving Yace. He was willing to do anything at this point, including racing the horses until their legs were nearly broken from overuse. Kipp would not try Irwin's suggestion to mutate into a bird, any bird! And though Irwin implored him to practice morphing his body; the Clan-Duin seemed to lack the motivation to try. He was so focused on Yace that imagining a large bird, other than a chicken, was apparently impossible.

This frazzled Irwin to the core.

And Kipp's ideas about how they should appear when arriving in Arenu Village grew increasingly outlandish. He had boldly suggested they drive into the village, with Irwin showing off his power. "That would intimidate everyone," Kipp crowed one afternoon.

Irwin hated being judged by his white skin, hated being recognized as anything other than Mortal. He could be as volatile as any other, but it wasn't in his nature to be so bold.

Kipp's excitement grew. "If we go in with a show, and Yace is still there, she would be drawn to the spectacle." Kipp suggested over and over that the wagon should be completely coated in metal, and Irwin too. And, if it was true what Arenu Village knew about Irwin, Kipp believed Irwin should reveal right upfront just how destructive he could be.

He could not.

I cannot be anything other than myself. If they want to judge me on how I look and not who I am, there is nothing else I can do. I refuse to be like my father.

He knew to remain rational with his ideas and thoughts. A million things could go wrong if he wasn't. He also knew that they would be watched intently, especially because of what the PCP knew about him. Every interaction in Arenu

Village needed to be as transparent as possible. He did not want to show off. No one needed to know what he was or what he could do. They would surely be judged by everyone with whom they interacted, no matter what happened inside the village walls.

Although it was considered a hostile place, Irwin understood that Arenu Village was exclusively for people with powers. It was one of the few places where those with Talents were allowed to be who they were. Everyone there looked down on Mortals. The Talented people who lived in Arenu Village valued one another to some extent. They had to, to ensure their very existence. This is what he had learned through the teachings Kipp had shared, and what he surmised.

He learned from Alio's stories that knowledge was key in the world of those with Talents. The more you know about others with powers, the more you respect them. Irwin figured that as long as he showed kindness to the people in Arenu Village, they would be kind in return. He also believed that every set of eyes would be watching him. He could not risk a misstep.

Those in Arenu Village would be attempting to telepathically probe Kipp's mind, too. Irwin figured those Telepaths would try to learn all they could about him from the Clan-Duin. And Kipp knew him very well. His link to Kipp would give those Telepaths more insight about his Metalist talents than they already knew, and this made Irwin want to plan for all things unforeseen. For now, their only plan was still to save Yace.

Yet Irwin was working on contingency plans. Since he did not believe that Yace would be in Arenu Village, there had to be other options. One plan was to keep the attention on himself. If everyone was watching him, no one would notice Kipp. The Clan-Duin could be like any other Clan-Duin and could just slip away from Arenu Village and continue on without him. That was a decent plan, but it needed more development.

He was used to being the focus of attention; in his youth, it was usually negative attention. Irwin's grandfather and father had taught him how to read and redirect people's perspectives. They had been cruel, sometimes unrelenting, in their mind games or sideways questioning. They would say one thing, or have one look, that would make him jump and do things automatically.

Am I nitpicking my childhood again? No, but I will use that same cunning and inventive style when dealing with the inhabitants of Arenu Village.

Although Kipp was willing to place some faith in the Telepaths there, Irwin did not trust them. After meeting and dealing with Lady Gretchen—hearing her rant—he knew more than ever to be extremely cautious.

It seems they know enough about me and my family. And if Yace is not in Arenu Village, we will need to contact Nonbry. I would like to believe, to hope, that there are powerful Telepaths, like Nonbry hinted, powerful enough to see Dephen. But what if they do not? What will we do then? Breathe. Keep calm.

He had learned how susceptible anyone could be to telepathic attacks. Even he had been taken.

I cannot allow that to happen again. No one is allowed to touch me. What about Kipp? He is taken so quickly each time. He needs to practice. But I cannot trust that he can keep himself safe from them. I despise Telepaths who want nothing but to control.

What is their motivation anyway? Why do they care to use and abuse? Are people of Urthis really so slow that they need telepathic guidance? Or maybe Telepaths are scared? Ha! Scared of having no control, maybe. Is that not how life works? It is either be in control or be controlled ... says the Metalist who has lost control.

He wanted to believe that there were other ways besides being a Metalist to keep the Telepaths at bay. Even though Kipp touted Alio's lessons about clearing his mind of thought, Irwin felt reticent about that tactic. He did not believe Clan-Duins could go on in a meditative-like state without thinking anything. They were animalistic and acted on their innate primary urges much of the time. At least that was what he had seen with Kipp.

He would never admit it to Kipp, but right now he felt as though he was in-over-his-head. And once they arrived in Arenu Village, around so many people—feeling all the Erthins and metals again—that would drive all that home.

Why could I have not just stayed in the mountains? Did I really need all this adventure? All I wanted was warmer weather and flat land. I am in over my head.

He had to calm his inner anxieties before they could see the village on the horizon.

I hope Arenu Village is just a village. Do not worry about the future until whatever happens, happens, it will always be uncertain. Dang it all, I hate life sometimes.

⋺⋲ ⋺⋲

On the third morning after leaving Lady Gretchen's nightmare, Irwin challenged Kipp's idea of keeping the wagon coated in metal. Though using the metal to reflect the day's heat was a clever idea, today he took it down, removed the coating. He used most of that metal to make a large lockbox—the length of the wagon, half the width, and it took the place of their makeshift bed. Topped with a layer of blankets and furs, the lockbox would appear to be their bed. And because it would be hidden, they could stash all their personal belongings in there while away from the wagon. He hoped the large box would be too heavy for any one person to remove, hoped no one could or would levitate it.

He knew not to display anything of value. Nor did he want to show off any form of his power. Lady Gretchen had done Irwin a favor by ranting on and on about having captured him. Even though he had been writhing in pain, he heard her. He recalled how smug she had been to have captured him out from under the PCP. All she had confessed after poisoning him was now a secret card up Irwin's sleeve.

Fog lingered along the edge of the coastline that morning. It was slow to break, but then it became a new bright and balmy day. The road followed the gentle contours close to the coastline, and they bumped along as always. The winds weren't as swift as they had been in previous days—a pleasant reprieve for their ears and windblown faces. Occasionally, there were large stubs of green grass tall enough for a horse to sway its head and take a bite. After being out in the harsh rusty-brown landscape, the sight of vibrant green grass was soulful comfort for now.

Soon they turned a lean corner and were heading true south. Now the roadway was better maintained, with less gravel and ruts to make it bump so much. The horses jogged at a good pace. They weren't too hot yet, but soon the temperature would rise. Far off in the approaching distance, a red tower pierced the blue sky like a phallic gesture—probably a lighthouse and a crow's nest for Arenu Village. From the fortress and on to the west, dark leafed trees lined the riverside.

"This is it," he said with a deep exhale.

Now the grasses grew thicker along the sides of the road. Far off groves of symmetrically planted fruit trees spread to the west. "There are Erthins at work here," Kipp muttered.

Irwin noticed Kipp becoming ever more uncomfortable as they surveyed the green landscape ahead. He put his hand on Kipp's arm. "Take a deep breath. Calm down. We are doing this for Yace. Nothing bad will happen to us. We will be safe. If you can think either nothing, or positive thoughts, that would be best." Irwin smiled at his partner—the same dopey smile the Clan-Duin had for the ladies. He erased that look from his face and stoically stared ahead.

"We're doing this for Yace," the Clan-Duin said. "We're doing this for Yace."

They rolled through a basin area—tailor made to suit the residents of Arenu Village. The landscape was perfect for growing food and raising animals. Toward the mountains to the west, the grass grew thick up to and around the long edge of a vast orchard of apples, pears, cherries and other fruits he could smell but not yet name. There were some grasses growing on the east side of the road too, but not as luscious as the west side. On the east side, through the sporadic sprigs of grass, there were foot trails that led through the sandy bluffs to the beaches below.

As they neared Arenu Village, the rocky fencing emerged once more, lining the roadway on both sides and creating a tight channel straight into Arenu Village. This road was clean of sprigs of grass. Nothing grew between cobbles. Not a rock or a bump hit their wagon wheels. There were no crossing avenues—no way to turn around. They had entered the point of no return.

Beyond the fencing, to the east, were half a dozen pregnant and nursing horses. There were also several dozen milking goats, with a horde of kids following along. Colts and fillies frolicked with goat kids. The animals were excited to see the approaching wagon, the horses, and the donkeys. Mares nickered at the geldings that pulled the wagon, and they called back. All of those curious animals followed their slowly moving vehicle alongside the rock wall. They were the first to greet the newcomers. Off to the west, dozens of cows and more goats grazed, but only a few lifted their heads. Too busy foraging, they did not come running.

Huge stone walls encompassed the fortress that was Arenu Village. All the buildings, except for the red tower, loomed stark gray and with no visible openings. This place was an omnipotent stronghold, dark and wary. A skywalk encircled the larger fortress wall. Suited men watched everything going on outside and inside the village. Not one window, balcony, door, or any other opening to the outside world could be seen along the tall, flat exterior facades. There was only one entrance, the one they were driving toward. Even the stone fences were without gates and flowed flawlessly into the heavy fortress walls.

Half a dozen golden eagles leered down at them from their high perches on the closest rooftop—massive sentries for Arenu Village. They were watching the two-horse-drawn wagon, the two young men, and the two donkeys being pulled down the channel of stone walls.

The looming rectangular fortress that was Arenu Village straddled a swift-flowing river and had a sizeable stable yard. Enormous walls ran east-west at least a thousand feet, and then north-south for about four hundred feet. Rocky bluffs along the eastern side hid the small harbor. Irwin would come to know that was the only other access point into the village besides a small entrance on the west side of the stable yard leading to the gardens. It was impressive to see that every inch of Arenu Village was created and maintained by Erthin power. This was clear to Irwin.

Kipp pulled on the reins, slowing their approach to the fortress. Cautious, they headed toward a dark tunnel that mysteriously opened as they drew near. Kipp white knuckled the reins and kissed at the horses to carry on into the dark passageway. Blacky and Roper timidly passed the threshold and clip clopped on through the building and then exited the corridor leading into a massive courtyard square.

Without warning, the stone wall closed behind them. The passage they had driven through ceased to exist. Now they were inside a stable yard of sorts.

Irwin saw three stories of living quarters above the stables—hundreds of rooms with a view of the busy storage yard. People wrapped in sarongs rushed here and there. The second, third, and fourth-story windows mirrored one another across all sides of the barnyard square. Their only uniqueness was their colorful curtains. On the ground level, long and short wooden doors were sporadically placed on each structure around the square. Open and enclosed stalls were separated by storage rooms, stairwells, and dark corridors. Every surface looked as if it had been chiseled from one solid piece of stone. Irwin and Kipp were both spellbound.

The ground they drove across was one long solid and impervious piece of stone—no doubt angled for rainwater drainage toward the closed opening they had just driven through. That stone curved up, forming uniform walls. Unlike the fortress's bland exterior, the anterior façade of the square exhibited a unique artistic flair. Mosaics mottled across the square's façade, from the second floor on up, highlighted openings and open spaces along the courtyard facing walls.

They saw glimpses of villagers working outside in the gardens and fields that lay further west and along the river's edge through a portal on the west side of the stable yard. It was obvious that crops flourished in this type of climate. There was no lack of produce, or work, for the residents of Arenu Village. Kipp looked at Irwin, probably wondering what to do. No one approached. A few people studied the wagon as it inched along. With the wall sealed behind them, there were only two other visible doorways. One led farther into the stronghold, the other headed west and did not appear tall enough for their covered wagon to get through. The stable yard was clean and barren except for two flatbed wagons and another longer wagon with tall wooden sides parked along the larger fortress wall.

"I don't see the carriage." Kipp circled the wagon around.

"Do not worry about it. Drive forward to those soldiers over there." Irwin pulled on the left rein as he ordered and pointed. He did not want them to appear hesitant.

The stone wall encapsulating the main part of Arenu Village loomed as high as sixty feet. At the southwest side of the fortress, the red stone tower stood strikingly tall. It protruded nearly three hundred feet into the sky, as if wanting to play with the sun. This wall of the mighty fortress was barren of openings along the ground floor. They gazed up at mosaics along the upper floors. The windows along those floors mirrored each other all the way around the stable yard wall. Most were bare of curtains, though a few had tapestries hoisted into place—probably to block out sunlight and prying eyes.

Not yet midday, it was already sweltering inside these dark stone walls where there was no breeze. The men they approached were muscular and looked to be cool and comfortable in their indigo sarongs. Their muscular dark-skinned bodies exhibited Clan-Duin traits, hairy arms and chests crowned in heavy black hair. Their brilliant green eyes focused on Irwin and Kipp as they drew near. Irwin made a mental note that the close-cut red hair spoke of Erthin powers. He expected that they would use their metamorphic abilities to intimidate any who approached.

They seemed to grow taller as the wagon rolled closer. They snorted at one another and turned to engage the newcomers. The older of the two stepped forward and held up his hand to stop the wagon. "Ten gold pieces," he said, and glanced back at his stout companion. "And your wagon will be parked here. Your horses and donkeys go in the stables over there." He pointed to each location.

"Twenty gold pieces and my wagon and animals will park in the village," Irwin said. "And we will clean up their excrement."

Kipp jabbed Irwin's rib with his elbow and gave him a look, suggesting they should not make such demands. But the soldiers were mulling over the offer.

They grunted at one another. "We'll let you pass for twenty-four gold pieces."

Irwin reached behind his seat for a pouch containing three gold pieces. He put his hand into the small satchel and created another twenty-one golden coins while studying the soldiers. He felt Kipp stiffen.

The first soldier chuckled as he walked up to the side of the wagon. "You play cards?" he asked with his hand out. Irwin handed over the pouch. "I wanna win more of your money!"

"I am not very good at cards. Indeed, you would win my money. Maybe I will play later. Then you can take all my money." Irwin grinned widely. "Is there a saloon inside?"

"Oh, yeah! Only da best saloon!"

"Excellent," Irwin said, and the soldier stepped aside. "See you later."

"What a stupid cuss!"

The soldier pointed at Irwin as the wagon began moving again. They looked inside the satchel. Irwin saw them split the satchel of gold coins and heard them chortling.

Kipp said, "Yeah, I'm starting to think you are a little stupid—"

"Kipp," Irwin squeezed his friend's forearm, "it is only metal."

Besides, I now have a beacon on those two.

31

EYES EVERYWHERE

They rolled past the soldiers and up through another dark corridor. There was a slight incline in the road as it spilled into the heart of Arenu Village. Beyond the shadowy passageway, there was a large stone courtyard abounding with extraordinary stonework and mosaics of various styles. Red, brown, and black stones marked the roadway heading due south and east toward the harbor. Walkways to storefront entrances, and the large open cobbled space between was filled with ornate rings. Checkerboard squares were lined with perfectly cut blue and white stones. The storefronts and windows and all along the upper walls of this interior fortress, seashells and translucent rocks and jewels, had been embedded across the uniform structures and shimmered in the sunlight. Aquatic mosaics of colorful fish appeared to float amongst different sizes and shapes of coral.

Arenu Village had been grandiosely enhanced by Erthin genius. How many years, how many minds, he wondered, did it take to create such vivid visual splendor?

They finally came to a place called the Gritty Titty Saloon—the only section projecting from the continuous flat exterior walls. Directly across from the ramp that sloped up and into the Saloon, Irwin noticed a southern-bound tunnel. He could see that the far end of that tunnel was closed off—not with a gate, but by a solid stone wall. Was that the only drivable exit south into the Jungle of Datzar?

Indeed, they were sealed inside Arenu Village.

There's no way out of here!

He looked at Kipp to see if he, too, noticed this. Not yet.

There was a forge near the center of the long courtyard, the only solitary building. Clan-Duin and Erthin men were working with hot metals inside the forge, and the hard twangs drilled into Irwin.

At this point, he wasn't sure which was worse, the metallic chorus or the fact that they were trapped. His brain swirled and his heart pounded.

Kipp put his free hand on Irwin's wrist. "Are you gonna be alright?"

Irwin took a deep breath and opened his now silvery eyes. "Yes."

Irwin let his eyes adjust, and then he shifted his focus upward to the metal-tipped arrows in the soldiers' quivers six stories above. He peered up at the soldiers as they walked along a catwalk high above.

Throngs and assortments of the Talented milled about. He felt their metal bore into him and felt his eyes turn an even deeper silver—even felt those down by the wharf. There was a constant buzz of banging metal and people talking and laughing.

"I will not go Onj Raha here Kipp, I promise."

"I trust you." Kipp looked here and there and around the long square. "But I don't see the carriage. Irwin, where's Yace's carriage?"

Where is that carriage? We calculated their arrival to be maybe a day and a half ago. What the shit! They were probably allowed to go on. What are we going to do? Keep our focus. Do not deviate from the plan. Breathe! But we are trapped. We are trapped!

"Let us not worry about the carriage. We need to keep our focus. We need to stay safe, or we'll never rescue her."

"But where is it?!"

A young telepathic man with long, sun-bleached hair approached. "We're glad to see you've arrived," he said.

Hearing those words sent a shiver down Irwin's spine. He tried to shrug off what he knew to be true—that the Telepaths knew their every move, knew they were here in search of Dephen and Yace. "Glad to see you too," he said. "Say, is this an acceptable place to park our wagon? The men at the gate said we could drive in, but said nothing about where we could—"

"Yes, we saw that exchange." The Telepath smiled, but there was spite in his eyes. "Welcome to Arenu Village. This is a special place for those with Talents." His lips twisted with annoyance. "There are rules here—but they're different from other places. We follow only two of Hakra's rules." He stared at Irwin, and he looked as if he wanted to say more but did not.

Kipp's voice wavered and cracked. "I'm fairly sure he hasn't killed any Mortals." The Clan-Duin's hand found Irwin's knee.

The Telepath raised a sculpted eyebrow. "What about killing people of Talent?"

"That was an accident," Kipp said, studying the Telepath. He squeezed Irwin's knee. "Besides, there is nothing against murdering soldiers. Hakra doesn't condone killing those of us who are considered Volatile. In fact, he promotes torture, maiming, and mutilation if they're considered miscreants."

Irwin said nothing. The horrifying truth sinking in.

Using his own innate magnetic power, Irwin rendered the Telepath momentarily powerless—unable to see into Kipp's mind.

The Telepath loosened his tone. "Make yourselves at home. There are many places to visit here. The shops, barber, the wharf's markets, bathing facilities, laundry services, and the Saloon are all available to you. Everything you'll ever need is here in Arenu Village." He pointed around the square. "But be mindful. You'll be watched."

Irwin tried not to add cynicism to his words, "Thank you for the welcoming."

"Clan-Duin," The Telepath was trying to peer into Kipp's eyes, trying to read his mind.

Kipp kept his hand on Irwin's knee.

"You do not have to be with this ..." The Telepath apparently was not finished with them. He studied Irwin, trying to find a suitable word to describe him. "... man, any longer. If you wish, we can find a place for you here in Arenu Village. Or you can take a voyage on one of those ships. You are a free man, Clan-Duin."

"What about me? Am I not free?" Irwin was not afraid, felt confident to push further.

"Admiral Ubic will want an interview with you when he's available. Until then, no!"

He scrutinized the Telepath and calculated his next words. Those blue-green eyes stared back.

Oh! Is that how this is going to work? I can stay here in Arenu Village, but I am not free? Interesting.

Kipp's hand gripped Irwin's knee, and he kept silent while his canine eyes watched the Telepath.

There was a long uncomfortable silence between the three of them before the Telepath spoke again. "I'm Donnolin. If you need anything, just say my name. I'll be quick to appear." He let go of a nervous chuckle. "Enjoy your time here." Donnolin eyed Irwin and turned and walked away.

Kipp peered into Irwin's eyes. "That was creepy! I'll be glad to get out of here, hopefully soon."

"Oh, that reminds me! Donnolin!" Irwin called out and immediately the Telepath stepped back into view. Kipp's fingernails nearly punctured Irwin's flesh.

Donnolin's blue-green eyes grew large, as did his greedy smile. "Yes?"

"Yes. I have a few questions. First off, I am wondering if once I am done speaking with the Admiral, that we may leave here today."

"Leave here?" Donnolin's face turned cold. "No. Only the Clan-Duin is free to leave. Admiral Ubic is busy this afternoon, or he would have the pleasure of speaking with you right now." He turned his head slightly. "I'm wondering, by the way, are you looking for something or someone?"

"Let us cut the crap. When did the carriage arrive? And when did it depart?"

"It arrived the day before yesterday in the afternoon." Donnolin chuckled. "We sent it on to Nuaki Village yesterday morning after filling it with rations for our neighbors there. They say you lust after precious metals. Why? What's your concern with that carriage?"

"Did all the Clan-Duin's arrive with the carriage?"

"Clan-Duins?"

"And the Daosian Princess?"

"Daosian Princess?"

Irwin was unrelenting. "Only six horses, right?"

"Six horses?" Donnolin scowled, clearly stumped. "There were ten."

Irwin continued, "Six Clan-Duins?"

Now agitated, Donnolin remarked, "Six Clan-Duins? There were only four soldiers with that carriage, and they were all Erthin."

"Ten horses and four soldiers? That is odd." Irwin was hoping to make Donnolin think about what the Telepaths had actually seen. "Did anyone inspect the interior of the carriage?"

"It was an elaborate carriage. Why would we—"

"Were the soldiers interviewed?"

"Soldiers interviewed? Why do you care about—what business is—"

Irwin sneered at Donnolin, "What about the liberated Clan-Duins?"

"Liberated Clan-Duins?"

"Have any arrived?"

There was a brief pause as Donnolin studied Irwin, no doubt hesitant to go into details. "There was word about Clan-Duins on the lam." His smile diminished, and he glanced up toward the rooftop. "But don't worry; our eagles are on the prowl. They like lamb."

Irwin understood the lethally cynical reference. "Rations for our animals will be where ... the wharf or barnyard?"

"Animal feed is in the barns. And Captain Karnsi is who you'll ask for once you're there. He should be able to help you." He waited for more questions.

"Thank you for your honesty, Donnolin," Irwin said with a nod. He appreciated this Telepath's candor.

"And you do know you need to pick up your animals' excrement, seen as how you're insistent to keep them here." Donnolin pointed to a pile of fresh manure.

"Consider it done," Irwin shot a quick glance at Kipp.

"Will there be anything else?"

"No, thank you." He watched Donnolin step away from the wagon. Irwin then made a metal bucket and a long-handled scoop appear behind the seat and passed them to his friend.

Kipp complied with Irwin's innate order and jumped down to clean up the road behind the horses. "Thank you, Kipp."

"Yeah! You're welcome." Kipp looked up at Irwin, a scoop filled with manure in hand.

He whispered, "When you are done, come touch me."

Kipp put the fresh manure into the bucket and then climbed back up to his perch on the wagon seat, placing his hand on Irwin's forearm. His brow deeply furrowed, the Clan-Duin said, "We need to get out of this place as fast as possible, Irwin."

"That will be difficult. There are solid stone walls between us and freedom, and they want to question me." Irwin moved in closer.

Kipp said nothing but was obviously stunned; he squeezed Irwin's arm.

Irwin let all the information sink in and said, "You did hear what Donnolin said? Four soldiers."

"I heard. Do you think the others hid in the carriage with Yace?"

"I do not think you were listening. There was no one in the carriage."

"Are you positive?"

"When I said Daosian Princess, that Telepath looked confused—as though I was crazed."

"You asked him a bunch of questions."

"Yes. And I asked them fast, and I mixed them up. I was trying to gauge his intelligence."

"And ...?"

"He is not smart enough to stop my questioning. But I believe he was mostly, if not completely, truthful with his answers. Of course, why would he lie? I imagine that this is the worst place to speak falsely about others. Here, you are dead if you lie."

"That does make sense."

"And since the carriage is not here, we will have to adjust our plans." They were clearly in a trap, and Kipp did not yet fully understand. "Let us get the Jennies and go to the markets at the wharf."

"It doesn't look very big. We probably only need to take one donkey. Besides, we can always come back and drop things off. It's not like it's a long walk or anything." Kipp was ingesting information. He looked confused.

Irwin tried to ignore the metal calling to him, and decided not to press the point about what a mess they were in. "I do not want to make more than one trip around the square."

The artistry of Arenu Village belied its danger.

Kipp will realize this soon enough.

32

TO THE MARKETS

The horses were watered and left to stand in the scorching sun. But shadows would soon draw across the ground to the east, lending a cool reprieve. Behind the wagon, there loomed a large carved wooden door twice the size of most men. This colossal tower felt menacing—a warning beacon, a place of caution.

Side by side, Irwin and Kipp walked away from the wagon. The two Jennies followed close behind. They strode toward a large gathering area—twice as long as it was wide. This communal area shared an interior wall with the angled tunnel they had driven through. A thin stone sun awning extended out into the square, opposite the Gritty Titty Saloon. Inside the large public space, there were wooden benches, chairs, and about three dozen tables scattered about.

Just beyond, there was a partially enclosed kitchen with shuttered windows above a lengthy wooden buffet. The aroma of searing meat wafted through the common area and massive square. About two dozen men were gathered at the tables, sharing bowls of fruit, and gawked at Irwin and Kipp. Irwin heard the word 'Mortal' and ignored the grumbles, scoffs, and vicious glares.

Kipp said, "We need to find out where Yace is. We need to know why she wasn't seen in that carriage. I know she was in there, Irwin; her scent can't lie to me. Maybe she stepped off the carriage when she saw all the green grass. Those beaches and bluffs would make a good hiding spot. But that makes no sense either. It's a wasteland out there. We want to be here, if only for the food and the reprieve from all that driving. But what I want to know is why—"

Irwin listened to Kipp carrying on, but he was also eyeing the Erthins and Clan-Duins staring at him. Many glared, not knowing what he was, or why he was allowed to be there. "We should not talk about this now, Hauss," Irwin softly replied, but Kipp didn't hear him; he was in his own world. Murmurs about Irwin's smell and his looks had already rippled around the square.

"—there were only four soldiers. I've smelled six all this time! Where do you think the other two went? I mean, they might be with Yace, might have snuck off the carriage with her before it got here. They probably hid on the beaches or something." Kipp drifted in and out of his hyper vigilance on Yace and her possible whereabouts. "No, she would stay with the carriage. Maybe she would hide. Maybe she would hide with the other two soldiers. They could've been hiding in the carriage somehow. A carriage that grand must have built-in hiding places. I know that several of the Gypsy's carriages and carts have false floors and secret hiding spots for children or skinny adults. That's where we hide the Cyclops."

Irwin said, "Look, Donnolin said there were four soldiers and ten horses. No one else. They did not see, or sense, Yace or any other soldiers. Though he is a Telepath, like I said, he has no reason to lie. He could withhold information, but he would not lie." He paused, and then said, "I would like to think that if the PCP are all so amazing, as you claim, then they should be able to sense another Telepath and two Clan-Duins hiding in a carriage. Nonbry told us that the Telepaths here are strong enough to spot a Coterie spell. Besides, if you can smell Yace, their Clan-Duins can too."

"But if they believe the carriage was being sent from one PCP Hall to another PCP Hall, they might not bother to look." Kipp was evidently trying to burst the bubble of positivity Irwin was attempting to create. "As you've said before, Dephen's smart. Probably smart enough to slip himself and two Clan-Duins past telepathic radar. I really hope you're not right about him sailing off!"

Irwin held back a smile. "If the carriage is considered a decoy, and they did not sense Yace or the other soldiers, then why send it on with rations to Nuaki Village?" He already had a few questions for Admiral Ubic. There would be more.

"That's what I wanna know too!" Kipp looked around, taking it all in. "I hate Erthins."

"We must continue to be wary." Irwin eyeballed each man they passed.

"They look powerful," Kipp whispered.

Irwin studied each Erthin. "Fire-water-wind. Wind-fire-earth. Water-fire-earth. Earth-fire. Water-fire. Wind-water-fire. Earth-spirit. Fire-wind-spirit. Water-earth-fire-spirit. Water-spirit. Fire-earth-water." He combed back his hair with his fingers and lifted his face to the sun. "You see, there are a lot of Erthins with triple powers here."

Kipp came forth from his own revelry and touched Irwin's arm. "Would you like a sweet roll?"

"Sure!"

It was warm inside the bakery. There were rolls and baguettes for sale. A skinny Clan-Duin baker's man with scruffy facial hair stood behind the counter. He stared at them, sneering at Irwin. He addressed Kipp. "Whatcha want?"

Kipp pointed. "Are those the sweet rolls?"

"We ain't got no more of them. Buttermilk rolls and flour baguettes is what we sell right now." The young baker's man smiled at Kipp and then glowered at Irwin.

Irwin eyed the fresh buttermilk biscuits. "When do you have sweet rolls?"

The young man again sneered at Irwin. He turned to Kipp and said, "I don't speak to stinky Mortals."

"Oh, he's far from Mortal," Kipp glanced at Irwin, then back to the baker's man. "He's got more power in his pinky than you have in your whole body."

"Hauss," Irwin said, hoping to diffuse the situation, hoping Kipp would not get too worked up. "Do not worry about it." His eyes settled again on the baker's man. "We will take two of the long roll baguettes."

The baker continued to grimace at Irwin, ignoring this 'Mortal' man.

Kipp stepped up to the counter, ready to fight the baker's man. He shot Irwin an angry glare and then turned to the young man behind the counter. "Two of those," Kipp pointed, "and four small rolls. How much?"

The man studied Irwin with a sour expression. "How much ya got?"

Irwin flipped four silver coins toward him, making them land one atop another. The coins were perfectly stacked face up on the countertop. The baker's man watched the coins magically levitate and then amass. Irwin and Kipp were gone before the man could say anything else.

"What an ass," Kipp said as they walked away and into the marketplace.

They bought boxes and boxes of supplies during their ensuing adventures in the marketplace, while Kipp struggled to keep Irwin from exploding. Insults about him being Mortal and stinky had flown wild everywhere they went. The sun was now hidden by the red tower, a slow descent to the far-off western mountains, and Kipp stared at Irwin while he secured the last box. "Why are we buying so much food? I don't eat this much in a moon's time."

"Actually, you do eat this much in a moon's time." Irwin reached over and touched his friend's hand. "We must be prepared for anything, and I need you to practice what Alio taught you."

"I *have* been!"

Irwin knew they were compromised every time they did not have contact. But he was wary to tell Kipp more than necessary. There were things they needed to buy, but large quantities of food supplies were not necessary. Both men were adept at conserving their meals and hunting if necessary. All this food was part of a contingency plan in case things went bad in a hurry. He did not want them to have to hunt down food if and when they left this place in haste. They must be well-prepared for anything. Kipp was becoming aloof again.

The Meat Market was next to 'Barber's Hop' where a line of men awaited getting their face and hair cleaned and cut. The barbers took their time, and only two were working. Just beyond that shop, there was a Healer's Home. Those who were sick or hurt went there to be nurtured back to health. Two Erthin healers, a man and woman, had their hands on a man who was yelling out in pain. Irwin learned that they also removed teeth at the barbershop.

Beyond the agony and howls of men in pain was a Masseurs Cove where petite women wearing nearly nothing were giving massages. There were raised beds and upright chairs that allowed patrons to sit or lay and have their aches rubbed away. A small line of those waiting their turn had formed.

Finally, they came upon a place called Cobblers Corner next to a place called Knotty Wicks and Sticks. The next open door was the Oracle's Domicile, and it appeared to be empty. The resident Telepath had just stepped out of the booth. Above each doorway, each business name was written in three different languages. All the establishments were open to the public, though some, such as the Oracle Domicile, had closed doorways and translucent windows for privacy.

Possibly because of the four ships moored out past the wharf, the markets were especially busy. Rows of merchants with crafts, treasures, personal items, and imported articles to be exported were displayed in mass quantities. They learned of a black market where high-strength alcohol, speculative medicinal tinctures, opiates, and other narcotics were available. Apparently, everyone in this market was willing to make a trade.

Two dark-skinned, large-bodied men walked side by side, blocking the market's widest corridor. They strode confidently toward Irwin and Kipp while navigating around sailors and merchants. The younger of the two enormous men, a partial Clan-Duin/Erthin, spoke to Irwin with bitterness in his voice. "I forgot how stinky Mortals can be." He pushed into Irwin's shoulder as he passed by. "Get out of my way, Mortal!" he shouted and pushed Irwin again.

Irwin pretended to grovel. "I am sorry, Sir."

"You better be sorry!" The second man was more Clan-Duin than Erthin, but he held fire and wind powers. "Or you'll be dead."

Kipp stayed close to the Jennies and behind Irwin. "Keep walking," Irwin whispered over his shoulder.

With a small use of his Metalist power, Irwin pulled on both men's coin-purses, diverting both their attentions. "What the ... who ... what?" They both spun around, trying to catch the fake would-be thief, and bumped their heads together instead.

That gave Irwin and Kipp enough time to escape. They hastened down a small alley away from the heavy congestion of the main market walkway.

Irwin stepped into a clothing booth. All the bright garments were artistically sewn and seemingly one-of-a-kind. He was drawn in by the smooth fabrics and wonderful embroidered details. He wanted to replace the red blouse he had buried in the manure pile at Lady Gretchen's.

He had looked at only a few shirts when the merchant began shouting, "No touch. No touch. Get out. Get out." Irwin abruptly left the clothing shop—he hoped he would find someone else selling apparel down some other alley.

"There's the cheese place," Kipp dropped the lead lines. The Jennies stopped. The two men walked into a tapestry lined alcove. It was at least thirty degrees cooler inside this merchant's stall.

There was one tall wooden shelving unit in the center of the shop with different sizes and flavors of cheese on display. An older partial-Erthin with orangish-red hair tied in knots sat in the corner of the booth. His clothing was patterned with colors and dark indigo splotches. He was chewing on a thick toothpick as he watched them enter.

The Erthin studied Irwin as he ventured inside to look at the cheeses.

"I do not serve your kind."

Irwin had reached his limit. He was ready to reveal himself. He knew keenly that showing any piece of his power would have an effect. He stepped closer to the Erthin. "And what kind do I look like?"

The merchant made a gesture to shoo Irwin from his shop. "Clan-Duin." The Erthin looked at Kipp. "Your Mortal servant is a displeasure to view." He signaled toward Irwin again, trying to direct him out of this cheese booth.

"I am anything but Mortal."

"Yeah," Kipp said, "I wouldn't cross him." He was gazing at the blocks of cheese, but Irwin knew he was also watching his and the merchant's exchange.

"A Mortal appears Mortal. A Talented man appears talented. What is your Talent, Mortal?"

"I am Erthin."

"Pah! You are not Erthin. I am Erthin. I would feel you if you were Erthin. I know Erthin, and you are no Erthin." The aged man's energy intensified, as did his wild green eyes. "Prove yourself."

Irwin inhaled and exhaled, trying to remain calm. He looked at the bricks of cheese and made an effort to get Kipp's attention. But his friend was on the other side of the display watching the Erthin. "How much for a two-pound brick?" He pointed at the wax-encased brick of cow cheese.

"Clan-Duin, I ask you again: remove your Mortal from my shop." His eyes slid from Kipp to Irwin, then back again. "And if he speaks again, I will summon the authorities. You should keep your Mortal on your ship. They are not permitted in a port such as this." He pointed toward the donkeys who stood with their lead lines on the ground. "Mortals should be kept on a line."

"I say decimate him, Samuel." He glanced over his shoulder to see if anyone was nearby. His voice lowered as he stepped closer to the Erthin. "No one will see it happen. They won't even hear you scream."

"I could absorb this Fire-Water-Wind Erthin. But really, all I want is some cheese."

The Erthin snorted, not impressed by either of these men. "That be a nice guess."

Irwin smirked. "We could play a game." Now he was dead serious. "But only if you want to." He wondered if this man might be one of those partial Telepaths who did not look telepathic and decided he was. "Alright, Fire-Water-Wind Erthin, let us see if you can light me aflame. Use your fire on me. See if you can incinerate me."

The Erthin cackled, "Oh! You like games, do you?"

Oh, the fun he could have with people who did not know him. Games like these were what his father had done to him. But his father's games had been more cynical, and sometimes life-threatening. But there had been lessons to be learned for Irwin. "I sure do. I am good at playing games." Irwin's eyes never left the Erthin's as the merchant jumped off his stool and stepped forth.

The Erthin's hands began to turn red hot as he churned his fire power within his flesh. He moved his glowing palm toward Irwin and then grasped his bicep.

Irwin cried out in pain. "Ouch!" But his outcry quickly turned to laughter.

Kipp threw a punch at Irwin's arm. "Dang it, Irwin!"

Irwin continued to laugh. "If you could see the look on your face, Hauss!"

The Erthin released Irwin and stepped back, looked at the reddened bicep where he had tried to ignite the Metalist from the inside out. Ideally, the skin was to boil first before the whole body became liquid fire and then vaporized. Instead, Irwin ground out the Erthin power and his flesh regenerated instantaneously. "You should be dead," The Erthin gasped. The merchant examined Irwin. "You say you are Erthin? Though, you surely do not look it. When did you realize you had this Talent?"

Irwin analyzed the merchant—an older local who appeared at ease with seeing the obscure. Even so, Irwin was clearly an oddity to him. The sight of him aroused the merchant and disturbed him at the same time. He chose his words carefully. "When a much younger Erthin than you attempted to ignite me."

"You were ignited?"

"He was trying to steal from me. He grabbed my arm, trying to ignite me like you just did. But all he did was singe my clothing. I was unscathed."

"I'll bet on you when you're Convoked." The Erthin merchant smiled. But Irwin did not respond. "I'm guessing you haven't been Convoked yet. I would've heard about it ... about someone fighting the Mortal." He continued to study Irwin. "Everyone hates Mortals here. But you are no Mortal." The merchant winked at Irwin. "And that will make the fight more fun. And if everyone bets against you, and I bet for you, the odds will be in my favor, mm-hmm."

"Convoked? I do not understand." He looked at the Erthin, then to Kipp.

Kipp said, "Basically someone calls you out to fight ... usually to the death. We've talked about it before, but I forgot what it was called in these places." He tried to remind Irwin about Alio's stories. "Let's hope you're not Convoked."

Irwin nodded.

"I will bet twenty percent of what you buy. And if you win, I will split the money! But you must first buy some cheese." The Erthin was trying to make a larger barter. "So, you just want two pounds of cheese?"

Irwin could see the merchant's angle. It was all about making money. "I was hoping to buy eight to ten pounds."

"That be five silver a brick. I think I still have four. Ah, take it all! I have goat cheese too. Aged to perfection; you'll never taste better. And in the jars is butter. It is the best butter too, made from our happy cows. And the ceramic jar it comes in is handcrafted by our woodworkers. The cork is the churner, a brilliant invention by one of our Clan-Duin friends." He pointed down below at ornately glazed jars.

Kipp's smile never left his face. It only grew wider when they talked about the cheeses and butter. "Oh, goat cheese," he drooled. "It goes great on everything: bread, fish, you name it. Patrice cooks with it all the time. And butter, oh butter, for the bread we just got. Oh, to dip it and lick it."

"Goat cheese is three coins, and the butter, two per jar."

Irwin allowed Kipp to grab all the cheese and butter he could gather. He paid the Erthin merchant and continued to be kind. He was done being heckled for the day, yet they still had to buy several more items before they were finished in the market. He was glad he told Kipp they were only walking around the markets once.

Moving on, further into the marketplace, he muttered, "Now we need oats or lentils or that rice stuff; you know, something of sustenance that we can eat in the mornings—and some fresh produce. Oh, and a bag of carrots, or apples for the animals; soaps and a new scrub brush too would be good."

The next merchant was an old blind-man with two young boys on-hand. They sold rice. The boys, Clan-Duin twins, hissed at Irwin, and the old man sniffed at him. He did not overreact, unlike the children. The elderly Clan-Duin did not seem to be unsettled by the Metalist's smell.

Irwin decided Kipp should take the lead for this transaction. So he stood next to the donkeys and played aloof. Kipp bought thirty pounds of rice while Irwin made up the money.

33
FEELING JADED

As they were loading up five-pound bags of rice, Irwin felt the eyes of a telepathic pirate. The bearded old man's clothing was whimsical and well-kept. Following behind him were four disheveled children of various ages and sexes. They were all dirty, tattered, and clearly tired. The pirate with darkened teeth glowered at Irwin, revealing a golden canine tooth gleaming in the sunlight. There were silver and gold rings on his fingers, and his ears were lined with golden hoop earrings. The old man's face had been tattooed, accentuating his weathered and wrinkled features. He pushed around Kipp and up to the rice dealer.

Why do pirates wear gaudy amounts of rings, jewels, and clothing? They remind me of raccoons, attracted to shiny things.

This telepathic pirate's attire was other-worldly with flaps of fabric that glimmered in the sun, like the gold in his teeth. He looked wicked and glared at Irwin and Kipp, visibly wanting them to leave.

He and Kipp had investigated nearly every shop in the busy marketplace by this time, and they had bought almost everything they would need. Though Irwin revealed no actual plan, he was working on a master plan as there was no Yace, no carriage, and for now, they were stuck in Arenu Village. All he wanted now was safe passage into Datzar Jungle so they could continue to chase the carriage. Their mission had not changed. They still had to rescue Yace. And presumably she was now heading south to Daos through the Datzar Jungle.

They spotted the sign for the Bath House above the market's fabric roofs and turned down one of the main walkways through the open markets and walked toward the southern courtyard wall.

"A bath sounds nice," Kipp said.

"We took baths two days ago."

"Yeah, I remember ... the cold ocean. I mean a real bath! Where there are seats and small pools and hot water ... a pretty lady to speak with and look at. You know, a bath!"

Kipp reached the end of the markets first. He paused when he saw several naked ladies on display. At the front of the stone-lined alcoves, the prettiest women were exhibited. The slave owners stood just beyond shouting for customers to come and see—to step into their well-lit rooms and pick out the best of the slaves. All the women were naked save a chain attached to their ankles. Most of them appeared Mortal—pale skin and dark brown eyes. They had numbers painted on them. The price for their souls was steep. There were Talented women too, their darker bodies had higher prices. A few were pregnant, and others were extremely skinny ... a depressing sight to see.

The next alcove was occupied by young girls. Their slave-trader was also a telepath, dark circles under his eyes, and piercing lips moved a little except when he saw Irwin and Kipp gawking. He shouted at them, telling them about the young girls, how good they were, how hard they worked, how they were in bed. Irwin averted his eyes and then spotted the next storefront filled with young boys from the age of about two to teenaged. The strongest of the boys were presented along the exterior wall—their slave-trader was negotiating with a pirate. Irwin's eyes locked with one of the younger boys who looked to be no older than five.

Horrific images flashed in Irwin's mind's eye.

He remembered, right after Great Grandfather Edwin's death, being forced into what his father had called 'lock down'. Every day when Albert and Jebadia went to the mines, they put Irwin in heavy ropes or chains. That was their way of making sure he behaved throughout the day without supervision. They left him with no food or water for hours at a time—left him to wait for over a day with no sustenance. He had called out, screaming for Edwin, longing for his suffering to end. He saw that same look on that young boy's face—knew the terror he felt.

Kipp kept Irwin from stopping, from staring. "Come on." Irwin stumbled forward.

He saw those haunted eyes staring back at him, scared, alone, wondering if the torment, torture, rape, and abuse would ever end.

I could buy them all. I have more than enough metal to do so.

So many of the boys appeared to be of Clan-Duin and Erthin descent, though there were a few young, naïve Telepaths and many more Mortals mixed in. He could not understand why the people of Arenu Village allowed this to happen.

These are no doubt all orphaned or unwanted children. It makes no sense that they cannot just live their lives. Who could allow such brutality?

Telepaths.

They were all doomed, no matter what he did.

"We can't stay here, Irwin. Come on!" Kipp pulled on him until Irwin walked on his own accord. "Like I said before, this is a place where slavery is common. In places like this, children and women are bought and sold like livestock. We must be cautious."

"I just did not think ...." Irwin's voice faded. He was sickened by the sight—now etched forever in his mind.

"Alright, so we walked through the markets and the butchery. We got rice and flour and all the salts and seasonings and herbs you need for cooking." Kipp ogled the netted bags waiting to be opened. "And I really want to just gorge myself. You better start thinking of other rations, or I'm gonna take you over to the Oracle's and have her mess with your mind so that you don't keep thinking about all the suffering and misery that happens here every day."

Irwin stared off, in his own world, his own memories.

I do not want others to know the suffering I endured. None of them deserve that type of life.

Seeing so many in chains, women and children, anemic and atrophying, made him want to do something. "I have to save them," he whispered.

"Alright, Irwin, enough with the saving of everyone. You cannot save them. Well, knowing you, you could. How about this: I don't want you to save those people!"

Irwin was quiet.

"Maybe you need to be thinking of where Yace might be; the lack of information about the carriage and its contents is annoying me!"

Hammering against metal at the forge had started up again. And the children and women in chains in storefront windows—it was all too much. Irwin's mind swirled. "Do you really want to know where Yace is? I will tell you where she is! She is on a ship bound for Daos, and we missed her by moments. Moments! We could have stopped her if we had any clue what Lady Gretchen was up to." His silver eyes glowed. Irwin erupted with anger as he thought about that ship that had been parked offshore. "On that last boat, there were eight men. Eight men. Why? You do not need eight men, especially if the other boats only have five. Four oarsmen and one manning the rudder. That's how those other boats with the goats and sheep were. Pigs are not labor intensive. They do not need eight men. Maybe sheep because they are stubborn. But not pigs. Not eight. Five makes sense when it comes to operating a small vessel full of animals. But eight is three too many!"

"Eight men? What are you talking about? Wait. We've had this conversation before. Yace would not get on a boat!"

Irwin growled at his Clan-Duin friend. "You are too far from reality sometimes. I would like to believe you could catch all the idiosyncrasies going on around us. Do you ever pay attention? The three extra was Yace and two of her soldiers. Dephen would not be caught here in Arenu Village. He would leave the land. He would take passage on a ship! And if my calculations are correct, that was the vessel that left Ahradah heading for Tresdahla with a brief stop in Daos. That was the same ship parked outside Lady Gretchen's, picking up food and three more patrons." He could see that Kipp was having a hard time following. "That was the boat you heard about in the game room at the last saloon where we ate in Ahradah."

Be calm. Be patient with Kipp.

"Even though the carriage continued on, Dephen left our trail back at Lady Gretchen's. He probably timed it so it would happen that way. And then he sent the carriage on as a decoy." He was making a point. "This is all a hoax, and Dephen plotted it all. He wanted us here in Arenu Village. And now we are trapped here. There is no way we can follow. I am sure they are planning to keep me here, and you want a bath!

"Dephen is smart. He hoped I would not be paying attention. He hoped I was stupid enough not to notice what was going on. And he knew you would follow your instincts. That is why you are being duped into believing she would be here. Nonbry said it best: his mother—Dephen's mother—sailed ships. Dephen is a sailor. He is not afraid of the sea!"

"Dephen can't fake her scent," Kipp barked back.

"He has before. He will do it again. He used it to his advantage in Ahradah."

"Her scent has been at each camp. It was old, but it was there. I don't believe your ship-sailing theory. You're wrong Irwin! Yace wouldn't travel by sea."

The clanking of metal stopped, and Irwin inhaled a deep breath. He wanted to trust the Clan-Duin's instincts. "You actually believe that she hid in the carriage?"

"Yeah! I do. My nose doesn't lie to me. If I smell her, then I smell her—end of story."

Irwin knew that being in Arenu Village was more than just a trap set by Dephen. He had made the PCP believe that capturing Irwin would be of their own doing. That action alone took Dephen's manipulation to a higher level.

I cannot think that this is the end of our journey. I must stay positive. Ha! Good luck with that, especially with Kipp being ... Kipp.

Shit. How will we get out of this?

"Look, unless you can think of anything else to buy, I think we are done with our errands."

Kipp looked around. "I'm not saying that Dephen wouldn't be going to Daos. All the signs seem to point to there. I just don't see Yace taking a ship." He motioned for the Jennies to follow.

Irwin was half a stride ahead and lost in his own thoughts. His eyes were focused on their wagon.

"Hey Irwin! Hey, we need to get oats for the animals."

Irwin turned to look at the weighted packs on his Jennies. "They need to be unburdened first." He was tired, and the hard inconsistent hammering of metal never ceased.

"Are you sure you're alright, Irwin?"

Irwin rubbed his face. "I have a headache." He glared at the forge as they walked past. The Erthin soldier who worked the metal noticed him. Each pang rang louder, making Irwin want to recoil into the wagon, only a few hundred feet ahead of them.

"I can get the grain after we dump all this stuff off," Kipp said. "And I'll take the horses down and stable them. Get them out of the sun. They'll probably want more water and oats."

"Good." Irwin was in pain ... mentally and physically. He wanted to lie down, but there were things that still needed to be done. He unhitched the tailgate from the wagon.

Without another word, they peeled off the bags and boxes of rations. Each man methodically packed and stacked everything into the wagon bed. The day felt long. The sun was still on the horizon but closing in on the mountain tops to the west.

Irwin eyed his friend. Kipp wanted to ask more questions, he could tell, but he was in no mood. They stacked everything precisely—behind the bench and alongside their bed, careful to leave enough foot space. Silently, Irwin converted another rock of metal into coins. He threw a heavy satchel of silvers to Kipp.

"That is two pounds of silver coin. It should be enough for four hundred pounds of oats. Donnolin said to go to the stable yard. You are doing this on your own. I need to rest."

"Are you gonna be alright?"

Irwin dismissed Kipp's question with a swipe of his hand. He needed time away from all these people and Kipp. He was being mentally bombarded by too many things, especially his repressed memories. The chained young boys and girls had set off a series of remembrances of the nightmares of his own childhood. “If you are not back soon, I will make these move.” He handed off two silver pieces. “Do not spend them. Always keep them on your person while away from me.”

Kipp studied the coins and Irwin retreated further into the covered canopy. He did not care if the wagon would become hot and stuffy. He pulled the front and back canvas curtains shut.

34
Quieting The Demons

He listened as Kipp led the donkeys away. The clopping of their hooves was not loud enough to muffle the clanging radiating from the forge area; he was tired of it all. They had lived with only the howling wind for many days before arriving here in Arenu Village. Now, even the sound of birds and rustling leaves felt deafening. The faintest murmuring of voices and the constant ringing and pulling of metal agitated him to his core. It was all too much.

Here and now, he understood why his father had always been on edge whenever they arrived in the small city of Kobiton. Irwin had not been this sensitive back then, the back then that felt like eons ago. But now the glares, murmurings, and vicious words only fueled his energy. He wanted to allow his wrath to take hold, but he had to hold back. If he allowed all those venomous people to provoke him, everyone would already be dead. He was better than that, and he had to remind himself of that fact every minute of every day here in this rough and rowdy city. This alone time was essential. He did not want to be consumed by his Metalist urges, but the raging tempestuousness was hollering at him, challenging him to unravel and destroy any hope they might have of getting out of there.

He wanted to meditate without being consumed by his compulsions. Taking deep breaths, Irwin pulled back the layers of blankets on the large metal lockbox. He lay down but left himself partially uncovered. He did not want Kipp to worry and hoped this would be enough of a clue for the Clan-Duin to know where he was. He took one more deep breath and then let the metal casket consume him.

He sank into the metal capsule. It was warm inside, airtight, but that did not matter. He made air holes up near his head along three sides of the box. They were small, but he made several for cross ventilation. Irwin had wanted to wrap himself inside this casket even before setting off around the square. Even then, the symphony of metal had been earsplitting. It was during their walk through the market that it had all become simply way too overwhelming.

Back at the markets, he used all his focus to retrieve their rations. What usually was a simple and fun task, had turned into a nightmare. He had masked his feelings during their excursion. But now, after all the exposure to negativity, disturbing sights, flashbacks to his past, and all that metal singing out of harmony, Irwin needed a positive recharge. He needed to collect himself. A piece of him wanted to run away from sounds he was not used to, away from all the over-reactive people. Again, he felt a sense of empathy for his father, now understanding why Albert had always exploded and acted so crazed when visiting civilization.

Here in this place, it is all a test. Everyone is watching me. I am constantly being scrutinized. They need to see me for who I am, a peaceful man. I must remain calm. But they want to know about me, my true abilities. I cannot show them my true form. I must remain calm.

He had to keep it together for Kipp, if no one else.

The humming of all the metals inside the lockbox: bronze, iron, copper, gold, aluminum, and silver were harmonizing at last. All the exterior noise ceased while he lay inside his chamber—a peaceful place where he could surround himself with positive thoughts and resonating metallic feedback. Expelling all the metal in his body, Irwin tried to meditate inside this protective casket.

The combinations of metal now surrounding him helped him center himself. He could calm his anxieties and inner fears.

He did not want to use his powers on these people as his father would have. Even so, a part of him wanted to show off—wanted to show everyone he was not Mortal. But that type of exposure would create fear.

Although these people do not fear Mortals, the fact that I am Volatile but do not look it might create unnecessary havoc.

One misstep before these Talented people could cause irrevocable harm.

I cannot be like my father. I will not be like my father.

He knew a situation might transpire that would boil beyond his control. He did not want to provoke, or to be provoked, but he had wanted to incinerate several of those men he encountered inside the labyrinth of markets. In the past, he had witnessed his father's and grandfather's wrath. Albert had been more unpredictable than Jebadia and would explode without forethought of consequences.

How many towns did Albert lose control in and 'blow-out'?

He took several deep meditative breaths, letting the metal nourish him. He hoped that the resonating songs would soothe him and help him feel whole again.

I am not my father.

He inhaled with each thought and became more calm with each exhale.

I can control myself. People react because of their fear of me, not because of me. I have done no wrong to these people. I will not wrong them. I will not harm them. They have no reason to harm me—besides the fact that I do not look right or smell right.

He was trying not to take what others said or did personally. What they said was of their own beliefs, not his. If his mind was calm, then he would be calm; he would be able to find other options to get them out of Arenu Village. Yet he knew there was no hope for a simple escape.

This experience has shown me many things. I now know how Kipp feels every time we go anywhere he is not welcome. Intolerance and ignorance is everywhere. Truth and knowledge are my guides. Intolerance comes about because people do not want to understand. Ignorance comes about when people do not have the knowledge. I want to understand others. I know knowledge is the key to better understanding. I must breathe and let things go.

He was drifting and relaxing, but could not let go of his thoughts.

Breathe.

Those with Talents are as ignorant as Mortals. Fear is what controls the people, not Telepaths.

Breathe.

I do not fear them; I pity them. They have negative feelings toward me. Ignore them. I cannot take their thoughts or feelings away. There is nothing I can do for them.

Breathe.

I must show kindness. I cannot save them from their ignorance. And I cannot show more of myself than I must. I must let this all go. I will not harm or kill anyone while I am here. Pity. I will take pity on those who do not understand. I must remember that I am not my father. I am not my father.

Breathe.

I am Samuel Irwin Miner.

Irwin rose from the metallic box much later, feeling barely rested, hungry, and anxious about something he could not name. Kipp was not in the wagon, but still within the square. He felt those two silver coins a few hundred feet away and summoned Kipp to return. In the meantime, he took an apple from their supplies, opened the bag of peanuts, and tore into one of the baguettes. He gulped warm water from the flask at his side while enjoying some of their bounty.

The wagon rocked as Kipp stepped up onto the front bench. He balanced well as he crept over the seatback. The Clan-Duin used his toes to guide him through the portal into the covered section—his hands were full of freshly cooked food.

With a bright smile, Kipp said, "These are for you. It's a honey-mustard-soy sauce. They've been marinating in it all afternoon. You'll like it. I brought you two."

"Thank you." Irwin noticed sauce marks on Kipp's chin and cheek. "How many have you had?"

"I've had two. Bought the last four of these so the Erthin Merchant could close up shop and go to das Grits Tits, as they call it."

"They?"

"The sailors and such."

Irwin took the skewered fish. "Out gallivanting, I see."

"You were nowhere to be found."

"Were you not worried that I was not here?"

Kipp shrugged. "It didn't smell like you had left the wagon. And there were no other scents. And I saw no foul play. I noticed the bed covers were pulled back. But no, I was never worried—maybe a little hopeful you wouldn't kill anyone or destroy the village."

Irwin took a bite of the sweet and sour skewered fish. "Where all did you go?"

Kipp took a deep breath and began to explain his afternoon, "Well after I hauled up the four-hundred pounds of feed I—"

"You did not haul it, the donkeys did."

"—I went past the Bath House, and woah they're busy! Told me we should come back tomorrow if we want a bath, and our clothes cleaned. Then to the wharf and was heckled, but I listened in on a few conversations, hoping to hear anything about Yace, or the ship, or the carriage, or any of it." He huffed and looked at Irwin like he was trying to remain calm. "Anyway. I went past the Oracle's office. She's a scary mystic with only one eye. The other is marbled, almost spins in that socket." He shuddered, then blew a breath that made his lips flutter. "Stopped off in the markets because you were shooed away from the booths and such. Went looking for a shirt for you. Oh, passed a tannery we hadn't seen before. Got a few things from there. Then I saw the Erthin cooking these things ...."

"How did you pay for these?"

"I took a dozen coins off the top of the bag you gave me for the grain."

"Why would you take money from the bag I gave you for grain? I would have given you a pound of coins to spend if you needed it." Kipp shriveled away when Irwin's voice rose. "Do you know why I have not haggled? Why I have been paying fair price for everything?"

"I thought it was because you were fearful of these people."

"No! It was so the people of Arenu Village would know I am a fair person—that my actions and words are worth something. I do not want to be seen as a liar or cheat or a person of anger or aggression. And if they see me as a fair person, then maybe I will be allowed that same respect."

"You think the people around here will respect you? These people are all for themselves, and that's why you'll never see a child running around free." Kipp spat and then pulled out a large, tied leather satchel from under his tunic. "Here are the things we didn't find the first time around the markets." Kipp smiled at Irwin and took an apple from the bag bought for the animals. The Clan-Duin leaned back against the tight canvas wall and bit into the apple.

Irwin finished the fish, licking his fingers clean, before opening the satchel Kipp laid between them—a large bag secured to one long leather tether. The bag was full of different lengths and widths of leather straps and pieces—everything he had been ruminating over, and more. "Oh good! I can repair my calf chaps and your boots. Thank you, Kipp."

"There's more."

At the bottom of the sack, folded up several times over, was a red silken tunic. The hemlines were sewn with purple thread and ornately put together. It had been the plainest of all the shirts in the clothing booth.

"I couldn't tell which one you liked, since that asshole merchant pushed you out earlier. But he was nice to me when I went back."

Irwin held back the urge to throw his arms around his friend. "Thank you, Kipp!" He patted the Clan-Duin's shoulder.

"Yeah, anytime." Kipp patted Irwin's knee.

"Well then, I should show you what I made for you." He summoned the silver coins from Kipp's pocket and motioned for him to stand up. Irwin knelt on the floor and pushed the blankets back. Placing the coins in the center of the metal box, he fashioned reliefs of them. Then he levitated the coins from their corresponding divots in the metal. The rectangular box's top sprang up and held there. "Your coins now have copper relays that make contact within these divots on top." Irwin demonstrated this by closing the box and putting the coins in the reliefs again. Metal clicked, and the box sprang open. "There are similar marks on the inside for exiting." He opened the lid all the way while holding onto their bedding. "If you are ever in a compromised position and need to get away, just slip right in here. I made air-holes at that end."

"Dang me, is this where you were?"

Irwin nodded and closed the metal lockbox.

"You fit in that! And how did you make it move like that?"

"It is called a hinge. Most doors have them."

"Impressive."

"Thanks." Irwin did not want to take too much credit. He sat back on the cushioned bed. "I made it just in case we need to put things in there, like our belongings, or maybe even one of us."

Kipp took his seat again. "Should I be scared?"

"Not of me."

"You alright?"

"For now, yes. So long as I am not heckled, or the forge starts up again."

"I think everyone is done working for the day. Well, all except the ladies in the Saloon. Speaking of which, I think you should put on that shirt and follow me over to da Grits Tits."

Irwin heard men shouting, laughing, and hoo-hawing. Most of the noise came from the Saloon.

He raised his hand and cupped his ear. "Did you not hear me? I do not want to be heckled. If I go into that Saloon, guaranteed I will be Convoked."

"More reason to go."

"Are you mad?"

"Are you allowing *Vols* who are less scary than you scare you?"

"No."

"Then what are you worried about?"

Irwin kept his lips tight.

They ate their food and drank from flasks of water in silence. Finally, the Clan-Duin said, "I can't believe you're willing to drink this shitty warm water when there is whiskey, or even wine, a hundred feet away."

"We bought you ale."

"It's not the same. I'd much rather be staring at pretty ladies than this stark canvas while I drink. Besides, when will we be in a place like this again?"

"Hopefully never."

"What is your suggestion then? Sit around, eat rations, drink warm water or ale? You don't even like ale! They probably have whiskey. Maybe they'll have wine too. How will we know if we don't go? All you wanna do is mope around." Kipp pointed toward the Saloon. "Those men are afraid because they don't know you. Like I said, if you'd come into Arenu Village all silvered out, there'd be no worries. They'd all know what and who you are. And if you're Convoked, so be it. Any person who decides to fight you will die! We both know that."

With a touch of sarcasm, Irwin replied, "Your confidence in me is overwhelming. If you want me to be like my father, then yeah, sure, I will go in there with you, let loose and lose control ... again."

"You're too calculating to lose control."

"And when it happens, you can bet all the silver we have that I will not be allowed to leave here with you. Not without a fight. And again, I do not want to fight, Kipp. You do not want to be a part of that either!"

Kipp rolled his eyes.

"And yes, I know I think about things too much—to a fault—but I also catch things you do not."

I do not need to be angry at my friend. Kipp just wants to enjoy himself.

"Besides, as long as I play along with what the Telepaths want, we can hopefully pass on through tomorrow morning without another glance our way."

"You're willing to play along with their shit?"

"It is better than the alternative."

"The alternative is to go in there and not worry about what others think. Enjoy ourselves for a change!"

"If I do that, you will be dead."

"For being as calculating as you are, you never factor living in the moment, do you?"

Spite grew between the two and their bags of fresh foods and dried fruits. They held their tongues and ate a few more bites.

The door at the base of the red tower opened and closed several times as men, mostly Telepaths, emerged from the building. Footsteps traipsed away.

I am ready to be done with this place.

"I wonder if the Admiral is ready to speak."

"I can't believe you really wanna speak with that man."

"I have a few questions for him," Irwin said, staring off. "I was hoping we would have that interview today."

"And if not?"

"Then we should seek out the Oracle."

If I cannot talk myself out of this situation, we will indeed need Nonbry's help.

"I'll want alcohol in me before we do that. There's no way I'll speak to Nonbry and tell him what we are heads-deep into without being drunk!"

"That sounds like a bad idea, Kipp."

"And going there sober is an awful idea. Put that shirt on and let's go find a woman worthy of you."

"I would need a lot of alcohol for that."

"Come on, Irwin, let loose for once. You can't let a few *Vols* get in the way of having fun. Yace would go with me."

"If Yace was here, I would not be."

"What are you saying, Irwin?"

"Go. Be with your people. I will wait here to speak with Admiral Ubic. When you are good and liquored up, maybe we will go find an Oracle and speak with Nonbry."

"They're your people too, Irwin. Now come on. Stop moping. Let's go have a drink."

All I want to do is speak with Admiral Ubic and be gone from this place.

Biting the insides of his cheeks, Irwin stared at Kipp. He did not want to fret over any of this. His mind and soul hurt. He took a long drink off the warm water and then corked the flask. He said nothing.

I'm doing this for Kipp.

He pulled off his dirty and sweaty sleeveless tunic and slipped on the red shirt, pushed his feet into his boots, and followed his friend out of their covered wagon, across the cobbles and into the noisy Gritty Titty Saloon.

35

The Gritty Titty Saloon

They walked over to The Gritty Titty Saloon from their wagon, Irwin half a step behind. Through the open windows and doors, they surveyed the barroom. It was busy with life, full of haggard pirates and sailors and some of the men and women who worked in the gardens. It smelled of fresh meat pies, baked bread, and salmon, and all those aromas intertwined with sour body odors. Voices boomed from games and arm-wrestling matches, but then fizzled.

From across the room, at the long and large wooden bar, a dockhand, clad in his orange sarong, jumped down from his seat and strode straight toward Irwin. Other patrons saw the 'Mortal' enter. They were ready for whatever might happen next, keenly alert and ready to fight.

"Das Mortals notss serveds heres!" The dockhand spat, pointed at the door. "Gits yas backs tas yas wagonsss!"

Irwin put his hands up, not wanting an altercation. Kipp stepped back. Their eyes locked, and then Irwin returned his attention to the dockhand. He forced silver to swirl around his eyes, occluding his iris.

"I am no Mortal. And I will not let you bully me."

"Proves sits!"

A dozen men, Clan-Duins and Erthins alike, moved away from their tables and card games. Others began shouting, standing up from their seats, attempting to diffuse the situation before it blew out of control.

"Calm down soldiers."

"DamnSonsABitchesShutsUps!"

"At ease men!"

A female bartender telepathically froze those crowding around Irwin and the dockhand. She shouted from the wooden bar, "All right you bastards!" A dozen large men, ready to fight, were frozen where they stood. Only their eyes could move.

The exotic beauty jumped over the large and long bar. Her forcefulness startled both Irwin and Kipp. She was short, dark-haired, with bright blue almond-shaped eyes. Her form-fitting dress moved with her as she pushed through the non-frozen men to get to those who were statues. "Back up already!" She shouted at the congregation of powerful men.

Two frozen Erthins loomed behind the Metalist. They had begun to churn their powers. Everyone could see their fire energy turning colors inside their hands.

Irwin's hands were still up, but then he lowered his arms. Those Erthins had wanted to touch him, incinerate him, but could not. Not with the short, powerful barkeep commanding. On the other hand, Irwin was ready to pull their fire power out of their hands. But refrained. He wanted to see how this female bartender could disperse the escalation.

"Stand down," she grumbled and pointed at the two Erthins. "If you don't withhold your powers, you'll no longer reside in Arenu Village. Understand!" Her eyes met Irwin's, but also sought out all the other men who were acting with hostility toward this newcomer.

"We don't want this man to prove he is Volatile. Trust me when I say he is. He has come here to seek asylum, much like the rest of yous! So, if you'll be kind to him, then we'll receive his kindness in return." She pointed at each face surrounding her. "You might as well leave while you still have privileges to visit this establishment." She telepathically released all the frozen men except the drunken dockhand. Most of them raced from the Saloon. Others returned to their card games.

The stinky dockhand was still frozen there by the door—only his eyes moved. Sweat dripped down his face and back. The barkeep released her frozen spell from him. He gasped, realizing he now had control of his body again. She open-handedly slapped the dockhand's face and shouted, "Get out of here Batton! I don't want to see you in here for a full moon's time." She spat at him. The dockhand lowered his head and moved around Irwin, not giving him so much as a glance.

Irwin smiled at her. "Thank you, but I could have handled that."

"I saw that situation going five ways to Daos. Too many would have died, and all for naught."

"No, only he would have died."

She rolled her eyes, turned away from Irwin, and went back to the bar. Irwin and Kipp walked together and took two seats at the bar. "You would have been part of the waste, but that's now in the past. What can I get you?" The barkeep said with a coy smile. She grabbed a glass from under the counter.

The few Clan-Duins who had been sitting near them moved away. Nearly half of the patrons had left by now.

The barkeep smiled at Irwin. "What's your drink of choice?" Her eyes were trying to see into him.

He knew her trick. "You probably do not have it." He said while looking at Kipp.

"We have many spirits to choose from. The hot libation for the night is a clear liquor with very little taste, but it will have you seeing double after one shot. We also have the usual ales, dark, light, porters and stouts, hard cider, and several superb wines."

"Do you have whiskey?"

She shook her head.

"What type of wine do you carry?"

"We have casks of white wine from Tietzah region and red wine from Gustin."

Kipp blurted, "That's where I'm from, a town outside of Indova, that is."

Irwin saw Kipp's glee, saw his puppy dog eyes plastered on the bartender. "I'll take a shot of the hot alcohol," said Kipp.

"And you, sir?"

"The red wine please and thank you."

She nodded and quickly poured Kipp his small drink. "Either of you interested in the carrot pig pie? It's local!"

"Local? How local?"

"I think you know how local." Her smile never wavered, but her left eyebrow raised high on her forehead.

Irwin tossed his head toward the patrons in the barroom. "Do they know?"

"They are hungry men. They eat what is given to them and don't complain."

"Hey, I am not complaining," Irwin smelled hot baked bread, saw a platter walk by and said, "Bread and cheese looks good. And a large glass, or carafe, of wine."

"My pleasure."

Kipp whispered to Irwin, "What an entrance."

"I had it handled. Though it was nice to see a woman assert herself." He watched their barkeep tap a new cask of wine.

"Yeah," Kipp stared lustfully at her and shot down his hot alcohol. "She'd be a fun one."

"I knew I would be confronted. I had it all figured out, but she took away my fun."

"Dang, this is good alcohol. It has hardly any taste. But, dang me, I'm feeling buzzy already."

"Buzzy?"

"Buzzy, fuzzy, oh so good," Kipp cackled.

Irwin leaned forward on the sleek wooden counter. A yellow-glazed carafe of wine was set before him. "Thank you." He took a taste. One drink led to another. "Damn, this is good. It tastes like grape juice and blackberries."

Their barkeep had a small mug of white wine. She pressed against the bar next to Irwin and he leaned back. "I like it too. Here's a taste of the wine from Indova." She passed it over, and Irwin took a sip.

"Ugh, that's bitter."

"Yes, it is. You picked a superb wine. And you're good at discerning flavors too," she clanked her small glass against his giant ceramic carafe, "Prost." She gulped down the bitter wine.

Irwin lifted the carafe, "Prost," and then took another large gulp.

Kipp could not resist his eagerness to play with the pretty bartender. "Why do you work here?"

"If I do not serve here, then I serve up there or out in the fields. Here, my body does not get beaten by the sun, nor does it tire from the men." She laughed a laugh that sounded like a tinkle in the breeze. She had all her teeth and a sparkle of life in her eyes.

"You don't seem jaded by this place." Kipp glanced in the direction of the wharf. "Aren't you afraid of those slave shops?"

"Those shops are for trade, nothing more. Those who end up there deserve better, but they're brought here for a reason. They will serve their purpose," she said with a touch of spite. "Many of us who live here are smart. I am smart. I found a way to satisfy men," she winked at him, "without being hurt too much." She turned to help another customer.

All the ladies who work downstairs showed telepathic traits, though not all had blue eyes or blonde hair. But that didn't matter, they moved like Telepaths. Irwin noticed his bartender work things to her advantage—the way she ran her hand through her hair, flipped her long locks across her shoulder, or the way she leaned in to push up her cleavage while engaging the customers. Her invitingly blue eyes, framed by her long black hair and lustful lips, hastened sales. She made people want to drink more. She had just received a silver piece for her smile. She glanced back at Irwin and Kipp and winked at them; then she served another patron a brimming mug of ale with one smooth motion.

A younger Clan-Duin waitress was bringing bar patrons their food. Their bartender pointed at Irwin and Kipp and spoke quietly to that waitress. After placing out her plates, the younger woman darted off toward the kitchen and returned with a plate of cheesy bread for the men. The bartender leaned in toward Kipp with an intense smile of satisfaction.

"Anything else I can get for you? You know you have wonderful eyes." Her voice was sultry in a way that made Irwin's spine prickle.

"So do you," Kipp smiled in his goofy way. "It's not often that there are women as pretty as you behind a bar. I can only guess they do not have anyone as stunning as you are up above."

She averted her eyes and blushed. "Thank you, and no," she laughed, "of course not. The prettiest of us are down here to lure you men in."

"Well, it worked," Kipp said with his puppy dog eyes on her. "Yeah, women like you are a rarity. I can only guess when another pretty woman comes into the Saloon, you're all on high guard—not wanting her to take away your station."

"Women do not come in and take anything around here. We earn our positions." She wiped off the bar counter. "But on occasion, we do get those who are all high-and-mighty. They are rare, but it happens." The waitress helping the bartenders heaved down two trays of cleaned glasses and one tray of freshly cleaned mugs.

The bartender quickly stacked them under the counter. "We're protective of those who are with us, though." With a chortle, she added, "The other day a female Erthin pirate came in fiery-red hair and attitude. She acted as if she owned the place, shouting at our patrons; she ordered around the waitress who was helping her and her men. And she gave much grief to the soldiers accompanying her. Oh, boy! Those Clan-Duin hybrids got drunk and gambled and arm wrestled ... and argued! They argued about everything, caused quite a ruckus."

A dark-skinned shipmate approached the bar, stepping next to Kipp, and slapped down a coin. "Rum!"

She filled a cup, pushed it into the man's hands, then regarded the open barroom before returning her attention to Irwin and Kipp.

"Yeah, the dockhands were hooting about that fiery-red woman," said Kipp.

"Her men were outrageous with their gambling and rowdy tones. And she was horrible to the women upstairs too. She paid to sleep with three at the same time," she snorted. "You know, I'm not sure she bought those men anything other than food and drink. I don't think they made it upstairs. But then again, they were too busy carousing with everyone down here." She tossed her hair, rolled her eyes.

"That fiery bitch took advantage of our best ladies. She broke Joslyn's arm and fractured Daneaha's pelvic bone, and she left Lenay unconscious. The two were screaming in pain, and, of course, the men all thought they were enjoying themselves. But that Erthin cunt left bruises and tore up those ladies. She didn't care. She fuked them until they were beaten and bloodied. It was worse than anything any of the men have ever done. I mean, sometimes they beat and leave bruises, but broken bones! That's just not allowed."

The barkeep stepped back, maybe assessing the impact of her story.

"Usually, we stop these sorts of things. Our women are amazing at what they do. And luckily, they don't have to do it all night. Definitely a blessing for them. In most saloons—as you both probably know—you can go all night and rough them up until they are bloody. Here, we don't let that happen. Time with the women is limited. They shouldn't have to deal with the bruits all night. This life we all share is cruel enough."

Irwin sat back in his chair, chewing on this story and another piece of cheesy flat bread.

"None of us suspected a woman could be that fierce. She was a shifty Erthin pirate, and a Telepath. None of us Telepaths sensed anything until it was too late. That's when we found out she was off-the-ship-crazed. If you know what I mean."

"Dem fiery reds!" Kipp grinned and took a sip off Irwin's carafe.

"Yes, that's what the men have been calling her. Some of them seemed to get a thrill from hearing the women screaming. It's just crazy though. For those of us who work here, and those privy enough, we didn't know what was going on until it was too late."

Irwin pressed, "Why not?"

"Well, she looked to be just another Erthin at first, definitely acted like one. But it's only after all that happened that we found out she was a Telepath too. And no one saw it. No one felt it, not even the men in the tower. Like I said, we defend one another here. And no one knew what was going on until after she left. No one knew what was happening until the screaming didn't stop. The servers and we bartenders tried to ignore it. We know how you men like to talk about wild women. But once the screaming didn't stop, we summoned the healers. It's been three days, and they are just now ready to go back to work."

Kipp said, "I don't understand how a woman can break another woman's pelvis?"

"Trust me, none of them recall how it all happened either. But it happened. We mended them and threw those pirates out of here. Those three are prohibited from stepping foot in any PCP-run port-of-call ever again."

Kipp glanced at Irwin and then at the barkeep. "They came on that south bound ship, destined for Ajihya, right?"

The friendly barkeep nodded.

Irwin was all ears. "An Erthin who did not appear telepathic, but was?"

Kipp moved his hand forward on the bar's surface. "Can you show me an image of that fiery Erthin?"

"Why?" She raised her left eyebrow. "Is that what gets you going: fiery Erthin women? If it is, we've several to choose from upstairs."

Irwin said, "That woman sounds like a woman we met at a saloon in Radia."

Kipp nodded. "Yeah, she does." He waited for the sultry barkeep to touch his hand.

She put her hands on Kipp's. "Have your hands ever seen rough work?" She looked his fingers over. "As young as you are, you need more dirt under those nails."

Irwin placed his hand on Kipp's arm, grounding out whatever extraneous telepathy the barkeep was attempting on him. "Show him the picture of the Erthin, please, and be done with it."

She recoiled from Kipp and addressed Irwin, "You're powerful indeed."

He did not want her to say those words too loud, so he withdrew his hand from Kipp's arm. "Please, show him."

She touched Kipp's hand and passed along the image. Kipp gasped, and she pulled her hand away from his. Her blue eyes never left Irwin's. "What type of being are you?"

Kipp gulped. "It's the Erthin we saw in that bar! Same woman, same clothes, the same luring look."

"Are you sure?"

"If I could smell the image I'd know for sure. Maybe she can show you the image." Kipp urged the barkeep who was turning away.

"So Yace was here." Irwin chuckled to himself. "She was on that ship, just like I said."

"What're we gonna do now?"

"I do not know. But we must continue south. Do any of those ships out there go south?"

"No, all the ones in port today are following the trade winds back to Al 'Lieur."

"Then the plan should remain in place," Irwin whispered to Kipp. "It is possible that they took the ship here and then sought refuge in the carriage." He mulled over the barkeep's story.

"How possible?"

Irwin took a long drink of wine. "Now I really need to speak to Admiral Ubic."

"What are you gonna tell him?"

The barkeep poured a glass of water for one of the other patrons.

"How are you two doing here? More of the clear stuff?" Her eyes were focused more on Kipp than Irwin.

"Wishing we could speak with the Admiral. I was told we would have an interview with him today," Irwin replied.

"Admiral Ubic? He's away for the day. He does that sometimes—especially when the pirates are here."

Kipp said, "We? I thought he was just speaking with you." He stared at Irwin.

"I think it would be better if we both went," Irwin lied, knowing this bartender would not know the difference.

"Because of what we just learned." Kipp kept the conversation going. "Of course, yeah. We know all about that fiery Erthin, Telepath. We know she's up to no good, as you all already know."

"Oh, the men up above," she pointed to the red tower, "They were quite studious of those soldiers with her. Those who defect to the sea and try to sneak back onto the land are usually watched." She stepped out of the way of the younger waitress darting through the bar area with full trays of dirty mugs and glasses. "Well, good luck speaking to the Admiral. He's usually a bear when it comes to new things. He prefers order to chaos."

Kipp slapped Irwin's back. "Much like my friend here. Sounds like you'll be having great conversations with the Admiral, Irwa-Samuel."

The barkeep turned away to help another patron.

Kipp whispered, "Do you believe Yace would take the carriage after being on the ship?"

"The barkeep's accounting says they threw the pirates—the Erthin and her two soldiers—out of here. Who is to say they did not sneak back on land? And I am curious to know why they sent the carriage on and full of rations. Are they still trying to lure me along, or is it some other ruse? I have much to discuss with the Admiral."

He took another drink from the carafe and set it down.

Kipp picked it up and poured a small amount into his empty glass. "You don't mind, do you?"

"No. But I might make you go retrieve those two empty jugs so I can take some with us."

"Or ask if they sell half casks of it? Dang me! For wine, this is good." He finished his glass.

The barkeep stepped up again. "I hate to break up conversations, men, but the upstairs will be closed once the night is truly black. You might want to get yourselves some women. If that's why you're here." She pointed toward the darkened square, signifying night was upon them, and turned away to stack more dirtied mugs.

Irwin examined the carafe. It was more than half gone. He looked at Kipp's emptied mug and poured it half full of wine. "I cannot drink all of this."

"Are you really up for a woman tonight?"

Irwin watched Kipp. Oh, how he wanted to be with him—to just lay with the Clan-Duin, smell his musky odor, and feel their bodies pressed against one another—to hear Kipp's heartbeat and feel his breath on his neck, in his ear, would be divine. But as always, he held back every urge. "Sure. As long as we do not share!"

The barkeep walked in on that part of their conversation. "Oh, how sweet! You two like to share ladies?"

"Only once, and all Samuel wanted to do was watch." Kipp winked at Irwin and downed his glass of wine. "Damn, that is good wine. Do you sell it?"

"At the wharf," she said. "Casks of it were traded this morning. Though, if you want a jug of it, and have a jug, I will fill it for you for twenty silvers."

"That sounds like a good deal, but only if I have a large enough jug," Irwin said. Then he enjoyed the last few sips from the carafe. He felt ready to ascend the stairs with Kipp. Although, as they stepped down from their bar seats, he began second-guessing his choice. He did not want a woman. He wanted Kipp.

Kipp patted Irwin's shoulder and pushed him on ahead toward the spiral staircase. "This will make you feel better. Dang it, it'll make me feel better!" He stumbled around empty chairs. "All our pent-up energy over saving Yace and killing Dephen is all for what? He's been trying to stop us every step of our way." He was clearly drunk. "I say we have this one small piece of victory. Yeah, we made it to Arenu Village. And we're alive! So, we haven't saved Yace. A minor hiccough, as you would say. And you haven't been taken away by the Admiral yet, so another, yeah! What we need is our fill of women and drinks and to enjoy this night." He touched Irwin's shoulder again.

"Yes, let us get you that woman," Irwin said as they reached the stairs.

"Wait. What! You don't want to enjoy yourself, you know, slap skin together?" Kipp pushed Irwin up the spiral staircase. "I don't know how you keep yourself so restrained. I mean, all those ladies below were ... their smell, how they looked. Our barkeep's hands were so soft ... and those Daosian eyes. We're going to the land of beautiful almond-shaped eyes."

"And in Daos they kill people like me."

"You're Mortal, Irwin. You've nothing to worry about."

"You must be drunk! Calling me Mortal."

A portly, brown-skinned woman in a lacy purple dress, blue eyes and whitening hair was sitting on a chair at the stair's landing. "What be your fancy?"

The room above the Saloon was open—couches, tables, chairs, pillows, women and men. Some were large, and some were skinny, small and tall, all shades of skin, all types of hair. They all wore wildly colored clothing, some laced, some sheer, some loose-fitting. Male and female whores sat together talking, brushing hair, knitting, or pretending to sleep. Many had scars, tattoos, and piercings; only a few were barren of brands.

"Wow," Kipp said, "what options. The barkeep lied. There are some beauties up here."

"Three silver for hand, four for mouth, six for bedtime," the large female told them, holding her hand out for payment.

Kipp turned to Irwin who stared at all the eyes looking back at him. He was not sure how they perceived him, but there were many curious eyes. Kipp tapped Irwin's shoulder. "Don't forget to pay."

"Pay for what you want. Find what you need," the woman told them.

"Irwin."

"Hauss." He glowered at Kipp who was drunk and forgetting himself again—calling him Irwin.

"Hey, I'm not forcing you to do anything, Samuel Irwin. Remember, this is supposed to be good for both of us. Don't get angry at me."

"I am sorry. But this brings up terrible memories for me."

Kipp whispered, "I only want four silvers worth. Just so you know, I don't trust any of their genitalia—being whores to so many shipmates. You better be buying yourself something too."

Irwin did not want to have any conversation about sex here before all these people. He did not understand why this was so important to Kipp—it was a Clan-Duin thing. But, as Irwin had witnessed many times now, this was considered and accepted as a typical male habit. He sighed and made up ten coins. He did not know what he wanted or needed. And he did not want to underpay for these people's time. "Here," he said, angered that he felt forced to have some sort of relations with a stranger.

This feels wrong.

Kipp began carousing with the women—smiling, flirting, trying to find the one he wanted.

Irwin ambled stiffly toward the females sitting on the couches. Several stood up and walked toward him. They talked seductively, trying to lure him in. His eyes bulged, and his spine tightened. Then a eunuch approached him, disarming him with a soft look.

"Hi. I'm Arrol." The deep voiced, pale-skinned Clan-Duin pulled his thigh-high silken robe closed. He was completely hairless except for well-kept facial hair and the black locks on his head. His light brown eyes had been darkened with a tattooed lining; faint, but it made his eyelashes appear thicker. "Would you like a drink?"

Irwin softened, and the women who had congregated then realized they were not needed.

Arrol's tone was kind and soft. "What do you prefer? We're allowed to serve white rum or red rum." He gently pulled Irwin away from the crowd.

"I am Samuel. Red rum please," Irwin glanced over at Kipp who was leaving with a woman.

Arrol brought Irwin a small shot of the alcohol. "To enjoying one another's company," the Clan-Duin smiled. He clanked his small cup against Irwin's and then gulped down his own drink.

Irwin watched Arrol, and then he too gulped the hot beverage. Then slowly, softly, the eunuch lured him away from the greeting area.

36

Finding Comfort

Arrol was not intimidating. He even smelled pretty. The eunuch had brought Irwin into his private chamber and closed the door. At first, he tried to encourage Irwin to sit on the soft bed, but Irwin chose to stand. He did not mean to come off as defensive, yet crossed his arms nonetheless and stayed close to the door. The eunuch smiled submissively. He patted his bed, urging Irwin to come sit by his side.

Arrol's voice was soft, and his light brown eyes were indeed inviting. "Don't worry, I don't bite." The robe slipped off his shoulder, exposing his hairless, light-brown chest.

"See, the thing is," Irwin said, "I am not really comfortable with anyone touching me."

I am overreacting. Breathe.

He relaxed a bit by taking a few breaths.

The eunuch was sweet-looking, almost like a boy but in a man's body. Arrol opened his arms. "You can sit or stand. I will do nothing unless asked. I'm not here to dominate you unless you ask. I'm here to comfort you, to put you at ease. All your stresses, all your worries, they can be gone while you are here with me."

There was something about Arrol that finally put Irwin at ease. He wanted to be on guard as he had been with Kipp, but Arrol did not know him. The calmness the eunuch exuded drew him in. "You are not telepathic, are you?"

"No, they don't allow Telepaths to be concubines. I'm partial Clan-Duin, but mostly Mortal." He smiled kindly at Irwin.

Irwin was hesitant, if only because he did not know what to expect. Arrol waited, just as Saryh would have—patiently, almost playful. And those light brown, almost amber eyes were inviting. After a long contemplative moment, Irwin moved forward and sat down next to Arrol on the bed.

"There, see, easy. I can see you work hard. Your muscles are tense. Would you want me to rub your shoulders?"

Irwin allowed his shoulders to slouch. There were many thoughts running through his mind, but none he would share.

"Would you like a hug?"

And then it dawned on Irwin, "Yes." He had always wanted this type of closeness with Kipp. He yearned for it. He wanted to feel a comforting embrace after all they had been through. All their time spent together in the saddle, by the fireside, trying to keep each other alive and sane, had been grueling. The two men had a closeness Irwin had never experienced with anyone, including his family members. How he felt about Kipp was unexplainable at times, but mostly joyful. Most of all, Irwin wanted physical contact with Kipp. His soul craved that connection. But he was afraid to ask for it.

Slowly, softly, Irwin descended into Arrol's chest. Arrol allowed their weight to pull them down onto the bed. He held Irwin, caressing him. Irwin closed his eyes and released a breath and slowly relaxed his many tight muscles.

Thank you, Kipp.

This was near ecstasy for him, and he allowed his mental fantasies to run wild.

"My brother Ron and I do this often," the eunuch whispered. "We lie in each other's arms and let each other know we are loved." He stroked Irwin's hair, face, and arms. "It's nice to know we are wanted, appreciated." Arrol kissed Irwin's forehead. "When you're with me, you're safe. I don't judge."

Irwin began to weep. He cuddled into this eunuch's embrace and felt his tightened body relax—a new sensation. He had not known how much he needed to feel that everything would be alright. He wanted so much to hear it from Kipp, but Arrol's soft voice was just as good right now. And for this moment, a wave of contentment washed across him.

Irwin descended the stairs with a lightness to his step. He had enjoyed every moment with Arrol; how right Kipp had been. It was then, as he stepped up to his best friend, that Irwin realized he was smiling. He had worn a scowl for a long time. He patted Kipp's shoulder and sat next to his friend who was talking with the exotic bartender.

Kipp cackled, his eyes sparkled gold. "See, I knew what you needed."

A spark had returned to Irwin's eyes. He could feel it. He smiled at the bartender and pressed into Kipp's shoulder. "Thank you." Maybe the Clan-Duin did feel an emotional attachment to him—understood how much of an oddity he was. Though bad things did happen to them, there was a silver lining. They had each other. Indeed, Kipp was watching out for him.

Kipp was playfully ogling the barkeep. "Another goblet of wine for my companion." It was obvious Kipp had been having fun conversing and flirting with her. And no doubt, he had gotten what he needed upstairs.

"Not until he pays for the earlier carafe." She held out her hand.

"Oh! I am so sorry. How much is it?"

"For that giant carafe, five silvers."

Irwin laid out eight coins. He felt bad for not paying before and added a gratuity. He turned to Kipp. "You are helping me with this next carafe."

The Daosian Telepath bent in seductively. "Those came quick. May I ask what your Talent is, Samuel?"

"I am Erthin."

"Funny, you don't look Erthin. You can keep your thoughts hidden, and you can protect others' thoughts with your touch. Those are not Erthin powers." She was trying to read his thoughts; those bright blue eyes were hungry to know more about him. "What's your real Talent?"

"I can heal myself. That is why you cannot hear my thoughts, and I keep those around me protected. I have been told it is called instant regeneration."

The side of the barkeep's face twisted. "Instant regeneration does all that? I don't think so." She called to an older, olive-skinned man a few tables away. "Lieutenant Bejorn, I have an Erthin question." The lieutenant put his cards face down on the table and looked at the Daosian barkeep. She summoned him with a flick of her fingers.

The man stepped up to the bar. "Yup. What is it?"

"Instant regeneration means an Erthin can heal themselves, but it doesn't keep their thoughts protected, does it?"

The Lieutenant's red hair was askew, and he looked to have come down from upstairs not too long ago. He was dressed in the southern uniform: an indigo sarong wrapped around one's mid-section and drew up along the back and over the left shoulder and tucking into the material along the front side. Bejorn's body was heavily tattooed. His chest, arms, and legs bore intricate designs. His olive skin shade made some of those tattoos stand out. Bejorn's hazel eyes stared lustfully at the bartender when he spoke. "Instant regeneration is the power to heal oneself, or others. You cannot ward off telepathy by regeneration."

She continued to pry. "What about the ability to block Telepathy? To himself and others, but only through contact."

"Never heard of that. I'd have to check the reference books in Nuaki to see if anyone's written about it."

She was still staring at Irwin. "Curious."

"Are you the man in question?" The lieutenant put his hand up. "I feel Erthin power within you, but it's unusual." He motioned for Irwin to put his hand up too. "Connection. Connection is necessary for me to confirm your Erthin origins."

Irwin squirmed as the Erthin moved closer to him. "Put your hand on his," the barkeep instructed. "He will feel your power. If you're indeed Erthin, Bejorn will know."

Irwin asked, "Are you a Telepath?" He could already tell that this Erthin held all five Erthin powers: water, fire, wind, earth, and spirit.

"Ha! I am an Elementalist."

"Elementalist? What is that?"

"I am a true Erthin," He haughtily shouted. "The rest of yas are bastards."

"The lieutenant is someone who can harness all five Erthin powers. And no one power is more powerful than the other," she said. "Lieutenant Bejorn can use all five of those powers at the same time." She grinned and smoothed her sides with her hands.

Irwin was curious to hear what this lieutenant would have to say about his newfound abilities. He placed his hand on the Lieutenant's.

Bejorn pulled back. "You're Erthin. But you don't look it. We'd need a blood sucker to know your true abilities."

Irwin and Kipp said in unison, "Blood sucker?"

The barkeep said, "A blood sucker is someone who can taste your family lineage by suckling your blood."

Huh. That is what Lady Gretchen did to me!

Another platter of cheesy bread appeared on the bar. Kipp helped himself to a piece. He leaned in close, listening to what the Lieutenant had noticed. "So, it's true, you're Erthin!" Kipp slapped Irwin's shoulder.

The Lieutenant confirmed, "Oh, yes."

The barkeep weighed in, "Could he be a weak, watered-down Erthin who's mostly Mortal?"

"He has the potential to be very strong. You've got the ability to harness all five powers. Someone like you needs an excellent teacher to show you all the ways of being an Erthin. You'd be able to use all five, if properly trained. But you'd need the highest of instruction—the kind you'd never receive in a Hall of *Vols*."

"Nuaki Village has some of the best teachers," she said. "That's why the *Shayot* live there—to learn from the best, or the worst."

Irwin glanced at Kipp, both bewildered by this new discovery.

So maybe I am Erthin? But how is that possible? Must be from my mother's side. Wait. Now I remember, Lady Gretchen said we were related—but I do not believe she was Erthin, but that is a possibility. She said she was related to Dephen. Could I be related to him too?

His heart skipped a beat.

He is half Coterie and did take hundreds of mistresses. And Coterie can supposedly harness all the known powers.

He let go of the impulse to question what he had just learned about himself. He sat back and considered the exchange, apprehensive about the findings. He took a bite of bread to help chew through his thoughts.

He shyly asked, "Are there blood suckers in Nuaki Village?"

Lieutenant Bejorn shook his head. "The nearest blood sucker is three days north of here."

Irwin recalled Lady Gretchen drinking his blood, enjoying the taste and ranting on about it. Feeling the heat of Bejorn's eyes boring into him, he changed the subject. "I have always regenerated quickly—my body, that is." He wanted to show off, but not too much. He was truly startled and stumped to find out he might be a powerful Erthin.

I remember father saying my mother was weak, but Erthins, even Coterie, are not weak. Maybe he absorbed her like what I have done to so many.

"This is what I can do." He pulled out his small knife and stabbed it into his forearm. The Lieutenant stiffened. Irwin winced as he forced the blade across his flesh. Puncturing his skin enough to draw blood, he had to concentrate as he retracted the blade. His body wanted the metal, but he could not, should not, show all his power.

Their bartender and the lieutenant were visibly stunned as Irwin's hand refused itself. Only a few drops of blood were left behind. "That's beyond Erthin." She eyed the Lieutenant for confirmation.

Lieutenant Bejorn nodded. "Only true Erthin Healers can mend that quickly."

"That's what I thought," she said, rubbing her own arm.

The Lieutenant was summoned back to the card game. "Lieutenant, thank you." She winked at the older Erthin. "Bejorn is fun. He taps into all elements, and all at the same time. He's pure Erthin. His skin and eyes ...." She placed a hand on her chest, heaved a deep sigh, then returned her attention to Irwin.

"Thank you, Samuel; that was a fun trick. Never have I met one as pale as you who might be more Talented than most." There was lust in her eyes. "That is really a unique trait. And so is your ability to hide your thoughts. Women must be fond of you."

He was stuffing a piece of cheesy bread into his mouth. "Huh?"

Kipp redirected the conversation. "Tell me, what do you know about Nuaki Village?"

"Nuaki?" She looked toward the Lieutenant and his comrades. "Lieutenant Bejorn is from Nuaki Village. Desolate place it is. Worst of the worst beings live there. And only men reside there. Every moon they have a lottery to decide who brings their trades to Arenu Village. Only four men are allowed to leave at a time. They come and stay four days. Many of the men who live in Nuaki are not normal *Volatiles*. They're quite Talented! Like you Samuel." She winked at Irwin who quietly drank his wine and ate his bread. She tried to jest with him, but Irwin ignored her.

She turned to Kipp. "No women are allowed in Nuaki Village. But Nuaki and Arenu Villages often trade food and spirits. The lottery allows the Nuaki men to visit civilization and have time with a woman, or a man.

"Corporal Teigahn or Lieutenant Bejorn can tell you more about Nuaki Village." She pointed over at the card game; the man she called Corporal appeared Mortal—brown hair, brown eyes, and pale skin—not the usual type of *Vol.*

Hearing his name, Corporal Teigahn stood and gathered the empty glasses cluttering the playing table.

The barkeep winked at him when he stepped up to Kipp's side.

He studied the two strangers with interest.

The Clan-Duin tried to ignore the Mortal-looking middle-aged man. If he came from Nuaki Village, it meant he was not Mortal, but he surely looked it.

"YouBeTheMortalThemSoldiersBeGrimacin'Bout?" The Corporal's eyes were on Irwin. "MaybeWeCanSee'BoutGettingYouToNauki. You'dBeBetterOffThere."

Confused by the Corporal's strange accent, Irwin and Kipp slouched forward trying to stay out of the conversation, especially with unsuspected Telepaths. They continued drinking and eating. Kipp moved over slightly, allowing Corporal Teigahn a better view of Irwin.

"Teigahn is right," she said. "Going to Nuaki Village, especially if you're more Talented than you know, would be a good thing. Around here, Arenu men are quick to anger, if you know what I mean." She winked at Irwin. "You be safer there than here."

37
Copper Bells

Irwin took another sip of his wine. "I am told I must speak with Admiral Ubic before I go anywhere."

Corporal Teigahn said, "Oh yeah? WhoSpokeToYouAboutAdmiralUbic?"

Irwin wondered if that was fire in his eyes.

He could barely follow what the Corporal was saying, but he got the gist of what was being asked. "Donnolin," he replied. "I was hoping to speak with the Admiral today. But the barkeep here says that he sometimes leaves when pirates are around. My companion and I ... we plan on going to Nuaki Village. We are hoping to leave first thing tomorrow."

Corporal Teigahn's voice rose with excitement. "Ah! AdmiralUbicHadMentioned .... YourAccompanimentWouldBeANiceAddition."

"Then it has been decided!" Irwin tried to muster some enthusiasm. "We shall join you on your voyage back to Nuaki Village tomorrow." He could tell Kipp was not sure about being included in the madness Irwin was trying to create.

"WeAreNotLeavingHereTomorrow. AndYourClan-DuinCounterpart," Corporal Teigahn made a long-winded sound as he pointed at Kipp, "Aaaeee .... He less than. HeStayHereInArenu. YouWillVisit. SaferForHimHere. MorePossibilities."

Kipp muttered, "I'm less than?"

One of the other men facing away from the bar whooped at the Corporal, "Teigahn! Play cards; don't cahoots with the enemy!"

"WeTalkLater." The Corporal returned to the card game.

Kipp said, "I'm not sure I want to go south with them, Irwaa-Samuel. That ass says I'm less than!"

Irwin watched the Corporal rejoin the card players. "He said that to rile you up. We both know that you are easily equal to, or better than, most of them. Besides, there are worse things to worry about than journeying south."

The short Daosian bartender returned to the countertop and leaned in close, nodded in the direction of the card game. "They know about *Uoala* an *Uere*, and *Arlo* and *Enoo*. If you plan on going to Nuaki Village, you need them! They keep you safe in Datzar Jungle. They know where to make camp. They know where fresh *Arlo*-free water is."

Irwin did not want to look as confused as he was. He looked to Kipp for an explanation. "*Arlo*?"

"She is talking about apes? Oh wait, you said *Arlo*-free water. *Arlo* is Alligator, right?"

Irwin whispered, "Alligator?"

"*Uoala* is what?" Kipp turned to their bartender for help, and Irwin knew his friend trusted this telepathic woman.

"*Uoala* .... ooouoala!"

"Ah, Ape! Got it, then *Enoo* is what? The only other great beasts that are feared are rhinoceroses and jaguars, right?"

The barkeep could not say rhinoceroses. "*Enoo*?" She hooked her finger and put it on her nose.

Confused, Irwin stayed out of their conversation; he finished the cheesy bread and enjoyed his carafe of wine.

Lieutenant Bejorn shouted over to the bar, "Soundin' a bit funny over there, Jyn!"

Kipp flirted with their barkeep, Jyn. "What language is that? Who named them *Enoo* and *Uoala* and such?"

"Those are Daosian words. I speak four languages."

"Four languages! How's it a beauty such as you is so multi-cultural?"

"My sire from Uriun, my dame from Daos. Uriun is across Bounen Ocean." She pointed in the wharf's direction.

Kipp leaned closer to Jyn again. "How'd you end up here, of all places?"

"Short story, pirates." Her smile flattened. "They raid towns, steal women; sell them as slaves in Uriun and they have children with men there. Bastard children are brought here for sale. I am a smart one, though. I got a job, and not as a sex-slave; I earn my living in other ways." She appeared smug about that. "Another carafe of wine?" Jyn asked, watching Irwin drink directly from the vessel.

Irwin was paying close attention, even if his eyes were not on Kipp or the bartender. "Ah, no, I think I am good. Kipp?"

The Clan-Duin belched and rubbed his stomach. "Yeah, I'm good. Oh, and if you can give her a few more silvers."

"Why?"

"The bread and cheese—the information and the cleavage. We need to pay her!"

"And what information was that?"

"About Yace. That fiery Erthin woman."

He passed more coins to Jyn. Kipp stood by drunkenly and he kept an eye on Irwin.

"I will defend you again, Samuel Irwin. Come back soon." Jyn blew Kipp a kiss and a wink.

Irwin felt Lieutenant Bejorn eye him as they walked past and out the door into the cool night air.

All the storefronts were closed, sealed by stone. The owners and employees were heading to the Saloon—the only place to find a cooked meal at this time of night. The mess hall across the square was closed, although baskets of food still lay out on the buffets for anyone to take. A few men sat in the shadows and around the tables in the common area. Telepaths mostly. They all had different shades of blue eyes and either blonde or whitening hair. And they all watched Irwin and Kipp walk past.

Irwin knew he was drunk and was ready to head back to their wagon. But then Kipp grabbed his arm and pulled him in another direction.

Irwin pulled back. "Where are we going, Hauss?"

"Oracle, remember?"

"Oh, yes, correct! Are we still doing that? You are quite drunk, but so am I. Nonbry might beat us for our blunders." They moved faster along the street and passed several groups of men conducting what looked to be insidious business. They saw a young child being offered as a trade to a haggard old man. They heard sounds of torture and rape as they hurried along the closed storefronts.

Kipp kept Irwin's arm looped through his and pulled him to the Oracle's door. The smell of sage lingered in the air. "You're back. And you brought your partner with ya." The Oracle smiled with a look of expectancy.

Kipp held Irwin close.

She smiled and waved for them to follow her inside. "You wanted to speak to your mother, is that correct?"

"That's why I'm here. I brought the necklace." Kipp pulled out the talisman.

Irwin liked the closeness, yet he wanted to question Kipp. A look from his friend told him not to. They helped each other into the soft chair, big enough for two drunken men.

"It'll be three silvers up front and then another two at the end of the session. And if it ends early, I don't give refunds." She reached out for payment and for the necklace. Irwin tossed her three silver coins. She stuffed them into her cleavage. "Oh! Wait. There is someone here now. You have a spirit following ... appears kind and nurturing."

"Yeah, that's probably my mother," Kipp said.

"No." She shook her head. "This is a young, young woman—your age, maybe. She says she knows you—you are friends." The Oracle closed her eyes. Her body jolted. "I can't control myself, Kipp," the woman began to speak, but she sounded like Yace. "He has my body. We fight, but I cannot get him to leave. He has horrific plans. He holds them back, but I see hints. He plans to murder many." A tear streaked down the Oracle's cheek. "I can't stop him. I need you, Kipp. Please don't stop looking for me. You're so close."

Kipp gasped, "Yace!"

Irwin cut in, "Why can you not take control? Why can you not stop him?"

"He forced me out." The Oracle squirmed. Her eyes moved like bees in a hive behind her closed eyelids. "He pushed me out of my body at Lady Gretchen's. She helped him with a spell! She's a mean Witchtress." The woman paused and looked at Kipp. "I miss my body. I miss the two of you so much. Please don't stop your hunt."

Irwin leaned forward. "Wait, Yace, where are you?"

The Oracle's eyes popped open. "I know she was not your mother. But she had a need to speak."

"Get her back." Irwin said, dead sober now. "We need to talk to her."

"I-I cannot. That entity has left." She clapped her hands together. "But I digress."

They both cried out at the same time, "Left! What do you mean?"

"I will not charge you for speaking to that young entity. You really came to me to speak to your mother, correct?"

Kipp growled, "You're telepathic! You can get that spirit back!"

"That spirit had a message to deliver, nothing more." The telepathic Clan-Duin Oracle shrugged as though Kipp had asked her for a weather prediction. "Sometimes they do that. She might've brought you the message in a dream, but instead she saw me as an open vessel. If you're not careful, I'll charge you another three silvers for her message."

Kipp's face turned red, and his body stiffened. "You're a Telepath, be ... do your telepathy!"

"You're right! I *am* a Telepath, and I can make you pay me all you have if I want. But I won't. Instead, let me do what you've asked. Just so you know, speaking to the dead can take time. I think you should relax. Be receptive to the entity we are trying to summon." The Oracle studied the wooden trinket.

Straightaway, the woman was overtaken. White eyes burst open and darted around the room. "We've been expecting you," Nonbry spoke in a way that had apparently scared Kipp. Irwin felt him shudder.

Kipp reiterated, "We?"

"Dana's here with me. She says Yace is with her now. She tells me Yace has spoken to you."

Irwin put his hand on Kipp's chest. "How can Yace be there when she was just here? Was that a Dephen trick?"

"Space and time don't affect spirits like it does us." The old man pointed a crooked finger at him and chastised, "You, Miner, caused much turmoil in Onj Raha. For now, all those with Talents are forbidden to enter or exit that city. For what it's worth, we're unable to take the southern passage at this time, so we won't. Are you anywhere close to retrieving Yace's body?"

Irwin did not mind being the gruff one this time. Kipp was fearful of Nonbry. Irwin feared no one but himself. "Would she not tell you if I was?"

"She says you've been close all along. She also says that you'll free her soon. But I don't know if I believe her. She's frantic. She's a spirit without a body. Should I guess where you are?"

Irwin persisted, "Is Lady Gretchen your sister? Or is she Ishik?"

Kipp's chin quivered, looking into the white eyes staring back. Nonbry summoned the answer about their location from Kipp who, terrified of the old man, gave him what he wanted. "Arenu Village."

"Lady Gretchen? Arenu Village?" Nonbry boiled. Those white eyes were more than enough to instill more fear into Kipp's heart, and Irwin's, too. The Oracle's body vibrated, and her muscles tensed. She looked ready to harm them. But her dainty female fingers were hopefully not strong enough. Nonbry shouted, "You fools! You were supposed to stop her by now."

Irwin leaned forward. "Has Yace confessed to you how much telepathic manipulation Master Dephen has accomplished using her powers? He has tried to have us killed multiple times! He convinced your sister, Lady Gretchen, to turn Kipp into a pig and bury me alive. Did Yace tell you about that? Did she tell you that he ordered his Erthin goons to suck all the water from every watering hole along our way to Arenu Village? Did she tell you about the doppelgänger she found to pose as a ruse for us back in Ahradah city?"

"Whoa, Irwin." Kipp raised his hand toward Irwin's face. "Let me do this." He took a breath as though entering a lion's den. "Well, did she?"

The white eyes spun back to their original deep blue. The Oracle pushed forth a smile. "This is different from I am used to." She muttered, and her eyes reverted to white again. "You're in Arenu Village now? Do you know you're speaking through a Telepath who is connected to everyone else there who is telepathic?! All those connected to her know about this exchange. They can hear everything."

Irwin felt Kipp shaking, heard him breathing heavily.

Nonbry ground out a reply. "Nonetheless, you must go on at all cost. Yes, things have happened in Onj Raha which now makes it more difficult for those of us with Talents. But that's our life's challenge. Make the most of what you have, boys. Oh, and while you are exploring Arenu and Nuaki Villages, inquire about the Cyclops. See if any have come through there in the last ten years. This is Dana's request."

The white eyes return to blue. The Oracle was still, perhaps recovering, and then she smiled at Kipp. "Is that it? Will there be anything else?"

Kipp turned to Irwin. "Just how was I supposed to disclose what we know? He knows those of us with Talents aren't allowed in Daos. Dang it! And that's where she's headed. We could be killed trying to rescue Yace, and he'd never know." Kipp fell back in the chair and heaved his breath. "Maybe he doesn't care."

Irwin believed something different. "No, he cares. He has asked us not to give up, to continue at all costs. He does not want Yace to be lost."

Kipp moaned, "But how will we make contact? How will he know when it happens?"

The Oracle interrupted, "Copper bells." They both blinked at her. "Even in places considered *Vol*-less, there are Telepaths. You might never see an Erthin or Clan-Duin, but Telepaths live everywhere." She nodded and then eyed Irwin. "Copper bells are the ones you can trust. They are in smoke shops, herb shops, and even knickknack shops." Her eyes were pinned on him. "Copper bells only; not tin, nor iron, nor silver. They can be decoys." She looked in the direction of the tower. "Never trust those."

Kipp said, "How many smoke shops are there in Daos Territory?"

She winked at him. "In Daos, every village has at least one smoke shop. But most won't have copper bells. Be watchful." She smoothed her skirt, pulling it over her knees. "Will there be anything else?"

Nonbry had spoken the truth. They had just put themselves, and the Gypsy, in harm's way by using this Telepath to make the call. And though she had not been present, this woman would probably know in one way or another of the conversation they just had with Nonbry. The community of Telepaths in Arenu Village would make sure of that. Kipp sat upright and inclined toward the woman. "Do you know of any Cyclops living around here?"

"I do not, but Nuaki Village keeps records of all travelers between the two territories. They have done this for hundreds of years." She shifted from her knees back onto her feet. "Anything else?"

Irwin decided to try a question: "Does it behoove us to go with the men who will be traveling back to Nuaki Village? Or should we take the road alone?"

"Ah, wary travelers travel warily together. Those who are alone, die that way."

Irwin tossed the Oracle three silver coins. "Thank you."

They left the small room. And though the scent of the room had masked the stench of the wharf, they were now back in the salty, fishy air. Kipp squeezed his nose, and Irwin tried to ignore the unpleasant odor. Retracing their steps, they went back to the far side of Arenu Village. Passing the forge again, Irwin slowed his pace.

He could not help but become hypnotized by the singing metal. He stared at the flattened façade and the extended roof that had been brought down to cover the forge. "Do not worry, Kipp, I will do nothing to jeopardize our mission." He paused. Touched Kipp's elbow.

Unless they do not allow you to leave with me.

It was time to head back to the wagon and lay their plan. Kipp clung to his arm, and for the first time in his life, Irwin did not mind being touched. He pressed into his friend's side; a momentarily lustful smile spread across his liquored lips.

I must not become attached to Kipp. He glanced at his friend, *But I want to.*

I cannot trust our safety while we are here. I need to speak with Admiral Ubic tomorrow. But if not .... I must stay positive. I must remember the plan; we cannot deviate from rescuing Yace. Either we will, or we will die trying.

If you're enjoying Irwin's journey, please leave a review at your place of purchase. If you want the next book, visit www.kdlumsden.com

<u>The Unusual Creatures Mentioned</u>

ANCIENT DWELLERS

<u>APPEARANCE</u>: Unknown

<u>UNIQUE TRAITS</u>: Deities who created the universes. They wanted life to happen; to experience love, hate, melancholy, triumph, and sorrow. Everything exists because of them.

CLAN-DUIN

<u>APPEARANCE</u>: brown skinned, black hair, hairy bodies, eye colors can be gray/ green/ brown/ amber

<u>UNIQUE TRAITS</u>: shapeshifters, can be feline, canine, raptor, bear, ape, and/or marine mammals. Are very loyal companions, prefer to live in packs, but can be loners. Linear thinkers, they can be stubborn and foolhardy.

COTERIE

<u>APPEARANCE</u>: pale-skinned, white to blonde hair, white to blue eyes, but can take on darker appearances if bred with other creatures, such as Clan-Duins or Erthins.

<u>UNIQUE TRAITS</u>: Blended children of the Guru, infused with Mortal DNA. Their abilities are similar to Guru, but can be limited by Mortal blood. They are considered bastard children of the Guru and are impure. Often arrogant and egocentric, they live anywhere/anytime.

ELEMENTALIST

<u>APPEARANCE</u>: grey to olive-skin color, auburn-orange to red hair, green-hazel eyes

<u>UNIQUE TRAITS</u>: can harness every element known to exist. They can create elements from within themselves, or through interaction with organic and inorganic life. They are known to have the ability to live out in space without

oxygen or nutrients, they can oxygen exist inside their lungs without taking a breath. It is said they were the first beings created by the Ancient Dwellers, that they were necessary for creating the known universes.

ERTHIN

APPEARANCE: grey to olive-skin color, auburn-orange red hair, green-hazel eyes

UNIQUE TRAITS: hybrid Elementalist and Mortal. They can harness the five most powerful natural elements: Air, water, fire, earth, and spirit. They can be pure-bred and have all abilities, or part-breed and have abilities specific to person (ie. the ability to harness only one element).

GURU

APPEARANCE: white skinned, white-ashen hair, white-blue eyes.

UNIQUE TRAITS: Direct descendants of Ancient Dwellers. They have can use any type of power (teleporting, telepathy, shapeshifting). Considered living gods, they hide in plain sight and across all the universes. They can live everywhere/anywhere/anytime.

GYPSY

An enclave of like-minded people, usually Talented, who tour Urthis rescuing other Talented people. They often take the rescued to sanctuary cities.

HAKRA (Urthis's God)

APPEARANCE: black-skinned, blue-eyes, hairless.

UNIQUE TRAITS: considered a living god who resides in Akarah City, capitol of Urthis. Has lain the groundwork for Telepaths to shape Urthis into an interstellar hub; keeps the general population subdue through religion. Every few years produces a Tome for the people to follow, hypnotizes the masses through telepathic ideology; zealot followers are devout enough to turn in their brother or neighbor if they believe they are Talented. Every few years his followers take pilgrimages to Akarah to stand in Hakra's presence with hopes to be bestowed a gift.

ISHIK EMPIRE

Current rulers of Doas Territory, the Ishik Empire have been in control for the last thousand years. Believed to be the last full-blooded Coterie family, they claim to be purebred; to couple with someone outside the family brings dishonor. They tout their land to be free of Talented people, yet employ Talented people to work at the palace. They maltreat their subjects, taking boys away from their families at 9-10, to work iron mines, daughters are married off by 8-9, families live in small dome-huts, and when compared to the rest of Urthis, Doas Territory is at least one hundred years behind in technological advancements.

METALIST

APPEARANCE: ashen skin color, gray hair, silvery-gray eyes

UNIQUE TRAITS: can harness all types of metal including, but not limited to; gold, silver, aluminum, nickel, iron, zinc, mercury, cadmium, cobalt, chromium, platinum, lead, etc. They can hold up to eight pounds of any given substance within their own flesh, flushed it under the skin to specific places. Their ability to manipulate metal starts with extraction, turning the metal into its liquid form, and integrating it back into its hard form, and can form anything imaginable with any amount of metal. They are known to give off a deathly scent when holding metal within. Direct descendants to Elementalist.

MORTAL

APPEARANCE: always pale-skinned, brown-eyed, hair light brown to dark-brown/black

UNIQUE TRAITS: Bipeds with no superhuman powers. One of the five eldest beings created by the Ancient Dwellers. They have been exported from their home world, brought to foreign worlds to repopulate but often exploited as cheap labor.

PLANETAIRY CONSTIBLE PATROL (PCP)

Comprised only of people with Talents. Telepaths are given powerful positions (Admiral, Captain, Colonel, Corporal, Sargent), Erthins can hold powerful positions (Lieutenant, Sargent), Clan-Duins are considered working soldiers or minions, but can be demoted and placed in a “court-yard sitter” position. Also called “Population Control Patrol”. They usually patrol in groups of four and are seen riding large “warhorses”.

SANCTUARY CITY

Not necessarily a city, but a place where people with Talents are safe from the PCP and Hakran ideology. Most don’t allow Mortals to reside. Most require those looking for permanent residency to prove they are a positive influence, that they will help protect others with Talents, regardless of abilities, and not cause issue within the community. There are rules within each community to adhere, and if someone breaks that main rule they can be banished from one, or all sanctuary cities. (*Note: All Sanctuary cities are interconnected by Telepaths.)

TALENT, PEOPLE OF (aka TALENTED)

Any being who possess supernatural powers.

TELECAPRITIAN

APPEARANCE: pale skinned, white to blue eyed, white to blonde hair

UNIQUE TRAITS: can use telekinesis and telepathy, can shapeshift appearance but only into same gender roles. One of the five eldest beings created by the Ancient Dwellers.

TELEPATH

APPEARANCE: pale skinned, white to blue eyed, white to blonde hair

UNIQUE TRAITS: hybrid of TeleCapritian & Mortal, they cannot yield telekinesis. There are many types of telepaths; dreaming (they see visions future or past based), some can hear thoughts, some can manipulate beings though 'telepathic' brain waves, others can only do this through physical touch.

TELEKINESIS

The ability to move objects at a distance by mental power or other nonphysical means.

URTHIS

Fourth planet from the sun in the Oska'al solar system and one of the many places in the known universe that hosts supernatural and natural powered creatures. It is the planet on which Samuel Irwin Miner lives.

VOLATILE

A derogatory word used against people of Talent. (see: Talent, people of)

Also By

The Metalist's Journey

(Prequel) Flight of Yellow Falcons (2025)

The Metalist's Journey Prologue

Secrets of Urthis

Elements of Power

Sleeper Assassin

Land of Cannibals

(+2 more at least!)

If you liked this book please leave a review!

Want more information about Irwin and the world of Urthis?
Join KD Lumsden's newsletter at https://www.kdlumsden.com/

About KD Lumsden

A lifetime reader and writer of fantasy, Secrets of Urthis is KD Lumsden's debut novel. She creates fantastic worlds while drawing up architectural designs, and dreams up unforgettable characters while maintaining an equestrian farm. Supported by her loving husband and imaginative son, they enjoy nature hikes and playing at the beach when the Pacific Northwest weather permits.

Back of Book Blurb

Their friend Yace vanished like a whisper on the breeze. Had Irwin touched her while she lay unconscious from the fright endured, he could have ground out the old entity, Lord and Master Dephen Ishik, from her body—from her mind. He hated regretting things he had not done. But worse, he hated hearing the maddening sounds from the metal that rang everywhere, like a terrible bout of vertigo followed by a throbbing headache. Bad things could happen if he didn't keep his Metalist powers in check, if they didn't stay out of PCP hands. But they must find Yace. With the chase begun, there are few breadcrumbs to follow; it seems that Clan-Duin birds have picked them up and scattered them to the winds.

In their frantic search for Yace, Kipp brings up past events, finding fault with Irwin's volatile actions. Doubt in one other will arise if they cannot come together with decisions, if they cannot trust each other. They cannot have doubt. If they do, then Lord and Master Dephen Ishik wins. And if the elderly Telepath wins, Irwin and Kipp will surely die.

Yet Irwin is resourceful, even when he feels overwhelmed by it all. He must be, or everything could crumble—or worse, they will be captured and locked away, taken to the worse place imaginable and killed. He knows to keep himself in check, but with soldiers surrounding, finding Yace's trail is a challenge. And the deeper into PCP territory they travel, the worse their odds of survival are. But if they don't save Yace from her mentally manipulative father, her odds of survival drop to zero. Will they be able to save her before that happens?

Don't miss this exhilarating continuation of The Metalist's Journey series. Get your copy of Elements of Power today and join Irwin and Kipp as they battle against the odds to save their friend and uncover the shocking truth that awaits them.

www.ingramcontent.com/pod-product-compliance
Lightning Source LLC
Chambersburg PA
CBHW071413200726
48294CB00002B/385

* 9 7 8 1 9 5 9 6 7 9 0 2 8 *